FROM RUIN
TO RICHES

The Regency Season

DANGEROUS DUKES

August 2017

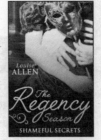

SHAMEFUL SECRETS

September 2017

BLACKMAILED BRIDES

October 2017

RUINED REPUTATIONS

November 2017

GENTLEMAN ROGUES

December 2017

PASSIONATE PROMISES

January 2018

SCANDALOUS AWAKENING

February 2018

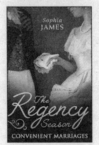

CONVENIENT MARRIAGES

March 2018

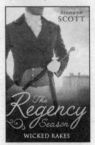

WICKED RAKES

April 2018

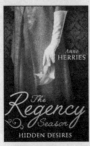

HIDDEN DESIRES

May 2018

FORBIDDEN PLEASURES

June 2018

DECADENT DUKES

July 2018

*To Dr Joanna Cannon for her invaluable advice
and insights into Will's illness.*

Louise Allen has been immersing herself in history, real and fictional, for as long as she can remember. She finds landscapes and places evoke powerful images of the past – Venice, Burgundy and the Greek islands are favourite atmospheric destinations. Louise lives on the North Norfolk coast, where she shares the cottage they have renovated with her husband. She spends her spare time gardening, researching family history or travelling in the UK and abroad in search of inspiration. Please visit Louise's website: www.louiseallenregency.co.uk for the latest news, or find her on Twitter @LouiseRegency and on Facebook.

Chapter One

16th June, 1814—Queen's Head Inn,
Oxfordshire

He was all power and masculine arrogance with the candlelight dancing on those long, naked limbs as he stood and poured ruby-red wine into the glass and tossed it back in one long swallow.

To be in his arms, in this unfamiliar bed, had not been what she had imagined it would be. Less tender than she had hoped, more painful than she had expected. But then, she had been very ignorant and she would be more realistic next time. Julia snuggled back into the warm hollow his body had made.

'Jonathan?' He would come back now, hold her in his arms, kiss her, talk more of their plans and all the uncertainties would vanish. On that headlong drive from Wiltshire he had ridden beside the chaise almost all the way and dinner in the public room below had not been the place to discuss their new life together.

'Julia?' He sounded abstracted. 'You can wash there.' He jerked his head towards the screen in the corner and poured himself another glass, his back still to her.

Unease trickled through the warmth. Was Jonathan disappointed in her? Perhaps he was simply tired, she certainly was. Julia slid from the tangled sheets, pulled one of them around her and padded over to the screen that concealed the washstand.

Making love was an embarrassingly sticky process, another small shock in an evening of revelations. That would teach her to think like a lovesick girl. It was about time she went back to being an adult woman making a rational decision to take control of her own life, she thought with a wry smile for her own romantic day-dreams. This was real life and she was with the man she loved, the man who loved her enough to brave scandal and snatch her away from her relatives.

The screen overlapped one edge of the window and she reached to twitch the curtain completely over the panes of exposed glass before she dropped the sheet.

'London Flier!' There was the blare of a horn below, too dramatic to ignore. Julia looked through the gap as, wheels rumbling, the stagecoach pulled out of the arch from the stable yard and turned right. In a second it was gone. *Strange. Now why do I think that strange?*

She was too tired to puzzle over odd fancies. Julia washed, draped the sheet more becomingly and came out from behind the screen, unexpected butterflies dancing in her stomach. Jonathan was half-dressed now, seated staring into the empty grate, the stem of his wine glass twisting between his fingers. His shirt lay open, revealing the muscular flat planes of his chest, the dark arrow of hair that disappeared into his breeches... Her eyes followed it and she felt herself blush.

How cold it was away from the heat of his body. Julia poured wine and curled into the battered old armchair opposite his. Jonathan must be thinking of the next morning, of the long road north to the Scottish border and their marriage. Perhaps he feared pursuit, but she doubted Cousin Arthur would trouble himself with her whereabouts. Cousin Jane would screech and flap about and moan about the scandal, but she would be more concerned about the loss of her drudge than anything else.

The wine was poor stuff, tart and thin, but it helped bring things into focus of a kind. It was as though her brain had taken a holiday these past days and she had become nothing but an air-headed girl in love instead of the practical woman she really was.

You are *in love. And you've thrown your cap over the windmill with a vengeance*, the inner voice that was presumably her conscience informed her. *Yes, but that does not mean I have to be a useless ninny*, she argued back. *I must think how to be of help.*

The jolting, high-speed ride across country had been straightforward enough once Jonathan had explained why they were not going directly north to Gloucester and the road to the Border. Cutting northeast to Oxford and then going north would confuse pursuit and the road, once they got there, was better. They had turned on to the Maidenhead-Oxford turnpike about ten miles back, but apparently Oxford inns were wildly expensive, so this one, out of town, was the prudent option for their first night.

She would look after the money now, budget carefully, save Jonathan the worry of sorting out the bills, at least. *North to the border. To Gretna. How romantic.*

The north. That was what was wrong. The wine slopped from her glass staining the sheet like blood. The stage was going to London and it had turned right, the direction they had been heading when they arrived here.

'Jonathan.'

'Yes?' He looked up. Those long-lashed blue eyes that always made her heart flutter were as unreadable as ever.

'Why were we driving south for ten miles before we got here?'

His expression hardened. 'Because that's the way to London.' He put down the glass and stood up. 'Come back to bed.'

'But we are not going to London. We are going to Gretna, to be married.' She drew two painful breaths as he did not reply and the truth dawned. 'We were never going to Scotland, were we?'

Jonathan shrugged, but did not trouble himself with denials. 'You wouldn't have come if you'd known otherwise, would you?'

How could the world change in one beat of the heart? She thought she had been chilled before, but it was nothing to this. It was impossible to misunderstand him. 'You do not love me and you do not intend to marry me.' There was nothing wrong with her thought processes now.

'Correct.' He smiled, his lovely slow, sleepy smile. 'You were such a nuisance to your relatives, clinging on, insisting on staying.'

'But the Grange is my home!'

'*Was* your home,' he corrected. 'Since your father died it belongs to your cousin. You're an expense and no one's fool enough to marry a managing, gawky, bluestocking female like you with no dowry. So...'

'So Arthur thought a scandalous elopement with Jane's black sheep of a third cousin would take me off his hands for good.' Yes, it was very clear now. *And I have slept with you.*

'Exactly. I always thought you intelligent, Julia. You were just a trifle slow on the uptake this time.'

How could he look the same, sound the same, and yet be so utterly different from the man she had thought she loved? 'And they made you seem a misunderstood outcast so that I felt nothing but sympathy for you.' The scheme was as plain as if it was plotted out on paper in front of her. 'I would never have credited Arthur with so much cunning.' The chill congealed into ice, deep in her stomach. 'And just what do you intend to do now?'

'With you, my love?' Yes, there it was, now she knew to look for it: just a glimpse of the wolf looking out from those blue eyes. Cruel, amused. 'You can come with me, I've no objection. You're not much good in bed, but I suppose I could teach you some tricks.'

'Become your mistress?' *Over my dead body.*

'For a month or two if you're good. We're going to London—you'll soon find something, or someone, there. Now come back to bed and show me you're worth keeping.' Jonathan stood up, reached for her hand and pulled her to her feet.

'No!' Julia dragged back. His fingers cut into her wrist, she could feel the thin bones bending.

'You're a slut now,' he said, 'so stop protesting. Come and make the best of it. You never know, you might learn to enjoy it.'

'I said *no.*' He was a liar, a deceiver, but surely he would not be violent?

It seemed she was wrong about that, too. 'You do what I say.' The pain in her wrist was sickening as she resisted.

Her feet skidded on the old polished boards, the hearth rug rucked up and she stumbled, off balance. There was an agonising jolt in her arm as she fell, then Jonathan's grip opened and she was free. Sobbing with pain and fear and anger Julia landed with a crash in the grate. The fire irons clattered around her, striking elbow and hand in a landslide of hard little blows.

'Get up, you clumsy bitch.' Jonathan reached out to seize her, caught her hair, twisted and pulled. It was impossible to roll away. Julia hit out wildly to slap at him and connected with a blow that jarred her arm back. With a gasp Jonathan released her. *Get up, run...* She rolled free, hit the foot of the bed, dragged herself up on to shaking legs.

Silence. Jonathan sprawled across the hearth, his

head in a crimson pool. Her hand was wet. Julia looked down at her fingers, rigid around the poker. Blood stained her hand, dripped from the iron.

Blood. So much blood. She dropped the poker and it rolled to come to rest against his bare foot. *Not my dead body—his. Oh, God, what have I done?*

Chapter Two

Midsummer's Eve, 1814—
King's Acre Estate, Oxfordshire

The nightingale stopped her. How long had she been running? Four days…five? She had lost count… Her feet took her up the curve of the ornamental bridge, beyond pain now, the blisters just part of the general misery, and, as she reached the top the liquid beauty poured itself into the moonlight.

Peace. No people, no noise, no fear of pursuit. Simply the moon on the still water of the lake, the dark masses of woodland, the little brown bird creating magic on the warm night air.

Julia pulled off her bonnet and turned slowly around. Where was she now? How far had she come? Too late now to regret not staying to face the music, to try to explain that it had been an accident, self-defence.

How had she escaped? She still wasn't sure. She remembered screaming, screaming as she backed away from the horror at her feet. When people burst into the room she'd retreated behind the screen to hide her near-nudity, hide from the blood. They didn't seem to notice her as they gathered round the body.

And there behind the screen were her clothes and water. She had washed her hands and dressed so that when she stepped out to face them she would be decent. Somehow, that had seemed important. She'd had no idea of trying to run away from what she had done so unwittingly.

Jonathan's pocketbook lay on top of his coat. It must have been blind instinct that made her stuff it into her reticule. Then, when she had made herself come out and face the inevitable, the room was packed and people were jostling in the doorway trying to see inside.

No one paid any regard to the young woman in the plain grey cloak and straw bonnet. Had anyone even glimpsed her when they burst in? Perhaps she had reached the screen before the door opened. Now she must have appeared to be just another onlooker, a guest attracted by the noise, white-faced and trembling because of what she had seen.

The instinct to flee, the cunning of the hunted animal, sent her down the back stairs, into the yard to hide amidst the sacks loaded on a farm cart. As dawn broke she had slipped unseen from the back of it into the midst of utterly unfamiliar countryside. And it felt as though she had been walking and hiding and stealing rides ever since.

If she could just sit for a while and absorb this peace,

this blissful lack of people to lie to, to hide from. If she could just forget the fear for a few moments until she found a little strength to carry on.

The tall column of grey shimmered, moon-lit, in the centre of the narrow stone bridge. Long dark hair lifted and stirred in the night breeze: a woman. *Impossible.* Now he was seeing things.

Will strained every sense. Silence. And then the night was pierced again by the three long-held notes that signalled the start of the nightingale's torrent of languid music, so beautiful, so painful, that he closed his eyes.

When he opened them again he expected to find himself alone. But the figure was still there. A very persistent hallucination then. As he watched, it turned, its face a pale oval. *A ghost?* Ridiculous to feel that superstitious shudder when he was edging so close to the spirit world himself. *I do not believe in ghosts. I refuse to.* Things were bad enough without fearing that he would come back to haunt this place himself, forced to watch its disintegration in Henry's careless, spend-thrift hands.

No, it was a real woman of course, a flesh-and-blood woman, the paleness of her face thrown into strong relief by the dark hair that crowned her uncovered head. Will moved into the deeper shadows that bordered the Lake Walk and eased closer. What was she doing, this trespasser far into the parkland that surrounded King's Acre? She must be almost a mile from the back road that led to the turnpike between Thame and Aylesbury.

Her long grey cloak swung back from her shoulders and he saw that she was tall. She leaned over the parapet of the bridge, staring down as though the dark waters beneath held some secret. Everything in the way she moved spoke of weariness, he thought, then stiffened as she shifted to hitch one hip on to the edge of the stonework.

'No!' Cursing his uncooperative, traitorous body, Will forced his legs to move, stumbled to the foot of the bridge and clutched the finial at the end of the balustrade. 'No…don't jump! Don't give up…whatever it is…' His legs gave way and he fell to his knees, coughing.

For a moment he thought he had so startled her that she would jump, then the ghost-woman slid down from the parapet and ran to kneel at his side.

'Sir, you are hurt!'

Her arm went around his shoulders and she caught him against herself in a firm embrace. Will closed his eyes for a moment. The temptation to surrender to the simple comfort of a human touch was almost too much.

'Not hurt. Sick. Not contagious,' he added as she gave a little gasp. 'Don't…worry.'

'I am not worried for myself,' she said with a briskness that bordered on impatience. She shifted her position so he fell back on her shoulder and then laid a cool palm on his forehead. Will bit back a sigh of pure pleasure. 'You have a fever.'

'Always do, this time of night.' He fought to control his breathing. 'I feared you were about to jump.'

'Oh, no.' He felt the vehement shake of her head. 'I cannot imagine ever being desperate enough to do that. Drowning must be such a terror. Besides, there is always some hope. Always.' Her voice was low and slightly husky, as if she had perhaps been weeping recently, but he sensed that it would always be mellow, despite its certainty. 'I was resting, looking at the moonlight on the water. It is beautiful and calm and the nightingale was singing so exquisitely. I felt some need for calm and beauty,' she added, with a brave attempt at a rueful laugh that cracked badly.

Something was wrong. He could feel the tension and the exhaustion coming off her in waves. If he was not careful, she would bolt. Or perhaps not, she seemed determined to look after him. As if he was dealing with a wounded animal he made himself relax and follow her lead. 'That is why I come down here when the moon is full,' he confessed. 'And Midsummer's Eve adds a certain enchantment. You could believe almost anything in the moonlight.' *Believe that I am whole again...* 'I thought you a ghost at first sight.'

'Oh, no,' she repeated, this time with a faint edge of genuine amusement that appeared to surprise her. 'I am far too solid for a ghost.'

Every fibre in his body, a body that he believed had given up its interest in the opposite sex long months ago, stirred in protest. She felt wonderful: soft and curved and yet firm where she still held him cradled against her shoulder. He managed not to grumble in protest as she released him and got to her feet.

'What am I thinking about, lingering here talking of ghosts and nightingales? I must get help for you. Which direction would be quickest?'

'No need. House is just—' His breath gave out and Will waved a hand in the general direction. 'If you can help me up.' It was humiliating to have to ask, but he had learned to hide the damage to his pride after long months discovering the hard way that fighting got him nowhere. She needed help, but he couldn't give it to her sprawled here.

'Stay there, then. I will go and get help.'

'No.' He could still command when he had to: she turned back to him with obvious reluctance, but she turned. Will held up his right hand. 'If you will just steady me.'

She wanted to argue, he could sense it, but she closed her lips tight—he fantasised that they were lush, framing a wide, generous mouth, although he could not be certain in that light—and took his hand in a capable grip.

'I suppose,' she said, as he got to his feet, 'that you would say you are old enough to know what is good for you, but I have to tell you plainly, sir, that wandering about in the moonlight when you have a fever is the height of foolishness. You will catch your death.'

'Do not concern yourself.' Will got a grip on the stone ledge and made himself stand steady and straight. She was tall, his ghost-lady, she only had to tilt her head back a little to look him in the face. Now he could see the frown on a countenance that the moonlight had bleached into ivory and shadow. He could not judge her age or see detail but, yes, her mouth was generous and curved, although just now it was pursed with disapproval. It seemed she liked being argued with as little as he did. 'I have caught my death already.'

He saw her take his meaning immediately and waited for the protests and the embarrassment that people invariably displayed when he told them the truth. But she simply said, 'I am so very sorry.' Of course, she would be able to see in the moonlight just what a wreck he was, so perhaps it was no surprise to her. It was a miracle that the appearance of a walking skeleton had not frightened her into the lake. 'I am trespassing on your land, I assume. I am sorry for that also.'

'You are welcome. Welcome to King's Acre. Will you accompany me back to the house and take some refreshment? Then I will have my coachman drive you onwards to wherever you are staying.' She bit her lip and her gaze slid away from his. It seemed he was not as harmless in her eyes as he felt. 'There will be whatever chaperonage you might require, I assure you. I have a most respectable housekeeper.'

His reassurances provoked a smile, as well they might, he supposed. He was deluding himself if he thought she had taken him for his regiment's most dangerous ladies' man, as his reputation had once been. Even the most nervous damsel would need only one glance to realise that the possibility of him ravishing them was slight.

'Sir, the question of chaperonage is the least of my

concerns at the moment.' There was a bitter undertone to her voice that made no sense. 'But I cannot trouble you and your household at this time of night.'

His breathing had steadied and with it, Will realised, his wits. Respectable young ladies—and his companion was certainly a lady, if not a very young one—did not materialise in the moonlight *sans* baggage or escort without good reason.

'The hour is of no consequence—my staff are used to my penchant for late nights. But your luggage, ma'am? And your maid? I shall have someone fetch them to you.'

'I have neither, sir.' She turned her head away and the effort to steady her voice was palpable. 'I am… somewhat adrift.'

She could not tell him the truth, Julia knew that, although the temptation to simply burst into tears, throw herself into the arms of this elderly man and pour out her story was shockingly strong. He was probably a magistrate and, even if he was not, he would be duty-bound to hand her over to the law. But she had been tramping across country, hiding in barns, spending a few coppers here and there on bread and cheese and thin ale, and she was exhausted, lost and desperate. Something of the truth would have to suffice and she must take the risk that she would prove to be a good liar.

'I will be frank with you, sir,' Julia said, grateful for the protection of the shadows. She wished she could see his eyes. 'I ran away from home. Several days ago.'

'May I ask why?' His voice, strangely young for one advanced in years, was as studiously non-judgemental as his haggard face.

'My cousin, on whom I am totally dependent, schemed to give me to a man who wanted only my... undoing. Running seemed the only way out, although I am just as effectively ruined as a result, I realise that now. I am sure you would not wish to entertain me under the circumstances. Your wife—'

'I do not have one,' he said, his voice cool. 'And I have no objection, only a regret on your behalf, ma'am, that you find yourself in such a predicament.'

He should not be talking. Julia had no doubt that he meant exactly what he said about his health: the man was desperately ill. His body when she had supported it had felt like bones and sinew contained in skin and expensive superfine. He was tall, over six foot, and in his youth must have been well muscled and powerful. Now his breathing was ragged and his forehead under her palm had been damp with fever.

He had come to her aid when he thought she was going to cast herself into the lake and he had not insulted her when she told him a little of her disastrous misjudgement. Now the very least she could do was to assist him home and risk the slight chance that the description of a wanted murderess had reached them here. Surely she was safe for a night? The authorities could not know her name and Jonathan's card case was with his pocketbook in her reticule—the local constable would have a nameless body to deal with, as well as a nameless fugitive.

This was no time to be scrupulous about accepting help. 'Come, sir. If you will not allow me to go for assistance, at least take my arm. I am certain you should not be out here tiring yourself.'

'You sound remarkably like Jervis, my valet,' the man said with an edge of asperity. For a moment she thought stubborn pride would win out over common sense, but then he let her put her forearm under his and take a little of his weight.

'This way, I think you said, sir?' She made her sore feet move, trying not to limp in case he noticed and refused her help.

'My name is William Hadfield,' he said after a few steps. 'Just so you know whom you are rescuing. Baron Dereham.'

She did not know the name, but then she was adrift more than a hundred miles from home and her family, although gentry, did not mix with titled society. 'My name is—'

'There is no need to tell me.' He was breathing hard. Julia slowed her pace a little, glad of the excuse to do so. She was tired and sore and almost more exhausted by fear than from physical exertion.

'It is no matter, my lord. I am Julia Prior. *Miss*,' she added bleakly. Live or die, she was never going to be anything else now. And then she realised that she had given her real name. *Foolish,* she chided herself. But it was too late now and it was common enough.

'Left here, Miss Prior.' Obedient, she took the path he indicated. To her consternation the ground began to slope upwards. How was Lord Dereham going to manage this with only her feeble help? As if he read her mind he said, 'Here is the cavalry, you need not carry me any further.'

Julia opened her mouth to protest that she was merely steadying him, then shut it again. There was enough edge in his voice for her to know the baron was not resigned to his condition and would bitterly resent any attempt to jolly him along. He must have been arrogant and self-assured in his prime, she concluded, to resent his decline so fiercely now.

'My lord!' Two men hurried down the slope from where a gig stood waiting. One, when he got closer, could have been identified as a valet at a glance: neat, dapper and immaculate, he was making clucking sounds under his breath. The other, in boots and frieze coat, was just as obviously a groom.

'Jervis, help this lady into the gig.' Her arm was released and Julia found herself being ushered into the humble vehicle as if she was a duchess and it a state coach. Behind, she could hear a low-voiced exchange that ended abruptly with a snapped command from the baron as he took the seat opposite her.

The groom went to the horse's head and led it on, the valet followed on foot. After a few minutes passed in silence they emerged on to a great sweep of lawn and then crunched across a gravelled drive.

'But it is a castle!' Startled out of her circling

thoughts, Julia blinked up at crenellations, a turret, arrow slits, all preposterously Gothic and romantic in the silvery light.

'A very small one, I assure you. And disappointingly modern inside to anyone of a romantic nature. The moat is dry, the cellars full of wine bottles. The portcullis has long since rusted through and we rarely pour boiling oil on to anyone these days.' He sounded as though he regretted that.

'Fetch Mrs Morley to Miss Prior,' Lord Dereham ordered as the groom helped her to descend. Her legs, she discovered as she stumbled, were almost too tired to support her. 'Tell her to place the Chinese bedchamber at Miss Prior's disposal and then have Cook send up a hot supper to the library.'

'But, my lord, it must be midnight at least—' He should not be worrying about feeding her at this hour, let alone housing her.

'I will not have you wandering about the countryside or going to bed hungry, Miss Prior,' he said as he climbed down, leaning on the groom in his turn. Here under the bulk of the building it was almost dark and she could not see his face at all, only judge his mood by the autocratic orders. 'You will oblige me by spending the night and tomorrow we can see what may be done.'

He will not have it, indeed! A forceful old gentleman, the baron, whatever his health, Julia decided. *But it is rather beyond his powers to find a solution to this problem. A new dawn will not make matters any better.*

'Thank you, my lord. I should not trouble you, I

know, but I will not deny that your offer is most welcome.' She had thought she could never trust another man, not after Jonathan. But the baron was advanced in years and could be no threat to her. Or her to him, provided he had no idea who he was sheltering.

'I will see you in the library then, Miss Prior, when you are ready,' he said behind her as she followed the valet into the hall.

'Just down the main stairs and the door to the left, Miss Prior.' The housekeeper stood aside as Julia murmured a word of thanks and left the warmth and comfort of the bedchamber for the shadowy panelled corridor.

The woman had shown no surprise at the state of her travel-worn clothes, although she had tutted in sympathy over the state of Julia's feet and had produced copious hot water, linen for dressings and salves. Now, clad in some borrowed undergarments beneath her brushed and sponged walking dress, Julia felt a new surge of courage. She had heard that prisoners were more easily broken if they were kept dirty and unkempt and now she could well believe it. She had felt her strength and will ebb along with her self-respect.

The house had been decorated a few years ago, she judged as she negotiated the broad sweep of an old oak staircase. All was in good repair with an intriguing glimpse of ancient baronial castle here and there beneath the modern comfort. Yet there was an impersonal air about it as though efficient staff kept it running, but the driving force behind it, the spirit that made it a home, had vanished.

It had happened at the Grange after her father had died and she had not had the strength to simply carry on as before. It had only lasted a few weeks, then she had made herself take up the reins again. Pride, and the refusal to let her cousin and his wife find the slightest thing to criticise when they came to claim their inheritance, had dried her tears and stiffened her will. Here, with the master dying, the staff were obviously doing the best they could, which argued loyalty and efficiency.

The heavy panelled door swung open on to a room that was all warmth: a fire in the grate despite the season, crimson damask curtains at the windows, the soft glow of old waxed bookshelves. The man in the chair beside the hearth began to get to his feet as she came in and the hound at his feet sprang up, her teeth bared as she ranged herself in front of her master.

'Down, Bess! Friend.'

'My lord, please—there is no need to stand.' Julia took three hasty steps across the carpet, dodged around the dog and caught the baron's arm to press him back into the seat. She found herself breast to breast with him, the light from the fire and the candelabra on the side table full on his face.

This was the man from the lakeside? The man she had held in her arms, the one she thought elderly and harmless? 'Oh!' She found herself transfixed by amber eyes, the eyes of a predator, and blurted out the first thing that came into her head. 'How old are you?'

Chapter Three

Lord Dereham sat down as she released his arm. His breathless laugh was wicked. 'I am twenty-seven, Miss Prior.'

'I cannot apologise enough.' Cheeks burning with mortification, Julia took a hasty step backwards, tripped over the dog and found herself sprawling into the chair opposite his. 'I am so sorry, I have no idea why I should blurt out such a impertinent question, only—'

'Only you thought I was an old man?' Lord Dereham did not appear offended. Perhaps in his currently restricted life the sight of a lady—*female*, she reminded herself—behaving with such appalling gaucheness and lack of elegance was entertainment enough to distract him from her outrageous lack of manners.

'Yes,' she confessed and found she could not look him in the face. *Those eyes.* And he might be thin and ill, but he was unmistakably, disturbingly, male for all that. She bent to offer an apologetic caress to the elderly hound who was sitting virtually on her feet, staring at her with a reproachful brown gaze.

'Miss Prior.' She made herself lift her eyes. 'You are quite safe with me, you know.'

Her head agreed with him. Every feminine instinct she possessed, did not. 'Of course, I realise that. Absolutely,' Julia said, in haste to reassure herself. Her voice trailed away as she heard her own tactless words and saw his face tighten.

He had been a handsome man once. He was striking still, but now the skin was stretched over bones that were the only strong thing left to him, except his will-power. And that, she sensed, was prodigious. His hair was dark, dulled with ill health, but not yet touched with grey. He had high cheekbones, a strong jaw, broad forehead. But his eyes were what held her, full of life and passionate, furious anger at the fate that had reduced him to this. Were they brandy-coloured or was it dark amber?

Julia could feel she was blushing as they narrowed, focused on her face. 'I mean, I know I am safe because you are a gentleman.' Safe from another assault, not safe from the long arm of the law. Not safe from the gallows.

She sat up straight, took a steadying breath and looked fixedly at his left ear. Such a nice, safe part of the male anatomy. 'You are being remarkably patient with me, my lord. I am not usually so…inept.'

'I imagine you are not usually exhausted, distressed and fearful, nor suffering the emotional effects of betrayal by those who should have protected you, Miss Prior. I hope you will feel a little better when you have had something to eat.' He reached out a thin white hand and tugged the bell pull. The door opened almost immediately to admit a pair of footmen. Small tables were placed in front of them, laden trays set down, wine was poured, napkins shaken out and draped and then, as rapidly as they had entered, the men left.

'You have a very efficient staff, my lord.' The aroma of chicken broth curled up to caress her nostrils. Ambrosia. Julia picked up her spoon and made herself sip delicately at it instead of lifting the bowl and draining it as her empty stomach demanded.

'Indeed.' He had not touched the cutlery in front of him.

She finished the soup along with the warm buttered roll and the delicate slices of chicken that had been poached in the broth. When she looked at Lord Dereham he had broken his roll and was eating, perhaps a quarter of it, before he pushed the plate away.

'And a very good cook.'

He answered her concern, not her words. 'I have no appetite.'

'How long?' she ventured. 'How long have you been sick like this?'

'Seven—no, it is eight months now,' he answered her quite readily, those remarkable amber eyes turned to watch the leaping flames. Perhaps it was a relief to talk to someone who spoke frankly and did not hedge about pretending there was nothing wrong with him. 'There was a blizzard at night and Bess here was lost in it. One of the young underkeepers thought it was his fault and went out to look for her. By the time we realised he was missing and I found them both we were all three in a pretty poor state.'

He grimaced, dismissing what she guessed must have been an appalling search. And he had gone out himself, she noted, not left it to his keepers and grooms to risk themselves for a youth and a dog. 'After four years in the army I thought I was immune to cold and wet, but I came down with what seemed simply pneumonia. I started to cough blood. Then, although the infection seemed to go, I was still exhausted. It became worse. Now I can't sleep, my strength is failing. I have no appetite, and there are night-fevers. The doctors say it is phthisis and that there is no cure.'

'That is consumption, is it not?' As he had said, a death sentence. 'I expect the doctors think saying it in Greek makes them seem more knowledgeable. Or perhaps it justifies a higher bill.'

'You have no great love of the medical profession?'

How elegant his hands were with the long bones and tendons. The heavy signet on his left ring finger was so loose that the seal had slipped round. 'No,' Julia admitted. 'I have not. No great faith, would perhaps be truer.' The doctors had done little enough for Papa, for all their certainties.

'You seem to understand that speaking about problems is a relief after everyone pretending there is nothing wrong.' He looked away from the fire and into her eyes and for a moment she thought the flames still danced in that intent gaze.

Jonathan's beautiful blue gaze was always impenetrable, as though it was stained glass she was looking at. This man's eyes were windows into his soul and a very unpleasant place it seemed to be, she thought with a shiver at her Gothic imaginings.

'Would it help to confide your story in a total stranger? One who will take it to—' He broke off. 'One who will respect your confidence.'

Take it to the grave. He was no priest bound to silence, she could hardly confess to her actions and expect him to keep the secret, but perhaps talking would help her find some solution to the problem of what she could possibly do now.

'My father was a gentleman farmer,' Julia began. She sat back in the chair and found she could at least begin as though she was telling a story from a book. The hound circled on the hearth rug, sighed and lay down with her head on her master's foot as if she, too, was settling to listen to the tale. 'My mother died when I was fifteen and I have no brothers or sisters, so I became my father's companion: I think he forgot most of the time that I was a girl. I learned everything he could teach me about the estate, the farm, even purchasing stock and selling produce.

'Then, four years ago, he suffered a stroke. At first there was talk of employing a steward, but Papa realised that I could do the job just as well—and that I loved the place in a way that an employee never would. So I took over. I thought there was no reason why we could not go on like that for years, but last spring he died, quite suddenly in his sleep, and my Cousin Arthur inherited.'

She would not cry, she had got past that. Just as long as the baron did not try to sympathise: she could not cope with sympathy. Instead he said, 'And there was no young man to carry you off?'

'I had been too busy being a farmer to flirt with young men.' He had seen, and heard, enough of her now to understand the other reasons no-one had come courting. She was hardly a beauty. She was too tall. And too assertive, too outspoken. *Unladylike hoyden*, Cousin Jane called her. *A managing, gawky blue-stocking female with no dowry,* that was what Jonathan had flung at her. He was obviously correct about her lack of attraction—it was quite clear in retrospect that she had been a complete failure in his bed.

'My cousins allowed me to stay because I had no-where else to go, but it was unsuitable for me to take any interest in the estate, they said, and besides, they made it very clear that it was no longer any of my business. Cousin Jane found me useful as a companion,' she added, hearing the flatness in her own voice. *A drudge, a dogsbody, the poor relation kept under their roof to make them appear charitable.*

'But then it changed?'

'They must have grown tired of supporting me, I suppose. Of the cost, however modest, and tired too of my interference in estate matters. There was a man—I think they intended to make it worth his while to take me off their hands. He did not offer marriage.'

* * *

A squalid story, Will thought as Miss Prior ran out of words. Those lips, made for smiles, were tight, and she had coloured painfully. It was unwise of her to flee her home, but the alternative seemed appalling and few unprotected young women would have had the resolution to act as she had done. 'You ran away, eventually found yourself in my parkland and the rest we know,' he finished for her.

'Yes.' She sat up straight in the chair as if perfect deportment could somehow restore her to respectability.

'What is their name? Someone needs to deal with your cousin. Even if he had not been in a position of trust, his behaviour was outrageous.'

'No! Not violence...' He saw her bite her lip at the muttered curse that escaped him. She had gone quite pale.

'No, of course not. You need have no fear that I might call him out. I forget sometimes that my fighting days are over.' *Damn.* And he hadn't meant to say that, either. Self-pity was the devil. 'I am not without influence. It would be my pleasure to make his life hell in other ways than by threatening him at swordpoint. Is his name Prior? Where is your home?'

She shook her head in silent refusal to confide. Will studied the composed, withdrawn, face in the firelight. He had never met a woman like her. Even in this state she seemed to have the self-possession of someone older, an established matron, not a girl of perhaps twenty-two or three.

In the candlelight her skin was not fashionably pale, but lightly coloured by the sun. Her hands, clasped loosely in her lap, were like her whole body—strong and graceful with the physical confidence that came from fitness and exercise. She moved, her cuff pulled back and he saw bruises on her wrist, black and purple and ugly. That a woman should be under his protection and yet he could not avenge such treatment was shameful. No, she must not go back to that, he could do that for her at least.

'I hope your father did not know that his heir would wilfully ignore the expertise you could have shared with him,' he said at last when a log broke in the grate, sending up a shower of sparks and jerking him back from his bitter reverie. 'I know all too well the character of my own heir, my cousin Henry. He'll squander away the lifeblood of the estate within a year or two—that's all it took him to lose what was not tied down of his own inheritance.'

'You are estranged from him?' Miss Prior's face was expressive when she allowed it to be. Now the little frown between the strongly marked dark brows showed concern. She was too tall, no beauty. One would almost say she was plain, except for the regularity of her features and the clarity of her gaze. And the generous curve of lips that hinted at a sensuality she was probably unaware of.

Will felt a *frisson* of awareness run through him, just as he had when she had held him in her arms on the bridge, and cursed mentally. He did not need something else to torture him and certainly not for his body to decide it was interested in women again. If he could not make love with the stamina and finesse that had caused his name to be whispered admiringly amongst certain ladies, then he was not going to settle for second best.

A wife, he had realised, was out of the question. He had known he must release Caroline from their betrothal, but it had shocked him, a little, how eagerly she had snatched at the offer amidst tearful protestations that she was not strong enough to witness his suffering. She was a mass of sensibility and high-strung nerves and he had found her delicate beauty, her total reliance on his masculine strength, charming enough to have talked himself half into love with her. To have expected strength of will, and the courage to face a husband's lingering death, was to have expected too much.

Miss Prior was waiting patiently for him to answer her question, he realised. Will jerked his wandering thoughts back. 'Estranged? No, Henry's all right deep down. He's not vicious, just very immature and spoilt rotten by his mama. If he wasn't about to inherit this estate I'd watch his antics with interested amusement. As it is, I'd do just about anything to stop him getting his hands on it for a few years until he grows up and learns to take some responsibility.'

'But you cannot afford to do that, of course.' Miss Prior had relaxed back into the deep wing chair. Another five minutes and she would be yawning. He was selfish to keep her here talking when she should be asleep, but the comfort of company and the release of talking to this total stranger was too much to resist.

'No. I cannot.' *I cannot save the only thing left to me that I can love, the only thing that needs me. My entire world. There must be a way.* In the army before he had inherited, and in the time he had been master of King's Acre, he had relied both on physical prowess and his intellect to deal with problems. Now he had only his brain. Will tugged the bell pull. 'Go to bed, Miss Prior. Things will look better in the morning.'

'Will they?' She got to her feet as the footman came in.

'Sometimes they do.' It was important to believe that. Important to believe that he would think of something to get King's Acre out of this coil, important to hope that the doctors were wrong and that he had more time. If he could only *make* time, stretch it…

'Goodnight, my lord.' She did not respond to his assertion and he rather thought there was pity in those grey eyes as she smiled and followed James out of the room.

The ghost of an idea stirred as he watched the straight back, heard the pleasant, assured manner with which she spoke to the footman before the door closed. A competent, intelligent, brave lady. Will let his head fall back, closed his eyes and followed the vague thought. Stretch time? Perhaps there was a way after all. Unless he was simply giving himself false hope.

Do things look better in the morning light? Julia sat up in the big bed, curled her arms around her raised knees and watched the sunlight on the tree tops through the bay window that dominated the bedchamber.

Perhaps she should count her blessings. *One: I am warm, dry and comfortable in a safe place and not waking up in another disreputable inn or under a hedge. Two: I am not in a prison cell awaiting my trial for murdering a man.* Because Jonathan was dead, he had to be. There was so much blood. So much… And when people had come, pouring into the room as her screams had faded into sobs, that was what they were all shouting. *Murder!*

And now she was a fugitive, her guilt surely confirmed by her flight. Julia scrubbed her hands over her face as if that would rub out the memories *Be positive. If you give up, you are lost…* Was there anything else to be thankful for?

Try as she might, there were no other blessings she could come up with. It was dangerous to try to think more than a few days into the future because that was when the panic started again. She had spent an entire morning huddled in a barn because the fear had been so strong that she could not think.

One step at a time. She must leave here, so that was the next thing to deal with. Perhaps Lord Dereham's housekeeper could recommend a nearby house where she might seek work. She could sew and clean, manage a stillroom and a dairy—perhaps things were not so very bad after all, if she could find respectable employment and hide in plain sight. No one noticed servants.

* * *

The baron came into the breakfast room as she was addressing a plate laden with fragrant bacon and the freshest of eggs. Her appetite had not suffered, another blessing perhaps, for she would need strength of body as well as of mind. *A mercy that I possess both.*

'My lord, good morning.' Lord Dereham looked thin and pale in the bright daylight and yet there was something different from last night. The frustration in the shadowed amber eyes was gone, replaced with something very like excitement. Now she could imagine him as he had been, a ruthless physical force to be reckoned with. A man and not an invalid.

'Miss Prior.' He sat and the footman placed a plate in front of him and poured coffee. 'Did you sleep well?'

'Very well, thank you, my lord.' Julia buttered her toast and watched him from under her lashes. He was actually eating some of the scrambled eggs set before him, although with the air of a man forced to swallow unpleasant medicine for his own good.

'Excellent. I will be driving around the estate this morning. You would care to accompany me, I believe.'

It sounded remarkably like a very polite order. He was, in a quiet way, an extremely forceful man. Julia decided she was in no position to take exception to that, not when she needed his help, but she could not spare the time for a tour. 'Thank you, I am sure that would be most interesting, but I cannot presume further on your hospitality. I was wondering if your housekeeper could suggest any household or inn where I might find employment.'

'I am certain we can find you eligible employment, Miss Prior. We will discuss it when we get back.'

'I am most grateful, of course, my lord, but—'

'Is your Home Farm largely arable?' he asked as if she had not spoken. 'Or do you keep livestock?'

What? But years of training in polite conversation made her answer. 'Both, although cattle were a particular interest of my father. We have a good longhorn herd, but when he died we had just bought a shorthorn bull from the Comet line, which cost us dear. He has been worth it, or, at least he would be if my cousin only chose the best lines to breed to him.' Why on earth did Lord Dereham want to discuss animal husbandry over the coffee pots? 'May I pass you the toast?'

'Thank you, no. I am thinking of planting elms on my field boundaries. Do you have a view on that, Miss Prior?'

Miss Prior certainly had a view on the subject and had left a promising nursery of elm saplings behind her, but she was beginning to wonder if the absence of a Lady Dereham was due to his lordship's obsession with agriculture and an inability to converse on any other topic. 'I believe them to be very suitable for that purpose. Marmalade and a scone, my lord?'

He shook his head as he tossed his napkin on to the table and gestured to the footman to pull back his chair. 'If you have finished your breakfast we can begin.'

Can we indeed! Was the man unhinged in some way?

Had his illness produced an agricultural mania? And yet he had shown no sign of it last night. As she emerged into the hall she saw the maid who had helped her dress that morning was at the foot of the stairs, holding her cloak, and a phaeton waited at the front steps with a pair of matched bays in the shafts. Her consent had been taken for granted, it seemed.

Julia closed her lips tight on a protest. Without Lord Dereham's help she was back where she had been the night before. With it, she had some hope of safety and of earning her living respectably. It seemed she had no choice but to humour him and to ignore the small voice in her head that was telling her she was losing control and walking into something she did not understand.

'I am at your disposal, my lord,' she said politely as she tied her bonnet ribbons.

'I do hope so, Miss Prior,' Lord Dereham said with a smile that was so charming that for a moment she did not notice just how strange his choice of words was.

Chapter Four

Were his words strange, or sinister? Or quite harmless and she was simply losing her nerve and her sense of proportion? Lord Dereham handed her up to her seat in the phaeton and then walked round and took the reins. The groom stepped back and the baron turned the pair down the long drive. They looked both high-bred and fresh. A more immediate worry overtook her concerns about his motives. Could he control them?

After a few minutes of tense observation it appeared that skill was what mattered. As Julia watched the thin hands, light and confident on the reins, she released her surreptitious grip on the side of the seat and managed not to exhale too loudly.

'The day I cannot manage to drive a phaeton and pair I shall take to my bed and not bother to rise again, Miss Prior,' he remarked, his voice dry.

How embarrassing, he must have sensed her tension and probably showing a lack of confidence in a man's ability to drive was almost as bad as casting aspersions

on his virility. And, safe as he was in his weakened condition, she had a strong suspicion that Lord Dereham's
prowess in the bedroom had probably been at least equal
to his ability as a whip. The thought sent a little arrow
of awareness through her, a warning that Lord Dereham was still a charismatic man and she was in danger
of becoming too reliant on his help.

She repressed a shudder at the direction of her
thoughts: she was never going to have to endure a man's
attentions in bed again. *Another blessing.*

'Cleveland bays?' she asked. Best not to apologise.
Or to speculate on the man beside her as anything but
a gentleman offering her aid. Or think about that inn
bedroom, not if she wanted to stay calm and in control.

'Yes, they are. They were bred here. Now, Miss
Prior, what do you think I should do about this row of
tenants' cottages?' He reined in just before they reached
a range of shabby thatched cottages. 'Repair them or
rebuild over there where the ground is more level, but
there is less room for their gardens?'

'Why not ask the tenants?' Julia enquired tartly, her
temper fraying along with the dream-like quality their
conversation was beginning to assume. 'They have to
live in them.' Really, she was extremely grateful to Lord
Dereham for rescuing her, but anyone would think she
was being interviewed for the post of estate manager!

He gave a grunt of agreement that sounded suspi-
ciously like a chuckle. Julia bristled as he drove past the
cottages with a wave of the whip to the women hanging
out sheets and feeding chickens. Was he making fun of

her because she claimed to have run her family estate? He had been polite enough about it last night, but most men would find her interest in the subject laughable, if not downright unfeminine.

'I also have views on poultry, the management of dairies, sawmills and crop rotation,' she said with false sweetness. 'I know a little about sheep, but more about pigeons, pigs and the modern design of farm buildings, if those are of any interest to you, my lord.'

Again that scarcely repressed chuckle. 'They are, but I think I had better explain myself before you lose all patience with me, Miss Prior. Would you care to look at the view from the temple over there?'

They had been climbing a low hill and the temple was revealed as a small folly in the classical style overlooking the lake. Julia closed her eyes and took a steadying breath. If she was not so tense and, under the surface, so scared, she would be able to cope with this perfectly adequately. Perhaps he was simply gauche and had no idea how to make conversation, although there had been no sign of that last night.

She mentally smoothed her ruffled feathers and replied with dinner-party graciousness, 'I am sure it will be a delightful prospect, my lord. And you have no need to explain yourself to me. I must apologise if my nerves are a little…'

'Frayed?' he enquired as he brought the pair to a standstill and climbed down. Julia sat tactfully still while he tied the reins to a post and came round to hand her from her seat. 'Well, I hope I may ravel them up again, a little. I have a proposition for you, Miss Prior.'

Proposition. That was a word with connotations and not all of them good. She closed her teeth on her lower lip to control the questions that wanted to tumble out, took his arm and allowed herself to be guided towards the curved marble seat at the front of the folly. She could at least behave like a lady for today—this was surely the last time a gentleman would offer her his arm. And if he proved not to be a gentleman?

When they were seated side by side Lord Dereham crossed one leg over the other, leaned back and contemplated the view with maddening calm.

Julia attempted ladylike repose at his side, but all that relaxation did was to allow the waking nightmares back into her head. 'My lord? You said you had a proposition? You have thought of some post I might apply for, perhaps?'

'Oh no, not…exactly. You, I believe, are in need of some time to recover from your precipitate flight, to rest physically and to collect yourself mentally.'

'Yes,' she agreed, wary. 'That would be an agreeable luxury, I must admit.'

'And I would appreciate the company of someone who is knowledgeable about estate management. I have ideas I would like to talk through. If you would accept my hospitality for, let us say, a week, it would give you breathing space and allow me to think of some respectable employment I might suggest.'

The baron did not look at her as he spoke and she

studied his profile as she considered, trying to imagine him with the weight back that he had lost, with colour in that lean, hard face and a gloss on that thick hair. He had been a very attractive man and his character still was. He might have autocratic tendencies, but he seemed understanding, intelligent and his actions, right from the start, had been gentlemanly and protective.

She would be in no danger from this man, she knew. But was it safe to stay, even for a few days? *Safer than wandering around with no plan and no money,* Julia told herself. 'Thank you, my lord. I would appreciate that and I will do my utmost to assist you.'

'Excellent. Shall we begin by being on rather less formal terms? My name is Will, I would like you to use it. May I call you Julia?'

In for a penny, in for a pound... 'Yes,' she said. 'I would like that. Can you not discuss your thoughts with your...I mean, the man who will...' Goodness, it was hard to think of a tactful way of saying, *The man who will take over when you die.*

'My heir, you mean?' His lips curled into a sardonic smile. 'Cousin Henry Hadfield. He has no interest in the land. He wasted his inheritance from his father on enjoying himself in town until his mother finally reined him in. Not a bad youth at heart—but if I were to talk to him about elm tress and field boundaries he would think me all about in the head.'

'Most people would, frankly, if they aren't practical landowners.' Julia got up and strolled a little way so she could look down on the lake lying below to her right and the edge of the park with the plough-lands beyond to the left. 'You have some long boundaries there. From all I have read elm grows fast and the roots go straight down and do not steal goodness from the crops or interfere with the plough. You raise a timber crop and waste no land. I have...I had started a nursery of cuttings from a neighbour's trees.'

'There's some land that might do for that,' Will said. 'Shall we drive on and have a look?'

They spent all morning driving around the estate and Julia gradually relaxed in Will's company. They did not agree about everything, but that, she supposed, was only to be expected and the mood was amiable as they finally returned to the house.

'I will take luncheon in my chamber, if you will excuse me. Then I have paperwork to see to in the library.' Will surrendered his coat and hat to the butler. 'Please feel free to explore the house as you wish. Or the pleasure grounds.'

It was a little like a fairy tale, Julia decided as she strolled through a rose garden. She had fled from evil and found herself in some enchanted place where the outside world did not intrude and everything conspired to make her comfortable and safe.

A gardener materialised at her side with knife and basket and asked which blooms she would like cutting for her chamber.

'Oh, I had better not,' she demurred.

'Lord Dereham sent me.' The man glanced towards

the house and Julia saw the silhouette of a man watching her from one of the long windows. The baron in his study, she assumed.

'Then thank you,' she said and buried her face in the trusses of soft fragrance.

At dinner she mentioned the roses, but Will waved away her thanks with a gesture of his long fingers. 'They are there to be enjoyed. What do you think of the gardens?'

'They are lovely. And the vegetable gardens are quite the most wonderful I have ever seen. You even have a pinery—I confess to quite indecent envy!'

The mobile mouth twitched a little at that, but Will only said, 'I haven't succeeded in getting a single edible pineapple out of it yet.'

'More muck,' Julia said. 'I was reading all about it and you need a huge, steaming pile of manure, far more than you would think.' She caught the eye of the footman who was bringing in the roast and he looked so scandalised for a second that she stopped with a gasp. 'I am so sorry, of all the things to be discussing at the dinner table!'

But Will was laughing. It was the first time she had heard more than a chuckle from him—an infectious, deep, wholehearted laugh—and she found herself laughing, too, until he began to cough and had to sip water until he recovered.

The next day was overcast with a cool wind so they had gone to the stables in the morning and walked slowly from box to box, admiring the mares and then smiling over the yearlings and the foals in the paddocks. Will had let her take his arm as though he felt at ease enough not to hide the fact that anything more than a stroll was tiring.

Julia explored the house in the afternoon. She found an upstairs sitting room with bookshelves and a deep window seat and curled up with a pile of journals and some novels, but after a while she realised that she was simply staring out of the window.

This place was still a fairy tale, a sanctuary from the dark that she had left behind, a place out of time with its prince, struck down by a wicked enchanter, but still strong enough to defend its walls and keep her safe.

The whimsy made her smile until the chill of reality ran down her spine. It could not last and she should not delude herself. Soon she would have to leave here and find employment and never, ever, be herself again. She had a week, and two days of that were gone already.

At dinner Will was quiet, almost brooding. *Tired, perhaps*, she thought and did not attempt to make conversation. When the footman cleared the plates and set the decanter at his elbow she rose, but he gestured her back to her seat.

'Will you keep me company a little longer, Miss Prior?' Before the servants he was always meticulous in observing the proprieties, she noticed. 'Thank you.' He nodded to the footman. 'I will ring if we need anything further.'

When they were alone Will said, without preamble, 'I have a proposal, Julia.'

'Another one?' Her heart sank for all her light words. He had changed his mind about the week's respite, found her some position as a housemaid...

'That was a proposition. This is literally a proposal.' He poured two glasses of port and pushed one across the table to her.

Bemused, she ignored the wine and studied his face instead. From the intensity in his expression she realised his calm was not quite as complete as she had thought. His voice, however, was quite steady as he said, 'Will you do me the honour of becoming my wife?'

Julia found she was on her feet, although she could not remember getting up. 'Your *wife*? Lord Dereham, I can only assume you are mocking me, or that your fever has become much worse.'

She walked away from the table on legs that shook and struggled for composure. It was safer for her self-control not to be looking at him. One could not be rude to an invalid as sick as he was, but how could he not realise how hurtful his teasing was?

'Miss Prior, I cannot talk to you if you stalk around the room,' Will drawled. The weak desire to cry turned into an itch in her palm and a disgraceful urge to slap his face. 'Please will you come back here so I can explain? I am not delirious and I have no intention of offering you insult.'

'Very well.' It was ungracious and she could not bring herself to return to the table, but she turned and looked at him, swallowing hurt pride along with the un-shed tears. 'Please explain, if you can. I find my sense of humour has suffered somewhat recently.'

But he was not smiling. The haggard face was as serious as if he truly was making a proposal of mar-riage, but his words were strangely far from the point. 'You know what I have told you about Henry. For the good of this estate and its people I need to prevent my cousin from inheriting until he is older, has matured and learned to control his spendthrift ways.'

'You believe he can?' Julia asked, diverted by scep-ticism for a moment.

'I think so. Henry is neither wicked nor weak, sim-ply spoiled and indulged. Even if he does not improve, the longer I can keep him from inheriting, the better. I need time, Julia.'

'And you do not have that.' Intrigued, despite her-self, she sat again.

'Do you know the law about inheritance when some-one disappears?' She shook her head. 'If the missing person does not reappear within seven years of their dis-appearance, the heir may apply to the courts for them to be presumed dead and for the inheritance to proceed.'

She began to understand. 'And you intend to dis-appear?'

'I intend to travel. I have always wanted to go to North Africa, Egypt, the Middle East. I hope I can make it that far, because once there, away from British au-thorities, I can vanish without trace when...when the time comes.'

Julia doubted he would make it across the Channel, never mind southern Europe, but if this daydream was keeping him going, who was she to disillusion him? She understood the power of dreams, the need for them. 'But what has that got to do with me?'

'I must leave King's Acre in good hands. I could employ an estate manager, but they would not have the commitment, the involvement, that a wife would have. I could not guarantee continuity and, if they left, who would appoint their replacement? And by marrying before I go I would remove the suspicion that my disappearance is a stratagem.'

Julia stared at the thin, intelligent face. His eyes burned with intensity, not with fever or madness. For a moment she thought she saw what Will Hadfield had looked like before this cruel illness had taken him in its claws and something inside her stirred in response. 'It matters this much to you?'

'It is all I have. Our family has held this land since the fourteenth century when it was given to Sir Ralph Hadfield as a reward for services to the crown—hence the name. I am not going to be the one who lets King's Acre fall apart.'

'And there is no woman you *want* to marry?'

The baron closed his eyes, not to shut out the world, but to hide his feelings, she was certain. 'I was betrothed. I released her, of course, and she was relieved, I think, to be freed from the burden of being tied to a dying man.'

Will opened his eyes and there was no emotion to

be seen on his face. Then he smiled, an ironic twist of the lips. 'Besides, she has no views on elm trees or cattle breeding.'

'So you only thought up this insane scheme when I stumbled into your life?' It might be insane, but, Heaven help her, she was beginning to contemplate it, look for the problems and the advantages. *Stop it!* Julia told herself. *It is an outrageous idea. I would be heaping deception upon deception.*

'That first night, after you had retired, I sat thinking that I needed a way to stretch time. Then I realised I might have had the answer sitting in front of me at my own fireside.'

The past days had been a test to see if she really knew as much as she said, to see if she had an attraction to this place. *And I have.* Then common sense surfaced. Fate would not rescue her so simply from the consequences of her own folly. 'Your relatives will never accept it.'

Besides, with the wedding her name would be known to all and sundry... *But Prior is quite common and Julia is not my first name. Lord Dereham seems to live fairly retired, this would not be a major society wedding to be mentioned in the newssheets. If I can ask him not to place an announcement, there is no reason to think it would ever be noticed in Wiltshire.*

'My relatives will have no choice but to accept it. I am of age, no one can suggest I am not in my right mind. They will be present at the wedding—along with my man of law and any number of respectable witnesses.

You will not be dependent upon them in any way. Only the land is entailed, so the income will be yours to spend as you wish until my death is finally pronounced. Then you will have the use of the Dower House for life and a very generous annuity in my will.'

'You would give me all this? I am ruined, an outcast from the only relatives I have. I have no material resources to bring to the marriage—not a penny in dowry.'

Arthur and Jane will not seek for me, they will simply be glad I am gone, she told herself. Would they even hear of Jonathan's death? He was a distant relative, she had left no identification in the inn. Perhaps they would think he had simply disappeared along with the money they had no doubt paid him to remove her.

'I am not *giving* you anything.' The amber eyes were predatory as they narrowed on her face. He knew she was weakening as a hunter knew when the prey began to falter. Again the sense of his power swept over her, the feeling that she could not resist him. 'I am purchasing your expertise and your silence.'

'People will talk, wonder where on earth I have come from. What will we tell them?'

'Nothing.' He had heard the capitulation in her voice, she realised, and he was right: she would do this if she could, snatch at this miracle. All that remained were the practicalities. Julia took an unthinking gulp of wine. 'Think of some story—or let them speculate to their hearts' content on where we met.

'There is little time to waste. I had asked you to stay

a week, but I have seen enough, I know you will be perfect for this. Fortunately the Archbishop of Canterbury is in the vicinity—he is staying with his godson, the Marquess of Tranton. I can obtain a special licence with no trouble and we will be married the day after tomorrow.' He stood up. 'Say yes and I will drive over tomorrow and see the vicar on the way back.'

Say yes, *say* yes *and accept this miracle.* What should she do?

Chapter Five

'**W**ill!' Julia came round the table and caught at his sleeve. 'It is impossible, I cannot marry you at such short notice.'

'Why ever not?' He put his hand over hers and she looked up into his eyes. There was only that mesmerising amber gaze full of passion and intensity, only the warmth of his hand, those long fingers closing over hers. Julia felt hot and cold and as disconcerted as the first time Jonathan had kissed her. This was a man, a young man, a man of passion, and something deep inside her responded to him.

She felt her lips part, her heartbeat stutter, then the grip of his fingers lifted and the illusion of intimacy fled.

'Had you some other plans for the day after tomorrow?' Will persisted.

Safe, protective irritation took the place of whatever insane emotions she had just been experiencing. *The man is completely focused on what he wants without a thought for me. It is a very good thing he is going away,* Julia thought, *otherwise we would be falling out for certain.*

'I haven't said *yes* yet,' she protested. He just looked at her. 'Oh, very well! Yes! But I do not have a thing to wear.' His eyebrows shot up. 'Except this.' She swept a hand down to encompass her skirts. 'I can hardly marry a baron in a creased, stained walking dress and old cloak.'

'Then go shopping tomorrow. I will give you money. There are no shops of very great fashion in Aylesbury, not even for ready to wear, but you will find something adequate and you can always go up to London shortly. Just hire a town house, if you wish, Julia.'

She had a sudden, welcome, thought. 'Everyone calls me Julia, but for the licence you must have my first name. Augusta.' She saw his face and almost laughed. 'I know. It was the name of my mother's godmother and they were in hopes of some generous present from her. No one ever uses it—in fact, I doubt anyone recalls it now.' Even if they saw any mention of the marriage in some newssheet, no one would think that Augusta Prior, making an excellent match to a baron in Buckinghamshire, might be Julia Prior of Wiltshire, fugitive.

'But what of your cousin?' she worried. 'I cannot help but feel we are cheating him.'

'If I had married as planned, I could have an heir due shortly and Henry's nose would be permanently out of joint. Or if I had not been caught in that blizzard I might be in excellent health now. What we are doing is ensuring that when he does inherit he will have an estate in fine heart and, I trust, the maturity to appreciate it.'

Julia prodded herself with the thing that was troubling her conscience, deep down below the worry and the fear. 'And I am being rewarded for sin,' she muttered as she sat down again. She had eloped with a man, slept with him out of wedlock and then, however unintentionally, killed him. She could not absolve herself from blame—if she had not done that first shocking thing, then Jonathan would still be alive.

'Sin?' Will Hadfield must have ears like a bat. 'Running away to save your virtue? And fleeing from physical abuse—I saw your wrist.'

Her fingers closed protectively around the yellowing bruises. *Eyes like a hawk as well.* 'It was poor judgement,' she argued. 'I had no plan other than escape. Goodness knows how I would have found a respectable way of supporting myself.' She had to remember the story she had told him, act in character. 'I should have thought of something else, something less shocking.'

After a moment she added, 'All you know of me is what I told you. I wonder that you trust me with this scheme of yours.'

'But *my* judgement, my dear Miss Prior, is excellent. I have watched you and listened to you. I have seen how you look at the land, how you talk to the people. I have heard how you think things through and deal with problems. I have every confidence in you—after all, once you are safely married to me, you will not be a target for predatory young men.'

He blithely ignored her sharp intake of breath and continued before she could reply. 'Will you go shopping tomorrow? I will send a maid with you and a footman for your parcels, and Thomas the coachman will deliver you to the Rose and Crown where you will find a private parlour and reasonable refreshments.'

'Thank you, I shall do as you advise. It seems you have thought of everything,' she added, managing with an effort not to allow her ungrateful resentment at his masterful organisation to show in her voice. It would serve him right if the archbishop refused to give him a licence and he found himself saddled with a fallen woman with a price on her head and a very large pile of bills.

And then her conscience pricked her. Will Hadfield was doing this because he was driven to it, he had been kind to her and now he was helping her out of danger in a way that was little short of a miracle. She wished she had known him before he had become ill, wished she could know him better now.

Or perhaps not. Even ill he was dangerously attractive. She did not want to grow to like him, to be hurt when he left, to agonise more than she would over the fate of any chance-met stranger.

'You have known my nephew for how long, exactly? I do not think I quite caught what dear William said.' Mrs Delia Hadfield had doubtless heard perfectly well everything that had been said to her and her façade of vague sweetness did not deceive Julia for a moment.

The widow, she was certain, was aghast that her husband's nephew had married and was consumed with a desire to discover everything she could about the circumstances.

Julia saw that Will was seated on the far side of the room, deep in conversation with the vicar. She could hardly expect him to rush to her side to rescue her. 'It seems only days,' Julia parried with an equally sweet smile and sipped her champagne. 'But it was something we simply felt compelled to do.'

'And we had thought him so happy in his engagement to Caroline Fletcher. Of course that could never be once he was so ill, but I had no idea dear William would prove so fickle. Such a *suitable* girl. So beautiful.' The widow's smile hardened and her eyes narrowed. *She thinks she is sliding her rapier under my guard.*

People were watching them, Julia could feel their curious stares like a touch. The salon was a long room, but even with the windows open wide on to the terrace overlooking the dry moat it was crowded with the wedding guests that Will had managed to assemble at such very short notice. She dared not let any of her true feelings show, but the recollection of the last time she had been in a press of people was making her heart beat faster and her skin feel clammy.

She made herself breathe slowly and shallowly. These people laughing and talking were nothing like that avid crowd and no one looking at her would guess that the new Lady Dereham in her pretty gown and elegantly coiffed hair was a fugitive with a deadly secret.

'I thought I loved another, you see…' Julia let her voice trail off artistically. 'And then…' *Really, where did I get this ability to play-act! I have been reading too many novels. Desperation, I suppose.* 'Then we found each other again, when Will's betrothal had been ended and I had realised that there was no one else for me but him,' she finished. 'So romantic, is it not?'

'So William knew you some time ago?' Mrs Hadfield was intent on pursuing this mystery.

'I would rather not talk about the past,' Julia murmured, improvising frantically. Will had assured her no one would ask awkward questions. He might have been correct so far as he was concerned, for she was sure he could depress vulgar curiosity with one look, but she had been an idiot to take his word for it and not prepare a careful story.

'I was sadly disillusioned in the man I thought I loved and that made me see Lord Dereham's qualities in a different light.' Set against a scheming, mercenary rake who tried to force her, she was certain even Will's undoubted faults would be preferable.

'Lady Dereham—or may I call you Cousin Augusta?' With an inward sigh of relief she turned to Henry Hadfield, Will's cousin and heir. She could see the relationship in the height and the straight, dark brows and something about the way his mouth curved when he smiled, but there was no strength of character in the handsome, immature, face. She tried to imagine those features superimposed on Will's strong bones and experienced a slight shock of…what? Attraction? Not desire, surely, not after what she had experienced.

The momentary feeling passed and she was able to concentrate again. It would not do to let her guard down with either of the Hadfields. Henry had not quite worked out what a threat to him she represented, but his mama would soon enlighten him.

'Why, Cousin, certainly. But Julia, please. I never use my first name.' She smiled. He was young and it was up to her to get to know Henry and to influence him if she could, instil in him a love for an estate she did not know and remain on good terms through seven long years of uncertainty.

The setting sun slanted in through the long windows, setting the silverware gleaming and painting a pink glow over the faces of the guests. Not that they needed much colouring, Julia thought. Will had not spared the champagne and cheeks were flushed and conversation still lively, although it was almost half past seven and the party had gathered to eat after the church service at noon.

'Friends.' Everyone turned. Will was standing in front of the cold hearth, a glass in his hand. Did everyone see how his knuckles whitened where his left hand gripped the mantelshelf, or was it only she who realised how tightly he was controlling himself?

The image of the statue of the dying Gaul that she had seen once as an engraving caught at her imagination. Will was still on his feet but only because of that same indomitable refusal to give up and die. What was it? she wondered. Pride? Anger partly, she was certain. Courage. He was fighting Death as though it was a person who had attacked his honour.

Her eyes blurred and she swallowed hard. If she had met him before he became sick... *He would have been betrothed to Caroline Fletcher*, she told herself with a sharp return to reality. And he would probably have been as dictatorial and single-minded as he was now.

'Firstly my wife and I must thank you for your support today at such short notice. Secondly, I must ask you for further support for Lady Dereham as I will be travelling abroad for some months and must leave immediately on the morrow.'

A babble of questions broke out and then the tall man who had come down from London to stand as groomsman, the friend from Will's army days, Major Frazer, said, *'Abroad?'*

'I intend to develop the stud here and I wish to purchase Andalusians from Spain and Arabians from North Africa.' The major said something in an undertone, but Will answered him in the same clear voice. 'My health? I am feeling much stronger. It is best that I go now while the weather holds. And finally, my friends, I must ask your indulgence if we retire so I can rest before the start of my journey.' He raised his glass, 'To my wife, Julia.'

'To Lady Dereham!'

Blushing, Julia made her way through the scarcely repressed whispers and speculation to Will's side. 'That has put the cat amongst the pigeons with a vengeance, my lord,' she murmured. 'I had no idea you intended to leave so abruptly.'

She saw with a pang of anxiety that the lines of strain around his eyes and mouth were even more pronounced than before. 'There is not a great deal of time to waste, is there?' he said with a wry smile. 'Come, let us go up.'

He was so determined. She felt sick at the thought of what he was going through, but there was nothing she could do to help him except what, for such selfish reasons, she was doing now.

People were considerate and did not detain them with more than a few words of good wishes. Julia made her way into the deserted hallway before she slid her hand from resting on Will's arm to a steadying pressure under his elbow. 'I will ring for your valet,' she said when they paused at the second turn.

'Jervis will be already waiting with your maid in our bedchamber.'

'*Our* chamber?'

'Certainly.' Julia looked up sharply and thought she caught just the faintest hint of a smile. 'In my state of health you surely do not expect me to be negotiating draughty corridors in the middle of the night in order to visit you?'

'Are you saying that you expect me to share your *bed* tonight?' It had never occurred to her for a moment that this marriage would be anything but one in name only. Surely a man in his state of health could not…could he? She stumbled on the next step with images, sensations, shuddering through her memory.

'Shh,' Will murmured as a door below opened and the noise of the dispersing guests filled the space. 'This is not the place to be discussing such matters.'

Julia swallowed, nodded and somehow managed the rest of the stairs without blurting out the protests that were on the tip of her tongue. When Will opened the door to the master bedchamber Nancy, the chambermaid, was waiting there, chatting to Jervis, filmy white garments draped over her arm and a wide smile on her lips. This was no place for that discussion, either. The servants had to believe this marriage was real as much as anyone.

'There you are, my lady! I've had hot water brought up to the dressing room for your bath and Mr Jervis will see to his lordship in here.' She swept Julia in front of her through another door into a small panelled room with a steaming tub standing ready.

'I've sprinkled that lovely nightgown with rosewater,' she went on chattily as Julia stood like a block to be undressed. She had indulged herself with a pretty summer nightgown and robe when she had shopped for her wedding clothes and the other wardrobe essentials in Aylesbury. What she had not expected was that anyone but herself and her maid would ever see them.

'Excellent,' she managed as she climbed into the bath and began to soap herself. From the other room came the sounds of conversation, the bang of a cupboard door closing, the rattle of curtain rings. Next door was a man, a virtual stranger, getting ready to go to bed and expecting her to join him. The last man with those expectations had played on every one of her love-filled fantasies, taken her virtue and then betrayed her.

This one, she reflected as she climbed out of the bath and was swathed in towels, had at least married her. But could a man in Will's state of health consummate a marriage? She had no idea how the mechanics of male desire actually worked, but the performance was certainly physically demanding. What if Will expected *her* to do something...? With Jonathan she had simply lain there, held him and tried to do what he wanted of her. It seemed from his words that she had not been very good at it. Julia pressed her hand to her midriff as if that would calm the rising panic.

Jervis bowed himself out. A moment later Nancy bustled from the dressing room with her arms full of towels, bobbed a curtsy in the direction of the bed and hurried after the valet. The outer door closed with a heavy thud, the inner one stood open on to an apparently empty room.

Will lay back against the heaped pillows and got his breathing under some sort of control. He was bone-weary, aching and the night fever was beginning to sweep through him, but he had to stay in sufficient control to cope with Julia who, it seemed, had not thought beyond the marriage ceremony. *She is a virgin,* he reminded himself.

'Are you still in there?' he enquired. 'Or have you climbed down the ivy to escape me?' There was a pause, then she appeared in the doorway in a gown of floating white lawn, her hair loose on her shoulders, her hands knotted before her. His breathing hitched. 'You are a white ghost tonight, not a grey one.' She was certainly pale enough to be a spirit.

Julia took one step into the chamber. Her feet were bare. For some reason that was both touching and disturbing. 'I had not realised that you would expect me to share your bed,' she said. Her chin was up.

'I am sharing my title, my home and my fortune with you,' Will pointed out, goaded by her obvious reluctance into tormenting her a little.

She went, if anything, paler. 'Of course. I have no wish to be difficult. It is simply that we had not discussed it.'

'True. I have to confess that I have no experience of virgins.'

'I am glad to hear it,' Julia said, with so much feeling that Will blinked. 'I mean, one would hope that a gentleman does not go around seducing virgins.' She bit her lip, then put back her shoulders, tossed her robe on to a chair and walked over to the bedside.

Will was powerfully reminded of pictures of Christian martyrs bravely facing the lions and felt a pang of conscience. For all her maturity and poise and her scandalous circumstances, Julia was an innocent and his own frustrations at his weakness were no reason to scare the poor girl. 'Perhaps I should make it clear that I do not expect you to do anything but sleep in this bed.'

'Oh.' Julia froze, one hand lifting the covers to turn them back. The colour seemed to ebb and flow under her skin and he wondered if she was about to faint. 'Truly?'

Her relief was palpable. Will told himself that he was a coxcomb to expect anything else: she scarcely knew him, he looked like a skeleton, he could hardly stand up half the time—why on earth would the poor woman *want* to make love with him? The very fact that she feared he might attempt it showed how innocent she was.

'Get into bed, I promise you are quite safe.'

Julia pushed back the covers, climbed in and sat upright against the pillows. A good eight inches of space and the thickness of his nightshirt and her gown separated their shoulders: it must be imagination that he could feel the heat of her skin against his. She smelled of roses and Castile soap and warm woman and her tension vibrated between them like a plucked harp string.

'It is important that no one can challenge this marriage,' he explained, more to keep talking until she relaxed than anything else. 'We have a licence from the Archbishop, we were married by the local vicar in the face of the largest congregation I could bring together and now both our houseguests and our servants will vouch for the fact that we spent the night in this room. If and when my aunt decides she is going to challenge your control of the estate, she will not be able to shake the legitimacy of this marriage or contest your position as my wife.'

'I see. Yes, I understand why it is necessary.'

It sounded as though Julia was having difficulty controlling her breathing. She was not the only one, Will thought with an inward grimace. The spirit was very willing indeed as far as he was concerned—but the flesh was certainly too weak to do anything to upset the composure of the warm, fragrant, softly rounded and very desirable female so close to him. She was not a beauty, but she was, he was uncomfortably aware, an attractive, vibrant woman.

'Go to sleep,' he suggested and reached out to snuff the candles.

'Goodnight,' she murmured and burrowed down under the covers.

Will willed himself to stillness as gradually her breathing slowed and he waited for sleep to take her. Then a small hand crept into his. He froze. After a moment Julia shifted, murmured something and, before he could react, she snuggled right up to his side, her cheek on the thin cotton of his nightshirt over his heart.

'Julia?' His heart pounded in his chest until he felt dizzy. Or perhaps it was simply the scent and the feel of her. Somehow Will managed not to put his arms around her and drag her tight against him

'I am sorry,' she said. 'I should have known I would be quite safe with you, that you are a gentleman. I do not want you to think I was unwilling because you are ill.' She wriggled and came up on her elbow. Before he realised what she was doing she bent her head. The kiss would have landed on his cheek—instead, as he turned his head, their lips met.

Soft warmth, the yielding curve of that lovely mouth he had been trying to ignore for days. The whisper of her breath between slightly parted lips, the hint of the taste of her—champagne, strawberries, woman.

Hell. The torture of this was going to kill him. He couldn't breathe, his heart would surely give out. He wanted to touch her, caress her, because he was suddenly acutely aware that this trusting sensuality *could* overcome his body's weakness.

But he had just given her his word. He pressed his lips lightly to hers and then murmured, 'Goodnight, Julia. Better that you sleep on your side of the bed or you will find me a very hot companion with this fever.'

'Is there anything I can do for you?' she asked. He could almost feel her blushes as she lay down a safe distance from him.

Yes, kiss me, touch me, let me make love to you. 'No, thank you.' Will closed his eyes and made himself lie still. It would be a long night.

Julia woke in the dawn light. Exhausted by fears and emotion and the strain of the wedding, she had slept as though drugged and Will had let her. 'Will?' Silence. As she turned something crackled on the empty bed beside her. The note when she unfolded it said simply,

Goodbye. I will write when I can. All the information and addresses you need are in my desk in the study. I have taken Bess with me. Good luck. Will.

A key slid out of the folds and fell into the creased hollow where he had lain beside her all night. She was alone. A widow in all but name.

Her fingers closed around the key as they had around

his hand last night. Will Hadfield had given her her life back, as his was ending. He had not realised what a gift he was making her, what he had saved her from, but he had shown trust and confidence in her and that was balm to her bruised soul. She had tried, in sheer self-preservation, to feel nothing for him but a polite, remote concern, but she was aware that somehow the essence of the man had touched her heart.

'Oh, Will.' Julia curled up on his side of the bed and buried her face in his pillow. Was it imagination, or did it still hold a faint warmth, a trace of the scent of his skin?

Chapter Six

Three years later, 21st June, 1817—
Assembly Rooms, Aylesbury,
Buckinghamshire

'Do try and look as if you are enjoying yourself, Julia!' Mrs Hadfield scolded in a whisper. 'Do you have a headache?'

'A little. I really do not think I should have agreed to come to this dance, Aunt Delia.' Julia eyed the noisy throng around them with misgiving as they made their way into the market town's Assembly Rooms. She tried to avoid any kind of large public gathering where she did not know everyone present. Even after three years she had nightmares of someone pointing an accusing finger at her, shouting *Murderess! Arrest her!* She made herself breathe slowly, shallowly, and focused on negotiating the steps up to the front doors. Usually the panic could be kept under control by such tactics.

It was a long time since she had attended a dance of

any kind, let alone a public assembly, and she should have known she would regret not standing up to Aunt Delia's bossiness. She cast around for an explanation for her subdued spirits. 'Under the circumstances—'

The older woman bridled. 'The circumstances are that my nephew took off in a most ill-considered manner three years ago. The fact that you have not heard anything from him for almost eighteen months does not mean you should be behaving like a widow.' The words *not yet* hung unspoken between them

On the surface Mrs Hadfield had mellowed since her first resentment over Will's marriage, disappearance and the events that followed. After nine months, when she finally appeared to accept that Henry's position was unassailable and that Julia was not doing anything to damage his inheritance, she unbent towards the younger woman, although her tendency to patronise and to attempt to organise her niece by marriage grated on Julia's nerves.

But she suppressed her own forceful nature and worked hard to foster good relations between the households. She suspected that the other woman, foolish though she was in the way she indulged her son, was both a realist and also potentially a danger.

Julia knew that Delia had demanded that the vicar show her the licence and Nancy had confided indignantly that Mrs Hadfield had questioned her about where her mistress had slept on her wedding night.

'And did you tell her?' Julia asked.

'I did that! She asked me about the sheets, would

you believe? I put her straight, interfering old besom,' the maid said darkly.

So, Julia reflected, the pain of jabbing a large sewing needle into her thumb and sacrificing a few drops of blood had been worthwhile.

Mrs Hadfield might have accepted the marriage, but she had a clear eye on the calendar, and had no doubt consulted her lawyer over the necessary action to take in 1821 in the absence of proof of Will's fate. She was intelligent enough to know that they must wait, even if she was probably crossing off the days in her almanac, and the fact that Julia made a point of consulting Henry upon every decision relating to the estate at least appeared to mollify her.

'I do not behave like a widow,' Julia protested now as they inched their way to the foot of the stairs, Henry protectively at their backs. 'I do not wear mourning.' She glanced down with some complacency at the skirt of her highly fashionable shell-pink evening gown with its daring glimpse of ankle and then the months when she had worn black, when her heart had seemed frozen with grief, came back to reproach her for her mild vanity.

She pushed away the memory of those months, of the child she had lost, and made herself focus on the present. 'I will not give up on Will until I absolutely have to.' And somehow that was true. A whimsical part of her mind had a fantasy of Will well and happy and living an exotic life as an eastern pasha although the letters, the straightforward letters sent via his lawyer saying where he was, had long since ceased. She had never written back for he made it quite plain he was constantly on the move and had nowhere to send the letters.

The fantasy Will was strong and handsome and responsible for some rather disturbing dreams about things that, in the cold light of day, she preferred not to contemplate.

'I go to dinner parties and hold them,' she went on, calmer now they were climbing the stairs and she had something to concentrate on. 'I attend picnics and soirées and musical evenings. It is just that this seems rather…boisterous.'

And exposed. And full of people she did not know, people from outside the small, safe circle of friends and acquaintances around King's Acre. Improbable though it was after three years that anyone would recognise a half-naked, distraught murderess in the fashionably gowned, utterly respectable, Lady Dereham.

'Boisterous? The young people may romp. I shall not regard it,' Mrs Hadfield observed. 'For myself I am just thankful to be out of the house now that wretched summer cold has left me. I confess I am starved of gossip and fashions, even provincial ones.'

A faint headache, irrational fears and a growing, inexplicable, sense of foreboding were no excuse to be churlish, Julia told herself. And the Assembly Room, when they finally managed to enter it, was certainly a fine sight with the chandeliers blazing and the ladies' gowns and jewels like a field of flowers in sunlight. She relaxed a trifle as Henry, on his best behaviour, found seats for the ladies and melted away into the crowd to find them lemonade.

'He wants me to agree to him going off to the Wilshires' house party next week,' his doting mama said. 'Which probably means there is a young lady he has his eye upon amongst the other guests.'

More likely some congenial company his own age and a tempting array of sporting pursuits, Julia thought cynically as one of Mrs Hadfield's bosom friends greeted her with delighted cries and bore down upon their alcove. Henry was maturing, but he was still not much in the petticoat line and far more likely to flee than flirt if confronted by a pretty girl.

'I will take a turn around the room, if you will excuse me, Aunt.' Mrs Hadfield, already embarked upon some prime character assassination, merely nodded.

Everyone was having a very good time. So why could she not simply settle down and enjoy watching? Or even dance, if anyone asked her? The familiar crowd-induced panic was gone, but there was still this odd feeling of apprehension, of tension. Perhaps she was coming down with something. Not Aunt Delia's cold, she sincerely hoped.

Julia stopped by a pillar halfway down the room and fanned herself, amused by the chatter of a group of very young ladies who could only just have come out that Season.

'I do not know who he is, I have never seen him before,' one said as she peeped through the fronds of a palm. 'But have you ever seen such wonderful shoulders?'

'So manly,' another agreed with a sigh. 'And his hair—so romantic!'

Julia looked to see the paragon who had attracted their wide-eyed admiration. *Goodness.* There was no mistaking which man it was as he stood surveying the room with his back to them. Silly chits they might be, but they could recognise a fine figure of a man when they saw one. *That certainly is a magnificent pair of shoulders.* And his glossy brown hair was indeed romantically long.

The young ladies were far too bashful and shy to do more than giggle and swoon at a distance. Julia told herself that she was a matron and therefore perfectly at liberty to wander closer to inspect this threat to female susceptibilities.

She was not given to admiring gentlemen. She was a respectable lady with a reputation to maintain and the loss of her virginity had taught her that yearning after a handsome face was one thing—the reality of amorous men, quite another. Her body might disagree sometimes, her dreams conjure up fantasies, but, waking, she knew better. A solitary bed at night was a positive benefit of life as a grass widow, as she frequently reminded herself.

Even so, this man intrigued her for no reason she could put a finger on. She paused a few feet away from him, swept her fan languidly to and fro and studied him from the corner of her eye. This was easier when the heroine of a romantic tale did it, she realised, eyes watering. What she could tell, without blatantly staring, was that his valet and tailor had between them contrived to send him forth outfitted to constitute a menace to any woman who set eyes upon him.

He was clad in a close-fitting swallowtail coat and skin-tight silk evening breeches that between them left very little of the gentleman's well-muscled form to the imagination. Julia glanced casually around the room and managed to register, in profile, tanned skin, an arrogant nose, a very decided chin and long dark lashes which were presently lowered in either deep thought or terminal boredom.

The knot of apprehension that had been lodged uncomfortably in the pit of her stomach all evening tightened. *I know you.* Which was impossible: she could not have forgotten this man. *I know you from my dreams.* He shifted, restless, as though he felt her scrutiny and then, before she had the chance to move away, he turned his head and stared right into her face. And he was not bored or thoughtful now for he was studying her with eyes that were the amber of a hunting cat's, the deep peaty gold at the bottom of a brandy glass.

They were the eyes she had last seen burning with scarce-suppressed frustration in the face of a dying man. The eyes of her husband.

Julia had always imagined that fainting was a sudden and complete loss of consciousness: blackness falling like a curtain. But now the margins of her sight began to narrow down until all she could see was the face of the tanned man, those extraordinary eyes locked with hers. *Will.* Then the only noise was the buzzing in her head and the blackness came and on a sigh she escaped into it without a struggle.

He could hold one tall, curvaceous woman without trouble. Will registered the fact with the faint surprise that still struck him when his body obeyed without faltering, when his sinews and muscles flexed and responded with their old confidence and power.

'The lady has fainted. There is nothing to be concerned about.' The cluster of helpful matrons surrounding him were still thrusting smelling bottles forwards, waving fans, calling for sal volatile. 'If someone could please direct me to a quiet retiring room with a couch?'

Several led the way, bustling around and offering advice until he secured peace by the simple expedient of shouldering the door shut behind him and leaving them on the other side. Julia slid limply from his arms on to the rather battered leather *chaise* and he shot the bolt to give them privacy.

They appeared to be in a storeroom, now doing service as a makeshift retiring room with a cheval glass propped against the wall, a few chairs and a screen. Not the place he would have chosen to be reunited with his wife, but it had the virtue of privacy at least.

It was not the time of his choosing either, which should be a lesson to him not to yield to sudden impulses. He should have stayed in his bedchamber and ignored the lights and music from the Assembly Rooms opposite and then, as he had planned, arrived at King's

Acre in the morning. So close now to his dream, so close to coming home.

He had been thinking of the morrow when something had made him look up, glance to the side. He had recognised her at once, although this was no longer the anxious, tired woman he had married, but a poised and elegant young matron. Her eyelids flickered as he watched her now.

'Will?' The whisper from the *chaise* was incredulous. He spun a chair round and sat beside her. No time for dreaming yet. This was not going to be easy for he had no idea of what his own feelings were, let alone hers. Julia lay still, her face white, but she was thinking, calculating, he could tell. She might have fainted, but she was not in a daze any longer. 'I thought you were a ghost,' she murmured.

'That was my line when we first met, if I recall. I am perfectly real, Julia.' He remembered the courage and the pallor and the height. He recalled his body's surprising arousal and, looking at her now, he was no longer so amazed that Julia had sent tremors of desire through a dying man.

'I am very glad. And you are perfectly well by the look of you, which is wonderful,' she said slowly, as though she could still not believe in him. 'But, Will, what happened? You were so ill, and there has been no letter from you for eighteen months at least. I am delighted to see you again, of course, but it is such a shock!'

The colour was beginning to come back to her

cheeks. Three years had indeed wrought changes in her. The clinging silks of her evening gown revealed lush curves, smooth skin. Her hair was fashionably dressed, glossy with health. Julia was not a fashionable beauty, but she was undeniably attractive. She caught her lower lip between her teeth, drawing his eyes to the fullness and sending a bolt of desire through him. This was his wife. The emotions that produced were confusing and not all welcome, not yet. She was real now and he was going to have to deal with that reality.

'Yes, I am completely well.' He might as well explain now and get it over with. 'I was very ill in Seville and the doctor that Jervis found, quite by accident, was one who practised Jewish and Moorish medicine. He gave me some drugs, but mainly he made me rest, out in the sunshine. He took over my diet and gradually the coughing stopped and the night sweats got less frequent. I began to sleep and gain strength.

'Then he sent me south to the coast and from there over to North Africa to a doctor he knew.' Will shrugged. 'There is more to it than that, of course. Exercise, massage, swimming to build up my muscles again, days when I feared I would never get back to how I was before.

'But the miracle happened, although for months I could not believe I was really cured. Every time I picked up the pen to write I did not know what to say. If I said I was getting better and it was just a false hope… I have been fully well for over six months but it is hard to believe it sometimes.'

It was no easier speaking of it than it had been to try to write. Eventually he would learn to accept that he was going to have a future. A life. 'I thought it would be better simply to come home.'

Julia sat up and swung her feet on to the ground. Pink satin slippers and a provocative amount of ankle showed beneath her hem. His wife had obviously decided it was far too early to go into mourning for him, or perhaps she had simply found it easier to forget him.

She is still damnably self-possessed, he added mentally as she studied him, her face almost expressionless. And yet, there was something beneath that cool scrutiny. *What is she thinking?* He did not like secrets. Probably she was still recovering from the shock of seeing him and that was all it was.

'Why are you here?' she asked. 'At this dance, I mean.'

'I intended to come to King's Acre in the morning rather than turn up on the doorstep when you were about to sit down to dinner. And then I saw the lights and heard the music and decided to dip my toe into English life once more. It never occurred to me that you might be here.'

'Aunt Delia persuaded me to come. I am not much given to large public assemblies.' Julia studied him. 'And you have had no news of home, of course.'

Something *was* wrong, he could sense it. 'I have had no news at all. I collect that you and Aunt Delia are on good terms?'

'We have learned to rub along together,' she said

drily. 'And I have learned to bite my tongue even if she still sees no need to hold hers. But I should not be disrespectful, I have found her kind on many occasions. This is going to be a considerable shock to her; she has quite decided that you…that Henry is definitely going to inherit.'

'Did you travel with her this evening?' Time enough tomorrow to face Delia and Henry and shatter their hopes.

'No. I used my own carriage. It is out of their way to collect me and I prefer to be independent.'

'Then we will go back together, you and I.' Now this meeting had happened there was no going back, no retreat into the neutral ground of a solitary inn bedchamber for the night. 'If Delia has not seen me there is no need to tell her I have returned, not until tomorrow. Are you well enough to find her and let her know you are returning home?' Julia nodded. 'Then I will go and settle my account, pay off the postilions and collect my baggage. Jervis and I will meet you in the yard of the Stag's Head opposite.'

Something flared in her eyes, but it was gone before he could analyse it. Julia pressed her lips together as if on a retort and nodded again. This was not the place to talk. Will got to his feet and let himself out, wary now that Delia or Henry might see him. A confrontation in a crowded ballroom would set the district on its ears for weeks. That was the only reason for the knot in his gut, surely? He would be home within the hour. His life could begin again—on his terms now.

* * *

Julia stared blankly at the battered door panels as the catch clicked shut. She was not a widow. She was not even the pretend-wife of a man who had vanished as though he had been a dream. Her husband was alive and fit and, as far as she could tell, in the very best of health. Which meant he would find out exactly what had happened at King's Acre in his absence.

She had no idea what Will imagined he was coming home to, but she rather suspected that he had not thought through the implications of surviving his hasty marriage. Finally she would find out exactly what manner of man she was tied to, for this was all going to shake him off balance enough to reveal his true character. The baby. Her mind shied away from how she was going to break that to him.

Think of something else. My goodness, but he is attractive. Julia jabbed loose hairpins in securely and told herself that physical attractiveness was no guide to inner character. And if Will Hadfield thought he was coming home to her bed tonight he must think again. There was far too much to be said, to work out, before things became that intimate. She swallowed. If they ever did. She was not at all certain what she wanted, although that was probably academic. Her desires were not going to affect Will's reactions. For all she knew he might try to repudiate her now he no longer needed her. He certainly might when he learned what had happened in his absence.

But that was something to worry about when she was

alone. Now she must leave without arousing Delia's suspicions. Julia opened the door and almost bumped into Henry. She slid her arm into his and produced a faint smile. 'Cousin Henry! Just the person I need. I have such a headache—would you be a dear and let your mama know I am returning home now?'

'Of course. Shall I go and call your carriage?'

He was a nice young man, Julia thought, watching him weave through the crowd to the front door. Still self-centred and inclined to believe that things would fall into his lap by right, but he would learn. Yet however little he wished his cousin ill, the discovery that he was not going to inherit King's Acre in a few years would be a blow that would set his world on its ear.

When her carriage pulled into the inn yard the footman jumped down from the box to open the door and let the steps down and almost fell over his feet when he saw the two men waiting. 'Mr Jervis! And—oh, my Heavens, it's his lordship! Thomas, look, it's his lordship just like he used to be!'

'Praise be!' Thomas the coachman must have jabbed the horses' mouths in his excitement. The carriage rocked back and forth and she saw Will grin in the lamplight. It was the first time she had ever seen him smile like that. How had she ever thought him old, even when he had been so sick? This was a man in his prime.

'Praise be, indeed, Thomas. Good to see you again, Charles. Now, load up the bags and let us be going. We can't keep her ladyship sitting around like this.' He climbed in, the valet on his heels.

'Good evening, your ladyship.' The valet sat down with his back to the horses, his hat held precisely on his knees.

'Good evening, Jervis. Welcome home. I am delighted to see you after all this time.' And thankful that his presence in the carriage would bar any but the most commonplace conversation. Shock was beginning to give way to apprehension. It was no more than that, she assured herself. There was nothing really to actually be *afraid* of. Was there? Only some very unpleasant revelations to deal with.

'You have bought a new team,' Will observed. Perhaps he too was glad of their involuntary chaperon. 'There will be more horses arriving in a few weeks. I bought an Andalusian stallion and two mares and a dozen Arabians.'

'Fifteen horses?' Julia felt a surge of excitement sweep back the fears into their usual dark corner. 'We will need new stabling. And to extend the paddocks,' she added. 'Thank goodness the feed stocks are so good and the hay crop should be excellent if the weather holds. We may need to hire new grooms.' Mind racing, she started to make lists in her head. 'I will get Harris the builder up tomorrow to discuss plans. Jobbins will have ideas about any likely local lads to hire, of course, but we will need someone used to stud work—'

'I have it all in hand,' Will said. 'You have no need to trouble yourself with such things now that I am home.'

'It will be no trouble,' Julia retorted. She knew exactly what state the grass was in, how much new fencing was needed, where an extended stable block would go and the strengths and weaknesses of the current stable staff. There was going to be a territorial battle, she could tell, because she was not prepared to let three years of hard work go and retire to her sitting room and her embroidery. But that was something else that could wait until the morning.

'We can have supper while they make up the bed in the master suite,' she said into the silence that had fallen. 'And make sure your room is aired, of course, Jervis.' In the gloom of the carriage she could sense the sudden sharpening of Will's attention. He was hardly going to discuss their sleeping arrangements now. When the time came to go upstairs she would just have to be very clear that she wished to be alone.

No doubt that would be another subject on which Lord Dereham had very firm opinions. And then there was the secret tragedy that, somehow, she was going to find a way to confess before anyone told him of it.

Chapter Seven

Will rolled over on to his back and opened his eyes. Above him, lit by the early morning light, was the familiar dark blue of the bed canopy. He blinked the sleep out of his eyes and focused on the stars embroidered in silver thread by some long-ago ancestress. Home. He really was home.

Without turning his head he stretched out a hand as he had every morning since he had finally accepted that he was not about to die. Beside him the bed was empty, the covers flat, the pillow smooth and cool. No one was there, of course.

Julia had not been very communicative last night, not after the brief verbal tussle over where he was sleeping. Which she had won, he reflected. For one night, at any rate. He was hard, aroused, but then he was every morning since he had recovered.

Will threw back the covers with an impatient hand and let the cool air of dawn flow over his naked, heated body. He had made his bed and now, he supposed, he must lie on it. Not that it would be such a hardship to lie with Julia. His mouth curved at the memory of her in that pink silk last night. He had thought about her these past years, but the memories had been of her spirit and her intelligence, not of her looks.

But marrying Julia had been a brilliant piece of improvisation by a dying man. A marriage of convenience that he had expected to last mere months. For a man with the prospect of a long life ahead of him it was a sentence to a loveless but solid and respectable future.

Or, given the hideous example of his own parents' *convenient* marriage, loveless and cold, although, if he had anything to do with it, not spectacularly scandalous. He winced at the remembrance of the raised voices, the banging doors, the sniggers at school and the oh-so-careful reports in the scandal sheets—*It is said that a certain Lady D—... It is the talk of the town that Lord D—'s latest companion...*

All those lies, all the pretence. His father pretending he was not unfaithful, his mother pretending her heart was not broken, both of them lying to him, fobbing him off, whenever he asked if anything was wrong, when Papa would be home, why Mama was weeping again. It had felt as though they simply did not care enough about him to talk to him, to explain, to comfort the confused small boy. Looking back, he saw no reason to modify that explanation.

Thousands married without love and managed to live perfectly affectionate, civilised, faithful lives, he knew that. But, for a man who had once dreamed of something more for himself, it was a damnably unpleasant place to be. He had lived with a vision of bringing love back to Knight's Acre and he had to accept that now he never would. He could sense that Julia would find it difficult to have him home and he could understand her feelings.

The night before he had told Jervis to leave the curtain drawn back. Now the sun flooded in through the window and he gazed down the long avenue of oaks towards the glimmer of the lake in the distance while he found his equilibrium again. He had managed to survive a death sentence, the loss of his betrothed and exile from the place he loved with a bone-deep passion. He had taken a gamble to save King's Acre and if he had not, and had stayed, he would be dead by now and Henry in his place.

You're an ungrateful devil, he told himself. He was alive, well and had an intelligent, attractive wife. King's Acre had been in good hands, he felt confident of that. Of course Julia had been cool and had wanted to sleep alone last night. After all, she was a virgin and was probably shaken to the core to have her virtually unknown husband turn up without notice. That would change and he would be careful with her. And she would realise this morning that the master of the house had returned and she could place all the business affairs in his hands and, no doubt, be glad to shed the responsibility.

But for now the house was quiet in the dawn light. Down in the kitchens a yawning scullery maid would be riddling the grate and making up the range to heat water for the other servants. Up here all would be undisturbed for at least an hour.

King's Acre lay open and waiting for him, like a mistress awaiting her lover's return, and he would savour it, rediscover it and his hoarded, happy memories. Will pulled on a brocade robe and, without bothering to find his slippers, opened the door on to his dressing room.

He wandered from room to room, looked out of windows, touched furniture, picked up trinkets. Under his fingers the house came to life again in a myriad of textures: polished wood and rough tapestry; smooth porcelain, cold metal; cut glass and ornate ormolu. His eyes lingered on favourite paintings, achingly remembered views, familiar spaces. In his nostrils was the smell of lavender and beeswax, wood smoke and, unsettlingly unfamiliar, a hint of the perfume he remembered from Julia's skin as he had carried her into the retiring room the evening before.

On this upper floor every door opened to him. At the other end of the main passageway lay the oak panels leading to the bedchamber Julia was using and he passed that by. Today she would move her things into the suite next to his and that would put an end to this nonsense of sleeping apart.

The final door, the one beyond her dressing room, did not open. Will twisted the handle, pushed, expecting it to have stuck. But it stayed firm. Beyond, he recalled, was a small room with a pretty curve to the wall where it fitted into one of the old turrets. There was no reason for it to be locked. Thwarted, he frowned. It could wait, of course. He would get the key... But the rest of the rooms had opened to him as if welcoming him back, giving themselves up again to their master. It jarred that this one remained blankly inaccessible.

Frustrated, Will hit the panels with his clenched fist. The sound echoed down the quiet corridor like a hammer blow.

A sharp intake of breath was all the warning he got that he was not alone. When he turned Julia was standing in the doorway of her room, her eyes wide, one hand clenched in the ruffles of her robe.

Will should not look so much bigger in a robe with bare feet and yet he seemed to fill the space. His eyes ran over her as she stood there in the flimsy summer robe until she felt naked and exposed.

'I am sorry, I did not mean to wake you. I was surprised to find the door locked.'

'There are just some things stored in there,' she said vaguely. 'Did you need the room? I will have it cleared.' *Oh, I am such a fool! Why didn't I do it before? I don't need an empty nursery to remind me of the child I lost. Can I tell him now? No.* All night she had tossed and turned, trying to think how she would break the news of what she had discovered after he had left.

'No, I don't care about the room,' Will said. 'But may I come into yours?'

'My bedchamber? But, why?'

'Why?' One dark brow rose and his smile became sensual. That look had been in Jonathan's eyes that

night in the inn. Her pulse spiked. 'I am your husband,' Will pointed out.

'But our marriage was only a sham, a device. You cannot expect to...to come to my bed just like that, without any discussion, without giving me any time—I hardly know you!'

'Then I suggest we make up for lost time.' His expression softened. 'I find you very attractive, Julia. Do I...frighten you? Is that it?'

He was so close she could see the individual stubble of his night-beard, see the crisp curl of hair in the vee of his robe. *He is naked under it, just as I am beneath mine.* He was a virile, attractive man. Head and heart and body seemed to be at war in her. Her feminine reactions to him were primal, she could not help them, she knew that. Even before, when he had been so ill, she had felt that flicker of heat, that attraction. And it was her duty to lie with him, she had taken everything he offered her and been grateful for it.

'No,' she admitted and saw the tension leave him.

But... She swallowed as he came closer still. She only had to close her eyes and she thought of Jonathan, his hands impatient, the painful thrusting into her body, his sneers, the betrayal. And he had left her with child.

Will reached out and pulled her against him and then there was nothing but those amber eyes holding hers as he lowered his head and kissed her. One hand slid up to hold her head and his fingers sifted into the mass of hair, loosened from its night-time plait. With the other arm he encircled her shoulders. She felt herself become stiff, unyielding, as reactions and instincts warred within her.

Will was overwhelming. Overwhelmingly big, over-whelmingly male. His mouth, as it crushed down on hers, was unlike anything she had experienced or imag-ined.

His tongue slid along the tight seam of her lips, seek-ing entrance, and she tasted him, felt his heat. *This is not Jonathan.* Suddenly her body was fluid, curving against his, only thin muslin and thick silk separating their bare flesh.

Jonathan had not seemed to want to kiss her much. There had been romantic, respectful kisses when he was courting her. Fleeting caresses that she now knew to be hypocritical ploys. When he had taken her to his bed she had ached for kisses, had wanted their reas-surance, but he had been urgent, focused on sheathing himself in her body and, she realised now, reaching his own satisfaction.

She tensed at the memory, transferring those feel-ings to Will, wanting to reject him, but her body was sending her clamouring messages of need, of surren-der. Of desire. He felt so strong against her. The thrust of his erection pressed against her belly. His skin smelt of musk and, faintly, of last evening's shaving soap. His morning beard was rough against her cheeks.

Her body wanted to be seduced. Her common sense, squeaking faintly to be heard against the clamour of emotion, told her that he was her husband, that she should simply allow herself to be swept off to his bed.

No. Will's tongue probed along her lips, seeking entrance. Some instinct that she did not dare to quite trust murmured that he would not force her. *But he will make my body force me*, she argued back. *He thinks he holds every card, the arrogant devil.*

Then take control, don't let him dominate you so. As she thought it she felt her body melting, answering him, demanding with as much urgency as his was. He used his strength and she could not match it, but she could use it against him as a wrestler uses his opponent's weight to overbalance him.

Damn you, Will Hadfield, Julia thought as she opened her lips, felt the triumphant surge of his tongue. *You will be my husband, not my master.* Rather than yield she would give as good as she got. Her own tongue met his, boldly, and then she lost track of time, of coherent thought and, certainly, of speech.

Will kissed as though this meeting of mouths was the sex act in itself: hot, demanding, intimate. She had no idea what she was doing as her tongue tangled and duelled with his, as the taste of him filled her and her ears were deafened by the sound of his breathing and her thundering heart.

His robe was too thick. *Touch him.* Julia pushed it back and found naked skin, hot and smooth over shifting, hard muscle. She wanted to bite, to kiss…

His hands came down, over her back, down to her waist and he pulled her against him and she felt the hard ridge of arousal pressed against her stomach and the memory of the pain came back, sweeping away the passion in a cold flood.

Will released her, stepped back his expression rueful. 'I *have* frightened you. For a moment I forgot you were a virgin, Julia. It will be all right, I promise you.'

'Yes, of course.' From somewhere she found a smile.

'Those few days we were together before we married—we are still those people. I have not changed so very much and I doubt you have either. We trusted each other. There was liking, I think. We can build on that. And attraction as we have just proved.'

Attraction, yes. She nodded, it was impossible to pretend otherwise. *Trust. But I lied to you. You married a woman who killed a man. I was a fugitive. And now I have to tell you I bore, and lost, that man's child and I have to beg you to acknowledge it as yours. If I let you lie with me then the marriage is consummated and I will have trapped you.*

'I'll let you get dressed,' Will said. 'We'll meet at breakfast and talk afterwards. You can move into the chamber next to mine and this will all be all right, you'll see, Julia.'

'Thank you.' Her smile was slipping, but it was only a few steps to her chamber. Julia closed the door behind her with care. She was shaking, but she made herself walk to the armchair at the window, not collapse on the bed. She would be in control, she would not panic.

Before she slept with him she had to tell him the truth. Not all of it, not that she was responsible for Jonathan's death, but about the elopement and about the baby. She owed it to him to be honest about that before he made love to her.

He would be angry, and shaken, but she had to hope he would understand and forgive her the deception because there was only so much weight her conscience could bear.

Once she had thought that the guilt and fear over Jonathan's death would lessen, that she could forget. But it did not go away. It was always there and so was the pain and loss of her child, the two things twisting and tangling into a mesh of emotions that were always there waiting to trip her, snare her, when she was least expecting it. And now Will was home there was the added guilt of keeping her crime from him. But it was not a personal shame like her elopement or the pregnancy. This was a matter of law and she could not ask him to conceal what she had done.

The sensitive skin of her upper arms where Will had held her still prickled with the awareness of his touch. Her mouth was swollen and sensitive and the ache between her thighs was humiliatingly insistent.

He was her husband. She owed him as much truth as she could give him and, unfair though it might be, she wanted something in return. *I want a real marriage.*

Papa had taught her to negotiate. *Know what your basic demands are, the point you will not shift beyond,* he had told her. *Know what you can afford to yield, what you can give to get what you want.* He had been talking about buying land and selling wheat, but the principles were surely the same.

Julia lay back in the chair, closed her eyes against the view of the garden coming to life in the strengthening ·

sunlight, and tried to think without emotion. She could not risk the marriage: that was her sticking point. She wanted her husband's respect, and equality in making decisions about their lives and that included the estate and the farm. She wanted him to desire her for herself, not just as a passive body in his bed to breed his sons. *Sons*. The emotion broke through the calculation. Could she bear that pain again? Could she carry another child, knowing what it would be like to lose it before it had even drawn a breath?

Yes. Because if I am not willing to do that, then the marriage cannot stand. I made a bargain and I cannot break it. She felt one tear running down her cheek, but she did not lift her hand to wipe it away.

Chapter Eight

$\mathcal{A}$t length Nancy, her maid, arrived. Julia bathed, dressed and, still deep in thought, walked to the head of the stairs to be greeted by loud wailing rising from the breakfast room. When she ran down and along the passageway she was confronted by a view of the door jammed with all three of their strapping footmen, craning to see what was going on inside. Julia tapped the nearest liveried shoulder and they jumped apart, mumbling shamefaced apologies.

The wailing female was revealed as Cook, her apron to her face, sobbing with joy on Will's shoulder. 'I never thought to see the day... Oh, look at 'im... Oh, my lord...just like when he was a young man!'

Will had the usual expression of a man confronted by a weeping female, one of helpless alarm, as he stood patting Cook ineffectually on the back.

'Mrs Pocock, do calm down!' The relief of having some ordinary crisis to take control of almost made Julia laugh out loud. 'Gatcombe, will you please find someone to take Cook downstairs and make her a nice cup of tea and the rest of you, get on and fetch his lordship's breakfast. He will think he has come home to a madhouse.'

'My lady, I must apologise.' The butler glared at the footmen until one of them helped Mrs Pocock from the room, then waved the others in with the chafing-dishes. 'Cook had retired to her room when you returned last night and the kitchen maids did not inform her until this morning of his lordship's presence and his good health.'

'Of course.' Julia took her place at the foot of the small oval table as Will straightened his rumpled neckcloth and collapsed into his chair. 'I had forgotten that Cook has known Lord Dereham for many years.' Gatcombe went out, closing the door on the sounds from the corridor and leaving them alone.

'Coffee, my lord?' Will looked decidedly off balance. Whatever he had been doing for the past three years, he had certainly not been gaining experience in dealing with difficult females. But then, since he had recovered his health, they had probably been all willing complaisance. Julia tried hard not to imagine just how her husband would have celebrated his returning health and vigour.

'Thank you.' The heavy-lidded look had shivers travelling up and down her spine, but all Will said was, 'You appear to have rather more control over the domestic staff than I have, my lady. Mrs Pocock would not stop wailing.'

'It is only to be expected,' Julia said as she racked

her brains to recall whether her husband took cream and sugar with his coffee. He could say if it was wrong, she decided with a mental shrug and simply passed the cup. 'They are all delighted at your recovery and as for control, I have been dealing with them daily for three years, after all.'

'I trust there will be no more weeping females today.' Will sipped his coffee without a grimace, so she had that right at least. None of the servants knew the true story behind this marriage, or even where they had first met—the more familiar she seemed with Will's habits, the better it would be.

'I doubt any more of the female staff will shed tears at the sight of you.' Julia studied him over the rim of her chocolate cup as Charles came in and began to serve Will breakfast.

As was her habit, Julia started her day with only chocolate, bread and butter and preserves, but it seemed someone had warned the kitchen and Cook had managed to at least put a decent breakfast for a hungry man in train before her emotions overcame her.

Bacon, eggs, a slice of sirloin, mushrooms. Will nodded thanks to Charles when his breakfast plate was finally filled to his satisfaction. The contrast with the emaciated invalid picking at a spoonful of scrambled egg during their first breakfast together could not have been greater.

'What are you thinking?' Will asked as he reached for the toast.

'Thank you, Charles, that will be all.' Julia waited

until he footman had closed the door behind her. 'I was reflecting that I would not have recognised the man I married if it were not for your eyes.'

'And that recognition was enough to make you faint?'

'You must know perfectly well how distinctive a feature your eyes are. I had thought you must be dead, although I never once admitted it to anyone else. To tell the truth, I was surprised to receive the letters for as long as you sent them. When you left I had not expected you would make it across the Channel. So the shock of seeing you again with no warning was…intense.'

Will pushed the empty plate away with sudden impatience. 'I will not beat about the bush. What is the matter, Julia? You know I am the same man you married, but you have changed. You are wary now and it is not simply the shock of seeing me. What else are you hiding from me?'

Hiding? For a moment Julia froze. Had Will the powers to read her mind? *Of course I am wary! A ghost appears, kisses me until I am dizzy with desire…and whatever happens I must reveal one secret that may break our marriage into pieces and hide another for my very life.*

Julia spread honey on a roll to give herself time to collect her thoughts, then answered as though the situation was as uncomplicated as everyone else believed it to be. 'Of course I have changed. I have been alone for three years and I have just had a severe, but very welcome, shock.' That was not entirely a lie. 'You try hiding so much as an extravagant piece of shopping with

Aunt Delia's beady eye on you.' Will gave a snort of laughter and she added, 'Any woman would be wary if her lord and master had been away for so long and then returned unexpectedly.'

He paused, one hand outstretched to the fruit bowl. 'Is that how you see me now you have had time to think it over? Your lord and master?'

'Certainly not,' she answered with as much composure as she could summon and was pleased to see the amusement vanish from his face. 'It is how society views you. I regard you as an unknown and very uncertain factor in my life.'

He was peeling an apple, his eyes clashing with hers as the peel ran slowly over his fingers. The chocolate threatened to slop over the cup. Julia put it down carefully before he noticed the effect he had on her. 'I have no idea if I will be happy married to you. Or you to me. But I will do my level best.' She braced herself for an explosion of wrath.

'Happiness? You aim high. I was hoping for mere contentment as a starting point. An absence of scandal would be desirable.' There was an edge to that, she noticed, puzzled. He could have no idea what she was hiding, so why the reference to scandal? 'Well, we will see. My experience of marriage is as brief as yours, but I have no doubt you will point out to me where I am going wrong.'

All very calm and polite, Julia thought, but under the civilised words was more emotion that he was keeping hidden from her. Which was fair enough, she supposed.

She had no intention of making her own emotions any more transparent than most of them undoubtedly were just now, not yet.

'Your own childhood memories will guide you, I imagine,' she replied with equal calmness.

'Do you? If you mean I should seek for a model of the ideal husband in my own parent I am afraid you would not be very happy with the result. He gave me these eyes and he left me the only thing I love: King's Acre. I suspect you would want something more from me in the way of conjugal virtues.' He drained the coffee and tossed his napkin onto the table. 'Have you finished, Julia?

'Certainly.' In the face of that matter-of-fact bitterness there were no words of comfort to offer to a virtual stranger. She waited as he came round to pull her chair back. 'What do you wish to do first?'

'Any number of things, but please do not let me interfere with your morning. I will go and speak to my steward.'

'Mr Wilkins will wait on us at eleven o'clock. Mr Howard from the Home Farm will be here after luncheon. I have sent for Mr Burrows, the solicitor, but I would not expect him until tomorrow.'

'You have been very busy, my dear.' The blandly amiable expression had ebbed from Will's face. Those strong bones she had been so aware of when he was ill were apparent still, the stubborn line of his jaw most of all.

'I habitually rise early,' Julia said. 'And not just because unexpected noises outside my room waken me.' Although not, normally, as early as she had got up that morning to pen letters to all the men of business who must wait on the returning baron. She had just sealed the last letter when the sound of his fist on the nursery door had brought her into the corridor. 'But before you do anything else we must call on the Hadfields.'

'Must we, indeed?' There was more than a hint of gritted teeth about his polite response.

Julia swept out of the breakfast room, along the corridor and into the library. 'If you are going to shout, please do it in here and not in front of the servants,' she said over her shoulder.

'Was I shouting?' Will closed the door behind him and leaned back on the panels. 'I do not think I raised my voice.'

'You were about to. We need to call because it will appear very strange if we do not, and as soon as possible.'

'You will find, Julia, that I very rarely shout except in emergencies. I do not have to.' He crossed his arms and studied her as she moved restlessly about the room. 'You are very busy organising me. I am neither an invalid nor Cousin Henry.'

'You have been away for three years.' She made herself stand still and appear calm. 'I am in a position to bring you up to date with everything. I am only trying to—'

'Organise me. I do not require it, Julia. I am perfectly fit and able. You have done very well, but I am back now.'

'Indeed you are, you patronising man!' The words escaped her before she could bite them back. 'I apologise, I should not have said that, but—'

At his back the door opened an inch and slammed back as it met resistance. Will turned and pulled it wide. 'Gatcombe?'

'I beg your pardon, my lord. Mrs Hadfield and Mr Henry have arrived and are asking to speak to you, my lady. I was not certain whether, under the circumstances, you are At Home.'

'Yes, we are receiving, Gatcombe.' Her stomach contracted with nerves. This encounter was not going to be pleasant, especially if Will continued in this mood. And if she could not keep Delia from blurting out something about the baby it might well be disastrous.

The butler lowered his voice. 'Mrs Hadfield is complaining about a stupid hoax and rumours running around the neighbourhood. I did not know quite how to answer her, my lady. I did not feel it my place to apprise her of his lordship's happy return.'

'I quite understand. You did quite right, Gatcombe. Where have you put them?'

'In the Green Salon, my lady. Refreshments are being sent up.'

'Thank you, Gatcombe. Please tell Mrs Hadfield we will be with her directly.'

'Will we?' Will enquired as the butler retreated. 'This is an uncivilised hour to be calling.'

'She is not going to believe it until she sees you with her own eyes,' Julia said with a firmness she was far from feeling.

'And she is not going to want to believe it, even then.' Will opened the door for her. He sounded merely sardonically amused, but she wondered what his feelings might be behind the façade he was maintaining. Her husband had come back from the dead and it must seem to him that the only people who were unreservedly pleased to see him were the servants.

She listened to his firm tread behind her and told herself that soon enough he would make contact with his friends and acquaintances and resume his old life. But he had come home to a sorry excuse for a family: an aunt and cousin who would be happier if he were dead and a wife who had fainted at the sight of him and who was very shortly about to release a bombshell.

'Good morning, Aunt Delia, Cousin Henry.' She tried to sound as happy as a wife with a returned husband should be.

'Have you heard this ridiculous rumour?' Mrs Hadfield demanded before Julia could get into the room. She was pacing, the ribbons of her bonnet flapping. 'It is all over the village! I had Mrs Armstrong on my doorstep before breakfast demanding to know if it true, of all the impertinence!'

'And what rumour is that?' Will enquired from the shadows behind Julia.

'Why, that my nephew Dereham is alive and well and

here—' She broke off with a gasp as Will stepped into the room. 'What is this? Who are you, sir?'

'Oh, come, Aunt.' Will strolled past Julia and stopped in front of Mrs Hadfield. Her jaw dropped unflatteringly as her face turned from pale to red in moments as she stared up at him. 'Do you not recognise your own nephew? Is this going to be like those sensation novels where the lost heir returns only to be spurned by the family? Well, if you require physical proof, Mama always said you dandled me on your knee when I was an infant. I still have that birthmark shaped like a star.'

He put one hand in the small of his back, where only Julia could see, and tapped his left buttock with his index finger. Mrs Hadfield was beginning to bluster and from behind his mother Henry was trying to say something and failing to get a word in edgeways. Julia decided it was time to support her husband.

'You mean the birthmark on your, er, *left posterior*, my lord?' she enquired. 'This is hardly the conversation for a lady's drawing room, but I can assure you, Aunt Delia, the birthmark is most assuredly where you will remember it.'

'Mama,' Henry managed finally. 'Of course it is Will—look at his eyes!'

'Oooh!' With a wail Mrs Hadfield collapsed onto the sofa and buried her face in her handkerchief.

'Aunt Delia, please do not weep, I realise what a shock it must be—we were going to send a note and then come and call on you later today.' Julia sat down and put her arms around the older woman. The main thing, she thought rather desperately, was to stop Delia saying something that must cause an irrevocable rift and to prevent her leaving and creating a stir in the neighbourhood before she had time to consider the situation rationally.

The men, as she might have expected, were absolutely no help whatsoever. They stood side by side, Henry looking hideously embarrassed, her husband, wooden. *'Will.'* He looked at her, his dark brows raised. 'You remember I was telling you how kind Aunt Delia has been to me and how helpful Cousin Henry has been with the estate.'

Henry, who, to do him justice, was no hypocrite, blushed at the generous praise. 'Dash it all, I only did what I could. You helped me far more with my lands than I could ever repay here, Cousin Julia.'

'You were very supportive to me. But indeed, Will, Cousin Henry has been making improvements on his own estate. Why do you not both go to the study and talk about it—and have a glass of brandy or something?'

Will looked from her to the clock, his brows rising still further. Admittedly half past nine in the morning did seem a little early for spirits, but she needed to be alone with Delia. Giving up on subtlety, Julia jerked her head towards the door and, to her relief, Will took his cousin by the arm and guided him out.

'Now then, Aunt Delia, you must stop this or you will make yourself ill. Yes, I know it is a shock and you could quite reasonably have believed that Henry would inherit the title and King's Acre. But Will is home, hale and hearty and quite cured by a very clever doctor in Spain, so you must accept it, for otherwise you will attract the most unwelcome and impertinent comments from the vulgarly curious. And you do not want our friends and neighbours to pity you, do you?'

Will's aunt emerged from her handkerchief, blotched and red eyed. 'But Henry—'

'Henry is a perfectly intelligent, personable young man who has started to retrieve the mistakes he made with his own inheritance, if you will forgive me for plain speaking,' she added hastily as Delia bristled. 'If he finds a sensible, well-dowered young lady to marry in a year or two all will be well.'

'But the title,' Delia muttered and then bit her lip.

'If Will had married before he fell ill then he would probably have his own son by now and you and Henry would never have had your hopes raised,' Julia said. There was no point beating about the bush. But Delia had been kind to her when she was pregnant, she reminded herself. She owed it to the older woman to help her through this and not condemn her for her ambitions for her son. 'You do not truly wish Will dead, do you?' she asked.

'No.' It was almost convincing. 'Of course not.' That was better. 'It was just the unexpectedness of it.'

'I know. I fainted dead away when I saw him. It is such a comfort to me to have a female friend at a time like this,' Julia said, crossing her fingers in her skirts. 'And, please, can I ask you and Henry to say nothing about the baby? I have got to break the news to Will and it will be a shock.'

The other woman nodded. 'Of course, you can rely on me.'

Thank Heavens! If she could only do this right, then Delia would leave the house convinced she had supported Julia in her shock, had greeted Will with open-hearted warmth and was a paragon of selflessness. It might help quell the rumour-mongers.

An hour later the Hadfields left and Julia followed Will back to the study. There were, indeed, glasses and a decanter standing on the desk and she felt like pouring herself a stiff drink, despite the hour and her dislike of spirits.

'He has improved,' Will remarked. He stood beside the big chair, the one she always used, courteously waiting for her to sit. Julia took the chair opposite—she was going to have to find herself a desk, they could hardly share this one. 'How much of that is due to your influence?'

Julia found herself studying the long, elegant figure, thinking how right he looked in the ornate chair. He sat with his fingers curling instinctively around the great carved lion heads at the ends of the chair arms. Her own hands were too small to do that.

'To me? The improvements in his character I can claim no credit for. I believe he is maturing as you had guessed he would once he began to escape from his mother's apron strings. He does not enjoy being made to think hard, or to face unwelcome truths, but he is learning.' She felt her mouth curving into a smile at the memory of some of their tussles. 'I do believe I would make a good governess after the way I have had to cajole, lecture and bully poor Henry.'

Will did not speak. A ploy to make her gabble on, no doubt. It was, unfortunately, working. The relief of having the dreaded encounter with Delia over with was having its effect. 'If he can just find a nice girl to marry, I think it will be the making of him, although he is still very shy of girls.'

'You think you can recommend marriage from your own experience, do you?' Julia glanced up sharply to find Will doodling patterns up the margins of the sheet on which she had been calculating wheat yields.

She would not let him fluster her. 'Hardly,' she said with a smile, making a joke of it. If he wanted plain speaking, he would get it. 'A husband who vanishes less than twenty-four hours after the ceremony and returns three years later with no warning is hardly a model of ideal matrimony.'

Will raised a quizzical eyebrow, prepared, it seemed to be amused. He steepled his fingers and regarded her over the top of them. 'You dealt with Delia very effectively. I must thank you for your support. The tone in which you said *left posterior* was exactly right, although it was a miracle I kept my countenance.'

'It was fortunate that it was you who raised the subject of birthmarks—if Mrs Hadfield had asked I would not have had the slightest idea what to say.'

The left side of Will's mouth quirked into a half-smile that produced, improbably in that strong face, a dimple. Julia stared at it, distracted by how it lightened his whole expression. 'I wouldn't worry about that kind of slip,' he said. 'She is perfectly well aware that for a couple married three years we have had only two nights when it was theoretically possible to see each other's…shall we say, *distinguishing marks*.' The smile slipped easily from amused to wicked. 'So far. And, for all my aunt knows, we might be a most prudish couple who retire to bed in our nightgowns and blow out all the candles.'

Julia's mood moved just as easily as that smile, from almost relaxed to exceedingly flustered. If Will was not regarding her so watchfully from those heavy-lidded predator's eyes she would think him flirting. Perhaps he was, or perhaps he was trying to unsettle her—and succeeding very effectively, she had to admit. The thought of being naked with him, in a well-lit room, brought back all the memories of losing her virginity and added an all-too-tangible layer of apprehension and embarrassment to the mix of emotions that were unsettling her breakfast.

'I will show you the books now to save time when Mr Wilkins arrives.' Accounts, rents and the problems of the unsatisfactory tenant of Lower Acre Farm should divert her thoughts from the bedroom most effectively. The clock struck the half-hour, reminding her that distractions only served to bring bedtime closer and she still had no idea how she was going to react when Will came to her chamber door. Or how she was going to tell him what she must.

'That can wait.' He stood up, long and lean and as disturbing as a panther in the civilised room. Julia sat quite still in her chair as he walked past her. If he was going out, it would give her a soothing half-hour with the books...

'You were very kind to Aunt Delia, although she cannot have been easy to get on with, these past three years,' he said. Right behind her.

'We have learned to rub along. Your return was a shock and I feel sorry for her—she knows Henry is slipping out of her control and she has invested all her energies in him. It can only get worse when he begins to take an interest in courting. She will be a lonely woman soon.'

'And you were not only supportive to my aunt.' Will must be standing immediately behind her. Julia imagined she could feel the heat of his body. The upholstered chair back moved slightly and she realised he had closed his hand over it, just beside her shoulder. 'You have been loyal to me. *Wifely.*' He seemed to find the word amusing: she could hear the smile in his voice.

'Naturally. I am your wife, after all. It is important to keep up appearances.' She was *not* smiling. In fact, even to herself, she sounded miserably priggish.

'You are anxious to make this marriage work, then?' A featherlight touch on her shoulder, barely discernible through the light muslin scarf that filled the neckline of her morning gown. *Imagination. No, real.* Now the finger was stroking across the muslin, touching the bare skin of her neck, lingering to explore the sensitive skin just behind her right ear.

When she swallowed he must have felt it. She hated to betray her agitation, even by a little involuntary movement. 'Of course I am.'

'What is this?' Will's breath stirred the fine wisps along her hairline. He must have bent close. If she turned, they would be face to face, their lips might meet…

Chapter Nine

$\sim\!\!\!\sim\!\!\!\sim$

She felt as though she was made of tinder and Will was holding a flame so close, so very close. Julia kept still with an effort and said lightly, 'The scar? I was chased by a bull and had to throw myself into a hedge. I emerged rather the worse for wear.' It was only a little scar, just a quarter of an inch long. She could feel it under her fingers when she washed or dabbed scent behind her ear. 'I had not thought it showed. Is it very red?'

'Not at all. I only noticed it because I was looking very closely.' The warm breath moved, trailed its caress right round to the other side of her neck. Julia rolled her eyes uncomfortably to the left, rigid with the effort not to shiver. Will loomed beside her.

After a moment, to her intense relief, he straightened up and strolled back to hitch one hip on the edge of the desk. 'Farming appears to be a dangerous operation when you undertake it. I never found it necessary to traipse around fields looking at bulls, let alone provoke them into chasing me.'

'Which explains why the one you had was an inferior specimen with an unreliable temper. Unlike my... *our* current bull.' From the way he narrowed his eyes at her Julia could only assume that criticising a man's bull was like criticising his own virility.

'It will not be necessary for you to get your hands dirty, or your shoes muddy, or to endanger yourself in any way connected with the estate from now on. Let alone indulge in such occupations as judging stud animals. Hardly a ladylike thing to be doing in any case.'

That was the attitude she had feared he would adopt. 'But I am good at it. And I enjoy it. All of it. It is, after all, why you married me.' She kept her tone free from any hint of pleading, or of aggression.

'But the situation has changed. And there are many things in life that we enjoy that it is not acceptable that we indulge ourselves in.'

Julia swallowed the very rude retort that sprang to her lips, although the impulse to demonstrate just how unacceptable her behaviour could be by going upstairs, changing into her divided skirt and boots and riding astride round the estate was almost overwhelming. She folded her hands neatly in her lap and remarked, 'That is the sort of remark that gentlemen make when they intend it to apply to wives and daughters, never to themselves.'

'Are you suggesting that I behave in a manner not befitting a gentleman?' The lazy amusement had quite vanished although Will still lounged there, apparently at ease.

Julia shrugged. 'Gentlemanly behaviour appears to encompass gaming, whoring and drinking. All wives can do about it, so I understand, is to hope that the mistresses are not too expensive, that the gaming is for low stakes and that the drinking does not lead to imprudent expenditure on the other two entertainments.'

'I see.' Will got off the desk and went back to his chair. All inclination to flirt, or tease her by caressing her neck, had obviously vanished. 'It is a little late to be enquiring about my character, don't you think?'

'If it was vicious, or your activities scandalous, I would doubtless have heard about it by now.' Julia got up and went to the pile of ledgers stacked on a side table. She knew where she was with those. They did not answer back, play with words or look at her with eyes that tried to strip her to the soul. She wanted to tell him that of course she knew his character was good, but she could not find the words.

'You may rest assured, my dear, that I dislike overindulgence in drink, I gamble well within my means and I am not in the habit of whoring.' When she did not reply Will added, 'I assume you also wish to know whether I have a mistress in keeping, but do not like to ask directly?'

She had not meant this to go so far, or even to mention the subject. Her back to him, Julia shrugged, pretending an indifference she found she certainly did not feel. What she felt was a surge of uncivilised jealousy at the very thought. 'I presume that you have.'

'No.'

The heavy cover of the ledger for the Home Farm slipped from her fingers and banged shut as she turned. 'But you have been gone three years.'

'Until I began to get better again I had neither the inclination nor the strength for…dalliance.' Will was doodling again so she could not see his face, but his voice was stiff. 'Since I regained both I have reminded myself that I am a married man who made certain vows.'

Oh. She believed him. It was not easy for a man to admit that his virility had suffered in any way, she suspected. But that meant her husband was not simply feeling normally amorous. He had been celibate for months, so the restraint he had shown with her so far was nothing short of amazing.

Will had made vows and so had she. She had no intention of keeping him from her bed, however frightened that made her. But she was *damned* if she was going to allow him to seduce her into being simply a meek little wife—in bed or out of it.

'Then I imagine I should be looking forward to tonight?' she asked. It came out sounding more flippant, or perhaps provocative, than she intended and she saw from the flare of heat in his eyes that she had both aroused and shocked Will.

'Julia,' he said, his voice husky, getting to his feet, 'you may be certain of a most appreciative reception.'

'Mr Wilkins, my la…my lord, I should say.' Gatcombe sounded unusually flustered. Julia could only hope it was as a result of getting in a tangle over who he should be addressing and not because he had heard anything of their conversation when he opened the door.

The steward was a wiry Midlander with a cautious attitude and a depth of knowledge that Julia admired. It had taken her several weeks to break down his reserve when he discovered he was expected to take orders from a woman, but the realisation that she knew what she was talking about, and was quite tough enough to hold her own in an argument, soon swayed him.

Now, she could tell, Wilkins was uneasy because he was uncertain who was in control. 'I'm right glad to see you back with us, my lord,' he said, when greetings had been exchanged. 'I've no doubt her ladyship's been telling you all we've been about while you've been away.'

'Nothing, beyond the fact that you have been most effective, Wilkins.' Will gestured to a chair. 'Come and brief me.' He stood up and smiled at Julia. 'Thank you, my dear.'

It was a polite dismissal she had no intention of accepting. Julia smiled sweetly back and feigned not to understand him. 'It was my pleasure,' she said, settling back into her own chair. 'Mr Wilkins, perhaps you could bring those ledgers over.'

For a long moment it seemed likely that Will was going to order her from the room, witness or no witness, then he smiled wryly and sat down again. 'Let us begin with the livestock, Wilkins. I understand we have a new bull.'

Julia had done a good job, Will had to acknowledge—it far exceeded his hopes when he had thought up this scheme in the first place. She had gone beyond offering Wilkins informed support, she had taken the lead and steered the rather cautious steward into projects and changes he would never have dreamt of on his own initiative.

But now she was not going to hand back control without a fight. Will let them both talk, interjected a question now and again and realised it was going to take a while to break Wilkins of the habit of looking to his wife for approval with every comment. He did not want to be unkind to her, or unappreciative, but damn it all, he was master here and he was going to make that clear. In the estate, on the farm, in the bedchamber.

'I have horses arriving in a few weeks,' Will said when they had talked themselves to a standstill.

'Fifteen, Wilkins,' Julia said. 'We are going to need new paddocks, stabling. More staff…'

'I have men coming with them,' Will overrode her smoothly. 'And plans for the stables. Where would you suggest for the paddocks, Wilkins?'

'To the west of the existing ones,' Julia answered before the steward could. 'I have been considering it. We can move the beef cattle down to Mayday Field and Croft Acre and—'

'We do not have fields with those names.'

'We do now. I bought Hodgson's farm when old Jem Hodgson died last year,' Julia said, as if purchasing a large farm was as simple a matter as buying a new bonnet. 'His son has gone into the building business and needed the capital urgently so we settled on a keen price. I had the house done up and I lease it and ten acres to make a small park to a cit called Maurice Loveday. It brings a good income and we've gained another mile of water meadows into the bargain.'

He had had his eye on that farm for years and old Hodgson had refused to sell. Now his wife had calmly snapped it up, at a bargain price, and secured the income from the house—which had never occurred to him as an asset—while she was at it.

Will trod firmly on what felt uncomfortably like jealousy and smiled at Julia. 'You must have had hardly a moment to yourself, taking so much responsibility. Now I am back you can relax and get back to all your normal pursuits.'

'Oh, but these are my normal pursuits,' she responded with an equally false smile. 'This is what I enjoy doing.' *And try to take it away from me if you can,* those grey eyes said, meeting his with flint-hard resolve.

One thing had kept him going in those years of exile. His love for King's Acre was real and solid and his control of it was not negotiable.

What his wife needed was something else to keep her occupied. Womanly things. A man in her bed, babies in the nursery. Both of those, he realised with some surprise, would be an absolute pleasure to provide.

Will had not been pleased with her contribution to the meeting with the steward. Nor with the free expression of her thoughts when Mr Howard from Home Farm arrived after luncheon. It was obvious that the deference those gentlemen showed to her opinions was also an irritation. There was no need for her to attend when he met tomorrow with Mr Burrows the solicitor, Will had informed Julia with a smile that had not reached his eyes.

The words did not pass his lips, but it was plain to her that he considered her continuing interest meddling and interfering. Her proper place, in his opinion, was in the bedchamber and the drawing room and the only servants she should need to concern herself with were the domestic staff.

I have been the regent while the king was in exile, she thought with a grim attempt at humour that evening. *The state has been well governed but now the queen must go back to woman's work and leave the serious business to the men.*

But kingdoms required heirs—that was what husbands wanted, whether they were King of England or Joe Bloggs at the village forge. She stared blankly into the mirror on her dressing table until her maid put down the evening gown she had been shaking out and said, 'Excuse me, my lady, but are you all right?'

'What? Oh, yes, perfectly, thank you, Nancy.' Julia went back to dabbing Warren's Milk of Roses on to her face. She was persevering with this infallible remedy for freckles and the effects of the sun on the complexion more in the hope than the expectation of a fashionably pale skin. The true remedy, of course, was to wear a broad-brimmed hat at all times, or, better still, as Aunt Delia so often told her with a sigh, to stay inside as a lady should.

If Will had his way, she would be as pale as a lily in no time. And drooping like one too, from sheer boredom. Her mind was still skittering away from contemplating the prospect of becoming pregnant again. It seemed very likely to happen quickly once her husband came to her bed: after all, she had lain just the once with Jonathan.

Her fingers fumbled as she tried to replace the top of the bottle and Nancy fell to her knees and started to search under the skirts of the dressing table for the dropped stopper. Julia had dammed it up so long—the shock when she had realised that the changes in her body were not the result of terror and distress, then the joy at the realisation that she was carrying a child and the appalled comprehension of what she must do if it proved to be a boy.

But, even with that hanging over her, the overwhelming emotion had been delight and love. If the child was a daughter, then she would not have to tell anyone, for a girl would be no threat to Henry's rights. And even if it was a boy, she would work something out to give him a future and happiness.

It never occurred to her, with all her worries and plans, that she might lose the baby. Now she wondered about future pregnancies. What if there was something wrong with her? What if she was not capable of safely birthing a child? She had not even considered it before, because she had expected to stay a widow for the rest of her days, contentedly farming King's Acre and then, when Henry inherited, buying her own land. But now she was no longer a widow.

'That lotion is working a treat, my lady.' Nancy sat back on her heels with the stopper in her hand and regarded Julia with satisfaction. 'I swear you're a shade paler for using it.'

'I fear it is simply that I have a slight headache, Nancy.' Julia attempted a smile. 'I will be better for a glass of wine and my dinner, I am sure.'

By the time her stays had been tightened and the gown was on and her hair dressed there was some colour back in her cheeks and at least the freckles were not standing out like dots on white paper.

It was a warm evening, almost sultry. Julia draped her lightest shawl over her elbows, chose a large fan and went down to the drawing room. Her first proper evening as a married lady, she realised as the butler opened the door for her and she saw Will standing by the long window that was open to the ground to let in the evening air.

He was dressed with as much careful formality as she. Julia admired the effect of silk evening breeches, striped stockings, a swallowtail coat that must have been bought in London on his way home and a waist-coat of amber silk that brought out the colour of his eyes and matched the stone in the stickpin in his neckcloth. Regarded dispassionately, she thought, her husband was a fine figure of a man. Discovering *how* to be dispassionate about him was going to be the problem. *A lost cause, in fact,* she told herself.

'Good evening, Lady Dereham.' He gestured towards the decanters set out on a tray. 'A glass of sherry wine?'

'Good evening, my lord.' She sat precisely in the centre of the sofa and spread her almond-green skirts on either side as though concerned about wrinkles. They covered virtually all the available seat and left no room for anyone to sit beside her. She did not think she could cope with any sly caresses just now. 'Thank you. A glass of sherry would be delightful.'

Will poured a glass for both of them, placed hers on the table beside her and went back to the window and his contemplation of the view, which allowed her the perfect opportunity to admire his profile. Dispassionately, of course.

'Did your meeting with Mr Burrows go well?' Julia asked after a few minutes' silence. She took a sip of her wine while her husband pondered his reply.

'It was most satisfactory, thank you,' he said politely and tasted his own drink.

If this continues, I may well scream, simply for the diversion of seeing the footmen all rush in, Julia decided. 'I have always found him extremely helpful.'

'He tells me you have not asked for any of the jewellery from his strong room.'

'I did not consider it mine to wear.' For some reason decking herself out in the family jewels had seemed mercenary in a way that taking all the other benefits of their arrangement did not. Jewellery was so personal.

'Besides,' she added in an effort to lighten the cool formality, 'think what a wrench to have to hand it all over after seven years when Henry inherited.'

'There was no need for such scruples. But you will wear it from now on, I hope.' She suspected that was an order. 'Burrows brought it with him.' Will gestured towards a side table and she noticed the stack of leather boxes on it for the first time. 'There is a safe in your dressing room. If there are any pieces you dislike they can be reset, or go back to the vault.'

There seemed a lot of boxes. Small ring boxes, flat cases with curving edges that must contain necklaces, complicated shapes that presumably enclosed complete parures including tiaras. Did Will expect her to pounce on them with cries of delight?

He thought she had only married him for purely mercenary reasons and to protect her good name, of course, so he must find her lack of interest in this treasure trove puzzling. She could hardly tell him that she did not want his money or his gems, only sanctuary from the law.

'Thank you. But I have not found a safe. Is it behind some concealed panel?'

'Behind a panel, yes, but in the baroness's dressing room. Nancy is moving your things there now.'

Somehow Julia kept her lips closed on the instinctive protest. Will was high-handed, insensitive, but, of course, he was in the right and she had agreed he would come to her bed.

He might not want her, of course, when she told him about Jonathan and about the child.

She pushed that thought and its implications deep into her mind. There were practical reasons also. Her place should be in the suite that was the mirror image of his: anything else would cause gossip and wild speculation amongst the servants. She knew, however loyal they were, gossip always leaked out to the staff in surrounding houses, then to the tradesmen and in no time at all the entire neighbourhood would know.

'Thank you,' she said with a genuine smile and was rewarded by the faint surprise on Will's face. He had expected a fight, but she was going to keep her opposition for the issues that were important to her. Jewels did not matter one way or the other, except that now she must make the effort to care for them and to select suitable ones for each occasion.

Julia exerted herself over dinner to make conversation and bring Will up to date with the local news. He would be riding round to visit their neighbours over the next few days, so she must set the scene for him. It also meant she could steer well clear of any personal matters. There was plenty to tell him about with a new curate, several marriages, some deaths, the strange case of sheep-stealing last year, Sir William Curruther's new wife's frightful taste in interior decoration and, of course, numerous births to the gentry community. She hurried over those and started enumerating the changes to their own staff while he had been away.

'Thank you,' he said drily when she reached the new scullery maid and the gardener's boy as the dessert plates were cleared. 'I will endeavour to recall all that tomorrow.'

Julia bit her lip—he made it sound as though she had been prattling on and not allowing him to get a word in edgeways. She had kept pausing, hoping Will would pick up his side of the conversation and tell her about his three years away. But he showed no sign of wanting to confide in her. 'I have got all the news I was saving for you off my chest,' she said. 'Tomorrow you can tell me yours.'

'I have told you most of what there is to know.' His long lashes hid his eyes as he looked down, apparently interested in the piece of walnut shell that lay beside his plate. 'I have no wish to revisit the past.'

'But your travels must be fascinating. I would so like to hear about them.' A neutral subject of conversation on an engrossing subject seemed like a godsend.

'I lost almost four years of my life to that illness,' Will said and looked up to catch her staring at him. 'I just want to forget about it and get on with living.'

She could hear the anger and the loss under the flat tone, see the heat in his eyes.

'Very well.' She had no wish to invite any further snubs. 'I will leave you to your port.' One of the footmen came to pull back her chair, another to open the door for her. Like all the staff, they were normally efficient and attentive, but somehow she sensed they were making a special effort to look after her at the moment, just as they had when she lost the baby. She could only hope that Will did not notice and feel they were being disloyal to him.

If she could just focus her mind on those sort of worries and not what was going to happen when the bedchamber door closed behind them, then she could, perhaps, remain her normal practical self. As she walked across the hall to the salon she could feel the brooding presence in the room behind her like heat from a fire. Common sense seemed as much use as a fireguard made of straw.

Chapter Ten

Will did not leave her alone in the salon for long. Julia had hardly picked up her embroidery, sorted her wools and begun on one of the roses that formed a garland on the chair seat she was working when he walked in, still carrying his wine glass, Charles on his heels with the decanter.

'What are you making?' He sank into the wing chair opposite her, stretched out long legs and sipped his port. Charles put the decanter down and took himself off. They were alone at last, with no servants present to keep the conversation on neutral lines.

'A new set of seat covers for the breakfast room.' She tilted the frame to show him. 'The existing ones are sadly worn and the moth has got into them.'

'My paternal grandmother made those.'

'I was not going to throw them away,' Julia hastened to reassure him. 'I will try to save as much of her embroidery as I can and perhaps incorporate it into window seat covers or something of the sort.'

'It is a lot of work for you.' Will was twisting the stem of the glass between his fingers, watching the red wine swirl in the glass.

'I do not mind. I dislike being idle.'

'Hmm.' It seemed her husband did not wish to make conversation. Perhaps he wanted her to retire. *Well, my lord, I have no intention of going to bed at half past nine so you can exercise your conjugal rights!* Nor was she looking forward to the conversation that she knew she must have with him first. She could not talk about it down here and risk being interrupted.

Julia executed a complex area of shading and worked on in silence attempting, with what success she had no idea, to exude an air of placid domesticity. At nine forty-five she rang for tea and contemplated her husband over the rim of her cup.

If she did not know better she would think him not *nervous*, exactly, but certainly edgy. Which was non-sensical—women were the ones supposed to be anxious about this sort of situation, not adult males with, she had no doubt, years of sexual experience behind them.

Now she had made herself nervous. Julia set down her cup with a rattle. 'I shall retire, if you will excuse me.'

Will stood up with punctilious courtesy and went to open the door for her. She had thought that she had got used to his presence, but the sense that he was too big and too male swept over her again and it was an effort not to scuttle into the hall like a nervous mouse. *Calm, seductive,* she reminded herself. *Make him want* you, *not just any wife.* But perhaps, when she had told him as much as she dare about Jonathan, he would not want her at all.

Nancy was waiting to help her undress when she made her way to her new suite. 'I've moved all your things, my lady. Such a nice spacious dressing room: there's plenty of room for your new gowns. And Mr Gatcombe brought all the jewellery boxes up and has put them in the safe. Shall we check the inventory to-morrow, my lady? I don't like to be responsible when we haven't got a list of what's there.'

'Yes,' Julia agreed, studying the room as if she had not seen it before. It was large with a deep Venetian window, a marble fireplace and a handsome bed in the classical style with pale-green curtains. The pictures were dull, she thought, attempting to divert her thoughts from the bed. There were others in the house that would look better here—that was something to do tomorrow. And there was the jewellery to look at. And she must think about new gowns for the entertaining Will was sure to want to do.

If she was not careful her day would become filled with all the trivial domestic duties her husband thought she should be engaging in.

'Such a pity we didn't know his lordship was coming home,' Nancy said as she picked up the hairbrush and began to take down Julia's hair. 'You could have bought some pretty new nightgowns, my lady.'

Now the butterflies really were churning in her stomach. She was about to sleep with a man for only the second time in her life. No, third, she supposed, although sharing a bed with Will on their wedding night had been sleeping only in the literal sense.

She was not in love with him and he was certainly not in love with her. She did not have a pretty new nightgown, and, rather more importantly to her confidence, she had carried a child to term, which doubtless would make her body less desirable to him.

When he learned that she was not a virgin perhaps he would expect considerably more sensual expertise than she could possibly muster. She was not at all sure what sexual expertise consisted of for a woman. Her resolve to make him desire her just as much as she desired him was beginning to look much like wishful thinking.

But sitting up in bed ten minutes later she did feel rather more seductive. If, that is, one could feel seductive and terrified simultaneously. Her nightgown might not be new, but the lace trim was pretty, her hair was brushed out smoothly about her shoulders and she could smell the scent of rosewater rising from a number of places that Nancy assured her were strategic pulse points.

All she needed now, Julia thought as Nancy left the room with a cheerful, 'Goodnight, my lady', was a gentleman to seduce. She kept her eyes on the door panels and tried to conjure up the image of Will to practise on. Smiling was too obvious. She tried to achieve a sultry smoulder. The nightgown was too prim. She unlaced the ribbon at the neck and pushed it down over her shoulders a little. Even without the help of stays her bosom, she decided, was acceptably firm and high. Men liked bosoms, she knew that much.

Now, all she had to do was to maintain that look and manage not to be sick out of sheer nerves until the door opened. Then she realised that she had her confession to make first and that to attempt seduction and *then* to reveal the unpleasant truths would seem as if she was trying to manipulate him. Julia threw back the covers to climb out of bed.

'Very nice.' The husky voice came from inside the room to her left.

Julia gave a small scream and twisted round to find her husband lounging against the frame of an open jib door she had quite forgotten about. Of course, she realised as she fought for some poise, it led to his dressing room, but it was so cunningly set into the panels it was almost invisible when closed. 'You made me jump.'

'And that was very nice, too.' He strolled into the room and closed the door behind him. His eyes were on her body and when she looked down she realised that her involuntary start combined with the loosened ribbon had revealed more of the swell of her bosom than she ever intended.

Will was still wearing the thin evening breeches and his shirt, but everything else had gone, the shirt was open at the neck and the cuffs turned back. The casual disarray seemed even more intimate than the silk robe he had been wearing that morning and the part of her brain that was not either panicking, or thinking shame-fully wanton thoughts, wondered if that was deliberate.

'May I join you, my lady?' His hands were on the open edges of his shirt.

'I… Of course. But not in bed. Not yet. I have to talk to you.'

'Talk? We have been sitting downstairs for some time this evening. I would have thought that the time for talking was past.'

Julia took a shuddering breath. 'This is not some-thing I wanted to discuss downstairs. This is in the na-ture of a confession.'

The amusement, and the sensuality, were quite gone from Will's face now. 'Confession?'

Julia took a key from the bedside table. 'We need to go back to my old room.'

'Very well.' His eyes were narrowed in calculation, or perhaps suspicion, but he waited while she tied her robe and led the way along the passageways until they were outside the door next to her room. She unlocked it and stood aside, feeling sick. With a sharp glance at her face Will pushed it open and went in.

What the devil was going on? Will had expected to be making love to his wife by now, not looking at spare rooms. He glanced around. When he had left this had been a sitting room, a little boudoir for lady guests using the bedchambers at this end of the house. Now there was a cradle draped in white lawn, a low nursing chair, a pretty dresser.

The nursery was up on the floor above. It still had, he recalled, his old crib, his childhood bed, his toys. What was this room doing furnished as a nursery? This *unoccupied* room? Behind him Julia was silent. Will opened a drawer in the dresser. It was full of tiny garments, a lacy shawl, little caps. One pile was weighted down with a rattle, silver and coral that jingled as he lifted it.

He dropped the rattle back into the drawer with a faint tinkle of bells, the realisation of what this meant stealing through his consciousness. He felt sick.

'Where is the child?' he asked as he turned back to the door.

His voice was perfectly calm, but Julia flinched as though he had shouted, struck at her. 'He was born dead.'

Will stayed precisely where he was until he got the flare of anger under control. If it *was* anger, that sharp nauseating pain under his breastbone. He had never lifted a finger to a woman in his life and he was not going to now. He was not his father: civilised men dealt with these things in a civilised manner. But he had not expected to be cuckolded, which, he supposed, showed a lack of imagination on his part, given the family history.

'Well,' he drawled, 'I have heard of some interesting accidents of birth, but I hope you are not going to tell me fairy stories. Whose child was he?'

'Yours,' Julia said flatly. 'In law. He was born nine months after I married and was bedded by my husband. By you. The law accepts any child born in wedlock as legitimate unless the husband refuses to acknowledge it. If you deny him, then you can only do it by revealing our marriage for the sham that it was.'

It took him a moment to find his voice. 'That little speech sounded rehearsed. Have you been lying awake all night fretting over how you were going to talk yourself out of this predicament? No wonder the door was locked. How long did you expect to keep me in ignorance?'

Julia pushed herself away from the door, walked across to the table set in the window alcove and began to shift things around with jerky, nervous movements. 'This is not how I meant to tell you. I could not find the words and now it has all gone wrong. But predicament? Is that what you call it? A child died. It was a tragedy.'

She started to turn away, but Will caught her wrist, the narrow bones delicate in his grip. She went white, but pulled against him with surprising strength. He stopped himself from tightening his hold, but he did not let her go.

'Whose child was he? Henry's?'

'Henry's?' Her expression was one of total shock. 'Of course not! How could you think I would do such a thing? He was the child of Jo—of the man I eloped with.'

'You eloped? You didn't run away from home to avoid a forced marriage as you told me? So what you told me was a lie?' What a fool he'd been. Respectable ladies did not run away from home like that. Of *course* there had been a man.

Julia pressed her lips together and her gaze dropped

from his. 'Yes. I…I thought you would not help me if you knew what I…the truth.' She was stumbling over the words, biting her lip. 'I thought he loved me, would wed me, but it was all a plot between him and my cousins to get rid of me. I lay with him before I realised he never had any intention of marrying me.'

'So you ran away from him soon after you had eloped?'

'Yes, the very first evening. When I realised we were not heading north I confronted him. He admitted he was taking me to London. I waited until he was…asleep and then I ran away.'

There was something wrong with the story, he could sense it. Not all lies, but not the whole truth either. 'And after one bedding you were with child?' To his own ears he sounded as sceptical as he felt. 'I do not think so. You ran off when he refused to provide for a fallen woman with a brat in her belly. It explains why you were so anxious to secure a husband.'

Julia flinched at his crudity and Will bit back the instinctive apology. 'You think *that* was why I agreed to your scheme?' She pulled back against his grip and this time he let her go, expecting her to retreat. Instead she stayed where she was, a puzzled frown on her face, as though she looked back to that night and was surprised at what she saw there. 'You may believe what you will, but strangely enough the possibility that I might be with child did not occur to me then. I was ruined and desperate: that was enough.'

No, my lady, I do not believe you, he thought. There

was something she was hiding, he could sense it, almost smell it. How the devil had he been so deceived that he had thought her an innocent, a respectable woman with nothing to hide except a bullying family? The memory of her reluctance to share his bed on their wedding night, of that innocent, trusting kiss came back. *Innocent*. He had been sick, exhausted, in a fever—he supposed that accounted for his lack of perception.

'Henry and Delia must have been frantic when they realised you were pregnant,' Will observed, finding a certain grim humour in the thought. He would have liked to have been a fly on the wall during that conversation—and yet Julia was on good terms with Delia now. That argued some clever diplomacy. Oh, no, it would not do to underestimate his wife. Not just another man's mistress and a liar, but as intelligent as he had first thought.

'They were as relieved as you obviously are that my child was stillborn, although at least they managed to conceal it decently.'

'And what would you have done if the baby had lived?' How subtly the colour ebbed and flowed under her skin, he thought, studying the curve of cheek that was all he could see of her averted face. She had grown into a kind of understated beauty that he could have sworn she had not possessed before. One tear trembled on the end of her lashes. Very effective, Will told himself, fighting the instinct to pull her into his arms and comfort her. That was what she wanted, hoped— to twist him round her little finger.

'If he had lived, I would have had to admit the truth. I was prepared for that: I could not have cheated Henry out of his rights.'

'No? You expect me to believe that you could deny your own child a title and an inheritance? Keep silent and you would have been the mother of the heir. You would have had another twenty-one years as mistress of King's Acre.'

'It would not have been right,' she said doggedly, as though she really believed what she was saying.

'So you would have bastardised your own son? Forgive me if I do not believe you.'

She swung back, control lost at last, her fury with him plain on her face. 'You think I could live a falsehood like that?' Her voice was low and shaking with vehemence. 'You think I could defraud a decent man of his inheritance and make my own child an innocent party to that for his entire life?'

'I have no idea what you might do, Julia,' Will said, as much to see the fire spark in her eyes—flint struck against steel—as to continue the argument. His body was beginning to remind him that he had been celibate for a very long time. Too long.

'Well, I could not do such a thing. You hardly know me, so you will just have to accept my word.' She caught her full lower lip between her teeth in a way that had him biting his own lip until the pain reminded his body just who was in charge. When he did not speak she turned and went to the dresser, smoothed her hand over the garments that lay inside the open drawer, then pushed it closed.

'Do I?' Will asked her unresponsive back. 'What if I chose not to accept it? What if I decide that you have lied to me, deceived me from the start in order to foist another man's bastard on me? What would the law's opinion of our unconsummated marriage be then, I wonder?'

Julia turned and looked at him steadily as though down the blade of a rapier. 'You think to cast me off? You may try if you are so unkind—and so uncaring of the world knowing you were incapable of making me your wife. But if you think to do it so you may court your pretty Caroline Fletcher, you will be disappointed. She is betrothed to the Earl of Dunstable who appears to be in complete possession of all his faculties and a great deal of money besides.'

Of course she is. Caroline had thought him dying and could not cope with that. Once she believed him dead she would not have gone into mourning. Curiously, he found he did not care in the slightest. Will shrugged. 'She is beautiful, richly dowered. It is a miracle she is not already wed. It is nothing to me.'

Julia turned towards the door. The white-muslin wrapper flounced around her feet as she walked, her steps rapid and jerky as though she really wanted to run and was holding herself in check. The sash was belted tight around her natural waistline and showed the curve of hip and buttock, the elegant line of her back.

His mouth dried and he had to moisten his lips before he said, 'We can hope that the next one is also a boy to put poor Henry out of his misery.'

'The next one?' Julia stammered.

She was going to refuse to sleep with him? 'You want to have it both ways?' Will demanded. 'You want me to acknowledge that I was the father of your still-born child, you want the rights of marriage and yet you would deny them to me?'

'You would not expose me?' She had gone bone-white, whiter even than when she had told him about the baby. The possibility of scandal seemed to terrify her.

Will shrugged. 'No, of course not. I am not attempting to blackmail you. But if you cannot be truly my wife, then we will have to end this marriage somehow for both our sakes. Coming back from the dead rearranges one's priorities somewhat. You'd be amazed what I find utterly unimportant now. What I *do* find important, what I have always, is that we have the truth between us. I will not be deceived and lied to, Julia. I grew up in a household of lies and deceptions and I'll not stand for it now. I cannot live like that and I certainly cannot bring up children in that atmosphere.'

Chapter Eleven

They stared at each other and gradually Julia found she could focus and move from blind panic to actually listening to what they were saying to each other. Will thought she was going to try to keep him from her bed and that was never what she had intended.

Julia swallowed hard. 'I have no intention of being other than a proper wife to you, if you will have me. I just needed a little time to come to terms with it, that is all. I am sorry if you cannot believe me about the elopement, but it was the truth.'

If only she could understand the roiling mix of emotions inside her. Over all of it was the terror that a public scandal would expose her and that she would be arrested for Jonathan's murder. Below that, like fish swimming in muddy water, were layers of other feelings. There was fear of the intimacy, of being hurt again, physically and mentally. And there was the attraction she felt for Will, due, she supposed, to him being such an attractive man. But if she became pregnant again, what would happen?

Could she carry the child safely? If she lost another...
Her mind shied away from the thought because it was
simply too painful to think about.

But she had her duty to her husband and she owed
Will a great deal. If it had not been for him, goodness
knows what would have become of her three years ago.
The fear and the pain and the doubt she would somehow have to overcome.

He was studying her with those dangerous amber
eyes. 'It was a shock,' he said eventually. 'If it had not
been for the baby, would you have told me about your
lover?'

'I do not know,' Julia confessed. 'Would you have
been able to tell?'

'Possibly,' Will said with a wry smile. 'Probably.'

'Shall we...I mean, do you want to...?' How difficult it was! To want something and yet to be so frightened of it.

'Yes, I want to,' he said. 'If you are sure.'

Julia nodded and walked before him, back to her
bedchamber. She turned when she reached the bed and
watched her husband as he closed the door and came
towards her.

*Courage. Seduce him. Oh, who do you think you are
fooling? You could not seduce anyone to save your life.
No, don't think that...*

One glance at those skintight breeches told her that
her husband did not need much encouragement. Of
course, he had been without a woman for a long time,
which would explain it. But she wanted him to want *her*,
not just any woman to slake his desires with.

What would he expect her to do now? Jonathan had simply ripped off his clothes, then her clothes, tossed her on to the bed and threw himself down beside her.

Will pulled the shirt over his head, dropped it at his feet, flipped back the covers and waited courteously for her to get into bed. 'Now that is a very piquant contrast,' he said as he stood and studied her. 'All that prim white cotton tight around your legs and all that slipping lace up above.'

Julia looked down. Her nervous shifting about had wrapped the nightgown around her legs. Then she looked up at Will. Looked properly and felt dizzy. When she had met him on the bridge that night and had held him in her arms she had felt nothing but skin and bone. Now she was contemplating muscle as defined as that on any classical sculpture of an athlete. Only this was not cold white marble, this was golden tanned skin, a dusting of dark-brown hair, the blue of veins, the nipples so much darker than her own.

Jonathan's body had not made that much impression on her, she realised. When he had first undressed it had all been so fast she had no time to look at him and afterwards… Afterwards she seemed to recall thinking that he was beautiful. But not with the emotions that looking at this man produced. Better not to think about Jonathan.

It was hard to think about any other man clearly at all with this one so close and so nearly naked.

'I am all in favour of piquancy,' she managed, her

gaze fixed firmly on his chest and the curls of crisp dark-brown hair.

'Good,' Will murmured, 'because I am intending to leave you nicely wrapped up for a while.' And while she tried to work out what that meant he slipped open the fastening of his breeches, slid them down his legs and kicked them away. Underneath he was quite naked. And quite magnificently aroused.

Will lay down on his side on the sheet, his body touching hot down the length of her. He propped himself up on one elbow so they were eye to eye, reached out, tugged one of the pillows away and followed her down when she fell back with a little gasp of surprise.

A gasp that left her mouth open, Julia realised as Will leant in and kissed her, his mouth warm and moist and tasting of brandy. The move had been assured and predatory and she found both amazingly arousing.

She had learned from that morning's kiss and had learned, too, what she liked. If she tangled her tongue with his then Will thrust more deeply, if she closed her lips a little then he would nip and nibble at them. She tried nibbling in return and felt his mouth curve in response. *He likes that.* She tried a little nip and was rewarded by a growl deep in his throat.

That was encouraging, she thought. He no longer seemed shocked or angry with her. But what now? Jonathan had been fast, and, she was beginning to realise as Will nibbled down the line of her jaw and sucked gently at the base of her throat with leisurely relish, not at all subtle.

She should be doing something seductive, but it was difficult when she was not at all sure what that involved and when her legs were restricted by her twisted nightgown and Will's arm was effectively pinning hers to the bed.

Julia moaned in frustration and arched up to try to free herself, squashing her breasts against Will, who was nuzzling into her cleavage. The effect was startling. He growled, twisted, seized the collar of her nightgown, ripped it clean down to her waist, then spread the two halves open and stared down at her.

Was something wrong? Why was he looking at her like that? It was her figure, that was it. She was no longer fresh and young and virginal... Just when she could not stand the suspense any longer he bent his head and licked, lavishly, slowly, over her right nipple. And then the left. And back. They went hard and tight and he caught first one, then the other in his teeth and Julia sobbed, arching again, wanting more. He increased the pressure until it was a tiny stab of pain that arrowed into her belly and became something else entirely: heat and weight and need. Then he licked again while his hand took hold of the torn edge of her nightgown and yanked down hard and it tore as far as her knees.

Now he would cover her with his body, push her legs apart, take her. She fought a silent battle with the memories and the fear. It had hurt and Jonathan had not been careful. And Will was very aroused, she knew enough to understand that. Julia tried not to let her apprehension show, tried not to freeze.

But Will kept on tormenting her breasts as he stroked down into the brown curls that were embarrassingly damp. *Wet*, she thought, shocked, as his fingers parted her and then she forgot to be self-conscious as the strange deep ache got worse and worse and she twisted, pushing up against the heel of his hand.

Am I supposed to feel like this? It was so much more than when she had lost her virginity. Then she had felt a little of this, but not the all-consuming desperate need for *something*. 'I want you inside me,' she gasped, beyond shame. That must be it, that was what her body was clamouring for.

'Patience,' Will said and blew on her nipples while his fingers played and teased and suddenly found a point of perfect, shocking pleasure.

'Will.'

He came to his knees, freed her completely from the nightgown and finally, *finally,* covered her with his body. But his fingers did not stop their torment and everything was tightening into an impossibly tangled knot and she did not know how she could bear it.

'Julia. Look at me.' Will's voice was husky and she dragged open her eyes and stared into the amber heat of his. 'Are you all right?'

'No! No, I'm not…I can't bear it. Please…' She had no idea what she wanted, only that she needed him inside her and his weight on her and his mouth on hers. And by some miracle he understood her incoherent plea. He lowered himself, speared his fingers into her hair, drove with his hips and filled her in one long, hard thrust. Everything unravelled, broke apart as she heard herself scream, felt her body close, tight, on Will as he moved and then he froze, shuddered under her clutching hands and collapsed on to her body.

Selfish bastard, Will thought as his brain stopped spinning. He lay pillowed on Julia's sweet warmth and contemplated her lover, the one she had eloped with, the one who had not, apparently, thought to give her any pleasure at all while he took what he wanted.

She had been as ignorant of what her own body could experience as a virgin. He smiled into the crook of her neck and lipped gently at the warm skin. Her arms were still around him and he became aware of the gentle movement of her fingers. She was stroking his shoulders lightly, as if exploring, like someone blind reaching out to map their world with their fingertips.

Had she any idea how seductive that innocence was? How sensual and responsive he found her? Of course not. Which was a very good thing, he decided, as he reached out a hand and pulled the covers over them. If she had any idea, then she would use it against him, use her feminine power to try to weaken and undermine him. It was bad enough having her fight him for control of every aspect of the estate without her deciding she could seduce him into letting her carry on being master here. Not that it would work.

Still, it was a pleasure how she had reacted to him. And fortunate, because after all those long months of celibacy he found it a miracle he had held out against his climax as long as he had. The next time—which had better be soon, he thought with a wry grin—would be even better. He was looking forward to teaching Julia the arts of love.

His harsh words when he had accused her of being another man's mistress, of lying about her lack of experience, came back to deliver a sharp jab to his conscience. Her story had obviously been true and he must make that up to her. If only he did not have this nagging instinct that she was still not being completely honest with him.

God, this is comfortable. I must be squashing her. He rolled off the soft fragrant body cushioning his so uncomplainingly and gathered her into his arms. She came with a little sigh, snuggled up against his chest and went quite limp. *Asleep.* It was endearingly trustful, the way she simply let go, just as she had on that strange wedding night so long ago. He should slide out of bed now, let her rest, go back to his own chamber. *In a minute...*

Her right arm had gone to sleep and there was a warm draught in her ear which tickled, but was oddly pleasant. And a strange beat under her ear. In fact, the pillow was rather harder than feathers and was not a pillow at all.

Julia blinked her eyes open and found she was wrapped in Will's arms, her cheek on his chest. He was asleep, breathing into her ear. And neither of them was wearing a stitch.

It was tempting to press her lips to his skin. She could smell the faint muskiness of sex and sleep and warm man and the nipple close to her mouth was puckered and hard, perhaps from her breath.

But if she did kiss him, then he would know how much she wanted him and she would only demonstrate all over again how inexperienced she was. She needed to think and she couldn't do it here with her body distracted by Will's closeness. He had not hurt her even though he had been so strong, so forceful. She could not quite believe it.

Her dreams had been as bad as always, the wisps of them still hung around her mind like dirty fog. The dream where she was running away on feet that were raw with blisters, the dream where she was so mired in guilt she could not move, the dream where they told her that her child was not breathing… But the waking memories were amazing. Would it always be like this?

Julia slid out of bed, held her breath until she could lower his arm to the mattress, and got to her feet. She would just tiptoe into the dressing room, put on her habit…

'Good morning.'

She turned to find Will regarding her with sleepy appreciation. There was nothing to wrap herself in. 'Good morning.' Julia began to back towards the door.

'Where are you going?'

'Riding. I wanted the, er, exercise.'

One eyebrow lifted in mocking disbelief.

'And the fresh air.'

'Open a window wider for the air and come back to bed for the exercise.'

'But I wanted to ride.' *I need to escape before you realise that you only have to touch me and I turn into melted butter. If you don't know that already.*

Will flipped back the sheet and lay back. 'Come here and I'll teach you to ride astride.'

There was absolutely no mistaking his meaning. Julia could feel the blush spreading from her toe-tips to her cheeks. She wanted to flee, she wanted to run to him. She tried to look as though it was actually a rational decision, as though she was in charge of her emotions. Julia held Will's gaze and walked back to the bed, tossing her hair back over her shoulder as she did so. His eyes narrowed and she saw a perceptible reaction in his already aroused body.

I please him. And despite everything, the fears and the dreams and the knowledge that Will still did not trust her, the realisation that this aspect of their marriage might be happy was like a benison. *If it lasts.*

Chapter Twelve

By the time she and Will sat down to luncheon Julia had managed to stop colouring up every time he looked at her. After a prolonged, very instructive and shatteringly pleasurable interlude in bed Julia had managed to take her horseback ride after all.

Nancy had fetched her conventional riding habit without being asked and Julia was glad to be saved the temptation to put on her divided skirt. She didn't want an argument with her husband to spoil the remarkable closeness their lovemaking had created. Will had accompanied her and even listened, without apparent irritation, to her comments on how the fields were being used and what the situation was with the tenants. He had admired the rebuilt cottages that replaced the row he had shown her that first morning and complimented her on the design of the well cover and the pigsties.

Perhaps, after all, things were going to settle down. He would accept her as a partner, her position would be safe and, with shared interests, they could begin to build a marriage.

And yet... She watched him from beneath her lashes. Will had been attentive, had listened and yet somehow she had felt that he was flirting with her, humouring her. He knew, because quite plainly he was a man of very considerable experience in these matters, that she was attracted to him, that she had enjoyed herself in his arms. *The balance of power,* she mused. *My lord and master. In bed and out of it—is that how he sees it?*

'I expect we will be besieged by visitors,' Will remarked now as he cut into a cheese. 'Aunt Delia will have spread the gossip all about the neighbourhood. We were spared all the bride-visits three years ago, but we are in for them now.'

'I suppose we will be.' People would soon sate their curiosity, surely? Then they would leave them in the peace she was used to, with only morning calls from close neighbours and her particular friends.

'We must hold a dinner party as soon as possible.'

'We must?' Will did not mean the informal dinners she enjoyed, with good plain food on the table and casual card or table games, music and gossip afterwards.

'Certainly. A series of small ones, I thought, rather than try to deal with everyone at once. In fact, I have a list of guests drawn up we can use to sort out the invitation list for the first one.'

A series of dinner parties would mean hours of planning. They would be an event in the neighbourhood and people would compare notes, which meant a different menu for each, and different table decorations. 'I will have to buy some new gowns.'

'Is that such a hardship? I never thought to hear a woman say that sentence in such a depressed tone of voice.'

Julia smiled and shrugged. 'It is simply the time, but I can go into Aylesbury tomorrow and order several.' She made no mention of the discomfort she felt walking around the crowded streets full of strangers.

Will had said nothing about pin money or housekeeping and she had no intention of bringing the subject up until she had to. It was not that she had been extravagant while she had sole control of the money, but she did not relish the thought of having to account for every penny spent on toothpowder or silk stockings. She had been earning the money that she spent so prudently. Now she would be beholden to her husband for everything.

'We will go up to town in the autumn,' Will said. 'Presumably you go fairly frequently.'

'No. I have never been.' Ridiculously it seemed more dangerous than any other place, as though Bow Street Runners would be waiting around every corner for her. Fingers would point, constables would pounce and drag her before magistrates…

'Why not? Is this another foolish scruple, like not wearing the jewellery?' Julia shook her head, unable to think of a convincing explanation, and Will frowned. 'Well, we will go up in a week or so. It will be short of company, but we can both shop, I can make myself known at my clubs again and so forth.'

'Of course. I shall look forward to it.' The irrational panic was building inside, beating at her, and Julia made herself sip her lemonade and nibble at a cheesecake. She needed peace and time to reflect.

The next day after luncheon Will rode off to interview the village blacksmith about the ironwork for the new stables. Julia waited until his long-tailed grey gelding had vanished from sight, then went into the garden to gather a handful of white rosebuds. Ellis the gardener controlled his usual grumbles about anyone picking 'his' flowers and gave her a smile as she passed him. He knew what the little bouquet was for.

The path wound through the shrubbery, past the vicarage and into the churchyard. The ancient village had been moved by some autocratic baron early in the last century when it got in the way of his new parkland. As a result the villagers found themselves with new homes, but a longer walk to the now-isolated church which also served as the chapel for the castle.

Julia made her way round to the south side and pushed open the ancient oak door. Inside the light was dimmed by the stained glass windows and the silence was profound and peaceful. She made her way to the Hadfield family chapel with its view through an ornate stone screen to the chancel.

The table tomb of Will's fourteenth-century ancestor, Sir Ralph Hadfield, stood in the centre. The knight, his nose long since chipped off, lay with a lion under his feet and his hand on his sword hilt. Beside him his lady, resplendent in the fashions of the day, had a lap-dog as her footrest.

Between the east end of the tomb and the chapel-altar steps was a slab with a ring in to give access to the Hadfield vault beneath. Delia always said the thought of the vault gave her the horrors, but Julia found the chapel peaceful. The ancestors beneath her feet, lying together in companionable eternity, held no terrors for her. It was quiet, cool, strangely comforting in the chapel as she gathered up the drooping roses from the vase standing on the slab and added the new flowers, then sat and let her tumbling thoughts still and calm.

That morning she and Nancy had folded and packed away all the tiny garments, the shawls, the rattle, the furnishings for the nursery. Now they were in silver paper and lavender, the cot stripped of its hangings, everything put away in the attic.

She had set the door wide open on to the room and left it for Will to find, or not. She did not feel able to talk about it. What if she was already with child again? All that pain to risk. Not the physical pangs, but the mental pain of nine months of anxiety and then...

But she was well and healthy now, she reassured herself, not the nervous girl who had spent those first months jumping at her own shadow, convinced that she would step out of her front door and find the constables waiting for her, her new neighbours pointing, crying, *Imposter! Murder!* Surely that would make a difference? And part of her ached for a child.

She was not sure how long she had sat there before

she heard the creak of the outer door being pushed open and footsteps coming down the aisle. The vicar, she supposed. Mr Pendleton was gentle and kindly; she did not mind his company.

The realisation that it was not the elderly scholar came over her with a sort of chill certainty. Julia did not turn, but she was not surprised when Will said, 'He is here, then?'

She should not have risked it, coming to the chapel while there was the slightest chance Will would find out. He would be furious that this was something else she had kept from him. He would insist that the interloper was removed…

'I know it is wrong.' She found she was on her feet, standing on the slab as though she could somehow stop this. Will stood with his hat in his hands, his face serious. 'I know he isn't yours and he has no right here. But he wasn't baptised, so they would have buried him outside the churchyard wall in that horrid patch under the yew trees and Mr Pendleton understood when I was distressed, so we put him here…'

'Does he have a name, even though he was never baptised?' Will said gently.

It was the last question she expected. 'Alexander, after my father,' she stammered.

'Alexander is very welcome here,' Will said and came to her side. 'Do you know who he is lying there with?'

'No.' He was not going to insist the tiny coffin was

taken and buried in that dark, dank patch with the sui-
cides and the other tiny tragedies?

'My brother and two sisters,' Will said and she saw
his fingers were curled tight over the edge of Sir Ralph's
tomb. 'The loss of two children after I was born shattered my parents' marriage.' His mouth twisted in a
wry smile. 'Not that it was well founded in the first
place. Afterwards things went from bad to worse. They
hardly communicated other than by shouting and the
third child, a daughter, was not my father's—or so he
always maintained. You may imagine the atmosphere.'

'Oh, the poor things!' Julia cried.

'The babies?'

'Well, of course. But for your mother to lose so many
and for your father… He lost two children himself and
then they were obviously not able to reach out and comfort each other or things would not have gone so wrong
between them.'

'You are an expert on marriage now?' Will asked
harshly. Was he recalling that she had taken a lover
before she had come to him? Might he fear she would
do what his own mother had done if she was unhappy?

'No.' Then she saw the pain in his eyes. How hard it
must have been to grow up in a household full of grief
and anger. 'No, but I can understand a little of what
your mother felt. If she had no one to talk to, the loss
of the children would have been so much worse.' She
hoped she had kept her voice steady and not revealed
how much this cost her to speak of.

Will half-turned away and stood staring down at his

long-ago ancestor, then he looked back at her as though he had been translating her words in his head and had just deciphered the meaning. 'And you had no one, had you? Even if Delia behaved decently, you would have known that in her heart she was relieved that Henry had not been displaced.'

'That is true.' She fought to find a smile. 'I managed.' *Somehow.* 'There was not much choice.'

'You should not have had to,' Will said roughly and the anger in his voice undid her in a way that gentleness would never have done. 'Damn it, I didn't mean to make you cry. Julia—' He pulled her into his arms and for the first time since he had returned there was nothing in his touch but the need to give comfort. He cupped her head with one big hand and held her against his shoulder. 'Perhaps it is not a bad thing if you weep now. Were you even able to cry properly after it happened?'

She shook her head, afraid to speak and lose control.

'Then do it now. Mourn for the first child of this marriage.' Julia gave a sob and then simply let the tears flow while Will stroked her hair and held her tightly and murmured comfort.

How long they stood there she had no idea. Eventually the tears ran their course and Julia lifted her head and looked up into Will's face. 'Thank you.' She became aware that her lashes were sticking together and she wanted to sniff and her nose was probably red. The breast of his coat was dark with moisture. 'Have you got a handkerchief?'

'Of course.' Will eased her down on to the pew, produced a large linen square from his pocket and moved away to study the memorials on the walls.

Julia put herself to rights as best she could and found she could express the anxiety that she had thought she could never speak of to him. 'Will, what if it happens again? What if I am not able to give you an heir?'

He came back and sat beside her, his hands clasped between his knees. He seemed to be engrossed in the design of a hassock. After a moment he said, 'I hope that is not the case, because I would hate to see you suffer such a thing. But if it did, then Henry, or his son, inherits. It is not the end of the world and besides, do not anticipate troubles. Now come back into the sunshine or you will get chilled. It is like an ice house in here and it is a lovely day outside.'

Julia took the hand he held out to her and went out, arm in arm with him as fragile hope began to unfurl inside her. Will understood how she had grieved and her need to weep and be comforted. He had been kind about letting her place Alexander in the vault and she had seen, with piercing clarity, just how wounded he must have been as a child by his parents' unhappy marriage.

Perhaps one day he might even come to trust her, even though she knew she would never be able to burden him with her secret. Perhaps, Julia thought optimistically as the sunshine and the relief of the tears did their work, this was the real beginning of their marriage.

'Will, how much did you understand of what was happening? When your brothers and sisters died?'

'Understand? Nothing. They told me nothing other

than that I was now the only son because my brother was dead so I must grow up to be the perfect Baron Dereham because there was no other option. They didn't tell me at all about the little girl my father said was not his. I only found out about that when I overheard two maids talking about it afterwards. I would have liked to have had a brother,' he added after a moment, his voice utterly expressionless. 'And little sisters. I asked my tutor what it meant when the maids said one of them was a bastard. So he told me and then I was beaten for eavesdropping.'

'That is outrageous!' Julia forgot her own melancholy in a burst of anger for the unhappy, confused small boy. 'They should have told you the truth, all of it, but kindly so a child could understand.'

He shrugged. 'Water under the bridge now.'

They walked on in silence, but it seemed to Julia that some of the tension between them had lifted a little. The roofs of the Home Farm came into sight to their right and Julia recalled that the workmen had finished building the foundations for the extension to the stables and were beginning on the walls. With the new horses arriving so soon Will had decided on a single-storied wooden building to save time and he had ordered the work without, of course, any reference to her.

Now, as they strolled back from the church, it seemed the time to build on the intimacy of the moment by showing an interest rather than offering suggestions. 'I would like it if you would show me the new stables. They seem to be coming along very well.'

Will changed direction and took the path to the farm. 'You have not been to look at them yet?'

'You made it clear that you did not require my interference.' She tried to say it lightly, but his arm stiffened under her hand.

'I am sorry you see it like that,' Will said. 'But there can only be one master giving orders or it confuses the servants and the workers. And I am the master.'

'I realise that.' Julia bit her lip. If he was prepared to be conciliatory, then she must not be grudging. 'And perhaps I had not taken that into account sufficiently when you came home. But this has been my life and my responsibility for three years. It is what interests me, what has always interested me. I do not want to displace you—I could not do that even if I wanted to—but I cannot bear to be shut out. May I not be involved? Can we not discuss things together?'

He was silent as he opened a gate for her. 'Will, I will go mad if you expect me to retire into the house and become a domestic paragon!'

'You seem to be that already,' he remarked. 'I do not recall the house ever looking better.'

'Thank you. But there is nothing left to do except maintain it, whereas there is always something with the estate.' He raised an eyebrow and she knew she was being too enthusiastic, but she could not help herself. 'I love it! There are always new things to try, experiments to plan, even a crisis or two to enliven the week.' They stopped abruptly, confronted by a six-foot wide patch of mire where the cows had churned up the entrance to the milking yard after an unseasonal cloudburst a few days before. 'See? This needs filling with rubble and tamping down.'

Will stopped, pushed his hat firmly on to his head, took her around the waist and swung her over the mud to a large flat stone in the middle, hopped across to it himself and then swore under his breath. 'I've misjudged this—there isn't enough room to stand securely and swing you across to the hard ground.' They clung together in the middle, swaying dangerously.

'You must let me go or we'll both fall in. We will just have to wade,' Julia said. Will was enjoyably strong and large to cling to, even if it did seem they were both about to land in the mud. *What we must look like...* 'I have old boots on.'

'Well, I have not!' Will protested as he took a firmer grip around her waist. 'These are Hoby's best.'

'They *are* very beautiful boots.' She had noticed. And noticed too how well they set off his muscular legs. 'If I go, then you will have room to get your balance and jump.' An irrepressible desire to laugh was beginning to take hold of her. Where on earth had that come from? Relief, perhaps, after the cathartic tears in the church.

'I am not going to leave my wife to wade through the mud in order to protect my boots,' Will said. Julia managed to tip her head back far enough to see the stubborn set of his jaw. There was a small dark mole under the point of it and the impulse to kiss it warred with the need to giggle. He sounded so very affronted to find himself in this ridiculous position.

'If we shout loudly enough, someone will come and they can fetch planks or a hurdle,' she suggested. 'Or is that beneath your dignity?'

'Yes,' Will agreed and she saw the corner of his mouth turn up. 'It is. I feel enough of an idiot, without an audience of sniggering farmhands. Can you put your arms around my neck?'

Julia wriggled to lift her arms. The stone tipped with a sucking sound. 'I think it is sinking. How deep can this mud hole be?'

'We are not going to find out.' Will put his hands under her bottom. 'Jump up and get your legs around my hips.'

'My skirts—'

'Are wide enough,' he said with a grunt as he boosted her up and then, with a lurch, made a giant stride to the milking-parlour threshold with Julia clinging like a monkey round his neck. She gave a faint scream as he landed off balance, jolting the breath out of her, then, with a ghastly inevitability, they were falling.

Will twisted and came down first into a pile of straw with Julia on top of him. 'Ough!'

They lay there gasping for breath until Will said, 'Would you mind moving your elbow? Otherwise we are endangering the future heir.'

Shaking with laughter, stunned to find she could laugh about it, Julia untangled herself and flopped back beside him. 'At least it is clean straw.'

'You find this funny?' He was grinning with the air of a man caught out by his own amusement. It was the first time she had realised that he had a sense of the ridiculous and it was surprisingly attractive.

'Exceedingly,' she admitted. 'Look at us! You have lost your hat somewhere, you have straw in your hair, your shirt is coming untucked from your breeches and, my lord, despite your exquisite boots, you look the picture of a country swain tumbling his girl in a haystack.'

'And what do you resemble, I wonder?' Will raised himself on one elbow and looked down at her. 'Your bonnet is no doubt with my hat in the mud, those boots are deplorable, your skirts are mired around the hem, your cheeks are pink and I do not blame the country swain for wanting to tumble you in the least.'

He leaned over and slid his hand into her hair, very much the lord of the manor exercising his *droit de seigneur*, she thought, rather than a farmhand. 'Now then, my milkmaid…'

He kissed her, laughing. She kissed him back, as well as she could. Will's weight pressed her down into the straw as his free hand began to creep up her stockinged leg. Julia's giggles turned into a little gasp of arousal. 'Will…'

Chapter Thirteen

'Coom oop, Daisy! Get along there, Molly!'

'What the hell?' Will sat up and Julia scrabbled at her rising hem. 'Oh my lord, the herd is coming in. Up you get.' He hauled her to her feet and began to bat at her skirts as Julia brushed straw off his coat-tails.

'Too late…here they come. For goodness' sake, Will, tuck in your shirt!'

The dairy cows pushed through the wide entrance from the field, bringing the smell of grass and manure as they stared with wide, curious black eyes at the interlopers in their milking parlour. 'Go on, get along with you.' Julia waved her hands and they wandered off placidly, each to its own stall, blinking with their preposterously long eyelashes.

'My lady! Oh, and my lord too. Never realised you was in here.' Bill Trent, the dairyman, stood in the doorway, staring at them with as much surprise, and rather more speculation, than his cattle.

'We came up against the quagmire out there, Trent,'

Julia said. 'And we rather misjudged the distance when we tried to get across it. Have you seen our hats? They must have fallen off when we jumped.'

'There they be, my lady.' Bill pointed to the ground behind the straw pile. There was no way the hats would have fallen in that position except from their heads as they sprawled there. On the other hand, she comforted herself as she went to retrieve them, Bill Trent was not perhaps the brightest of the farm workers and might not have the imagination to draw the very obvious conclusion about what the baron and his wife had been doing.

'Come along, my dear.' Will sounded so pompous that she could not decide whether he was perishing with embarrassment, fighting the urge to laugh or was unfairly furious with her for landing him in such a position.

'Of course. Thank you, Trent.' Julia managed as dignified a nod as she could under the circumstances and let Will usher her out of the milking parlour into the main yard. Fortunately there was no one in sight and Will strode across to the drive with Julia in tow. 'Oh dear. I am afraid that was not very decorous.'

'It was, however, exceedingly amusing.' His voice was shaking with laughter.

'Will!'

'And arousing. I assume, my lady, that you will now find it necessary to take all your clothes off in order to remove the lingering traces of the farmyard?'

'Indeed, my lord. And you will doubtless wish to take off your clothing also to assure yourself that no harm has come to those fine boots. Or your breeches. And I fear your shirt may be torn.'

'Quite. This is obviously an emergency. Can you walk any faster?'

'No, but I can run.' Julia took to her heels with Will beside her, burst through the front door and was half-way up the stairs before Gatcombe emerged to see what the commotion was.

'My lady?' He took one look at Will and effaced himself.

'We will have scandalised the entire staff at this rate.' Julia fell panting on to her bed as Will came in behind her and turned the key in the lock.

'I have no intention of having anyone else as an audience,' he promised as he threw his coat on to a chair and began to untie his crushed neckcloth. 'One yokel and one butler is more than enough.'

Julia watched appreciatively as he dragged his shirt over his head, then bent to unlace her boots. 'I am not a very dignified baroness, am I?' she asked, studying the muddy, battered footwear. A real lady would not have been seen dead in those boots, or in a cow shed, either. She would probably have no idea how milk was extracted from a cow and would faint at the sight of a dung heap.

Julia chided herself for the negative thoughts. *For the first time I feel at ease with him, for the first time this feels like a normal marriage.* They had shared secrets and painful memories and, for the first time, Will had been clear about his feelings over the management of the estate.

If only she did not feel so guilty whenever she thought about the secret she was keeping from him. He was coming to trust her and yet what she was hiding from him was awful beyond anything he might imagine.

'Do you think so?' Will said, jerking her back to the moment. What had she said? Oh, yes, something about not being dignified. He sat down to pull his own boots off. The muscles in his back rippled as he moved and tugged and Julia felt her mouth go dry. 'Rolling about in the straw is not dignified, I will agree, but it is perfectly suitable for a milkmaid and her rustic swain. Why do you want to be dignified, anyway? I don't want you to turn into a sober matron, Julia.'

'My clothes are not very... I suppose I should dress better.' Julia pulled up her skirts and untied her garters, conscious of Will's eyes on her hands.

'That footwear is suitable for walking around the yards or the fields,' Will said, standing his boots by the chair and pulling off his own stockings. 'But do you not want to buy new gowns? Or slippers or hats? Some feminine frivolity?'

'Frivolity,' she said blankly, then hauled her concentration back from the contemplation of Will's bare feet—who would have thought that feet could be so attractive?—and thought about his question. 'I did not like to spend the money on frivolities. It did not seem right.'

He had saved her life, given her hope. It had seemed immoral to indulge in what seemed like luxury with his money into the bargain. And even the fleeting thought of wandering around a large town, visiting shops amidst a crowd of strangers, brought back that feeling of panic and foreboding. She shrugged. 'I do not like shopping much.'

'I cannot believe that I have married the only woman in the country who doesn't enjoy it.' Will stood up to unfasten the fall of his breeches. His eyes narrowed and she realised she had run her tongue along her lips in anticipation. 'We will go shopping together in Aylesbury and then in London and I will teach you to be frivolous.'

'You want me to buy lots of new clothes?' She slid off the bed as he came towards her.

'Oh, yes,' Will murmured, turning her so he could undo the buttons at the back of her gown. 'Then I can enjoy taking them off you. Silks...' he pushed the sensible heavy cotton off her shoulders and it fell to the floor '...and satins.' He began to unlace her stays. Julia shivered despite the warmth. 'And Indian muslins so fine they are transparent.' The practical, sensible petticoat joined the gown on the floor. 'And when I get down to your skin, like this...' he began to nuzzle along her shoulder and into the crook of her neck '...there will be the scent of edible, warm woman, just as there is now, and perhaps just a hint of something exotic and French.'

Julia reached behind her and found the waist of his unfastened breeches and pushed down, her palms running over the smooth skin of his hips as they fell. Against her bare buttocks she felt the heat of his arousal branding her with its length and pressed back with a little wriggle.

Will groaned, pushed her forwards so that her hands were on the bed, and then entered her from behind with one swift stoke. *'Julia.'*

The blatant carnality of his need, her own excitement, the overwhelming sensations the position produced, all sent her tumbling helplessly over the edge with dizzying speed. She heard Will gasp, his hands tightened on her hips and then they fell on the bed in a panting, uncoordinated tangle of limbs.

Will rolled on to his back and pulled Julia against his side. It was not easy to find words and he was not certain she wanted any just now as she relaxed confidingly in his arms. Something had shattered the pane of glass that had been between them ever since he came home. Was it that shared laughter, or his realisation of how deeply she had been hurt by the loss of her child? Whatever it was, the results felt good. That hollow well of loneliness inside him that had ached ever since he had been given that death sentence by the doctors was being filled with something warm and soothing. He grinned at the whimsical thought. He had not realised just how much the loss of his siblings, the lies and secrecy, had hurt him until he had told Julia about it.

'You are quiet,' Julia said, her breath feathering across his chest.

'Just thinking.' He wasn't ready to share that feeling of loneliness with her yet. It felt like weakness: a man ought to be able to look death squarely in the eye and not fall prey to self-pity.

'I had never heard you laugh like that before.' Julia sat up, curled her arms around her legs and rested her chin on her knees.

'I'm sorry, I hadn't realised I had been so dour.' When he looked back he could not recall laughing about anything since he had fallen ill. Things had amused him occasionally. The discovery that he was recovering and would not die within months had filled him with happiness, but not laughter. Not the healing, playful laugher that they had shared that afternoon. Perhaps today he had finally accepted that he had his life back to live.

'It was the release after the sad things we spoke of earlier, I expect,' she said. 'Sometimes laughter brings healing.'

Will sat up too and tipped his head to one side so he could see her face. 'I am glad you talked about it to me and that you understood about my parents. I am glad that you could trust me. That is important to me.'

'Trust?' She slanted him a look.

'Yes. I suppose it comes from growing up in a house-hold with so little honesty and so many secrets. You must not think it was the fact that you had a lover before that disturbed me when I found out. It was the fact that you had not told me the truth about how you had come to be by the lake that night.' Julia went very still. 'That was all it was, wasn't it? A reluctance to tell a stranger about how you had been led astray and betrayed?'

'Of course,' she said and smiled at him, her eyes clear and limpid. So why did a drop of doubt send ripples to mar his certainty that his marriage was, finally, in calm waters?

'And you have no secrets from me, do you?' she asked, her voice light as though she was merely teasing him.

'Of course not.'

'So you have no regrets that we have consummated the marriage?' She was staring at her toes now. 'There are no possible grounds now to set it aside.'

Something knotted inside him. Did he regret it? No. He did not love Julia. But he liked her, he admired her. He certainly desired her. She would make a good mother.

'Of course I have no regrets,' he said firmly and saw her shoulders drop a little as though she relaxed with relief. Some demon of impulsiveness made him add, 'Are you asking if I still love Caroline? Of course I do not. I never did—it was a suitable marriage, that was all. That is over and done with.'

Julia stiffened slightly, or perhaps it was his imagination. 'I would not dream of prying into your feelings for Miss Fletcher.'

Will opened his mouth and shut it again. *I protest too much. I should never have mentioned Caroline.*

Julia slid off the bed. 'Look at the time! I must wash and dress.' She seemed perfectly composed and yet something in the relaxed atmosphere had changed.

Will gave himself a shake. Imagination and a slightly guilty conscience at his ineptitude just now, that was all it was.

* * *

'Is it this morning that you were going to call on Colonel Makepeace about the pointer puppies?' Julia enquired at breakfast as Will broke the seal on the last of his post. Every month on this day she had been helping Henry with his accounts and it had not occurred to her to write him a note and say that now he should come and ask Will for his counsel instead of her. Henry was not comfortable with his cousin yet and she had no idea how patient Will would be with him.

One more time, she told herself. Henry would turn up this morning as usual, full of his usual mixture of enthusiasms, doubts, hare-brained ideas and, increasingly, thoughtful insights into his responsibilities. Will would be safely out of the way and she could persuade the younger man that her husband would not scorn his efforts to deal with his debts and the needs of his own estate.

Will looked up from the letter. 'Yes, it is. Do you want to come along? Or was there something you need me to do?'

'Oh, no, I was just wondering.' She did not like prevaricating, but if he did not know she was still helping Henry he could not tell her to stop. Which was a very dubious argument, she knew.

An hour later she was profoundly grateful Will had gone out. Henry was pale, distracted and seemed almost on the verge of despair, however hard he tried to cover it up.

Eventually Julia gave up on the accounts, put down her pen and demanded, 'Henry, what on earth is the matter with you?'

For a moment she thought he would deny anything was wrong, or refuse to answer her, but he slammed the ledger closed and said, 'It's Mama. She is match-making again, only this time she's invited Mary...this young lady and her mother to stay. She's never done that before and it is so marked an attention when there are no other guests that I know they will be expecting a declaration from me!'

'That is somewhat obvious, I agree. Have you shown any interest in this girl?'

'No!' Henry looked positively flustered.

'Is there someone else? You must tell your mother if you have formed an attachment elsewhere.'

Henry got to his feet and went to look out of the window without answering. The tips of his ears had gone red.

'So there is someone? Someone unsuitable,' Julia guessed. She got up and went to sit on the window seat, close, but not crowding him.

'God, yes.'

'Has it been going on for long?' He turned his head away so she added, 'I swear I will not mention a word to a soul. You know I keep my promises, Henry.' It would not do, of course, this attachment to an ineli-gible woman, but there was no need to add to his misery by telling him that, he obviously already knew it perfectly well.

'A year.'

Serious, then. 'Is it a courtesan, Henry?' Perhaps he had sought to deal with his shyness with girls and had become attached to the professional he had gone to. A vehement shake of the head. 'An older woman?' He shot her an incredulous look. 'Someone not of your station?' He bit his lip. Ah, that was it. 'Someone of the merchant class? A servant?'

He had gone white now. 'A servant. I cannot tell you, Julia. You will be shocked.'

'No I will not, truly I will not, Henry. I have not led a very sheltered life, you know. Tell me about her, do.'

Henry sat down abruptly next to her, his hands fisted on his thighs as if to stop them shaking. He seemed unable to speak and a suspicion began to creep over her. 'Henry, is it a young man?'

'How did you—?' He broke off, his face stark with the realisation that he had given himself away. Julia managed to keep the shock out of her voice. Henry was confessing to something that could, at the worst, see him go to the scaffold.

'I just guessed. Henry, is this serious? Who is he?'

'A valet. I met him at the Walsinghams' house party and then… Well, you don't need the details. But it *is* serious, Julia. I love him and he loves me and I don't know what to do. Mama keeps on about me marrying.' He seemed to run out of words.

Yes, it was serious, she could see that. Lethally serious, if not for him, a gentleman, but certainly perilous for his lover. And Henry looked desperate enough to do something foolish. This was no time to be shocked and uncomprehending—she had to help him.

'How often do you go up to London?' she asked, thinking aloud. 'Quite a lot, don't you?' He nodded, bemused. 'Where do you stay?'

'Hotels, sometimes with friends. But what—?'

'It would be more economical, and an investment, if you bought a small apartment,' she suggested. 'You would need a manservant, of course, to maintain it while you were not there and to look after you while you were in town. Many young men do just that and no one thinks anything of it. A young man trained as a valet would be ideal, don't you think?'

'Julia, that is brilliant!' Henry took her hands and beamed at her. Then his face fell. 'But Mama keeps on trying to pair me off with girls.'

'Learn to flirt,' Julia said with sudden inspiration. 'Cultivate a reputation for being dangerous and the mamas will flee at the sight of you. Become a rake and a ladies' man. Your mother will be furious with you, but it should disarm all suspicion.'

'Will you show me how?'

'Certainly not! You'll have to be observant and work it out for yourself. Oh, Henry, don't—' There were tears in his eyes despite his smiles. 'Just do be careful, my dear. It will be more than just a scandal if you are discovered.'

'Thank you. Oh, thank you, Julia.' The next thing she

knew she was in Henry's arms and he was hugging her with desperate affection, his cheek pressed against hers.

The door banged closed. Henry started and clutched her tighter. 'A touching scene,' Will remarked. 'Henry, get your hands off my wife and come here.'

'Will—'

But Henry was already in his feet. He tried to thrust her protectively behind him even as she resisted him. 'Don't you dare look at Julia like that, as if she could do something wrong—as though she would dream of it! You can name your seconds, Cousin!'

'And cause a scandal? I don't think so. And as for my wife's capacity for wrongdoing, well, *Cousin*, you have a far longer and more recent acquaintanceship with her than I have.'

Henry went very still. 'You are just like your father,' he accused. 'I can remember him all too well and you—'

'That is enough, both of you.' Julia stood and put herself between Will with his clenched fists and his hard, angry eyes and Henry's rigid form. 'I have just given Henry some advice with a difficult problem that was worrying him and he was relieved and grateful. If you believe I would be unfaithful to you, and with a young man I regard as a brother, then, my lord, I am sorry for you.'

'What problem?'

Beside her she heard Henry's sharp intake of breath. 'That is a confidential matter. I do not break confidences, my lord. Not yours, not anyone's.'

The dangerous silence stretched until she thought she would faint from holding her breath, then Will said, 'Very well. Keep your hands off my wife in future, Cousin. I do not care how *grateful* you might be feeling.' He turned on his heel.

'I think it might be best if you come here only in company for a week or so,' Julia said as the door closed with exaggerated care behind her husband. 'Will does not like secrets.'

Chapter Fourteen

The evening gown was the most fashionable garment she had ever possessed. Julia regarded the sweep of silken skirts, the elaborate ruffles around the skirt and the tips of her sea-green slippers peeping out below the hem with some satisfaction.

She had shaken off Will's attempts to take her into every shop in Aylesbury—and probably Oxford and Thame, too, if he had his way—by the simple expedient of sending to the best local dressmaker and requesting that she attend her at King's Acre with patterns and samples. When the fabric was chosen she had charged Madame Millicent with taking a sample to her usual shoemaker and with bringing a selection of ribbons and artificial flowers with her to the first fitting.

With the addition of her gauze scarf and silver-spangled fan she was elegantly outfitted from head to toe without the stress of a visit to the crowded shops and was able to contemplate the thought of the first dinner party of their married life with composure.

It had taken some time to arrive at that state. Will had been punctiliously polite since the scene with Henry, although an attempt to discuss it was met by his assurance that he had no intention of prying into her affairs, but that it might be sensible not to be alone with an impressionable young man. This advice was delivered in such a patronising manner that she went from apologetic to thoroughly irritated and made no attempt to raise it again. There were moments when she wondered if that had been his intention. She also wondered uneasily if his insistence on her buying clothes in such a lavish manner was a way of asserting his ownership.

Now she did her best to push such thoughts away and rehearsed the guest list in her head. She knew almost everyone. There was Aunt Delia and Henry, of course. That might be awkward, although Delia would have been affronted not to be invited to the first dinner after Will's return. Then there was the vicar and his wife; Major Frazer, Will's groomsman and old army comrade and Mrs Frazer; the Marquess of Tranton and Lady Tranton, with whom the archbishop had, so providentially, been staying three years ago, and Caroline Fletcher and her parents, Viscount and Lady Adamson, along with her betrothed, Andrew Fallon, Earl of Dunstable.

Will had combined the highest ranking of their neighbours and those with a special connection to the wedding and she could not fault his reasoning, even if it brought her face to face with not only Henry, but also Miss Fletcher, in Will's presence. But Caroline would be accompanied by Lord Fallon so really, Julia scolded herself, there was absolutely no reason to feel any awkwardness. That betrothal was long over.

Her seating plan had required some thought, and Gatcombe's assistance, but she was pleased with the result. Thanks to a strict adherence to the rules of precedence, Miss Fletcher was almost the length of the table away from Will and separated from Julia by the marquess.

Julia swept downstairs, reminding herself that she really was the Baroness Dereham and not an interloper. Three years of grass widowhood running the estate was no preparation for an evening of entertaining a marquess, an earl and a viscount, but they were all pleasant, civilised people, she assured herself.

Will looked up as she entered the dining room, her seating plan in his hand. 'This looks perfectly all right,' he remarked, scanning it as she made last-minute alterations to the flower arrangements in the epergne in the centre of the table.

'I do hope so.' Julia went to the head of the table and tried to see whether the flowers would obscure Will's view of Miss Fletcher. She rather thought they would. It was not irrational jealousy, she told herself, merely what any wife would do when confronted with an acknowledged beauty in her own dining room.

'What are you looking so smug about?'

Julia wrinkled her nose at him. *Smug* was an unpleasant word. She was merely being tactical. Since that strange day with its tears, laughter and explosion of passion she had been unable to clarify her feelings about her husband. His furious reaction to seeing her in Henry's arms had not helped either. Possessiveness, or genuine jealousy?

He was evasive on the subject of Caroline Fletcher, she had noticed. But whether that was because he still wanted her or whether it was simply that he felt he had let Caroline down by breaking the engagement she could not fathom.

But she had told him she trusted him and that was the important thing, to be true to that. Trust was obviously a sensitive point with Will and she could hardly fret about any lingering feelings he might have for Miss Fletcher and forget the secret she was keeping from him herself, or Henry's worrying revelation.

Comparing her mild unease about Caroline Fletcher to the secrets she was keeping was like comparing the nearby Downs with the Alps, she thought with a sudden, familiar, lurch in mood. A rapid mental calculation and she realised it was, indeed, familiar. Unless she was very much mistaken her courses would start tomorrow, which meant she was not carrying Will's child.

The mixed feelings took her by surprise. Regret she had expected. But relief that she had another month's respite before facing that fear took her by surprise. She wished she could confide all that in Will, but she feared she could not articulate it without breaking down.

Gatcombe was hovering and probably thought she was finding fault with the table. Julia told herself to stop fussing and followed Will to the salon so she could pass the time with an unexceptional piece of embroidery until her guests began to arrive.

Will seemed on edge, but that was doubtless her wretched imagination playing tricks on her, Julia decided, and managed to stab herself in the thumb with her needle. He shook out the pages of *The Times* and began to read, creating an effective barrier between them. *And that is just your foolish fancy,* she told herself, sucking at the tiny wound. *Just as you are imagining that things are different in the bedroom.*

Ever since that afternoon when they had tumbled laughing on to her bed and made frantic, urgent love, it had seemed to her that Will had changed. His lovemaking was polite, restrained, considerate. He always left her satisfied…and yet it was as though he was holding something back from her. Had she revealed too much that afternoon? Was he shocked, on reflection, by her abandoned behaviour? Was he retreating back to a safe emotional distance? Or did he still harbour suspicions about Henry?

The French knot she was working had become tangled. Julia tried to unpick it, but the light was bad, or perhaps her vision was blurred. *Or perhaps I am just weepy because of the time of the month,* she told herself.

'I hear carriages.' Will folded the paper and got to his feet to stand by the hearth, facing the door. Julia rose, too, and went to his side. How very handsome he looked in the severe evening clothes. Her sea-green skirts brushed against his legs as she turned to take up her position and she saw him close his eyes for a moment.

'I feel as though a portrait painter will come through the door at any moment and set up his easel. *Baron Dereham and His Lady* about to be immortalised in oils,' she said.

That provoked a snort of laughter from Will and they were both smiling and relaxed as Gatcombe announced, 'The Earl of Dunstable, Viscount and Lady Adamson, Miss Fletcher.'

Julia fought to keep every iota of that smile on her face as she realised that four pairs of eyes were trained, not on them as a couple, but on Will. The earl, Lord Fallon, had that focused look she had learned to recognise in men who were on their mettle, even spoiling for a fight. The earl was on tenterhooks to see how Will reacted to Miss Fletcher, and how she behaved in her turn. Lord and Lady Adamson, she saw in an instant, were on edge, no doubt catching the tension emanating from Lord Fallon in the presence of the man who should have been their son-in-law by now.

And Miss Fletcher? Julia had met her several times before Will's return and knew her a little, but not well enough to sense whether her instinctive dislike was simple prejudice because Caroline had not fought to stay with Will when he had thought himself to be dying, or whether she would have found her uncongenial under any circumstances.

There was an infinitesimal pause, then Will stepped forwards to greet their guests and Julia lost the ability to detect anything but conventional social greetings and the exclamations of pleasure at Will's safe return.

Will was not looking at Caroline. Caroline was carefully not looking at Will and Lord Fallon was watching both of them like a hawk. Julia stepped between the two men. 'I am so pleased you could come, Lord Fallon. Will you be staying long at Heathfield Hall?' She turned a little as she spoke and he had, out of simple politeness, to follow her.

'For several weeks, Lady Dereham. We are making wedding preparations, as you know, and that takes a great deal of planning.'

He began to prose on about the guest list. Julia fixed a smile on her lips. At least she had succeeded in creating space for Caroline's parents to talk to Will and, as she suspected, there was long acquaintance and considerable liking between them.

'Mr and Mrs Pendleton. Mrs Hadfield, Mr Hadfield.'

Delia, unconsciously doing the tactful thing, swooped on Miss Fletcher and began to interrogate her about her trousseau. Henry, who had met Lord Fallon on the hunting field, came up with a question about a horse and, with a sigh of relief at the thought of another awkward confrontation averted, Julia was able to slip away and greet the vicar and his wife.

The big salon filled up quickly and Julia relaxed. Will had hardly so much as glanced in Caroline's direction and both he and Lord Fallon appeared to have decided there was no need to bristle at each other. Will had even spoken civilly to Henry and the younger man had relaxed from an all-too-obvious tension into his usual cheerful self.

* * *

By the time she walked through to the dining room with the Marquess of Tranton, Julia realised that she was actually enjoying herself.

'I hear that you are expecting a positive herd of horses shortly,' the marquess remarked as the soup was served.

'Indeed, yes. Lord Dereham purchased some very fine animals while he was in Spain and North Africa. We have had to extend the stables to accommodate them all. I will let you know when they arrive, if you are interested, my lord.'

'That would be a pleasure, thank you.' He passed her the pepper, then remarked, 'My steward tells me that you have been managing the estate here in Dereham's absence with remarkable success.'

'It is kind of him to say so.' The Tranton farms were famous—praise from that quarter was praise indeed.

Julia had been having qualms about entertaining a marquess and what topics of conversation might interest him. She had not been expecting him to show so much approving interest in her agricultural endeavours and the meal seemed to fly past in a highly satisfactory sequence of courses and a lively buzz of conversation.

Julia's other big fear had been that she would forget to rise and take the ladies out at the appropriate moment, but even that went smoothly without Delia having to shoot dagger-glances down the table to remind her. Will caught her eye and nodded and she felt the warmth of his approval.

The ladies settled in the salon to gossip and await the tea tray. Julia relaxed, then tensed in surprise as Caroline Fletcher settled beside her.

'I was amazed that Lord Tranton should have chosen to talk so much about farming.' She gave an artistic shudder. 'Why, he hardly spoke of anything else and I am sure he has all the Court gossip at his fingertips. You must have hoped to forget such tiresome things as cows and corn at dinner, Lady Dereham.'

'Not at all, Miss Fletcher. I was flattered by his interest. He is very knowledgeable.'

'I have never understood why you had to be involved with it at all. Could you not have hired a man instead of labouring over something so…unfeminine?'

'If I was both ignorant, and idle,' Julia riposted with a smile, 'I would have done. As it happened I knew what I was doing and I find it of great interest. Beside which, I considered it my duty to look after King's Acre until Lord Dereham returned.'

'You expected this miracle cure, then?' Caroline enquired, making no effort to hide her scepticism.

'I never gave up hope.'

To anyone knowing the history it would seem an implied criticism and Caroline certainly took it as one. Her eyes widened and her lips tightened as the colour slashed across her cheekbones. 'You must be congratulated upon having no imagination, Lady Dereham,' she riposted. 'To marry under the circumstances must have required the most ruthless control of whatever sensibility you possess.' Her smile indicated that she thought Julia had none.

'My sensibility goes with refined taste in all matters, I believe,' Caroline continued with staggering complacency. 'I cannot tell you what a pleasure it was to be in London the past few weeks. One may find the very best shops there.' Her gaze slid over the bodice and sleeves of Julia's gown. 'I could not bear to have to rely on provincial dressmakers. Do let me know if there is anything I may purchase for you when I return, dear Lady Dereham. Skin creams, for example.'

'That is so kind of you,' Julia said warmly. 'I am sure you must have experience of a *very* wide range of cosmetic aids. Do excuse me, there is something I have remembered I need to tell Mrs Frazer.'

If she did not remove herself she was going to say something she would regret. Anyone would think that she was some sort of threat to Caroline's position as reigning local beauty.

The men entered the room as she was crossing it. Mrs Frazer was deep in conversation with Lady Tranton but, having told Caroline she intended to speak with her, she could hardly walk away. Julia sat down beside them and sought some composure for Caroline's little barbs were beginning to get under her skin. Will had married her for her knowledge of estate management—he had never expected to have to live with her or for her to be the mother of his children. Did he now see her as some sort of rural bumpkin he was ashamed to come home to?

Julia swallowed the lump that had suddenly appeared in her throat. Is that why Will had seemed mysteriously remote since the incident in the milking parlour? He had been swept into thoroughly unseemly passion—was he now regretting it and despising her for her enjoyment? Had she seemed like nothing but an ill-bred romp foolish enough not to be able to manage Henry's youthful affections? Was his generosity with clothes and jewels an attempt to make her more *comme il fait*?

Imagination, just foolish imagination, she told herself and looked around for Will. There was no sign of him, or of Caroline Fletcher.

The room was full now and conversation was lively and general. It was doubtful that anyone had noticed who was missing, but that could not last for long. Instinct told her it was not coincidence and that she had to get one or other of them back into the salon as soon as possible.

What were they doing? *No, don't think about it, just find them.* Julia slipped out of the room and began to search. There were servants clearing in the dining room, the breakfast parlour was empty, the hall and billiards room were quiet.

Please not the bedrooms. The thought was so strong in her mind that, when she opened the door into the library, the sight of Will and Caroline, locked together in an embrace, was almost a relief. At least they were not on one of the beds.

They did not hear her open the door and she stood there, her hand on the latch, frozen into silent immobility, while she absorbed the shock that followed the relief. Somehow part of her had not quite believed she would find them like this. Caroline had her arms around Will, her head rested on his chest and he was holding her against his body, his cheek crushing the elaborate curls of her coiffure.

The only sound was of muffled sobs, the only movement, Caroline's shoulders shaking and Will's hand stroking her back. Julia found she could not stir. Certainly she could not speak, even if she had any idea what to say. Then Will opened his eyes and looked straight at her.

Chapter Fifteen

The spell broke as she met Will's gaze. It held nothing but a desperate appeal for help. Julia found her voice. 'I suggest that you go back to the salon as soon as possible, my lord, before someone notices exactly who is missing.'

Caroline went rigid. Will dropped his hands from her and turned. 'Julia.'

'Leave her. Go back now—do you want to make a scandal?' Will did not move and Julia's tenuous hold on her emotions gave way. *'Go,'* she hissed. 'It is quite safe to leave her with me, I am not going to start a cat fight!'

He shot her another harassed look, then strode past her without another word and she was alone with Caroline who stood, head averted, face buried in her hands.

'Do you need a handkerchief or to wash your face?' Julia demanded. 'Or are those crocodile tears?'

The other woman dropped her hands to show dry eyes, an unmarred complexion. 'You have no *feelings*!'

'No, apparently not. But I do have a quantity of common sense. It may be a cliché, but you really cannot have your cake and eat it, Miss Fletcher. However delightful it is to use your powers on Will, you risk a scandal and if that happens you would lose your earl and a great deal of money.' Caroline's big blue eyes filled with furious tears. 'For goodness' sake, do not start crying now! Do you want people to feel sorry for you?'

'*What?*'

'It will seem that you cannot bear to see Will healthy and happily married.' Julia shrugged and turned to the door. 'I was going to say your flounce had snagged and torn and we were pinning it up, but if you want to make an exhibition of yourself—'

With a gasp of outrage Caroline pushed past and swept down the corridor towards the salon. Julia caught up to her and linked her arm into hers as they entered the room.

'Such a pity if that has damaged your lovely gown,' she said clearly as they entered. 'I am not surprised you were upset.'

Caroline glared at her and swept away to her mother's side.

Spoiled little madam, Julia thought, trying to feel sorry for the other woman, shocked to realise that she had been suspicious when she had found them both gone and that she was jealous and upset now.

Ridiculous, she scolded herself. She trusted Will and, if he had been misguided enough himself to offer his ex-fiancée some comfort then who was she to complain? He had hardly protested his love and devotion to her, had he?

Will was standing before the fireplace, staring at her as he might at a bomb with a hissing fuse. He started across the floor as, behind her, salvation arrived.

'The tea, my lady.'

'Thank you, Gatcombe. Over there, if you please.' She turned to Will. 'Have you come to help me with the cups?' Faced with two full teacups, he had little choice but to take them. The surface of the liquid shivered as she handed them to him, and his hands, it seemed, were no steadier, but the vibration was not visible and he, too, kept his poise.

The clock struck twelve before Will could finally make his way upstairs and along the gallery to his room. The last guests had gone. The little crisis with the trace on the vicar's carriage snapping had been dealt with by sending them home in his own vehicle. The servants had been thanked and the house was secure. Now there was nothing between him and the confrontation with his wife and the consequences of his own actions.

Nancy passed him, her arms full of linens. 'Her ladyship's retired for the night, my lord. She's not feeling quite herself, you understand.'

For a hideous moment he thought Julia had confided in her maid, then he saw there was no accusation in Nancy's expression, only mild concern. Julia must have said she was suffering from a headache.

'Thank you. Goodnight.' He went into his own room

and endured Jervis's punctilious attentions for twenty minutes until finally, mercifully, alone he went and listened at the jib door between their dressing rooms. Nothing. He opened it, half-surprised to find it unlocked, and went through. The door into her room was unlocked too. Will tapped and entered.

'Julia?'

She was sitting up in bed, her hair in its night-time plait on her shoulder. 'Come in.'

Will had not known what to expect. Reproaches, certainly. Tears, probably. Accusations, of course. Even, although he had never seen Julia lose her temper, things thrown at his head. He deserved the lot, especially after the scene he had created when he found her with Henry. What he had not expected from his wife was calm.

'I am sorry,' he said, knowing it was insufficient but that it had to be said. 'That should never have happened. I had no intention that it should.'

'But Miss Fletcher waylaid you, threw herself on your chest and sobbed?'

That was exactly what had happened. Caroline had followed him when he went out to fetch a book he thought the vicar would be interested in and the next thing he knew he was in the library with the door shut and feeling more confused than he could ever remember. Short of violence he had no idea how to detach her and he had absolutely no experience in dealing with a sobbing woman. He shoved all the explanations away and said, 'I cannot lay the blame on Caroline.'

'It was inevitable, I suppose, given her refined sensibilities,' Julia remarked as though he had not spoken. 'Will, I do not blame you for embracing her, I just wish it had not happened where it would have been so easy for you to have been discovered.'

'You do not mind?' He stared at her, his mind going back, as it so often did, to the day he had found her in the chapel. After that rough, impulsive coupling she had slipped from the bed cool, collected, distant. She had been through an emotional storm in the church and the laughter, the passion afterwards, had been a reaction to that, he supposed. And when she had come to herself she had been disgusted with his crude lovemaking and his lack of tact in mentioning Caroline minutes later— he had seen it in her reserve, the way she had distanced herself from him emotionally and physically.

He had been very careful with her ever since, even after the scene with Henry when he had wanted to find the comfort and forgiveness in their lovemaking that he could not bring himself to ask for in words.

But this? It seemed as though Julia was not even remotely jealous, simply annoyed that he had risked a scandal. But what did he expect? Their marriage had been a sham from the start, there had not even been acquaintanceship to precede it. He had made no bones about his reasons for marriage, she had been betrayed and discarded by a lover she had given up everything for. So why then, when he could perfectly understand her indifference, was it so painful now?

'I am not in love with Caroline,' he said.

'You do not have to tell me whether you are or not. It

is not my business. And I do not believe that you would do anything…dishonourable.' Julia studied her hands as they lay on the lace edge of the sheet. She was twisting her wedding ring round and round her finger.

'But I am glad if you are not breaking your heart over her, because I do not think she is worth it. She is very lovely, but there is far less to her than meets the eye.' She laughed, a small, breathy sound. 'Listen to me! That was a catty remark if ever I heard one.'

'I think you are entitled to be as catty as you wish, Julia,' Will said. His chest hurt with guilt and tension and something else that he did not recognize, but which was damnably uncomfortable. 'It is unfair that you should be made in any way distressed. I promise that I did not seek a meeting alone with her and that all I did was to try to comfort her.'

He sat on the edge of the bed and reached for her hand—for the reassurance of touch, to still that endlessly turning ring, because he wanted to hold her. Because, surely, he had hurt her.

'I am sorry, Will.' Both hands vanished under the lace. 'I am not… Tonight I cannot…' He stared back, appalled that she should think him so crass as to try to make love to her moments after they had been confronting his indiscretion with another woman. Julia cleared her throat, her cheeks pink, her gaze still firmly fixed on the sheets. 'I mean my courses have started.'

It took him a moment to realise what she was talking about. Then it dawned on him that was what Nancy had hinted when he had passed her just now. Probably,

Not feeling quite herself was code a husband was expected to understand.

'Of course.' He couldn't even begin to explain why he had reached for her, what he wanted. How could he? He had no idea himself. Will stood up. 'You are tired, I won't keep you awake any longer. That was a fine dinner party, thank you. Goodnight, Julia.'

'Goodnight, Will.'

He closed the dressing-room door and leaned back against it to steady himself. It was as though a gulf had just opened up in front of his feet and he was hanging, dizzy, over it. What the devil had he thought this marriage was about? He had come home intent on seizing back his old life, taking control of King's Acre, putting his convenient marriage firmly into its rightful place. He had been confronted by the evidence of Julia's heartbreak and loss and he had seen everything through the lens of himself and his feelings.

With a muttered curse Will pushed away from the door and went through to his bedchamber. It had all seemed to be going perfectly well. He had acknowledged the child and, by doing so, tied himself to Julia. She had, after some resistance, come to his bed and now she seemed to enjoy his lovemaking. And he had thought that was all there was to it! Marry: tick that off the list. Sire an heir: working on it. But, be happy? Make Julia happy? Were those on the list too?

What did she want? Not, apparently, *him*, or not enough to be distressed when she caught him with his arms around another woman. *Arrogant devil*, he told himself as he threw off his dressing gown and lay down. *You expected her to be jealous, you* wanted *her to be jealous. Why should she be? She isn't in love with you and there isn't one reason why she should be. But your pride is hurt because of it, just as it was hurt when you found her comforting Henry.*

He punched the pillows, snuffed the candles and lay staring up at the underside of the bed canopy, lost in the dark. He had got what he needed: an attractive, intelligent, socially adept and unbelievably forgiving wife. So why, then, did he still feel that pain in his chest?

'The horses are here!' Will burst into the bedchamber like a strong gust of wind. Nancy gave a squeak and dropped the hairbrush. It took Julia a moment to take in what he had said, she was so surprised to see him there. Ten days after the dinner party he had not returned to her bed and it was proving remarkably awkward to find the words to ask why not. Was it guilt keeping him away or did he simply not want her any more? But he wanted an heir and he had never seemed to find her repellent...

'What, with no warning?' He was dressed in breeches and boots, his hair was tousled by the morning breeze and the lines of tiredness she thought she had discerned lately around eyes and mouth had quite gone. It must have been her imagination, for what could have been keeping him up at night? It was certainly not her!

'I heard from my agent in Portsmouth two weeks ago to say they had just landed and he intended to rest them, then start hacking them up in easy stages once he was certain they were all sound. But Phelps's letter saying they had started must have gone astray. Look.'

Julia could feel the excitement running through him as he took her arm and drew her to the window. It was an almost sexual force, that energy, and her body responded, warming, softening. If Nancy had not been there, she would have leaned into him and snatched a kiss. And would then no doubt have regretted it if he had failed to respond.

Instead she looked out at the sweep of parkland and the horses approaching at the trot. Julia narrowed her eyes against the morning sun: five riders, each leading two horses. Even at that distance she could see the quality of the animals in the way they moved.

'They look fresh. They must have spent the night close by.'

'Thank goodness the stables were finished yesterday,' Will said. He released her arm. 'I must go down again.'

'But your breakfast…' The door swung to behind him. Julia managed a rueful smile for Nancy's benefit. 'Men! I shall have to have something sent down to the stables.'

She supposed she should not feel awkward about going down to look at the new arrivals. 'My riding clothes, please, Nancy.'

'Which ones, my lady?'

'My old habit,' Julia said. Since that first time she and Will had never ridden together. Whenever they had travelled around the estate it had been in a gig. He knew she had her own horse, of course, and he had probably not noticed the other saddle hanging beside the side saddle. Would he be angry when he discovered she rode astride around the estate?

Somehow, without any formal agreement, they had arrived at a working compromise over responsibilities. Julia looked after the tenants' welfare, the dairy herd, the chickens, the gardens both decorative and productive, the house and the indoor staff. Will controlled everything else. So far there had not been any discussion about the housekeeping allowance or her own pin money, so Julia just kept on spending at the same level as she had before, maintained her scrupulously accurate accounts and waited to have those removed from her control too.

As with the subject of the bedchamber, and the events of the dinner-party evening, it seemed that they existed most harmoniously without confronting the issues. But it was an uneasy peace. Julia felt she was cramming unwieldy truths into a cupboard and sooner or later the door would burst open and release all of them.

Nancy fastened the divided skirt at the waist and then helped Julia into the coat. Really she was perfectly decent, she thought, bracing herself for the confrontation. Perhaps it was as well to have it while he was distracted by the horses. Perhaps he would not even notice. That was a melancholy thought.

Julia arrived at the new stables with a bite of roll and a mouthful of coffee inside her. Will was standing in the middle of the yard, talking to a wiry individual, while around them four grooms she did not recognise stood holding the horses. She stopped, knew her jaw had dropped and did not care.

'What's wrong?' Will turned at the sound of her gasp.

'Love at first sight,' Julia breathed. 'They are beautiful!'

'They are that, ma'am.' The grizzled man pulled off his hat. 'His lordship's got a fine eye for a horse.'

'Lady Dereham, this is Mr Bevis, who has had charge of the horses since Portsmouth. So you like them, do you?'

The Arabians were elegant, with their fine bones and dished faces. Will had told her he intended to breed them with thoroughbred stallions for speed and endurance as well as looks. The three Andalusians were very different and they drew her as though they called her by name.

They were not big animals. The stallion was about fifteen two hands, she supposed, his three mares a little smaller. They all had deeply arched necks, long, rippling manes and all were a perfect dapple grey in colour with iron-grey manes and tails.

Four pairs of dark, liquid eyes watched her as she approached and held out her hand to the stallion. He snuffled at her fingers, then stood rock-still as she bent and blew lightly into his nostrils. He blew back and butted her gently with his head.

'Do you wish to ride him, my dear? One of the grooms can get your saddle.'

Julia managed not to gape at Will. It never occurred to her for a moment that he would give her the first ride on any of the new animals, let alone allow her on the stallion.

'He's not used to a side saddle,' Bevis warned.

Oh well, it was now or never. Will was not going to create a scene in front of all these men. 'It is quite all right.' She took the reins from the groom and led the stallion over to the mounting block, adjusted the stirrup leathers and swung into the saddle before anyone appeared to realise what she was doing. 'What is his name?'

'He hasn't got one yet, my lady. He's got the manners of a gentleman, that one.' Bevis was carefully not staring at her legs as she adjusted the folds of the divided skirt. The horse stood still and patient, mouthing gently at the bit.

Will walked over and put his hand on the pommel. 'You, my dear, are full of surprises,' he said softly. She could not tell whether he was angry or not.

'I only ride astride on the estate. And my legs are better covered than they would be side saddle.' She tried not to sound defensive. It was not the actual degree of decency or coverage that was the question, she knew that. It was the shock of a woman imitating a man, the unspoken, sexual, connotations of being astride.

'I am not objecting.' He moved his hand to rest on her thigh then, as she was absorbing the surprise of that, raised his voice back to normal conversational levels. 'Would you like to name him?'

'Me? But I thought… He is a stallion, he will be your horse. Do you not want to name him yourself?'

'I realise I have never given you a wedding gift. It is rather late in the day for one, I know, but you seem to like him. He is yours.'

Chapter Sixteen

There did not seem to be any words, none Julia could say without bursting, ridiculously, into tears. What was the matter with her? Her fears over their marriage? Her state of physical frustration or Will's sudden wild generosity? Julia laid her hand over his and squeezed and then, ignoring their audience, bent from the saddle and kissed him on the cheek. 'I shall call him Angelo.'

'A Spanish angel? I hope he proves to be so.' Will grinned at her.

Emboldened, Julia murmured, 'Not many men would give their wives a stallion.'

'Perhaps they do not feel very secure about certain things and feel they have something to prove,' he suggested. 'I intend continuing to ride Ajax.' That was his raking thoroughbred gelding. 'I may be flattering myself, but I do not feel that puts my masculinity at question.' The look in his eyes was decidedly wicked.

Julia felt herself growing warm. 'I have missed you,' she whispered.

'We need to talk.' His eyes said that he meant with more than words. 'Why not try him in the paddock and then we'll see them all settled in?'

Mr Bevis was right, the powerful stallion had perfect manners and a soft mouth. He curvetted slightly, showing off, as he went past the mares, but answered her hands on the reins and walked past into the paddock.

'You are not to flirt,' Julia scolded and he put one ear back, listening politely. They circled at the walk, then the trot, Julia rising in the saddle as a man would, enjoying the stretch in her leg muscles, wondering if she was shocking Will and rather hoping that she was. When she settled into the saddle and pressed with her heels Angelo went into a perfect canter and then back to the walk as she reached the gate again.

'He is superb,' she called and reluctantly turned back into the yard.

The sun was warm and Julia went to sit on the mounting block, her elbows on her knees, and watched the men taking the horses to their appointed boxes. Everything was a controlled bustle, the sound of hooves on the stone setts, men giving orders, stable boys running back and forth, and yet she felt filled with the kind of peace she had experienced after she had recovered from the loss of the baby. In those months before Will returned she had come to feel she belonged here, that she was in control and understood what she was doing.

And then she saw Will walking towards her. He was hatless, his coat hooked on one finger over his shoulder, his shirtsleeves rolled up. He looked big, physical, intelligent, this man she was married to, had made love with, hardly knew.

'A penny for them. In fact...' Will put one foot on the bottom step and regarded her, head to one side '...I may offer two pence, your thoughts seem so deep.'

'I was thinking that I feel as I did just before you came back,' Julia said without calculation. 'As though I belonged here.'

'And when I came back, you no longer did.'

'Yes. That is exactly how I felt.' She had said it now, the hurtful, tactless thing. It was out in the open and they could no longer pretend that everything was just fine.

A shadow passed over Will's face. He would turn away now, deal with this in a civilised manner by ignoring it as usual. The loneliness and regret washed through her like the winter sea.

Will stood very still, studying her face, then, to Julia's surprise, came and sat next to her, hip against hip. 'We have not talked, have we?' It was a statement and he sounded reflective, not angry or hurt. Julia shook her head. 'There were the really big things,' Will continued. 'We talked a little about those, of course. The baby, Caroline. We could hardly avoid those subjects, although there is much more that could be said.'

'And we spoke of your love for this place and your parents. As you say, the big things, the difficult things, but not the small things,' Julia agreed. There was no tension. It seemed natural to lean against his shoulder as they sat there. 'I do not know how much housekeeping money I have, or pin money. We simply fell into some kind of division of responsibilities. You were surprised by the timing of…my cycle. We have been married for three years and yet we know nothing about each other. What are your political opinions? What is your favourite meal? Do you read novels or are the ones in your library there because you buy all the latest books?'

'I did not know how to open negotiations again,' Will said, surprising a laugh from her. 'I made such a mull of things with Caroline and Henry. I knew I must have hurt you, if only by my sheer clumsiness. And then I could not come to your bed and somehow I did not like to simply make assumptions and walk in after I thought the timing would be right. Perhaps it was a good thing or I suspect I would have tried to make up by making love and we would have talked even less.'

That was true. Lovemaking was something they could use to avoid confrontation as much as to give and take pleasure. 'You know who you are, don't you?' Julia asked. 'You know you belong here, you are so secure in being a man that you can give me a stallion to ride while you keep your gelding, you can admit when you are wrong and try to solve things by talking.'

'Are you implying that I am perfect?' She shot him a sideways glance from narrowed eyes and saw his mouth was curling into a smile.

'Not at all. You had not given a thought to what you were going to do about me when you came home.' She realised something as she studied his profile, the sensitive, mobile mouth and the stubborn chin. 'You thought that because I love this place, too, there must be a power struggle over it. But that's idio—I mean, there is no need for that. It is yours, I would just like to share it. And you do that typically male thing of ignoring uncomfortable things until they are pushed under your nose.'

'Ah. An idiot and a typical male?' He was still smiling. 'Do you think we can make this work, Julia? If you can overlook my idiocy and kick me when I'm ignoring things?'

'I can do that. But a marriage takes two people. What are my faults that must be addressed?' She was certain he would have a list as long as her arm. Julia braced herself.

'I want you to be honest with me.'

The cold grabbed her stomach as though she had swallowed a lump of ice. She had not expected that. 'What do you mean?'

'Don't hide things and bottle them up because they are difficult to talk about.'

'You think I do that? I cannot break Henry's confidence, you know that.' *I cannot tell you about the weight on my conscience, the dreadful thing I have done.* Julia got down from the mounting block, the urge to twine her arm into his and lay her head on his shoulder vanishing. 'I am starving. Shall we have an early luncheon? You had no breakfast.'

Will fell into step beside her as she walked towards the house. 'Yes. I would like to eat and, yes, I do think you hide things from me. I don't mean my cousin's secrets. You were terrified of what I would do when I discovered where little Alexander was resting. You didn't tell me that your lover was such a selfish lout. No wonder you were reluctant to come to my bed if your previous experience had been so bad.' She must have gasped because he added, 'You didn't need to tell me about it, I could see that from your reactions. But I would rather have known so I could have been more…sensitive.'

Julia found she was speechless. Will opened the front door for her. 'Gatcombe, we'll take an early luncheon if Cook can manage it.' When they reached the landing Will drew her into his chamber and closed the door. 'I am just a man and sometimes we need things holding up in front of our faces. Will you promise to tell me when you are unhappy, when things worry you? Don't have secrets from me, Julia, not about the things that will hurt this marriage.'

'Oh, Will.' She stood on tiptoe and curled her arms around his neck. His honesty, his willingness to admit his own faults, touched her. As their lips met she whispered, without thinking, 'No secrets, I promise.'

Will reached out and turned the key in the door, then simply walked backwards, still kissing, so she followed him until they tipped back on to the bed. 'At the risk of making Cook irritable, I think we should seal our new resolutions, don't you?'

'Oh, yes.' Julia rolled on to her back and lay looking up at him. *New resolutions, a new beginning.* And then as he sat up to work out the complexities of the closures of her divided skirt, the cold realisation gripped her again. *I promised, but—Jonathan. I cannot tell him about what I did to Jonathan.* If she told Will, even if he could accept why she had done it, that it was an accident, it would make him an accessory after the fact. His choice would be to become as guilty in law as she was or to hand her over to the magistrates.

And I have promised to be open with him. Yet there was nothing to be done but break that promise and keep her secret, or hand herself in or run away and disappear. Naked in Will's arms, Julia acknowledged that she did not have the courage to confess and take the consequences and she could not bear to leave King's Acre. *Or Will.*

Her body rose to his, cradled him, her arms and legs curling around him as though they were one and she would not let him go. As he sank into her and she felt him inside, as she gripped him with those internal muscles that made him groan as he stroked, tormenting himself as much as her, she knew she did not have the strength to do anything but stay. And lie to him.

'Do you mind if we go to London in a couple of days?' Will looked up from a large and imposing letter. It crackled expensively as he spread it out on the cloth amongst the breakfast things. 'My lawyer wants me to sign papers and I need to discuss investments with my banker, Jervis tells me that my shirts are a disgrace and he is ashamed to be known as my valet and I need new boots.'

'It sounds as though you hardly require me.' Julia sorted through her own post. Household bills, a letter from a friend in the next village, a note from the vicarage about the Sunday School, an account from an Aylesbury milliner. 'You will be far too busy on your own account.' The county newspaper was at the bottom of the pile and she turned to the inside page and the local news.

'You need a complete new wardrobe—stop putting it off,' Will said. 'I promised myself the fun of taking you shopping and you are not going to wriggle out of it, my lady.'

'But it is August. Nothing will be happening.'

'We can go back in the winter for parties and the theatre. But now it will be quiet and we can explore. You do not know London, do you?'

'No. Not at all.' Julia smiled at him. He was obviously set on going and looking forward to treating her. It was cowardly, and churlish, to refuse. 'Of course I will come with you: I will enjoy it.' She ran her eye down the columns of tightly packed type, skimming the stories. An unseasonable storm of hailstones had flattened just one field of hay at Thame. A small boy had been saved from drowning in a village pond. A calf with two heads had been born at a local farm and was being exhibited for a penny and a woman who had killed her husband had been hanged outside Aylesbury town hall and her body given to the surgeons to be dissected.

The room seemed to be full of buzzing, as though a swarm of bees had filled it. The print blurred before her eyes and Julia realised she felt hot and then cold and sickeningly dizzy.

She gripped the edge of the table as Will said, 'Good.

We'll stay at Grillon's in Albemarle Street and look for a house to hire for the Season while we're up there. Is the day after tomorrow all right for you? I'll send to the hotel today.'

'Lovely,' Julia managed as she closed the newspaper and folded it with trembling hands. A woman hanged. Was that where they would hang her if they caught her? In front of the town hall before a mob jeering and shouting and making a holiday of it?

'Julia? Is anything wrong? You have gone quite pale.' Will was half out of his seat. She waved him back to it and, from somewhere, found a smile.

I killed a man. For one terrified moment she thought she had said it out loud. 'Just the most alarming bill from a milliner! What a good thing we have not yet discussed allowances or I am sure I would be asking for an advance already.'

Will chuckled and sat down again. The room stopped swaying. She made herself open her clenched hand. Her mouth was dry, she felt sick with dread and the temptation to tell him was almost overwhelming. But she could not put him in that terrible position. Julia forced herself to calm. It was just the shock of seeing that gruesome report and the way her conscience was troubling her for breaking her promise to Will. She was in no more, or less, danger than she had ever been.

'I must spend the morning on my accounts,' she managed.

'Mmm?' Will glanced up from his post. 'Don't forget to tell Nancy to start packing.'

'No. Of course not.' *It will be all right. I have noth-ing to fear after all this time. Forget it and it will just become a bad dream.*

'You are very pensive, Julia.' Will took her hand as the chaise pulled up at the King's Arms in Berkham-sted for the first change of horses.

He had been as good as his word, those few days since their conversation in the stable yard. They had talked—or rather Will had talked and she had forced herself to respond. The housekeeping was agreed, her generous allowance settled. They discussed who would do what with the estate and what Will felt comfortable with letting out of his control.

If she was only able to sleep without nightmares, Julia knew she would be happy. It was as if she had cursed herself with that resolution to make those dread-ful memories only dreams. Now her nights were made hideous by images of blood. Never of Jonathan, but al-ways of blood. On her hands, on her body, curling like seaweed into the water in the wash bowl.

She leaned against Will's wonderfully solid and re-assuring shoulder. 'I am just a little tired with all the preparations.'

'And I have been keeping you awake at night,' he teased.

Julia felt herself blushing. Even with the fear gnaw-ing at the back of her mind of what would follow when she slept, their lovemaking was perfect. At least, it seemed so to her. Drowsing in his arms, her body limp and replete, she felt so safe that just for a while she could believe nothing could hurt her. But in the cold light of dawn she knew even Will's strength and courage could not protect her from the terrors in her own mind.

'It would have been a saving to have taken the carriage instead of two chaises,' she said repressively. Across the yard the other vehicle with Nancy and Jervis had just drawn up.

'I wanted to be alone with you,' Will said.

'In the chaise!'

'What a very wicked mind you have, Lady Dereham.' He chuckled and dipped his head to give her a fleeting kiss on the lips. 'I meant so we could talk. There is something I wanted to know and a journey means we can be uninterrupted. You have been remarkably quiet about your life before we met by the lake.'

It was so apposite to her thoughts that his remark almost struck her dumb. 'What…what do you want to know?'

'What your home was like, the estate. Tell me about your parents. Did you have a dog, a pony?'

'Oh.' The relief was physical and air rushed back into her lungs. 'You want to know about my childhood.'

'I was not intending to interrogate you about your lover,' Will said drily as the chaise left the yard and turned eastwards.

'Thank you, although I do not mind speaking of him…a little.' She did not want to leave Will with the impression that she had anything to hide from him. 'He was a mistake. A terrible mistake.'

'What is his name?'

'He was...*is*...called Jonathan.' She remembered how Will had not believed her story when he had first come home. Suddenly it was important to tell him as much of the truth as possible. 'When you first found out about him, you did not believe that I had only been with him a short while—a day and not quite a night. But that was honestly how it was. Before I ran away he had always treated me with respect, courted me with propriety. I truly thought we were eloping, I believed he would take me to Scotland and marry me. We lay together only the once.'

'I know.' His voice was firm and definite.

'How can you know? Or are you simply trusting me?'

'I would trust you, of course I would.' Was he trying to convince himself as much as her? She could sense a slight reservation. 'I know you now, Julia. Before, when I was so disbelieving, it was simply the shock of coming home, of being alive, of hearing about the baby. I was not thinking straight. But when I made love with you, I realised. It was all very new to you, was it not?' She bit her lip and stared out of the window and tried not to remember. 'It was not simply that he was too selfish to make it good, it was all unfamiliar because you were so inexperienced.' She nodded.

'Then we can forget him. Pretend he doesn't exist,' Will said. 'That's all behind you now unless there is anything it would help to talk about?'

'Yes, I can try to do that,' Julia said. *Pretend he doesn't exist. That is easy, he doesn't, because I killed him. He was a wicked man, but he did not deserve to die for it.* 'But I cannot promise that his ghost is not going to haunt me sometimes.' *Every night.*

'It will have to get past me,' Will said. 'Now, forget him and the past. I'll not stir that up again. Can you read in the chaise without getting sick? Because my London agent has sent me details of a number of eligible houses he thinks would be suitable to rent for the Season. See what you think.'

'How exciting.' Julia took the portfolio he handed her and infused her voice with as much enthusiasm as she could. Will was looking forward to London, to the London Season in the new year, to the sort of married life a man of his station should expect. And she could bring it crashing down around his head at any moment if she did not have the courage to keep her mouth shut and the intelligence to hide the truth. Whatever happened, she must make his happiness last as long as she could, she owed it to him.

'My goodness.' She riffled through the stack of papers. 'The addresses all sound very grand. I like the sound of this one.'

He took the paper. 'Half Moon Street? Why? It might be a trifle small, I thought.'

'I like the name.'

As she guessed it would, that made him laugh. 'Julia, you are a delight of a wife.'

And she laughed, too, as her conscience tore at her.

It was only half an hour later as she laid the stack of house particulars on one side that Will's actual words came back to her. *A delight of a wife.* Did he truly mean that? She watched him as he studied the work he had brought with him, his dark head bent over the papers, his face remote and intelligent as he studied the pages. She had wanted him to want her as his wife, to build a relationship with him. Certainly things were good in the bedchamber and harmonious in everyday matters. She believed he would be faithful. That was all she had hoped for, surely, so why did her heart beat faster at his affectionate teasing? Did she want him to fall in love with her?

Julia stared out of the carriage window at the passing landscape. *Do I? Am I in love with him?* She was not certain what that meant any more. She had thought herself in love with Jonathan, so much in love that she would trust her entire future to him, and yet that feeling had evaporated the moment she realised his deception.

And what she felt for Will was nothing like that lightheaded, romantic dreamy feeling. She liked him, she respected him and she desired him, but she was no longer so naïve that she thought a woman must be in love in order to ache for a man to lie with her. She felt for Will, in short, all those things that a woman making a marriage of convenience would hope that she would come to feel for her husband.

But it was not love. That was just a romantic dream and a sure way to a broken heart, Julia decided. And why should she want to be in love with her husband in any case? If she was fortunate, there would be children who would be healthy and strong and she would experience all the love she could want with them. Julia closed her eyes for a moment in silent supplication that if she was fortunate enough to become pregnant again then all would be well this time.

But even so, when Will looked up and caught her studying him, and his eyes crinkled with amused affection, her heart made that foolish little leap again. 'Your hair needs cutting,' she said prosaically. 'You must add that to the list of things to do in town.'

Chapter Seventeen

Will was as good as his word about the shopping. He gave Julia one day to settle into Grillon's Hotel in Albemarle Street while he had his hair cut, ordered his boots from Hoby's, wrote to summon his tailor and sent messages to his lawyers and bankers, then the next day swept her out to, as he put it, discover the lie of the land. With Nancy in attendance, so she knew where she was going when Julia wanted to shop in future, they explored Bond Street, located Harding, Howell and Company in Piccadilly, scanned the myriad of temptations in the Parthenon Bazaar and came home loaded with bandboxes and armed with the latest guidebooks.

Julia was thrilled to discover that King Louis XVIII had stayed at Grillon's Hotel in 1812 and even more excited to discover they were opposite the offices of James Murray, the publisher. It was only when Will pointed out that she would not recognise any of her favourite authors if she saw them that she could be persuaded away from the window.

'Would you like to see the City?' he asked over dinner. 'St Paul's Cathedral, the Royal Exchange, the Bank of England? We could even climb up the Monument if you feel really energetic.'

'Yes, please. All of those are on my list and I am hardly a quarter of the way through the guidebook yet.'

'I am not certain we can do all of them in one day. I must call on my bankers in the morning and then my lawyer, who is in Amen Corner.' He grinned at her expression. 'It is by St Paul's, which I suppose accounts for the name. We can decide what to do when we see what the time is, but we can certainly fit in the cathedral.'

Julia had tried to be patient, but an hour sitting in the banker's outer office, even sustained with coffee and ratafia biscuits and the copy of *La Belle Assemblée*, which she had prudently brought with her, was more than enough tedium.

As the hackney carriage made its way along Paternoster Row she asked, 'Is there any reason why I cannot walk around outside with Nancy while you are with the lawyer? The sun is shining, the shops seem to be cheaper than they are in Mayfair...'

Will nodded as they drew up in a narrow lane. 'I do not see why not. You can hardly get lost, not with the dome of St Paul's to act as a landmark. Shall we say you will be back here in an hour?' He helped them both out, making Nancy blush at the attention, then pointed. 'Go down Ave Maria Lane there and turn left and you'll find all the shops around St Paul's Churchyard.' He felt in the breast of his coat and handed her some folded banknotes. 'Do not let anyone see you have that.'

'Thank you.' Julia cast a quick look round, found the lane almost deserted and stood on tiptoe to drop a swift kiss on Will's cheek.

'Cupboard love,' he said with a smile and paid off the cab.

The previous day had been unalloyed pleasure. Julia had not felt at all alarmed in the fashionable streets, despite the numbers of people. On Will's arm, and in such fashionable lounges, her fears seemed foolish. Now she set off with confidence, Nancy at her side. They emerged from Ave Maria Lane to find themselves on a busy street with a pronounced slope. 'Ludgate Hill,' Julia said with the certainty of someone who had studied the map.

'My lord said to go left,' Nancy said as Julia turned downhill.

'I know, but see this silversmith's shop—is that not a delightful ink stand? I think something like that would make an admirable present for Lord Dereham.'

And the next shop down was a print seller with amusing cartoons in the window. And the next a jeweller's, its window stuffed with enticing oddments.

'My lady, it is getting rather crowded.'

Julia looked up. In front of them a press of people were heading into a street parallel to Ave Maria Lane. They were noisy, a motley crowd of working people and tradesmen, men and women. They seemed in good humour, but Julia's old fears came flooding back to cramp her stomach.

'Yes, we must turn back.' As they did so another crowd swept down the hill towards them. 'Nancy!' Julia was jostled, caught up. She struggled to find her feet and fight her way back, but she was carried, like driftwood on a stream, down the hill and round the corner.

Julia tried not to panic, knowing if she struggled she would simply exhaust herself or fall and be trampled. She let herself be borne along and tried to think coherently. Nancy would be all right, she was sure, for she had been further up the hill. If she could just get to the end of this street and turn right, go uphill again, keeping St Paul's in sight and then turn right, surely she'd be back in Ave Maria Lane?

Then the movement began to slow. She was still crushed against unwashed bodies and rough clothing, but at least there was no longer any danger of falling over and being trampled. Julia stared around and found the street had widened into a square shaped like a funnel. The crowd milled about, elbowing for room, but everyone faced the building that towered over them on her right. Wedged in place, she had no option but to turn with them. In front of her was the massive bulk of a grim stone building.

'What is that?' she asked the man at her side, a prosperous shopkeeper, she guessed.

'Why, that is Newgate Prison, ma'am. Aren't you here for the hanging, then?' He pointed and her reluctant gaze followed. High above the heads of the mob, the scaffold and the noose stood waiting for their first victim of the day.

'Let me out!' Julia turned and burrowed through the tight-packed spectators, fear and desperation lending her strength as she used her elbows and pushed, shoved, wriggled through every tiny gap that opened up, like a mouse through long grass with a hawk hovering above. Her bonnet was dragged off, she lost a shoe, but there was a thinning of the crowd ahead of her and she fought her way towards it.

Laughter, improbable in this mayhem, made her glance up to the right. There was an inn and, surrounding the swinging inn sign, its windows were crowded with people laughing and chatting as if they were in the boxes at a play. *Horrible*, she thought. *How could they?* And then a woman turned and nudged her husband and pointed at her and she found herself staring up at Jane and Arthur Prior, her cousins.

Julia gasped, stumbled and when she looked up they had gone. It was imagination, that was all, she told herself as she struggled on, the panic beating in her chest like a trapped bird against a window. With shocking suddenness she was finally out of the press, stumbling on the uneven cobbles. Her unshod foot jarred against a stone and she fell, throwing out her hands in a vain attempt to save herself.

The cobbles were rough, disgustingly dirty and wet. Her hands hurt. Almost winded, Julia lay where she was, felt the blood oozing through the split in her glove and wondered if her heart was going to burst.

'Julia! Sweetheart, it is all right. I'm here. Are you hurt?'

And, miraculously, there Will was, gathering her up

in his arms. Julia turned her face to his shoulder and clung on as he lifted her, then carried her to a hackney carriage where Nancy waited, white-faced.

'My lady—oh, your poor hands.'

'Just grazed. I am not hurt otherwise,' she managed to reassure them as Will gently opened her fingers and wrapped them in his handkerchief, still holding her hard against himself. 'Are you all right, Nancy?' Concern for someone else helped, she realised. The panic was ebbing, her breath was calming.

'I am fine, my lady, just all shaken up. I didn't know what to do, I couldn't reach you, or see you, so I ran back to the lawyers and made them get my lord. What was it, my lady? A riot?'

'No, a hanging.' She would not be sick, not if she closed her eyes and thought of nothing but Will's arms around her, keeping her safe.

'It is Newgate Prison,' he said, his voice grim. 'I should have warned you not to go that way, it isn't very salubrious at the best of times, but when there's an execution it is a glimpse into hell.'

'People were watching from the windows, as if it were a play,' she managed. *Jane and Arthur. It couldn't be. It was my imagination, my fear, a couple who looked a little like them. I haven't seen them for almost four years*, she comforted herself. *They will have changed, I wouldn't recognise them now if I really saw them. I am safe with Will, I don't imagine things when he is here.*

'It is disgusting,' Will muttered, his voice rough with anger. 'They moved the hangings from Tyburn because it was supposed to be more *civilised* to do it outside the prison instead of parading the condemned through the streets to the place of execution. It is not my definition of civilised. Just try to relax, sweetheart. I've got you safe.'

'I know,' Julia murmured and closed her eyes so that her entire world became just Will. She inhaled slowly and there was the familiar smell of his skin, of clean linen and the sharp male edge of fresh sweat. He had run, and run hard, to reach her. The feel of him was familiar too, the strength that made her feel so safe, the warmth of that big, desirable body under fine linen and smooth broadcloth. She listened to the sound of his heartbeat against her ear, a little ragged still. *Home. I am home when I am with him.*

Will cared for her, he was angry for her. He shifted a little to hold her more securely and she felt his cheek press against her hair and something happened in her chest as if a bell had tolled silently, reverberating through her whole body.

I love him. She felt herself go still as though to move would shatter the moment, break the spell. This was nothing like her emotions for Jonathan, this was a deeply complex, rich emotion like velvet swirling around her feelings. It was not about desire or liking or respect, although those were all in there somewhere. It was inexplicable and unexplainable and that, she supposed, was how she knew it was love.

She would tell him this evening when they were alone, when they were in bed together: it would be the naked truth, after all. He did not love her, she knew that, but that was all right. Well, no, perhaps not all right exactly. But she could not hope for the moon and the stars. She would explain to him that she did not expect him to feel the same way, that she was not asking him to pretend and to lie to her.

'Better, sweetheart?' Will murmured in her ear.

'Much, thank you, Will. You keep me safe.'

'Always,' he said and his arms tightened around her.

'I will sleep in the dressing room,' Will said from the open door of the bedroom as the clocks in their suite struck nine. 'You should be asleep.' Julia was pale against the heaped pillows. He wished he had her home again where she would feel safer as she recovered from her ordeal and not here, in a strange place.

'I have slept, for hours,' Julia protested. And she did look better, despite the pallor. 'That hot bath was like taking laudanum! Come to bed, Will.'

'You are still nervous? Then of course I will sleep with you.' He closed the door behind him and watched her carefully as he shed coat and waistcoat. No wonder she was so reluctant to go into the neighbouring towns for anything but the most essential shopping if crowds made her so frightened. Some people had a fear of them, he knew. It was like the fear of heights, or spiders—not something that seemed to be rational to anyone else, but very real to the sufferer. And a public hanging was probably, short of a riot, the most frightening mob to find oneself in.

'I wish you had told me how you felt about crowds,' he said as he pulled off his neck cloth.

'It was so irrational, I thought you would think me foolish,' she said, not meeting his eyes. 'I pride myself on common sense and keeping calm and then to experience such panic when no one means me any harm...'

Her voice trailed away and he bit his tongue on the reproach that she had kept this a secret from him. It was not a rational fear, he reminded himself, so perhaps she found it harder to confide about it.

'We all fear something,' Will said and sat on the edge of the bed to pull off his boots.

'What do *you* fear?' Julia curled round on the pillows and watched him as he tossed his stockings aside. 'I did not think you were afraid of anything.'

'Lies and powerlessness,' he said instantly, then stopped undressing to think about what he had said. 'Not seeing the whole picture when there is something to confront, so all the time you think there is something worse lying in wait. I think that was what was so dreadful with my parents when I was growing up: I did not know what was wrong, no one would tell me the truth and admit that the marriage was a sham. I was expected to act as though we were a happy family and nothing was amiss, yet I sensed the world as I knew it was all falling apart.

'And then at first when I was ill, no one would tell me the truth—or what they thought was the truth. In my heart I believed I was dying and yet I could not face it, deal with it, because the doctors insisted I would be cured in the end. I have no idea why they wouldn't tell me. Perhaps they thought I couldn't cope with it, or perhaps they thought I was a better source of income if I was hoping for a cure! It took three months before they would admit the truth, that they were certain there was no hope.'

'Was it any easier after that?' Julia asked. She reached out a hand and laid it over his on the bedspread. She did nothing except press lightly, but it was curiously comforting. Will curled his fingers into hers and dug deeper into his feelings than he had for a long time.

'It made the dying easier,' he confessed with a grimace. 'Which seems strange, but I suppose I had suspected the worst for so long it was a relief to know what I was dealing with. But then the powerlessness over King's Acre, that was terrifying.'

Julia's fingers closed tighter. 'You are in control of all of it now.'

All of it except my wife, Will thought wryly. He honestly had no idea what Julia would do next or how she would react to what he said or did. Most of the time that was refreshing, but there was still some secret, deep down, he was certain of it and it nagged at the foundation of trust that he thought they were building together. At least he understood her reluctance to leave the estate now if crowds brought on attacks of panic.

She began to stroke the inside of his wrist and Will lost the thread of his thoughts as desire began to build, hot and heavy. He tugged his shirt over his head and let Julia pull him back on to the bed. 'Nothing is going to get you in here,' he protested.

'I am not afraid,' Julia murmured, running her nails lightly down his torso. 'I am…' She blushed.

'Lustful?' Will suggested as he rolled over on his back and began to unfasten his breeches. It was not the easiest thing to do flat on his back, with an erection and with a wanton wife crawling over him.

'Will! Amorous sounds better.'

'Both of them sound good to me,' he growled as he kicked his legs free and sent the breeches flying. Julia gave a soft *huff* of laughter as he rolled over on top of her, but as she lay looking up at him the laughter ebbed away, leaving her serious. It was on the tip of his tongue to ask her what was wrong when she pulled his head down and lifted herself to kiss him.

It was the first time she had ever taken the initiative in their lovemaking. Before she had been responsive and willing to follow wherever he led, but he sensed that this exploration with soft lips and delicate strokes of her tongue was different.

Her hands drifted down his rib-cage, down his flanks, stroking in fluttering caresses that made him want to purr like a big cat and then to plunge into her to assuage the ache that gripped him. He was almost impossibly hard, aroused, simply by a sweet kiss and gentle hands. This was some enchantment she was weaving, it had to be.

Without freeing his mouth she wriggled, almost tipping him over the edge beyond control, then wrapped her legs around his hips so he was cradled against the hot, wet centre of her. Will tried counting backwards, then doing it in Arabic. He was going to lose his grip any moment and behave like an animal and it was obvious from Julia's gentle, languid movements that was not what she wanted.

It was also obvious she had no idea whatsoever that she was driving him to the brink, he thought in despair as she fastened her teeth on his earlobe with a delicate nip.

Then she wriggled again, and tilted her pelvis and he realised through the fog of desire that she knew exactly what she was doing. They were positioned perfectly for her to arch up and take him into her in a smooth, seductive glide that had him gasping for mercy until, somehow, he wrenched some self-control back.

And then he found that he could slow down, be as gentle as she was, make this exquisite pleasure last and last until there was nothing in the world except for their ragged breathing and the scent of arousal and the sound of their bodies moving against each other.

'Will.' She shuddered under him, around him, the force of her orgasm caressing him until he was falling with her. He knew he called her name, knew he found her mouth and stifled both their cries with his kisses, and then the world was still again.

'Will.' Seconds later, hours later? He had no idea. All he knew was that was the most perfect physical experience he had ever had in his life and that, somehow, it went beyond the physical into emotion. He opened his eyes and raised his head from the softness of Julia's breast and saw her eyes were wide and dark as her mouth trembled into a smile. 'I love you.'

It took a long moment before her words sank in. 'Julia—' He did not know what to say, what to feel.

'It is all right,' she murmured, lifting one hand to brush his hair back from his face. 'You don't have to say it too. I know you don't love me, but I had to tell you. How could I keep that a secret from you?'

He was squashing her, Will thought distractedly. But if he rolled off her she would think he was avoiding meeting her eyes. Those painfully clear, honest eyes. Will took more weight on his elbows and sought for the truth. 'I don't know about love,' he said at last. 'I was not in love with Caroline, I know that. Just dazzled and charmed and rather a lot in lust.'

That made her laugh, a soft gurgle of amusement. 'I know you were not. That is why I was not more angry with you after the dinner party. And I want you to be honest. I would hate to think you were telling me you love me and lying to be kind.' She hesitated. 'That would *not* be…kind.'

'I know.' How did he feel? 'I desire you more every time I lie with you, every time I kiss you. I like you. I miss you when we are not together. I admire your intelligence and your strength of will and I like that you need me to protect you sometimes despite it. I do not know what that adds up to, sweetheart.'

'Enough for any woman,' Julia said. 'I can live with that and be happy, believe me.'

'I believe you,' Will said, knowing in his heart that it was not enough but that he could not give her what he did not possess or understand. He pulled her with him as he rolled over, then gathered her against his chest. 'Go to sleep now, Julia.'

So that was what the secret was that she had been keeping from him, he thought as he began to drift off to sleep. She had needed the shock of that day's events to give her the courage to tell him how she felt. Perhaps he did love her. If only he knew what it felt like so he could recognise it. But whatever this was, he decided as Julia's breathing became slow and her body relaxed against his in complete trust, it was the start of happiness. A more complete happiness than he had dared hope he would ever find.

Chapter Eighteen

Will looked content, Julia decided, watching him over the breakfast table the next morning. She felt wonderful, strong enough to keep the key turned in the lock of that dark little cupboard buried deep inside her, the one where the memory of Jonathan's death lurked along with the new acceptance that she loved a man who, however fond he was, did not love her.

We are content, that is enough.

'Excuse me, my lord, only there's a message from the desk downstairs: there are visitors asking for you.' Nancy closed the door on the uniformed page who waited on the landing.

'What name?' Will folded his paper with a sigh and slapped it down beside his plate. 'This is very early to be calling. I suppose it might be about an investment I was particularly concerned about. Hapgood must have thought I was impatient for news of it after our discussion yesterday. I will come down.'

'No, don't do that.' Julia laid her napkin aside. 'We

have finished our breakfast. If it is Mr Hapgood and he wishes to talk business you can give him a cup of coffee and I will go into the bedroom. I have lots of things to sort out.'

'Very well.' Will looked resigned to business. 'I will not take long, I promise, then we can resume our interrupted sightseeing. Ask them to come up, if you please, Nancy.'

It would be the banker, or perhaps the lawyer, Julia thought, finding a clean cup and saucer from the tray for the visitor. After all, they knew no one else in town.

The door opened as she bent over the coffee jug to make sure there was enough. 'Mr and Mrs Prior,' Nancy announced.

For a moment she thought she was imagining things. Julia looked up and found herself staring into the face of Cousin Arthur and, beside him, smiling smugly, Cousin Jane.

She was going mad, seeing visions. Julia clutched the edge of the table and was dimly aware of the sound of falling china.

'Good morning, Cousin Julia,' Arthur said. 'What a relief to find you well and safe. You can imagine the worry we have been in, you wicked girl. What a terrible, terrible thing to have done! And now what are we to do?'

'And who the blazes are you?' Will demanded as Julia's knees gave way and she fell back onto her chair.

It had not been an hallucination yesterday. She had seen them and they had seen her and somehow discovered where she was.

'Lord Dereham, I presume?' Arthur advanced with an outstretched hand that Will completely ignored. 'I must make allowances for your natural agitation, I can tell. I am Arthur Prior, Julia's cousin, and this is my wife, Mrs Prior. I cannot begin to describe to you the anguish we have experienced since Julia ran away three years ago! To see her yesterday from the window of our lodgings was such a shock I hardly know how we had the presence of mind to send the lad to follow the hackney carriage and establish where she had gone.'

Will turned on his heel to face her. 'Is this the cousin who inherited your father's estate? The one who laid violent hands upon you?'

'Yes, he is my father's heir. But he never—'

'Violence! Is that what the wicked girl is saying?' Jane reeled back into the nearest chair and fanned herself with a napkin. 'Nothing but kindness she received from our hands. And how did she repay us? By running off with my uncle's stepson, despite being told what a wicked rake he was. The poor, poor boy.' She glowered at Julia who stared back, unable to form a coherent sentence.

'But it seems as though she's fallen on her feet here, has she not, Mrs Prior?' Arthur demanded with a rhetorical flourish.

'Before you go any further,' Will said in a voice that somehow managed to convey a threat of violence under a coating of ice, 'I should tell you that I am perfectly aware of my wife's elopement and of the reasons behind it. I can see no purpose in this call—she most certainly does not wish to receive you, now or in the future. Good day to you.'

'Not so fast, my lord.' To do him credit, Cousin Arthur was standing his ground against a man who Julia hardly recognised. Will looked bigger, angrier and more frightening than she had ever imagined he might. She struggled to find words, but she had no idea what to say, what to do in the face of this utter disaster. 'We have been to a lot of trouble and expense trying to find Julia and I consider you would be doing only the right thing if you were to recompense us for that. And our silence of course.'

'Your silence?' Will enquired dangerously. 'About what, exactly?'

'I cannot imagine you would want the truth about Lady Dereham to become common knowledge, would you? You might be able to gloss over the elopement, I suppose. But the violence?' He smiled slyly. 'I'll not pretend Jonathan Dalfield was anything but a sinner, but did he deserve such treatment? His poor head…'

Julia found her voice and the strength to stand. 'I never meant to kill him,' she said. 'Never. He was trying to rape me. It was an accident. I did not realise the poker was in my hand.'

The room went utterly quiet. Will turned slowly to face her, his eyes wide and dark with shock. 'You *killed* a man?'

'You did not know, my lord?' Arthur interjected. He was white and flustered, but he gabbled on. 'Of course, I should have realised you'd never keep such a thing quiet, not a gentleman like you. But it won't look good for you if it all comes out, now will it, my lord? Many will not believe you. And it puts us at great risk, always has. But you could be assured of our silence, my lord. We would be very reasonable. Five thousand pounds and no one would ever know and you would never hear from us again.'

Without taking his eyes from her face, Will said, 'You despicable, blackmailing worm.'

'Hard words don't break my bones, my lord.' Arthur had recovered some of his poise. 'But a hempen noose will snap your wife's neck if we aren't all very careful. And it wouldn't look good for you, would it? Accessory after the fact, they call it. I'm no lawyer, but I think that's a capital offence as well, my lord.'

'Julia, go to the other room,' Will said, his voice as soft as if he invited her to sleep with him. Beneath it she could hear the anger beating like a tocsin, his eyes blazed gold, and the skin was tight over his cheekbones as though he was a wolf with its hackles laid back.

Without a word she got up and went into the bedchamber. Now the worst had happened she felt strangely calm. It was shock—she recognised it from when she had killed Jonathan and it was strange to be able to diagnose it now as though she was an observer examining herself at arm's length.

What would Will do? Pay what Arthur demanded? But they would never be safe either from betrayal or from more and more bloodsucking demands. Will was a law-abiding English gentleman: his duty was to hand her over to the authorities, whatever the damage to himself. It was not even as though he loved her, she thought bleakly, sinking on to the edge of the bed to await his judgement. She should not put him in this position, make him decide what to do. She should walk out of here, surrender herself.

There was a door in the far corner of the dressing room concealed by a screen. It gave on to the service stairs and Nancy used it to bring hot water and to take away the slops. She could use that route, ask at the desk for the nearest magistrates' court and be there before Will realised what she was doing.

It all seemed very simple and easy now there was no choice. The important thing was not to think about what would happen afterwards.

The sound of voices from next door ceased. The outer door closed. Silence. Julia got to her feet and found her reticule. Her cloak and bonnet were on the chair. She should just—

The bedchamber door opened and Will stood there, framed in the opening. He looked, she realised with a twisting pang of guilt and shame, as though someone had dealt him a mortal blow and he had not yet realised it. 'I knew you were keeping a secret from me,' he said, his voice as steady as a judge. 'I should have listened to my instincts.'

'I could not tell you.' She found she was on her feet. 'It would have put you in an impossible position.'

'Not unlike the one I am in now?' he enquired and walked into the room, pulling the door to behind him with a savage slam that was like a gunshot, terrifying in contrast to his utter calm. 'I was happy last night, this morning. Pathetic, is it not? I thought we could be content together, I believed my wife loved me.'

'I do!'

'But instead,' he went on as though she had not spoken, 'she tells me of her love, so sweetly, so innocently, because she has seen her relatives and knows what will happen when they find her. Did you really think that telling me you loved me would stop me doing the right thing?'

'No,' Julia protested. 'Of course not! That is not why I told you. I said it because it was true. I saw them yesterday, I admit it, but I thought I was seeing things in my panic, that they were not real. I always expect to see people accusing me, pointing me out, calling the constables. That is why I am so afraid of crowds.' The tears welled up and she fought them back with savage resolve. She had to make him believe that she would not use those words to him so cynically. 'I would not lie to you, Will. Not about that.'

'No? Just about the important things, then? The fact you killed a man?'

'Love is the important thing! Will, I had discovered Jonathan had deceived me. I was in shock, he tried to drag me back to the bed. I refused, but he did not care, he was going to rape me. He dragged me by my wrist and I fell into the hearth amongst all the fire irons. He bent to pull me to my feet and I hit out to stop him. I did not realise the poker was in my hand until it struck him.

'There was so much blood. So much. On my hands, on my body. I screamed. Then I had to wash it off. All that blood. There was a screen half-hidden in the corner concealing the wash stand and water, my clothes. I washed my hands and dressed. I could not bear to be dragged away like that.

'They all came pouring in—the inn guests from the bedchambers, the maids, the innkeeper, everyone. I heard them, but they didn't seem to notice the screen, or if they did, to realise someone was behind it. And then…'

'Then?' Will demanded as she faltered to a halt. 'You tell me no-one saw you at all?'

'They were all crowded round the…body. And a woman had fainted and it was chaos. I came out in my cloak and bonnet and no one looked at me. I moved into the room and became just one of the crowd. Then I slipped downstairs and hid in a cart and escaped. It is the truth,' she added flatly.

Will did not comment on that. She noticed and it cut like a knife through her shocked numbness. He did not believe her at all. He thought she had meant to kill Jonathan, perhaps in revenge at his betrayal.

'There was no identification?' he said. She realised he had been analysing her story.

'I took it all. I burned his cards.'

'Very cool and calm. One could almost say professional. You were certainly composed enough when I found you. I must have seemed like a godsend. I have never considered myself a flat before, an easy mark. It seems I was wrong.'

'If taking pity on someone who needed help and offering them food and shelter makes you a flat, then that is what you were. All I knew was that I was exhausted, frightened, utterly adrift. You offered me respite, a chance to regain a little strength and calm. And then you made me that offer…'

Will sat down on the nearest chair as though standing was no longer an option. He passed one hand over his face, rubbed his eyes and answered with the weariness of a man who had fought to a standstill but must keep battling on. 'I made you an offer you could not have dreamt of. You must have been beside yourself with delight.'

'Yes,' Julia agreed. 'I was so relieved. I saw some hope. And I knew I could do what you needed in return. Do not pretend I did not,' she threw at him, some spirit flaring deep inside her. 'I looked after King's Acre with devotion. I did my best to help Henry become a worthy heir for you.'

'It would hardly have been safe if you'd been arrested for murder.' Will pronounced *murder* as if the word hurt him to utter.

'I considered the odds as best I could. My first name is one no one even thinks of me by. My surname is commonplace. I was hundreds of miles from home. Because of your situation the marriage was not reported outside the neighbourhood. I thought it safe and, if it were not, the authorities would believe I had deceived you.'

'The poor dying man deceived by the wicked murderess?' Will's mouth twisted into an ugly smile. 'And when I returned you were terrified that I might seek an annulment. Of course—that would have made a scandal indeed and it was not my good name you were worried about. How you must have quaked until I consummated the marriage and you were safe. And to think that the worst I considered was that I had been cuckolded in my absence.'

'Yes, I was fearful of a scandal. I will not lie to you. I knew I could not tell you.' His face darkened. 'Will, if I had not married you then you would be dead now. Henry, with no guidance, would be ruining King's Acre.'

'So dragging my name and honour in the gutter was actually a favour to me?' He looked down at his clasped hands. 'Finding that the woman I was becoming...attached to had killed and lied and deceived me was not supposed to hurt?'

'You never truly trusted me, did you? Julia said. He had become *attached* to her. 'Thank God you never grew to love me.'

'Thank God, indeed.' He stood up and went to the door. 'You will stay here.'

She would not beg him to save her. How could he, even if he wanted to? And besides, she had deceived him and, perhaps, brought him to ruin. 'I did not think it would come to this. I thought that if I was discovered it would be by the authorities and I would have some warning to be able to vanish before they could catch me and hurt you. What are you going to do?'

Will looked back at her and suddenly she saw him as he had been when she first met him, when she had thought him an old man. The skin was tight over those strong bones, the colour had left his face, his eyes were stark and full of anger. 'I have no idea. Think, I suppose. I have promised those bloodsucking relatives of yours that I will write to them by the end of tomorrow with my decision.'

This time he closed the door slowly, quietly, behind him. The key turned. He thought he had imprisoned her.

Think. She must think, too, and not give way to the tears or the paralysis of fear. Jonathan was dead. Nothing she could do would bring him back. He had no family in need to whom she could make some restitution. She would be hanged, of course, but the person who would have to live with this was Will.

The only question that mattered was how to inflict the least damage and pain on Will. Once she put it like that, then the answer seemed clear: not to drag his name through a public trial, an even more public hanging. She must vanish. But to do that she must silence the Priors and the only way she could think of was to hold over them the threat that they, too, would appear as accessories.

She would tell them that, rather than let Will pay blackmail money for the rest of his days she would surrender herself and then she would have killed their golden goose for them. If they did not believe her, called her bluff, then she would have to decide what to do— give up and surrender or run and try to hide. But she would deal with that if she had to.

Will would go to the authorities himself, of course, but then he would be seen as someone deceived, some- one doing the right thing as soon as he found out the truth. His pride would be hurt, but that was better than the alternatives.

But she needed time to compose herself and think this through, to make certain Will did not try to find her. There was one certain way of doing that, she sup- posed. If she could make Will believe that she had taken her own life he would not search for her. But she would not lie to him. Never again, even in this.

Julia went to the desk, pulled a sheet of paper to- wards her and dipped the pen in the inkwell. She wrote:

Dearest Will,
When you read this I will be beyond the reach of the law and beyond the capacity to cause you any more pain or scandal. I am too much of a coward to take poison. I have heard that the river is the last resort for many of London's despairing souls.

There is nothing to say except that I am sorry and that I never meant to hurt you. You will go to the authorities with this letter—I know that you are too honourable to break the law over such a matter. I will not write anything to embarrass you

more, except that I love you. Believe that if you
believe nothing else.
Julia.

There was a small portmanteau that she had pushed
into the bottom of a larger one, anticipating having
to pack more clothing on their return than she had
when they arrived. He would not notice that it had
gone. Julia changed from the smart morning gown
into a plain walking dress, put on strong half-boots
and packed a change of undergarments that hopefully
Nancy would not notice were missing. A handkerchief,
a comb, her reticule. She must take nothing that would
be missed or, if it was, be unlikely that a woman going
to drown herself might take out of habit.

Money she would need. She doubted Will had
counted the notes he had given her the day before, or,
after all that had passed, even recalled doing so. Julia
unfolded it: twenty-five pounds, a year's wages for
many people. She put it in the reticule, then checked
every pocket, all her other bags, and found another two
pounds in small coin and a crumpled five-pound note.
She had enough to get a long way away.

'I love you,' she murmured, one hand flat on the
door panels, as close to him as she would ever be again.
'Goodbye, Will.' Halfway to the service door she turned
back and took another two handkerchiefs from the
drawer. She would need them.

Then, feeling as shocked and desperate as she had
when she had stepped out from behind the screen in that

inn room, she slipped into the dressing room, went behind the screen in the corner, eased the door open and tiptoed down the back stairs.

Chapter Nineteen

Will splashed brandy into a glass and tossed it back in one swallow, poured another and stood gripping the glass as he stared down into the busy street below.

His mind could not seem to get past the fact that Julia had killed her lover. It seemed utterly out of character—everything about her spoke of the need to nurture. He had obviously not understood her at all and it was no wonder he had sensed that she was keeping something from him: any other secret he could conceive of paled into insignificance beside this horror.

Nancy came in and he snarled at her so that she fled, white-faced. He could not bring himself to explain. Not yet. Outside the traffic built as the morning progressed and his mind became as tangled as the mass of hackney carriages and carts, pedestrians and riders down below.

His name would be ruined. King's Acre would always carry the stain of this scandal. And his heart... Well, thank heavens his heart was not engaged, that was the only mercy in all this. What if he had loved his wife as she, the deceitful witch, had said she loved him? The pain in his chest was anger and betrayal, nothing more.

The glass was empty. He filled it. And again. It did not help, all it did was to fire his memory. The pale ghost on the bridge over the lake who had run to his aid. The desperate, grieving mother who had been so afraid he would evict that pathetic little coffin from the vaults. The intelligent farmer arguing for some improvement to the farm, the mistress that the staff, indoor and out, loved and supported with devotion.

Julia in those scandalous divided skirts riding the stallion with such skill and teasing him about his manhood as she did so. Julia, passionate and sensual in his arms.

Julia. And all he had been thinking about was how this was going to affect him. The empty glass dropped from his hand and he stared at it as it rolled on the carpet, wondering at his own selfishness. He believed her when she said she had not meant to kill. You could not live with a woman as closely as he had with her and not know whether she had a capacity for violence or not. *He dragged me by the wrist.* He had seen the bruises, savagely black and blue, that first evening. *He meant to rape me.* He knew from her responses in bed that the man had been a selfish lout. Of course she had tried to fight back.

And the story of her escape was probable. He could imagine the scene, the chaos, the gawping crowd avid for sensation. The body would have been the focus of all attention. Julia, almost sleepwalking with shock, could well have dressed in that simple grey cloak and plain bonnet and merged into the crowd until she vanished.

He believed everything she said, he realised. And that meant he must believe her when she said she loved him. The knife that was carving its way through his chest gave a sharp stab.

Julia had been abused, ravished and then threatened with more violence by the man she thought loved her. What had happened to him had been an accident and, if anyone was to blame it was Jonathan Dalfield. And now, with every excuse never to trust a man again, never to allow herself to love, she had given him, Will Hadfield, her heart.

And in return he had accepted the worst of her without question, verbally attacked her, locked her in her room, left her in fear of the worst kind of justice. Will was across the room, unlocked the door, flung it open, all before the thought was even finished.

The bedchamber was empty. He found the service door and then the note lying on the pillow. *Dearest Will.* His hand was shaking so much he had to sit on the edge of the bed and steady himself before he could read on.

He was halfway down the stairs before any kind of rational thought hit him. He sent the hall porter sprawling as he barrelled his way through the crowded lobby, down the steps and into the road under the nose of a startled cab horse.

'Westminster Bridge, at the gallop and there's five pounds in it for you,' he yelled at the cab driver, who shut his mouth on the stream of invective and whipped the horse up before Will could get the door closed.

He clung by on instinct as the cab swayed and swerved across Piccadilly, down St James's Street, across Pall Mall and into St James's Park. Westminster was the closest bridge and she would need a bridge to be certain of falling into the deep, lethal water. The banks were too uncertain, the water slower, there were too many people to stop her, to pull her out again.

Will was not conscious of any plan at all in that wild ride, only the knowledge that he must be in time, that if he lost her he would not be able to bear it. The cab pulled up in the middle of the bridge and he leapt out, stared along the length of it. And saw nothing. No hubbub as there surely would have been if a woman had jumped off in broad daylight. No sign of anyone resembling Julia.

'Well, guv'nor? What about my fare, then?'

Will pulled out his pocket book and handed up a note without looking at the driver, his eyes scanning the northern approaches of the bridge. 'Wait.'

'For that money, guv'nor, I'll sit here all day.'

Will gripped the parapet and tried to assess what was best to do when all he wanted was to rush on to Blackfriars Bridge. She did not know London, but she had read the guidebooks, would know that Westminster was the nearest bridge to Mayfair. And she could expect to get here before he found the note. But she should have arrived by now, even at the normal pace of a cab horse.

He would have to risk leaving his post here. 'Black-friars. As fast as you can make it.'

Up Whitehall, along Strand, down the hill to the foot of Ludgate Hill and then down to the river and the bridge. Again, only the bustle of everyday life greeted him. Will stood looking down at the dark water rushing beneath and thought about his first sight of Julia, a pale grey ghost in the moonlight, leaning on the bridge over the lake. And he had feared she would jump and drown herself, of all the ironies.

It was as though he could hear the nightingale again, feel her arms around him, holding him against her warm body. And as if she spoke in his ear he heard her voice.

I cannot imagine ever being desperate enough to do that, she had replied when he told her he had thought she was about to jump. *Drowning must be such terror. Besides, there is always some hope.*

Will dragged the note from his pocket and smoothed it flat on the worn Portland stone. The threat to kill herself was a feint, a clever bluff, all implication. And no lies. And he had fallen for it. The hope that surged back into him made him dizzy for a moment until he realised he still had no idea where to find Julia.

'You all right, guv'nor?' When Will looked up at him the driver scratched his stubbled chin and frowned back. 'Not choosing the best bridge to jump off, are you?'

'No. I have lost someone,' Will said. He needed help. Rushing about like a headless chicken was not going to answer in a city the size of London. 'Take me to the Bow Street offices.'

* * *

A busy coaching inn was the ideal hiding place, Julia realised as she closed the door of the cramped chamber and listened to the bustle and racket from the yard below. It was the one place where a woman alone was not conspicuous, for it was full of them, some modestly bonneted and cloaked, clutching their battered portmanteaux—servants and governesses, she supposed. Some were fine ladybirds, dressed to the nines and out to attract attention, others were harassed wives and mothers with a baby in their arms or fractious children at their heels.

The coaches came and went, the tide of passengers ebbed and flowed and she felt safe from detection for the first time in hours. Desolate, lonely, heartbroken and frightened. But at least no one would find her here.

What was Will thinking now? How was he feeling? Betrayed, of course. He believed she had deceived him and she had. He believed she had lied about loving him and that, Julia realised, hurt more than anything. And he loved King's Acre and he was having to face the fact that the woman he had thought would help him save it would smear it with the stain of blood and disgrace.

She wanted to write to him, to justify herself, to try to convince him that she truly loved him. But that would not help him, all it would be was a small, selfish, balm to her smarting conscience. Now she had to plan for where she would go to if she could silence Arthur and Jane and what she should do if she could not.

* * *

Bow Street was home to the Runners, and they would be a danger, but it also attracted a motley crowd of thief-takers and informants who hung around in the hope of commissions, legal and semi-legal. They would think nothing of being sent to every coaching inn in search of a carefully described woman who had bought a ticket and left town that day.

Will had paid twenty of them better than they asked and promised more for results, then went to the hotel to wait. The inaction was hellish. Worse was the nagging fear that he might be wrong, that Julia might even now be floating in the muddy waters of the Thames.

No, he told himself for the tenth time. She would not give up, she was a fighter. But man after man came to him and reported nothing. Women answering her description had been seen, but not buying stage or mail-coach tickets. Nor had any of the carriers sold places on their slow, heavy wagons. She was still in London and that, he was all too aware, would make her far harder to track.

Will paid them, then sent them back out to check again in the morning, pushed his dinner around the plate, left it away uneaten and tried to rest. He could not let her hang, he knew. Whatever the cost, whatever the consequences, he would find her and get her out of the country.

Why? he wondered, suddenly shaken out of his circle of dark thoughts. Why risk everything, his good name,

King's Acre? The answer came with shocking clarity. *Because I love her and nothing else matters.*

He needed to rest because Julia needed him. Will took off his boots and his coat, lay down on the bed, tried to come to terms with that shattering piece of self-knowledge and attempted to sleep through nightmares of Newgate and the gallows, the look of stunned misery on Julia's face as he had hurled those bitter words at her that morning, the smug, blackmailing faces of her cousins.

There was something there, something his mind fretted at and yet could not quite grasp. In the floating state somewhere between sleep and waking Will lay still and let his thoughts chase the puzzle. Something had not been right, something had been out of kilter. But when? The answer flicked out of sight whenever he seemed close, like a shadow vanishing from the corner of his eye when he turned to confront it.

Surprise. It had something to do with surprise. Shock. No, that was not quite right, he was missing the point somehow. Frustrated, Will thumped the pillow, turned over and, somehow, managed to sleep.

The sun was bright on the gilded cross atop St Paul's as the Mail clattered on to the yard of the General Receiving Office. Julia joined the crowd of travellers emerging from the numerous inns all around making their way towards the Receiving Office to take the morning coaches out, or to continue their journey by hackney carriage or on foot. A restless night had left her aching and weary, but Julia set off towards the great dome, thankful at least for a landmark. Once she found the cathedral then she only had to go down Ludgate Hill and turn into the Old Bailey and there would be the inn where she had seen her cousins watching the execution.

Her tired brain went over and over the arguments she had worked out during the long night. Firstly she would appeal to their good nature, then to the threat of scandal to themselves, tarred by association with her. If neither of those worked, well, then she would threaten to hand herself in at Bow Street and to implicate them as accessories.

And if that failed? She still did not know whether, if that happened she would have the courage to surrender herself and trust to a jury to believe she had acted in self-defence. But if she did not, could she spend her whole life running?

Whatever happened, she thought as she trod across the cobbled path through St Paul's churchyard, Will could not be implicated. It was bad enough that he would be seen as a man deceived, but she would not allow him to become implicated as the scandalous baron who knew of his wife's crime, but who did nothing.

There were the shops she had stared into so light-heartedly only a few days ago. There, busy now with the passage of lawyers, servants with their marketing baskets, bankers and tradesmen, was the opening into the Old Bailey. There were no hangings today and if it were not for the ominous bulk of the prison at the end of the street, and the stench in the air when the wind changed to blow from that direction, she would think it a pleasant enough district.

Opposite her was the King's Head and Oak, its sign of the crowned oak tree that had sheltered Charles II swinging in the light breeze. No baying onlookers hung from the windows. It looked respectable and well kept, a suitable lodging for minor gentry come to the city.

There was a bay tree in a pot by the front door, she saw as she hesitated there. Perhaps this was the last time she would walk outside as a free woman. Julia reached out and broke off a twig, crushed the aromatic leaf between her fingers as she entered and summoned up the dregs of her courage.

'Mr and Mrs Prior, if you please,' she said to the man who came out of the taproom as she entered. 'Tell them Lady…tell them Miss Prior is here.'

They kept her waiting only a few minutes, which was a mercy for she was not certain which would go first: her nerve, to send her fleeing down towards the Fleet, or her legs, to leave her huddled on the floor.

The man came back before either happened. 'You're to follow me, if you please, miss.'

The old wooden stairs were well waxed, she noted as she climbed. Every trivial detail was imprinted on her senses. The man's apron was clean, but his shoes were dusty and he had been eating onions. That picture hanging on the wall at the head of the stairs, so dirty it was impossible to tell the subject, was crooked. They were boiling cabbage below in the kitchens. Her guide tapped on a door, opened it and she stepped into a small parlour. Her relatives regarded her with identical expressions of supercilious amusement as she tried to control both her breathing and her face.

'I'll not pretend I am not surprised to see *you*,' Cousin Jane said, her over-plucked eyebrows lifting as she took in the sight in front of her. 'Where's his lordship?'

'I am here on my own account.' Julia looked at Arthur, who lounged in a carved chair before the empty hearth. He had not troubled to get to his feet as she entered and the deliberate insult somehow steadied both her nerve and voice. For three years she had been Lady Dereham, used to receiving respect and courtesy—she was no longer the poor, subservient, relation.

'I am sure that, having thought this over, you cannot wish to betray me to the law, not when you know full well I was deceived and forced by Jonathan Dalfield.' That was her first suggestion, the one she knew they would ignore.

'There's no evidence of force. No one else was in the room, were they? No witnesses.' Arthur folded his hands over his small paunch and smiled benignly. 'You're all alone, Cousin. Left you, has he? The baron, I mean. Can't stomach what you did, or just doesn't like being tricked into marrying used goods?'

Julia ignored him. Jane, after all, was the one who always wanted to keep up appearances. She tried her next bargaining chip. 'Do you want the scandal to attach to your name, Cousin Jane?' she demanded.

'We will appear as the poor, deceived relatives who

took you into our home and were grossly imposed upon,' Mrs Prior said, perfectly composed. 'How were we to know that you were a vicious, immoral little slut who was capable of such things?'

Well, that seemed to dispose of both appeals to their good nature. Time for threats. 'If you hand me over to the law, then my husband will not pay you a penny and I will tell the magistrates that you were accessories.'

Arthur shrugged. 'Your husband will pay up, never fear. That sort will do anything to safeguard their honour and good name.'

That seemed to dispose of the one feeble threat she could make. Julia realised she was not surprised. Her stomach felt entirely hollow and yet she had passed beyond fear. 'Very well. I shall go to Bow Street and surrender myself. And while I am at it I will report you both for extortion.' *Would I?* She realised she simply did not know.

Then, as Arthur still smirked, Julia's fragile hold on her nerves snapped into temper. 'I mean it. I will not have you threatening and impoverishing the man I love and as the only way to avoid that seems to be to expose this whole dreadful situation I will do my damnedest to see you are dragged down with me. And I promise you, Lord Dereham will make your life hell on earth from now onwards.'

That got through. 'Wait.' Arthur rose to his feet. 'Now there's no need to be hasty.' With a glimmer of hope she saw there was sweat beading his brow now.

'You want to negotiate, do you?' Julia said. 'Unfortunately I do not deal with—'

The inner door opened and a man strolled out from the bedchamber beyond. *Will*, an irrational voice in her head said and her heart leapt. Then he stepped fully into the room and she saw his eyes were cold, unreadable blue, not hot amber fire. This was a tall, dark ghost with a streak of pure white slashing through the forelock that fell on to his brow.

'Perhaps you would like to deal with me instead, Julia,' Jonathan Dalfield said and smiled as the room swirled around her.

Chapter Twenty

I will not faint, Julia thought grimly and spun round to the door. Jonathan reached her before she could lift the latch, his strong hands turning her, dragging her up against him. He smelled as she remembered, of lime cologne and the Spanish snuff he favoured and the oil he used on his hair. It was a scent that had once made her head spin with desire.

'You are alive.' It was foolishly obvious, but it was hard to believe that this was a flesh-and-blood man. Not so hard to believe was the remembered pain of his grip on her wrist. So close she could see that the line of his jaw had softened, that there were pouches under his eyes. He looked more than three years older, more dissipated. If he had approached her now, she would have seen him for what he was.

'Alive, but no thanks to you, my dear.' His smile was feral, bitter with all semblance of charm vanished. Once she had thought herself in love with this man. She must have been desperate indeed.

How had he survived that blow to the head? There had been all that blood. But she did not believe in ghosts—her wrist hurt with an exquisite pain that told her she was not dreaming, so it must be true. 'Then let me go. You'll have no money for blackmail now, Jonathan. My husband knows I was no virgin when I came to him, he'll give you not a penny for whatever feeble scandal you think you can stir up.'

'So I will have to get my recompense for *this* some other way, Julia my dear.' He pushed back the hair from his forehead and she saw the scar, a red, puckered dent two inches long. 'Pretty, isn't it? And the headaches are not pretty either.'

'It is your fault, Jonathan Dalfield,' Julia threw at him. She felt giddy with relief that she had not killed him, but she could feel no regrets now for having hurt him—the man was even worse than she had thought. 'You deceived me, ravished me, tried to rape me. Do you believe I had no right to fight back?'

'Women don't fight back, they do as they're told,' he said and smiled as cold ice trickled down her spine. Her anger was congealing into fear and she struggled not to let that show on her face. Bullies fed on fear, she knew that. 'I didn't get much fun for my pains last time. Now, I can only hope you've learned a trick or two from your baron.'

Julia saw it in his eyes, the truth that he was more than capable of dragging her into that bedchamber and ravishing her all over again. No one who cared for her knew she was there, Will thought she was dead, she had walked into this trap of her own volition. No one was going to get her out of it if she could not.

Julia curled her free fingers into talons and lashed out even as she realised that Jonathan had been expecting just that. He caught her arm and pulled her in close, so tight she could hardly struggle, then freed his grip on her wrist so he could hold her with one arm while he forced her chin up. She bared her teeth at him.

'You'll smile for me nicely, my dear, unless you want gaps in those pretty teeth,' he said. 'And if you bite, I can promise you a whipping.'

He bent his head and took her mouth with his, the same mouth she had sought to place shy, loving kisses on when they were courting. Julia tightened her lips, resisted the thrust of his tongue. She was going to survive this and she would see him brought to justice for what he had done. Now she could only endure.

At her back the door slammed open like the crack of doom. 'Jonathan Dalfield, I presume? Take your hands off my wife or I will break your neck,' said a voice she scarcely recognised.

Jonathan freed her with a shove that sent her reeling across the room hard against Will's chest. She grasped his forearms, looked up into burning amber eyes and saw nothing but murder there. 'Will, thank God—'

Will glanced down at her, one searching, scorching stare. 'Thank God I've found you. I did not expect to find you here.' He touched one finger to her cheek. 'He had his hands on you. His mouth.' Then he pushed her gently into the arms of the man who had followed him into the room and took a step forward.

'Will!'

'Never fear, Lady Dereham, you are safe now,' the man holding her said. He tried to bundle her out of the door but she stuck in her heels.

'Major Frazer?' How on earth had he got here? 'No, please stop pushing me, I must stay with Will.'

'There will be violence, ma'am,' the major said pedantically. 'It is no fit place for a lady.'

She simply ignored him. The Priors were standing together close to the bedchamber door, their faces white. Jonathan had backed up as far as the table and stood at bay, his hand at his side as though trying to grip the sword that was not there.

'You think that even if we had weapons I would duel with you as though you were a gentleman, a man of honour?' Will's voice dripped contempt.

'Julia ran back to me of her own free will,' Jonathan said. 'Why do you think she is here? Your quarrel is with her.'

'You seem to have a death wish,' Will observed. He pulled off his gloves, finger by finger, tossed them on to a chair, shrugged out of his greatcoat, laid that on top and added his hat, for all the world as though he was settling down for a comfortable chat. But Julia could read him now and what she saw was cold, focused fury.

'Don't kill him,' she gasped.

'You see?' Jonathan's sneering voice was at odds with his white face. There was a nerve twitching in his cheek and he did not seem to know what to do with his hands. 'She would protect me.'

'Lady Dereham appears to think that you are not worth hanging for. She is probably correct.' Will took a step forwards. 'So I will just have to deal with you some other way. Frazer, get her out of here.'

'No!'

'I am very sorry, Lady Dereham.' Major Frazer picked Julia up bodily and marched out of the door, pushed it shut with his shoulder, then leaned against it when she lunged for the door handle. 'I apologise for the liberty, but that is no place for a lady.'

'There are three of them in there and Jonathan Dalfield will not fight fairly,' she panted, trying to reach the door handle, but the major was almost as solid as Will. There was a crash from inside the room.

'Will won't be fighting fairly either,' Major Frazer said with a grin that faded as he took in her distress. 'You forget I knew him in his army days. He duels like a gentleman, but he fights scum like a gutter rat. There is no cause for alarm, I promise you. Ah, landlord.'

Julia turned as the man came running up the stairs. 'What is going on, sir? I'll not stand for fighting and my rooms being smashed up! I'll call the constables, I warn you.'

'Excellent idea,' the major said. 'Send for them at once. Your guests have set on this lady's husband in an unprovoked manner—I can only hope they have sufficient money to pay for the damages.'

'But if the constables come they might arrest Will,'

Julia protested, as the man turned and ran downstairs, shouting for the pot boy. The door at the major's back was hit with a massive crash that had him rocking on his feet.

'When they come, if we are still here, they will be met by me, in my capacity as a London magistrate, investigating a case of extortion and the forcible imprisonment of a lady. With any luck, we'll be away before it comes to that.'

'You are a magistrate?'

He nodded, his head half-turned as though listening. It had gone very quiet. 'Will knew I was at my town house. Ah, here we are.'

He stepped away from the door and Will came out. One eye was half-closed, there was a cut on his right cheekbone and his lip was split. 'Right, come on.' He clapped his hat on his head, shrugged into his greatcoat and took Julia's arm. 'My thanks to you for your support, Frazer. I owe you a good dinner, but you'll forgive me if we leave at once.'

'Will, your face—'

'Not here.' He took her arm and went briskly down the stairs and out onto the forecourt.

The major tipped his hat to Julia. 'Obedient servant, ma'am. Dereham.'

Will hailed a passing cab, bundled Julia into it without ceremony and called up, 'Grillon's Hotel', before climbing in beside her.

The vehicle rattled away down Ludgate Hill and Julia, speechless, simply stared at her husband. He was here, she was safe. She had killed no one. Julia dug her handkerchief out of her reticule and sat with it clenched in her hand, waiting for the tears of sheer relief to come. Strangely, they did not, nor did the rush of relief she experienced when she dreamed that everything was all right.

Will tossed his hat on to the seat beside him and took the handkerchief when she held it out to him. He dabbed at his cheek with some caution. 'Are you all right, Julia?'

'Am *I* all right!' She found her voice in a flood of anger that encompassed fear, anguish, anxiety and shocked relief all in one muddle of feeling. 'Yes, of course I am. Will, you might have been seriously injured, even killed.'

He raised one eyebrow, gave a wince at the unwary gesture and grinned, somewhat lopsidedly. 'That is not very flattering, my dear. Your Mr Dalfield is licking his wounds and contemplating the warning I gave him and your cousins: go back to where they came from and never speak of this or approach you in any manner. If they do not comply, they will have a respected magistrate to vouch for their attempts at extortion.'

'Then it is really all over.' It did not seem possible that the nightmare that had haunted her waking and sleeping for over three years had simply dissolved into thin air.

Will nodded. 'I am hoping this is the last of your deep dark secrets, my love.' His face was serious, but his eyes smiled at her.

'I promise.' Had he really said *my love*? Most likely

it was a careless endearment, or wishful thinking on her part. She was certainly feeling very strange. Light-headed, in fact, although with that came a certain clarity of thought. 'You were not surprised when you came into the room just now, were you? You said Jonathan's name without even having to think about it. How did you know?'

'I realised he was not dead in the early hours of this morning.' Will got up and changed seats so he could put his arm around her. Julia tried not to lean into him, anxious about cracked ribs, but the warmth of his body was like a balm to her own aching one.

'It was all about surprise, that was what had been niggling at the back of my mind ever since your cousins came to Grillon's. Their purpose was to blackmail us, of course. But all they threatened us with at first was scandal about your elopement and the fact that you had struck Dalfield. *Violence*, they said. Not murder, not killing. No one said anything about death or murder until you blurted out your confession. They mentioned Jonathan's *poor head*, not his dead body.

'They had come all prepared with a shocking tale of a woman who had lost her virtue and assaulted, and probably scarred, a man. They threatened to paint you as a woman who had run away from home, one whom society would be appalled to find as a baroness. They expected me to pay up simply to preserve our good name from unpleasant slurs.

'And then you said what you did. I was stunned. But

so were they and that must have registered with me without my grasping the significance, fool that I am.'

'You could hardly be expected to notice nuances when you had just been told your wife had killed a man,' Julia said.

'I suppose not,' Will agreed. 'But Mrs Prior gasped and Prior was struck silent. It only took him a moment to recover his wits and for her to at least regain some composure, but it obviously registered somewhere in my brain.'

'I was not looking at them,' Julia murmured, and turned so she could see his profile. Will was miles away, looking back on that appalling scene, she could tell. 'I heard them but I was watching you.' *Only you, while my heart broke.*

'They had thought I would pay them a few hundred pounds to shut their mouths and go away, I'll wager that was the sum of their ambition. And then they found that you believed you had killed your lover. I have to give Arthur Prior credit, the man can think on his feet. With a brain like that he should be a lawyer. It was a gift to him and he knew what to do with it at once: tell the big lie, ask enough money, and it all becomes that much more convincing. And you, my darling, could not but help them because you believed it and I, knowing you were still hiding a secret, had believed the very worst of you.'

'How could I have been so mistaken?' Julia felt her mind clearing, her strength returning. Perhaps, like Will, she was having to come to terms with the fact that she had a future. The certainty she had lived with so long like a leech on her conscience had been disproved. It was hard to believe she was free. 'Jonathan looked so…dead.'

'All head wounds bleed dreadfully. You saw an unconscious man lying face down, his head laid open by an iron poker. He must have sprawled as still as death amidst scattered fire irons on the hearth. There was blood everywhere. You had experienced betrayal, fear, violence, all within minutes and you had done something utterly alien to you—struck another person. The room was suddenly full of cries of *Murder!* from an ignorant, excited crowd. I can see it as plainly as if I had been there.'

'If I had not assumed the worst and fled—'

'You might have been taken up for assault, for it would have been his word against yours and he was the one with the cut head. And besides, I would never have met you,' Will said as the carriage came to a halt. 'Of course, you may well say that all these years of anxiety and guilt were not worth it, but selfishly I hope you will come to think they were.'

Julia looked at him sharply, but Will was already on the pavement handing up money to the driver. 'Now, to get ourselves back up to our room without setting the entire place on its ear. If the manager gets sight of me, we will find ourselves and our bags out on the pavement, I have no doubt!' he added as he tried to cover the worst damage on his face with the linen square.

'I do not think I look much better,' Julia confessed

as a page, trying hard not to stare, came to take her small valise. Mercifully, although there were hotel staff a-plenty to negotiate, they did not encounter the manager or any guests on their way up to the room.

'Oh, my lady! My lord. I was that worried, I didn't know what to do!' Nancy, started to her feet as they entered their sitting room. She had a basket of mending at her feet, but it did not seem she had been doing much to it.

Julia did her best to calm her down, although for the life of her she could not think of a convincing explanation to offer the maid other than a rather garbled story of family emergency and footpads.

Her head spun with suppositions and hopes and fears, but she allowed Nancy to lead her away to bathe and to change, leaving Will to deal with his own *toilette* in the minuscule dressing room. She suspected they both needed time before the full meaning of these revelations could be faced and she sensed that her husband did not want wifely fussing over what he was trying to dismiss as minor injuries.

'You are a pearl amongst wives,' Will said. He laid down his knife and fork after what she supposed was a cross between breakfast and luncheon and lifted his wine glass in a silent toast to her.

'I am?'

'You do not prattle and cling when the sensible thing to do is wash and change and eat.'

'Now I may do more than prattle,' Julia said. 'I do not know where to start.'

'At the beginning,' Will suggested. 'We have our lives back, both of us. Do you want to live the remainder of yours with me?'

'Of course.' That was the last question she had expected him to ask. 'I love you—do you not believe me?'

'I was just getting used to the idea when you ran away from me.' But he was teasing her, she could see. All the darkness was gone from his eyes and his mouth curved in a smile despite its bruising.

'I could not let you suffer for what I thought was my crime,' she said.

'I know. I am not sure what I have done to deserve that you should put me first, before your own safety, your own life.'

How do I explain to a man why I love him when I cannot even analyse it myself? 'Will, you do not even seem angry with me after all I have put you through.'

Will stood up, took her hand and led her through to the bedchamber. 'That must be because I am in love with you,' he remarked as he closed the door.

'What?' Julia spun round so fast she lost her balance and sat down on the end of the bed. 'Did you say—'

'I said I was in love with you.' Will sounded thoughtful. 'Actually, I should have said *I love you* because I believe there is a difference. I have never felt like this for any other woman. Nor will I,' he added. 'I suspect I have been lamentably slow in realising it, my love.'

'When did you? Realise it, I mean.' *After he realised I was innocent—or before?*

Will turned the key in the lock. 'The sooner we are

back in our own home and our own bed, the better,' he grumbled as he began to undress. 'When did I realise? I will tell you in a minute, but let me try to recount this as it happened. None of it was a blinding revelation, more a piecing together of pieces. After I had left you in this room, after I had said those things to you that I hope you have it in you to forgive, I sat and drank brandy and realised that you could never have killed a man in cold blood, or even intended to kill him in hot blood either. I realised that it must have been an accident and once I saw that I could understand how it all followed on—your flight, why you had kept it a secret.'

He trusted her. He had trusted her even when he believed she could bring his world crashing down around his ears. How could she not love him?

'When I found that note I believed it, at first. You frightened me half to death with that tarradidle about suicide and the Thames.' He heeled his boots off with scant regard for scratches on their glossy finish and tossed them across the room. 'Hell, woman, I was on Blackfriars bridge before I started to think straight and remembered what you said about throwing yourself in the lake when we first met. And then I looked at the letter and saw it was so very carefully constructed not to tell any lies.

'I did not think you would risk trying to hide in London, so the next thing was to see if you had taken a stagecoach out of town. I had men checking every ticket office. They drew a blank so I knew you must still be in town, but I didn't understand why.' Will sat on the bed beside her to roll down his stockings.

'I knew then that if I lost you nothing would ever matter again. Not my own life, not an estate, however much I loved it. Even a block-headed male can put two and two together faced with that realisation. I went to sleep despite the shock of realising that I loved my own wife and woke to the realisation that the Priors knew Dalfield was alive.'

He rubbed one big hand over his face, betraying in that gesture the hours of anxiety, the lack of rest. 'I still had no idea where you were, but I thought I had best deal with the Priors first, so I told Neil Frazer all about it and enlisted his help as a magistrate in case I needed more than brute force. And there, thank God, you were.'

Julia stroked her hand down his cheek, gently over the bruises, feeling the morning stubble prickling under her palm. *He loves me and he would love me even if the worst had been true.* She supposed it was possible to feel this happy and for it not to be a dream. 'You found me. I think you would always find me.'

Will pulled off his shirt and stood to unfasten his breeches. Julia scrambled out of her own clothes, careless of pulled buttons, and looked up from unlacing her stays to find him naked, bruised all over his torso and flagrantly aroused. 'Those bruises! Will, they must hurt so—'

'Then take my mind off them and do not try to test your theory that I can always find you by running away again. It ruins my sleep,' he added as he joined her on the wide bed.

Julia gave a little snort of laughter and kissed his collarbone, the nearest part of him she could reach. *Ah, the smell of his skin...*

'That is good—I was wondering if I would ever hear you laugh again.'

'I like this, having you naked and at a disadvantage,' she murmured, pursuing the line of the bone to the point of his shoulder and biting gently. 'Tired and battered, my poor love. I can have my wicked way with you.'

'Disadvantage?' He rolled her over with a mock growl and pounced, wrestling with the squirming, laughing, woman and the loose tapes of the corset. 'It would take more than a few bruises and a disturbed night to weaken me.'

Julia lay back with a contented sigh of agreement as Will began to kiss his way down her body. He paused to twirl his tongue in her navel, which always made her giggle, then raised his head. 'Talking of disturbed nights, do you feel any more comfortable with the idea of children?' He spoke lightly, but she could sense his underlying hesitation in case he hurt her.

'I feel very comfortable with that idea, my lord,' she said. 'In fact, I think we may have already begun the process. I am not certain, but I have hopes.'

Will moved so fast she hardly had time to blink. One moment she had been sprawled in sensual abandon, the next she was under the covers in Will's arms and he was holding her as cautiously as he might a basket of eggs. 'Will! I am not fragile.' Julia twisted to try to caress him, show him that she wanted, above everything, to make love.

'Are you sure you are all right?' His forehead was furrowed with worry lines she had never seen before. 'It must have been bad enough, these past days, but to have gone through all you have if you are carrying a child—'

'I am fine,' Julia said. 'And I might not be expecting, we need to wait a day or two more in case it is simply stress disrupting my system. But I do not want to wait to make love to my husband.'

Will's face relaxed. 'I suppose we could. Just in the interests of securing the succession, you understand, now we cannot rely on Henry.'

The words *You know?* were on the tip of her tongue. Julia bit them back just in time, but Will smiled. 'That was another thing that I thought about yesterday. It helped distract me when I was going insane worrying about you. I realised, when I was thinking with my heart, instead of…other parts of my anatomy, that I trusted you. I also thought about Henry dispassionately and not as simply my rather irritating heir and put two and two together. I may have made six, of course.'

'No, you have not.' Julia snuggled close against Will's flank and inched her fingers across his flat stomach. 'It will not be easy for him, but I have encouraged him to take chambers in London, where the presence of just one close servant would not be remarked upon. Are you shocked? I am sorry if you do not approve.'

'I am not shocked, so much as anxious for him. But

you have given him good advice. And now, having settled Henry's love life to your satisfaction, might we resume our own?'

'I thought I was,' Julia murmured, closing her fingers
around the evidence of her husband's desire.

Will laughed and rolled on to his back, taking her
with him. 'Ravish me, then.'

His eyes were golden, laughing, clear of any shadow.
She had never seen them like that, Julia realised as she
knelt astride the slim hips and took him into her body
with a sigh of pure happiness. 'I cannot remember when
I felt so content, so free of anxiety. So *joyous*. I love
you very much, Will. I thought I would never be able
to make love with you again.'

He pulled her down so he could raise his head to
meet her lips and smiled up at her. At the look she
melted, yielding and as boneless as a swathe of velvet.
'We've been though hell to get here, my love. I think
we are owed our little piece of paradise on earth. We
will kiss and we will love and then we will sleep and
then we will go home and be happy.'

'For ever?'

'I am prepared to devote the next eighty years to it,'
Will said. 'We can review things after that.'

'Very well, my lord,' Julia agreed and sank into his
arms and his kiss and delicious contentment.

Author's Note

My grateful thanks go to Dr Joanna Cannon for her explanations of how the symptoms of severe post-viral syndrome would have been interpreted by Regency doctors. With no concept of the condition they would have confused it with *Phthisis*, the normal term at the time for consumption, or tuberculosis, which was fatal throughout the nineteenth-century. Will's recovery would have been greatly hastened by the treatment he received—rest in a warm, dry climate, a good diet and skilled medical attention.

Julia was right to fear the consequences of the law if she had killed Jonathan Dalfield, however unintentionally. The reference to the woman hanged, whose body was then handed over to the anatomists in Aylesbury, is to the real case of the sister-in-law of one of my Regency ancestors who appears to have snapped after years of abuse. Society's horror of such 'unfeminine' violence is reflected in the severity of the sentence.

* * * * *

SCANDAL'S
VIRGIN

To all my friends in the
Romantic Novelists' Association.

Chapter One

April 1816—the park of Westerwood Manor, Hertfordshire

Keep still! The circular image shook, swooped over immaculately scythed grass, across flower beds fresh with young growth, over a flash of bright blue cotton… *There.*

The watcher's hand jammed so hard against the branch that the rough bark scored the skin from the knuckles. *Yes.* Glossy ringlets the colour of autumn leaves, determined little chin, flyaway brows over eyes that must surely be clear green. *Beautiful. She is so beautiful.*

And then the girl smiled and turned, laughing as she ran. The telescope jerked up and a man's face filled the circle. Hair the colour of autumn leaves, stubborn chin, angled brows, sensual mouth turned up into a smile of delight.

'Papa! Papa!' The child's voice floated back through

the still, warm air. The man stooped to scoop her up and turned towards the house as she buried her face in the angle between neck and broad shoulder and clung like a happy monkey. Her laughter drifted on the breeze towards the woodland edge.

The telescope fell with a dull thud onto the golden drift of fallen beech leaves and the woman who had held it slid down the tree trunk until she huddled at its base, racked with the sobs that she had stifled for six long years.

'You saw her then.'

'How did you guess?' Laura Campion let the door slam shut behind her.

'Look at the state of you. All blubbered up. You never could get away with tears, my la—ma'am.'

Trust Mab to exhibit the delicate sensibility of a brick. The scratch of wicker on wood as the maid pushed aside the mending basket, the sharp tap of her heels on the brick floor, the creak of the chain as she swung the kettle over the fire, all scraped like nails on a slate. But the words steadied her as gushing sympathy never would have done. Mab knew her all too well.

'Yes, I saw her. She is perfect.' Laura pulled out a chair and sat down at the table. Her boots were tracking leaf mould across the floor and she tugged them off and tossed them onto the kitchen doormat without a glance. 'She looks like Piers. She looks like *him.*'

'You just said.' Mab slopped hot water into the teapot and swirled it round.

'No, I mean she looks like the Earl of Wykeham.

Piers's cousin Avery.' Laura tightened her lips, stared round the kitchen of the little house that had been home for just two days and fought for enough control to continue. 'She calls him *Papa*.'

'Aye, well, that's what he says he is.' Mab Douglas dug a spoon into the tea canister. 'I only had to ask at the shop who lives in the big house and they were all of a clack about it. How his lordship came here just a month ago from foreign parts with a love child and no wife and doesn't even have the grace to be shamefaced about it.'

'Foreign parts!' Laura tugged at her bonnet strings. They'd do nicely to strangle *his lordship* with. 'He stole her from Derbyshire, though I expect that's foreign enough for them around here.'

'They won't know nothing about that, it was six years ago and he must have taken her abroad with him right away. He's been at that Congress in Vienna, and then he stayed on to help sort out some political nonsense in the Low Countries, so they say.

'Besides, Mr Piers is dead and Lord Wykeham is head of the family, after all. In the village they say he's spending money on the estate.' The boiling water splashed onto the tea leaves. 'Perhaps he thinks he should be responsible for Mr Piers's child as well as his old home.' Mab, at her most infuriatingly reasonable, being devil's advocate.

'That might be the case, if the child did not have a mother.' The bonnet ribbon tore between Laura's twisting fingers. 'But she does.' *Me.*

'Aye, and there's the rub.' Mab poured two cups of

tea and brought them to the table. 'You drink that up, now.' She sat down, five foot nothing of plump, middle-aged, bossy femininity, and shook her head at Laura with the licence of a woman who had looked after her since she was ten years old. 'He knows you're the child's mother, but he thinks *you* don't want her. He doesn't know you thought she was dead. The question is, where do you go from here now you've found her?'

'He has never met me.' It was time for calm thinking now the first shock of emotion was past. Laura smoothed her palms over the dull fabric of her skirts. She was so tired of the black she had worn since her parents died of influenza fifteen months ago. She had been about to put her mourning aside and return to society, but that had been before the bombshell that had rocked her world. Now the solemn garments made the perfect disguise.

'There is no reason he would suspect I am not who I say I am—the widowed Mrs Caroline Jordan, retired to the country to regain my strength and spirits before I re-enter society.'

'And how are you going to meet an aristocratic bach-elor who lives in the big house in the middle of a park?' Mab was still being logical. Laura didn't want logic. She wanted a miracle or, failing that, to sob and rant and… 'And what are you going to do if you do get in there? Snatch the child?'

'I do not know!' Laura closed her eyes and dragged in a steadying breath. 'I am sorry, Mab, I didn't mean to bite your head off. All I knew, right from when I dis-covered those letters, was that I had to find my daughter. I did not dare plan beyond that. Now I have found her and I have no idea what happens next.'

'He called her Alice,' Mab said and laid her hand over Laura's. 'They told me in the village. Miss Alice Falconer. That would have been her proper name if you'd married Mr Piers, wouldn't it?'

It was hard to speak around the thickness in her throat, to find the words in the confusion of her mind. When they did spill out they seemed unstoppable. 'She is six years old. I heard her cry, just once, before they took her away and then they told me she was dead. I heard her say one word today and you tell me her name, the name strangers told you. I should be so happy because she is alive and healthy and yet I feel as though I have lost her all over again. How could they do that?'

How could her parents—the respected Lord and Lady Hartland—have told her the baby had died? How could they have secretly given the child—their granddaughter—away? Admittedly, their chosen recipients, the Brownes, were respectable tenant farmers on one of the earl's distant estates, but even so…

'They thought they were doing the right thing for you,' Mab soothed. 'You were only just eighteen. What they did meant you could have your come-out two months later and no one any the wiser.'

'Really? What, I wonder, was I supposed to say to the nice young men they expected to propose to me? *So sorry, my lord, but I'm not a virgin. In fact, I've given birth.* I could hide the one—I gather there are shabby tricks, straight out of the brothel—but did they hope I'd find a complete innocent who wouldn't notice something amiss?' She knew she sounded angry and bitter and those weren't nice things, either of them. But she did not care. Being angry and bitter had got her through five London Seasons as the most notorious débutante of them all.

Scandal's Virgin, they called her, which was an irony if ever she heard one. But Lady Laura Campion, daughter of the Earl of Hartland, had the reputation of being frivolous, flirtatious and outrageous. And, to the intense frustration of the men who pursued her and the chagrin of the matrons who decried her behaviour, no one was ever able to say she had taken that one fatal step to ruin.

Yes, she would drink champagne on the terrace at a ball. Yes, she would slip away into the shrubbery and allow kisses and caresses no innocent should allow. And, yes, she would wear gowns more suitable to a fast young matron, ride with careless abandon and dance four times in an evening with the same man, if the fancy took her.

Any other young woman after five Seasons would be considered to be on the shelf, unmarriageable, the subject of pity. *But...* No gentleman could ever claim she had given herself to him, despite the wagers in the betting books of every club in St James's. No one had ever managed to catch her doing more than kissing a rake behind the rosebushes. And no one could deny that she was beautiful, amusing, loyal to her friends and the daughter of one of the richest and most influential of peers. Despite the nickname and the shocked glances from the chaperons' corner, Scandal's Virgin continued her apparently heedless way though the social whirl and no one guessed that her heart had shattered at the death of a lover and the loss of his child.

'If the man loved you, he might not care,' Mab ventured.

Laura snorted. She had hoped that, once. But observation soon taught her that men were hypocrites. That theoretical lovelorn suitor would care, for certain.

In January of 1815, just as she was preparing for yet another Season full of distractions to stop her thinking of the hollowness inside, her parents succumbed to the influenza. It was sudden, shocking and completely unexpected, but within ten days of the first fever they were gone. Laura, draped in black veils, retreated to Hartland Castle and the virtual solitude of mourning, interrupted by the occasional descent of Mr Bigelow, the lawyer, and letters from Cousin James, the new earl, apprising her of his efforts to sell out of the army and return home.

He was grateful, he wrote, that Cousin Laura continued to oversee things at the Castle and urged her to call upon whatever resources from the estate she saw fit to transform the Dower House into her new home.

Eventually she made herself order the work, advertised for a lady companion, failed to find one she liked, shrugged and decided to do without for the present. Mab was all the company she needed. Finally, a year after their deaths, she gritted her teeth and started to go through her parents' personal possessions, the things that were not entailed with the estate.

Mab had fallen silent while she sat lost in memories. Now Laura was vaguely aware of her gathering together the tea things and stoking up the fire. 'Why do you think Mama kept them?' she asked abruptly.

'The letters?' Mab stirred a pot and shrugged. 'No one thinks they are going to die suddenly and that someone else will go through their possessions, do they? And they had to do with her granddaughter, after all.'

The box had been inside a locked trunk under a stack of old accounts, dog-eared notebooks of recipes, bundles of bills for gowns going back years. Laura had almost ordered the whole thing taken down and burned unsorted and then she had seen a few sheets of music, so she dragged those out and put them aside.

Once her father had allowed an antiquarian to excavate an ancient mound on the estate and Laura thought of him as she dug her way down through paper layers of history, rescuing the music, smiling over a recipe for *restoring greyed hair to a perfect state of natural glory* and finally breaking a nail on the hard, iron-bound surface of a smaller chest.

It was locked, but she found the key on the chatelaine her mother had always kept about her. When the lid creaked open it revealed a neat bundle of letters. She began to set them aside for the fire unread, thinking they must be old love letters and recoiling from the ghosts of someone else's old romance. She had enough spectres of her own. Then something about the handwriting caught her eye.

Muddy brown ink, a hand that was not so much untutored as unpractised, and poor quality paper. These could not be *billets-doux* or family letters. Puzzled, Laura drew them out and began to read. Even now, knowing the truth, it was hard to withstand the emotional impact of what was revealed. Laura stood, left the kitchen for the back parlour of the little rented house and paced over the old Turkey carpet until her stomach stopped its roiling.

First, the joyful shock of discovering that her baby had not died. Then the monthly letters, three of them, from the farm in the Derbyshire Dales. The child was thriving, the money was arriving, the Brownes, who had just lost a newborn, were very grateful for a healthy babe to raise as their own and for his lordship's generosity. And then, May the fifteenth 1810, the news that she had caught some fever, they knew not how, and had sickened rapidly. *The little mite passed on peacefully in the early hours this morning,* Mrs Browne wrote in her spiky hand. *We will see her decently buried in the churchyard.*

It had taken a day and a sleepless night to recover from the shock of hope snatched away just minutes after it had been given. The next morning, still stunned into a strange calm, Laura had ordered her bags packed and a carriage prepared. At least there would be a grave to visit, not the vague assurance that her child had been discreetly secreted amongst the coffins in the family vault, unnamed, unacknowledged.

When she and Mab had arrived at the solid little greystone farmhouse she simply walked straight in, her carefully rehearsed words all lost in the urgency of what she had to say.

'I am Lady Laura Campion and I know the truth. Where is she?' she had demanded of the thin, nervous woman who had backed away from her until she simply collapsed onto a chair and buried her face in her apron.

Her husband moved to stand between Laura and his sobbing wife. 'He said no one would ever know. He said he was her cousin so it was only right she was with him.'

'What?' This made no sense. They had written that the child was dead…

'He said no one would ever find out if we said she had died and we just kept our mouths shut.' Browne shook his head, shocked and shamefaced. 'I knew we never ought to have done it, but he offered so much money…'

'She is not dead.' It was a statement, not a question. Laura had stared at him, trying to make sense of it all. *He? Cousin?* 'Tell me everything.'

A gentleman calling himself Lord Wykeham had come to the farm unannounced. He had known everything—who the baby's mother was, who was paying them to look after her. He had shown them his card, they saw his carriage with the coat of arms on the door, they were convinced he was the earl he said he was. He had a respectable-looking woman and a wet nurse in the carriage and he had offered them money, more money than they could imagine ever having in their lives. All they had to do was to write to Lord Hartland and tell him the child was dead.

'Babes die all the time,' Mrs Browne had murmured, emerging from the shelter of her apron. 'All ours did. Broke my heart…' She mopped at her eyes. 'I still had milk, you see. Her ladyship, your mother, made sure I could feed the little mite.'

They lived remotely in their distant dale. No one knew that they had a different child in the house, it had all been so simple and Wykeham had been so authoritative, so overwhelming. 'You'll want the money,' Browne said, his weather-beaten face blank with stoical misery. 'It was wrong, I know it, but the milk cow had died and the harvest was that bad and even with what your father was paying us...'

Laura had looked at the clean, scrubbed kitchen, the empty cradle by the fire, the grey hairs on Mrs Browne's head. *All her babies had died.* 'No, keep the money, forget there ever was a child or an earl in a carriage or me. Just give me his card.'

Now Laura took the dog-eared rectangle from her reticule and looked at it as she had done every day of the eight weeks it had taken her to track Wykeham down, organise her disguise, create a convincing story for her staff and neighbours.

She had wanted evidence she could hold in her hand of the man who had stolen her baby, stolen every day of her growing, her first tooth, her first steps, her first word. Piers's cousin, the rich diplomat, Avery Falconer, Earl of Wykeham. Now she no longer needed a piece of pasteboard: she had seen him, that handsome, laughing, ruthless man her daughter called *Papa.* The calling card crumpled in her hand as Laura tried to think of a way to outwit him, the lying, arrogant thief.

'Papa?'

'Mmm?' Saying *yes* was dangerous, he might have

missed the whispered trick question. That was how the house had become infested with kittens.

'Papa, when may I go riding?'

Avery finished reading the letter through and scrawled his signature across the bottom. Sanders, his secretary, took it, dusted over the wet ink and passed the next document.

'When I am satisfied that your new pony is steady enough.' He looked back to the first sentence and tapped it with the end of the quill. 'Sanders, that needs to be stronger. I want no doubt of my opposition to the proposal.'

'I will redraft it, my lord. That is the last one.' John Sanders gathered the documents up and took himself and his portfolio out. The third son of a rural dean, he was efficient, loyal, discreet and intelligent, the qualities that Avery insisted on with all his staff.

'But, Papa...'

'Miss Alice.' The soft voice belonged to another member of his staff, one possessed of all those qualities and more. 'His lordship is working. Come along, it is time for a glass of milk.'

'I will see you before bedtime, sweetheart.' Avery put down his pen and waited until Alice's blue skirts had whisked out of the door. 'Miss Blackstock, a word if you have a moment.'

'My lord.' The nurse waited, hands clasped at her waist, every hair in place, her head tipped slightly to one side while she waited to hear his pleasure. She was the daughter of his own childhood nurse and the only one of his staff who knew the full truth about Alice. Blackie, as Alice called her, had been with him when he had finally tracked the baby down to the remote Dales farm.

'Please sit down. I think it may be time for Alice to have a governess, don't you think? Not to usurp your position, but to start her on her first lessons. She is very bright.' *And impetuous. As her father had been.*

'Indeed, yes, my lord.' Miss Blackstock sat placidly, but her eyes were bright and full of questions. 'You'll be advertising for someone soon, then? I'll speak to Mrs Spence about doing out the schoolroom and finding a bedchamber and sitting room for the governess.'

'If you would.' Avery looked out over the rolling lawn to where the parkland began at the ha-ha. It was small but beautiful, this estate he had inherited from his cousin Piers and which he had signed over to Alice along with its incomes. He would do his utmost to give her all the standing in society that he could, and this place restored to prosperity as part of her dowry and an education with an excellent governess would be the start.

'There is no hurry to arrange the accommodation here. However, will you ask her to arrange the same thing at the Berkeley Square house immediately?'

Miss Blackstock stared at him. 'You are taking Miss Alice to London, my lord?'

'I am. I intend staying there for the remainder of the Season.' There was no reason why he should explain himself, even to an old retainer, but it would help if she understood. 'I plan to marry.'

'But, my lord…' Miss Blackstock hesitated, then

opted for frankness. 'Might Miss Alice perhaps…discourage some of the ladies?'

'Her existence, you mean?' Avery shrugged. 'I would not wish to marry a woman who thought less of me because of one, much-loved, child. Anyone who will not accept Alice is simply unacceptable themselves.'

'It will certainly winnow the wheat from the chaff,' the nurse murmured. 'When will you go up to town, my lord?'

'In two weeks. Late April.' *Wheat from the chaff, indeed.* Avery's lips twitched as the nurse shut the door behind her. It was a long time since he had been in London for the Season, it would be interesting to see what the quality of this year's crop of young ladies was like.

Chapter Two

'April in England. Can't be bettered.' The spaniel stopped and looked enquiringly at Avery. 'You agree, Bet, I can tell. Go and flush a rabbit or two.'

The shotgun, broken open for safety, was snug in the crook of his arm, just in case he did spot one of the furry menaces heading for the kitchen garden, but it was really only an excuse for a walk while the sun was shining and the breeze was soft.

I'm getting middle-aged, he thought with a self-mocking grin. *Thirty this year and enjoying the peace and quiet of the country. If I'm not careful I'll turn into a country squire with a placid wife, a quiverful of children and the prospect of the annual sheep shearing for excitement.*

After an adulthood spent in the capitals of Europe, in the midst of the cut and thrust of international diplomacy, he had thought he would be bored here, or that country life would bring back unpleasant memories of his childhood, but so far all he felt was relaxed.

The parkland was in good order, the Home Farm and the tenant farms thrived, as his regular rides around the surrounding acres showed him. Piers would have been pleased, not that he had been much interested in farming. Army-mad, he had been since boyhood.

Relaxed but randy, he amended. It was easy to maintain a mistress in the city and keep his home life separate, but a remote country manor and a small child were a combination guaranteed to impose chastity. And decency told him that setting up a London mistress at the same time as hunting for a wife was cynical.

Still thinking vaguely about sex, Avery rounded a group of four beeches and stopped dead. A dry branch cracked under his booted foot.

'Oh!' The woman in black sitting on the fallen trunk of the fifth tree jumped to her feet, turned and recoiled at the sight of him, her eyes wide in her pale face. He had an impression of fragility, as much of spirit as of form, although she was slender, perhaps too slender. Her eyes flickered down to the gun and then back to his face and her hands, ungloved and white against the dull sheen of her walking dress, clenched together at her waist.

'I beg your pardon, madam. I had no intention of frightening you.'

'I suspect I am trespassing.' Her voice was attractive, despite her alarm, but there was a huskiness in it that made him think of tears. She was in mourning, he realised, not simply soberly clad, and there was a wedding ring on her finger. A widow. 'I was told in the village that there was a public path across the estate, but

I saw a deer and went closer and then I lost sight of the path… If you will direct me, I will take myself back and cease my illegality, my lord.' Now she had recovered from the shock her tone was cool and steady.

'You know who I am?'

The spaniel ran up, ears flapping, and sat at her feet. She bent to run her hand over its head with the confidence of a woman used to dogs, but her dark eyes were still on Avery. 'They described you in the village, Lord Wykeham.' There was nothing bold or flirtatious in her study of him, she might as well have been assessing the tree behind him, but heat jolted though him like a sudden lightning flash and was gone, leaving him oddly wary. His thoughts had been sensual, but this was as if a fellow duellist had lifted a sword in warning.

'You have the advantage of me, madam,' he said, and knew his diplomatic mask was firmly in place.

'Caroline Jordan. Mrs Jordan. I have taken Croft Cottage for a few months.' She seemed quite composed, but then she was not a young girl to be flustered by a chance meeting with a stranger. She was a young matron, twenty-four perhaps, he hazarded. And a lady of breeding, to judge by her accent, her poise and the expensive sheen and cut of the black cloth. Standing there under the trees in her elegant blacks, she looked as much out of place as a polished jet necklace on a coal heap.

'Then welcome to Westerwood, Mrs Jordan. You are indeed off the path, but I believe I can trust you not to kill my game or break down my fences. You are welcome to roam.' Now what had possessed him to offer that?

'Thank you, Lord Wykeham. Perhaps you would be so kind as to point me in the direction of the path back towards my cottage.' She moved and again he was conscious of a stab of awareness, and this time it was most certainly sensual, even though she had done nothing flirtatious. A disturbing woman, one who was aware of her feminine allure and confident in it to the point where she felt no need to exert it, he surmised. Yet her eyes held a chill that was more than aloofness. Perhaps she was completely unaware of the impact that she made.

'It falls along my own route, if you care to walk with me.' He kept his voice as polite and reserved as her own as he skirted the fallen trunk, whistled to the dog and walked towards the path, trodden down by his own horse. He did not offer his arm.

'Is it you who jumps this?' she asked, with a gesture to the hoofprints dug deep in the turf in front of the trunk she had been sitting on. 'Not an easy obstacle, I would judge.'

'I have a hunter that takes it easily. You ride, ma'am?' She kept pace with him, her stride long and free with something about it that suggested she would be athletic on horseback. *And in other places,* his inconvenient imagination whispered.

'Before I was in mourning, yes.' She did not glance at him as she spoke and Avery found himself wishing he could see the expression in her eyes, the movement of her mouth as she spoke, and not merely the profile presented to him, framed by the edge of her bonnet. Her nose, he decided, was slightly over-long, but her chin and cheekbones were delicately sculpted. Her cheek, pink with exercise, showed the only colour in her face beside the dark arch of her brow and the fringe of her lashes.

'Was it long ago, your bereavement?' he ventured.

'Some time, yes,' she said in a tone of finality that defied him to question further.

Well, madam, if that is how you wish to play it, I will not trouble you further! He was not used to being snubbed by ladies, but perhaps it was shyness or grief. He was more used to diplomatic circles than London society and the ladies who inhabited those foreign outposts were no shrinking violets.

'This is where our ways part.' The path had converged with the ha-ha where the stone slabs set into its side provided a crude set of steps up to the lawn. Bet, the spaniel, was already scrambling up them. 'If you take that path there...' he pointed away towards the edge of the woods '...it will take you back to the lane that leads to the church.'

'Thank you, my lord. Good day to you.' She turned away as Bet gave a sharp yap of welcome. It made her start and stumble and Avery put out a hand to steady her.

'Papa! There you are! You will be late for tea and we are having it on the lawn.'

Mrs Jordan turned to look at Alice as she stood on the brink of the drop and the movement brought her into the curve of Avery's arm. He loosened his grip and for a moment she stood quite still where she was, so close that he could swear he heard her catch her breath. So close that a waft of lemon verbena teased his nostrils.

'Ma'am? Are you all right? I apologise for my daughter's abrupt manners.'

It seemed the widow had been holding her breath, for it came out now in a little gasp. 'It is…nothing. I turned my ankle a trifle when I twisted around just now.'

'Is the lady coming for tea, Papa?'

'No…I…'

Damn it, she's a stranger here, she's in mourning, she knows no one, what's the harm? 'Would you care to join us, Mrs Jordan? Perhaps you should rest that ankle a little.' When she still stood there, unspeaking, he added, 'And we are eating outside.' Just in case she thought he was a dangerous rake who employed children as a cover for his nefarious seductions. He was even more out of touch with country manners than he was with London ones.

'Thank you, Lord Wykeham, I would enjoy that.' She tipped up her head so she could look directly at the child above them. 'Good afternoon,' she said, as serious as if she was addressing a duchess.

'Good afternoon, ma'am.' The girl—*my daughter,* Laura thought—bobbed a neat little curtsy. 'I am Alice.' She was bare-headed and dressed in a green cotton frock with a white apron that showed evidence of a busy day's play.

'Allow me,' Lord Wykeham said before Laura could respond. 'These steps are more secure than they look. If you take my hand as you climb, you will be quite safe.'

'Thank you.' She put her ungloved hand in his,

her fingers closing around the slight roughness of the leather shooting gloves he wore. Her fictitious twisted ankle and the awkwardness a lady might be expected to show in climbing such an obstacle would account for her unsteadiness, she supposed, as she set foot on the first step.

As she reached the top Alice held out her hand, her warm little fingers gripping Laura's. 'Let me help.'

The shock went through her like a lightning strike. Laura tripped, fell to her knees and found her fingers were laced with Alice's. *'Oh!'* Tears welled in her eyes and she blinked them back as she fought the instinct to drag her daughter into her arms and run.

'Your ankle must be more than just turned.' That man was bending over her. She hunched her shoulder to exclude him from the moment. 'Let go, Alice, and run and tell Peters to bring out a chair and a footstool for Mrs Jordan.'

Laura could have snarled at him as Alice loosed her grip and ran up the slope of the lawn. Somehow she turned the sound into a sob of pain.

'Allow me.' Before she could protest he swept her up into his arms and began to follow the child. 'I will send for Dr Pearce.'

'There is no need.' The words emerged sounding quite normal. Laura tried to make herself relax as much as any lady held in the arms of a complete stranger might. She could not follow her instinct and hit out at him, slap his face, call him all the words that buzzed like furious hornets in her brain. 'I am certain it will be better for a short rest.'

'Even so, I will send for him.'

Not a man who accepted disagreement with his opinions, but then she already knew he was arrogant and ruthless.

'Thank you, but, *no*.'

'As you wish.'

I do. Does no one ever say no *to you?*

Laura dredged up some composure from somewhere and tried a tiny barb. 'Lady Alice is a delightful child.'

There was a pause, so slight that if she had not been attuned to his every reaction she would never have noticed, then, without breaking stride, Lord Wykeham said, 'She is not Lady Alice, simply Miss Falconer.'

'Oh, I beg your pardon. I thought in the village they said you were an earl. I must have misunderstood.'

'I am an earl. However, I have never been married and certainly not to Alice's mother.' He must have interpreted her small gasp of surprise at his easy admission as one of either shock or embarrassment. 'I see no reason why the child should suffer for the sins of her father. I will not have her pushed into the background as though she is something I am ashamed of.'

'Indeed not.' Laura fixed her eyes on the sharp edges of waistcoat and coat lapels and added, with malice, 'And she looks so very like her father.'

That went home. She felt the muscles in his arms contract for a moment, but his breathing did not change. 'Very like,' Lord Wykeham agreed, not appearing to notice the strange way she phrased the comment.

It was so strange, fighting this polite battle while in the arms of her opponent. With a less-controlled man, and probably with a less-fit one, she might have expected his body to betray his feelings even though he commanded his expression and his voice. He could have no suspicions of her, so this composure must be habitual. And she need not fear betraying anything by being so close against his body, for he would expect any lady to be flustered by such an intimacy.

He was warm and smelled not unpleasantly of clean linen, leather and man. She had missed that, the intimate scent of male skin, the feel of muscle against her softness, the strength that was so deceptive, so seductive. It turned a woman's head, made her believe the man would keep faith with as much steadfastness.

They had reached the top of the slope. Laura risked a glance forward and found any danger of tears had gone, banished by anticipation of the secret, one-sided duel she had just begun to fight.

The lawn levelled off beneath the spreading boughs of a great cedar. Windows stretching to the ground had been opened to the spring breeze and a table and chairs brought out to stand beneath the tree. A maid set out dishes on the table and Alice was speaking to a footman who stooped to listen, his face turned to see where she was pointing.

'What a charming house.' It should have been her home. Her home, Alice's home. She had never been there, but Piers had described it to her in those brief, breathless days of their courtship. It would be their love nest, away from the smoke and noise and social bustle of London, just the two of them. She had spun fantasies of making a home in this place so that when her hero returned from war he would find love and peace here. She could almost see him now, long legs stretched out as he sat beneath the cedar, so handsome in his scarlet regimentals.

'Yes, it is pleasant and well laid out. A little on the small side compared to Wykeham Hall and the estate is not large, but it is good land.'

'This is not your principal seat, then?' Laura asked as they reached the table.

'No. I inherited it from a cousin. Here is the chair for you.' He waited while the footman put down a sturdy one with arms and Alice, staggering a little under the weight, dragged a footstool in front of it. 'There.'

Lord Wykeham settled her into place with a brisk efficiency that, unflatteringly, showed no reluctance to yield up possession of her. Laura watched him from beneath her lashes as he went to take his own seat. And why should he wish to keep hold of her? She had exerted none of her powers to attract him, all she had done was to suppress her instincts to storm at him with accusations and reproaches.

And if I find it necessary to charm him? Can I do that, feeling about him as I do? Why not? I am a good enough actress to attract many men when all I want to do is play with their hearts a little. It would be no hardship to look at him, that was certain. He was as handsome as Piers had been and more. This was not a young man, still growing into his body and his powers. The earl was mature and powerful...and dangerous.

Laura smiled at Alice and felt the frost that grew around her thoughts when she spoke to Wykeham thaw into warmth. She had every excuse to look at her daughter now and to talk to her. *If only I could hold her.*

'Thank you very much for fetching me the footstool.' She lifted her foot onto it and caught a flickering glance from the earl before she twitched her skirts to cover her ankle and the high arch of her foot in the tight ankle boot. *Hmm, not so indifferent after all. Useful...* Was that shiver at the thought of flirting with such a man or disgust at herself for even contemplating such a thing?

'Does your foot hurt very badly?' Alice stood right by the chair, her hands on its arm, and regarded Laura's face intently. Her eyes were clear and green. On her, as with her true father, the winging eyebrows made her seem always to be smiling slightly. On the earl they added a cynical air that only vanished when he smiled.

'No, it is much better now I am resting it, thank you. I am sure it is only a slight strain.' Was there anything of her in the child? Laura studied the piquant little face and could see nothing that would betray their relationship except, perhaps, something in the fine line of her nose and the curves of her upper lip. Alice had none of her own colouring—dark blonde hair, brown eyes, pale skin. Perhaps, as she grew towards womanhood Alice would develop some similarities. It was dangerous to wish it.

'Why are you wearing a black dress? Has someone died?' Alice asked.

'Alice, that is an intrusive question.' The earl turned from the table, displeasure very clear on his face.

'It is all right.' It was easier to establish her story in response to the child's innocent questions than to attempt to drip-feed it into conversation with the earl. 'Yes, Alice. I lost my husband.' It was true in her heart: Piers had been her husband in everything except the exchange of vows in church. 'And then my parents died.'

Alice's hand curled round her forearm, small and warm and confiding; the touch so precious that it hurt. 'That is why you have sad eyes,' she said, her own lip quivering. 'I lost my mama. Really lost her, because she isn't dead. Papa says she had to go away and won't come back.'

I can't bear this. I must. 'I am sure your mama would if she could,' Laura said and touched her fingertips to the child's cheek. 'I am certain she will be thinking about you every day. But we cannot always do what we wish, even if it is our heart's deepest desire.'

'Alice, run inside and ask Miss Blackstock to join us for tea.'

Laura glanced at Alice, but the child did not appear frightened by Wykeham's abrupt order or the edge to his voice. It did not seem that she felt anything but trust and love for the man she believed was her father. She waited until the small figure whisked through the window and then said what she was thinking without pausing to consider. 'Why did you not tell her that her mother was dead?'

Chapter Three

Lord Wykeham did not snub her as he had every right to do. 'I will not lie to her,' he said abruptly. 'Do you take cream or lemon with your tea, Mrs Jordan?'

'Lemon, thank you.' Laura was hardly aware of the automatic exchange. 'But you—' She caught the rest of the sentence, her teeth painful on her tongue. *But you let her think you are her father.* 'You do not think that is more difficult for her to accept?' His expression became even more sardonic. 'I beg your pardon, my lord, it is not my place to speak of it.'

'Alice likes you,' he said without answer or comment on her question. 'Have you children of your own, Mrs Jordan?'

'I lost one child. I have no others.' It was quite safe to mention that she had given birth to a child, he would never associate her with Alice's mother, of that she was confident. His natural supposition, should he trouble to think about it, would be that she had married perhaps three or four years ago, some time after her first come-out to allow for the normal processes of upper-class courtship and marriage. She was almost twenty-five now, and her mirror told her that she did not look older.

'She is a naturally loving and friendly child, I imagine.' He nodded and passed her a plate of small savouries. 'Has she many playmates in the neighbourhood?'

'No, none. Alice has lived virtually her entire life abroad. We have only been back from the Continent for just over a month. There has been a great deal to do, but you are right to make the point, Mrs Jordan, I should make the effort to socialise locally in order to find her some friends of her own age.'

'My lord, I had no intention of criticising.' Which was an untruth. How fast he caught her up. As a diplomat the man was used to watching faces, listening to voices and hearing the reality behind the facade. She would have to be wary. She glanced towards the house, then quickly away. He must not see the hunger she was certain was clear in her eyes.

'Hinting, then,' he said with the first real smile he had directed at her. Laura felt her mouth curve in response before she could stop it. When the man smiled he had an indecent amount of charm. And that was confusing because there should not be one good thing about him. *Not one, the child-stealing reptile.* She dropped her gaze before he could read the conflict.

'Papa! Here is Blackie.' Alice, who never seemed to walk anywhere, bounded to a halt in front of Laura. *That energy is so like me as a child.* The pang of recognition was bittersweet. 'Mrs Jordan, this is Blackie.'

The nurse bobbed a neat curtsy. 'Miss Blackstock, ma'am.'

'Miss Blackstock. Miss Falconer is a credit to you.' *And you are a credit to Lord Wykeham's care for Alice,* she thought, reluctantly awarding him a point for the care of the child. Not such a reptile after all, if Alice could love him and if he could choose her attendants with such care. Being fair was unpalatable, she wanted to hate him simply and cleanly.

'Thank you, ma'am.' There was a stir as the nurse took a seat beside Alice, then a small tussle over the need to eat bread and butter before cake. All very normal for an informal family meal and not at all what she had expected and feared she would find. And that, Laura realised as she nibbled on a cress sandwich, was disconcerting.

She had been braced to rescue her child from some sort of domineering, manipulative, bullying tyrant and found instead a happy girl and, she was coming to suspect, a doting father behind the facade of firmness.

Tea was finished at last, a final sliver of cake wheedled out of the earl despite Miss Blackstock's despairing shake of the head, and Alice wriggled off her chair. 'May I get down, Papa?'

'You *are* down,' he said.

Alice dimpled a smile at him and came to gaze earnestly at Laura. 'Will you come and visit again, Mrs Jordan? We are very cheerful and there is always nice cake and perhaps you won't feel so sad then. You could play with my kittens.'

'Miss Alice!' Miss Blackstock got to her feet with an apologetic look at Laura.

'It was indeed very nice cake and I feel very cheerful now after such good company,' Laura said. Could she come again? Dare she? She must not promise the child something she might not be able to fulfil.

'Jackson!' A footman came striding across the grass in response to the earl's summons. 'Send to the stables and have Ferris harness up the gig to take Mrs Jordan back to the village.'

'Please, I do not wish to be a trouble, I can walk,' she said as the man hurried away across the grass to the side of the house. 'My ankle feels quite strong now.'

'I cannot countenance you attempting it without an escort and it is probably best if we do not emerge from the woods together.' The smile was back, this time with a hint of something that was not exactly flirtation, more a masculine awareness of her as a woman.

'As you say, Lord Wykeham.' To drop her gaze, to hide behind her lashes, would be to acknowledge that look. She sent him a carefully calculated social smile that held not one iota of flirtation. 'Thank you.'

'I do not know what to do.' Laura paced across the parlour and back, her black skirts flicking the bookcase at one side and the sofa on the other as she turned. 'I thought she would be unhappy and lonely, but I think she loves him and he loves her.'

'What were you planning to do if she'd not been happy?' Mab demanded. 'Kidnap the poor mite?'

'Go to law, I suppose,' Laura said. 'And, yes, I know

it would ruin my reputation, but it is the only remedy I can think of. This isn't a Gothic novel where I could snatch Alice and hide in some turreted castle until my prince came along and rescued us both.' *Not that I have a prince. Or want one.*

'But she is happy and well cared for and loved, so why not leave things be?' her henchwoman demanded, fists on hips. 'I can't be doing with all this handwringing, I've my dusting to get on with.'

'Because he doesn't deserve her! He lied, he deceived and he bought a child as if she was a slave. He has no right to her.'

'She's base-born,' Mab stated, attacking the bookshelves with a rag. 'No getting round that. He's family and she's better off with him, provided he's kind to her. He can protect her better than you can.'

'He is rich, he is privileged, he is—'

'And so are you,' Mab pointed out with infuriating logic. 'But he is a man so he can protect her in ways that you cannot. His reputation isn't going to be dented by having an acknowledged love child, but yours would be ruined and all the influence you can muster goes with it.'

'I do not like him.' Laura flung herself onto the sofa and slumped back against the cushions, exhausted by tension.

'What's that to do with the price of tea?' Mab demanded. '*You* haven't got to live with him. Alice has.'

'*I am her mother.*' The words were wrenched out of her. 'All those years when I thought she was gone. And then to find that she hadn't died, and to have hope and to have that wrenched away and then to discover she was alive after all. And now... Now I have got to do what is best for Alice. But it hurts so, Mab. It hurts.'

'Oh, lovie—' Mab tossed the rag aside '—don't you be crying now. You've done too much of that these past months.'

'I'm not crying.' Her eyes were dry. It was inside that the tears flowed. Or perhaps she was bleeding where some organ she could not put a name to had been wrenched out. It could not be her heart, she could feel that beating, hard and fast.

Mab stomped across the room and sat down on the sofa. 'She loves him and he'll do the best he can for her by the sounds of it. He'll be one of those gentlemen who'll stick by family come hell or high water—it's part of their pride. You've just got to be glad for her and get on with your own life. He'll be off abroad again soon, those diplomatic gentlemen are all over the place. Think of all the sights she'll see, the things she'll do. And when she's all grown up he'll give her a big dowry and find her a nice man to marry and she'll be happy, just you see.'

'I know.' *I know. It is the right thing. I am happy that she is alive and so clever and bright and kind and lovely. But she will never know that Piers was her real father, she will never know that her mother loved her and wanted her.* 'I am going to stay for a week. Just a week. I will see her again, I will make certain she is truly safe and happy and then I will go back to London and take off my blacks and rejoin society.'

'A good thing, too. But who's going to chaperon you,

then?' Mab asked. 'You turned down all those fubsy creatures that came in answer to the advertisement.' She stood up and administered a brisk pat on the shoulder before going to hunt for her duster.

'I have written to my mother's cousin Florence. She is a widow and she isn't in very comfortable circumstances. She says she'd be delighted to be my companion.'

'What? Lady Carstairs? The one your mama always said had feathers for brains? She'll be no use as a chaperon.'

'I am too old to need one of those. I just need a lady companion to give me countenance.'

'Huh.' Mab snorted.

'Yes, I know, I am shockingly fast and have no countenance to preserve, some would say, but I am not seeking a husband. So long as I am received, I really don't mind.'

'There'll be many a man who'd overlook a slip-up in your past.'

'For the sake of my bloodlines and dowry, you mean?' Just as there would be gentlemen who would overlook Alice's birth when the time came, all for the sake of her powerful father and the money he would dower her with. 'I don't believe there is and I don't want a man who would *overlook* something for anything but love.' And none of them would get close enough to her heart to arouse such emotion. She did not have the courage to risk it, one more wound would kill her.

Coward, a small voice jeered. Once she had been prepared to do anything for love. Not now. Now the only

battle she was prepared to fight and be hurt in was the
one for Alice's welfare

Mab suddenly slapped her own forehand with the
palm of her hand. 'I'll disremember my own name one
of these days. You had some callers while you were out.
It went right out of my mind when you came back just
now in that smart carriage, white as a sheet. They left
their cards. I'll go and get them.'

'Three.' Laura picked up the cards and found all were
from married ladies and all had the corners turned to
indicate that they had called in person. 'Your visit to
the village shop has obviously caused some interest.'

'A right gossipy body she is behind the counter, so
she'll have told everyone who came in. I was careful
to say who you were so they'd know we were respectable and there'd be no problem with credit. Who you are
pretending to be,' Mab corrected herself with a sniff.

'Mrs Gordon, The Honourable Mrs Philpott and
Mrs Trimmett. She is the rector's wife, I assume, as
the address is the rectory. I will call on them tomorrow, they all have At Homes on Tuesdays according to
their cards.'

'What, and risk them finding something out?'

'Why should they suspect I am not who I say? I am
not pretending to be someone whose status might ex-
cite their curiosity and it will look strange if I do not.'
Laura fanned out the cards in her hand and realised
she had reached a decision. 'I will stay for a week and
I will find out all I can about Lord Wykeham. These
ladies and their friends will be agog about his arrival
and full of information.'

'You always say you despise gossip,' Mab muttered.

'And so I do, but I will use it if I have to. I'd wager a fair number of guineas that all these ladies know just about everything there is to know about what goes on at the Manor. All I have to do is give them the opportunity to tell me.'

One of the disadvantages of her disguise was not having a footman in attendance, or a carriage to arrive in, Laura reflected as she rapped the knocker on the rectory door the following afternoon.

'Madam?' The footman who opened the door to her was certainly not a top-lofty London butler, which was a relief. She could hardly assume the airs of an earl's daughter if he snubbed her.

Laura handed him her card. 'Is Mrs Trimmett at home?'

He scarcely glanced at the name. It was certainly more casual in the country. 'Certainly, Mrs Jordan. Please enter, ma'am.' He relieved her of her parasol and flung open a door. 'Mrs Jordan, ma'am.'

There were two ladies seated either side of a tea tray. One, grey-haired and plump, surged to her feet. 'Mrs Jordan! Good day, ma'am. How good of you to call, please, allow me to introduce Mrs Gordon.' She had all the rather forceful assurance of a lady who knew her position in the community was established and who spent her life organising committees, social gatherings, charity events and the lives of anyone who allowed her to.

Laura and Mrs Gordon—a faded blonde of indeterminate years—exchanged bows and Laura sat down.

Two birds with one stone, she thought with an inward smile. 'I am so sorry I was out yesterday when you were both kind enough to leave your cards. As a stranger to the village it is most welcome to make new acquaintances.'

Over cups of tea Laura endured a polite inquisition and obligingly shared details of her fictitious bereavement, her depressed state of health and her need to have a change of air and scene before facing the world again. The two ladies tutted with sympathy, assured her earnestly that Westerwood Magna was a delightful, healthful spot where she would soon recover both health and spirits, and delicately probed her background and family.

Laura shared some of her invented history and nibbled a somewhat dry biscuit.

'You will find everyone most amiable and welcoming here,' Mrs Gordon said. She was, Mab had reported, the wife of a city lawyer who had retired to a small country estate and spent his time fishing and breeding gun dogs.

'I do hope so,' Laura murmured, seizing her opportunity. 'I fear I may have inadvertently inconvenienced the lord of the manor yesterday.'

'Lord Wykeham?' Both ladies were instantly on the alert.

'Yes, I became lost crossing his park and strayed off the footpath. The earl came across me and I was startled and turned my ankle. In the event he was kind enough to offer me refreshment and send me home in a carriage.' It was impossible to keep that sort of thing secret in a small village and she saw from the avid look in their eyes that they had already heard that she had been seen in a vehicle from the Manor.

'Well! How embarrassing for you,' Mrs Trimmett remarked with ill-concealed relish as she leaned forward in an encouraging manner.

'It was a trifle awkward, but he acquitted me of trespass. Oh, you mean the refreshments? Just a cup of tea on the lawn with one of the female staff in attendance. I would not have gone inside, naturally.'

'Naturally,' they chorused, obviously dying to do just that themselves.

'Do tell us,' Mrs Gordon urged, 'what is the earl like? My husband has left his card, of course, and they have met, but he has not yet called.'

'He was perfectly punctilious and civil, but I found him arrogant, you know. Perhaps it is just those devilish flyaway eyebrows—'

The two ladies opposite her went very still, their eager expressions frozen into identical stilted smiles. Too late Laura felt the draught from the opening door on the nape of her neck.

'The Earl of Wykeham,' the footman announced.

Chapter Four

It seemed impossible the earl had not heard, which left two alternatives, once Laura had stifled the immediate instinct to flee the room. She could apologise and probably dig herself even deeper into the hole or pretend the words had never been uttered.

'My...my lord.' Even Mrs Trimmett's self-assurance seemed shaken. 'How good of you to call. May I make Mrs Gordon known to you?' The matron managed to utter a conventional greeting. 'And Mrs Jordan I believe you know,' she added as the earl moved into the room.

'Mrs Gordon. And, Mrs Jordan, we meet again. Are you quite recovered from your fall yesterday?' His voice was silk-smooth, so bland that Laura was suddenly doubtful whether he had heard her *faux pas* after all. Willing away what she was certain must be hectic colour in her cheeks, she sipped the cooling tea. *Thank Heavens he has been seated to one side of me!*

'I have no pain at all now, thank you, Lord Wykeham.' Laura shot a glance at the clock, mercifully in the opposite direction to the earl. She had been there twenty minutes which meant, by the rules governing morning calls, Mrs Gordon should be departing soon, her own half-hour having passed. 'I was just telling the ladies that I trespassed in your delightful park yesterday.' She smiled and shook her head at Mrs Trimmett's gesture towards the tea pot. She would finish this cup and then could most properly make her escape. Mrs Gordon was obviously determined to hang on now this intriguing visitor had arrived, never mind the etiquette of the situation.

'No trespass at all and my daughter, Alice, was delighted to meet you.'

Both the older women stiffened and the polite smiles became thin-lipped. *He has done that on purpose,* Laura thought. *It wasn't thoughtless—he wants to see how they react.* Then the realisation hit her. *That is my daughter they are pokering up with disapproval over.*

'Miss Alice is a delightful child,' she said. 'Such charming manners and so pretty and bright. A credit to you, my lord. I do hope she soon makes some little friends in the area. Do you have grandchildren, Mrs Trimmett?'

The vicar's wife looked as though she had been poked with a pin. 'Er...no, they are all in Dorset. Such a pity.'

'Mine will be coming to stay next week,' Mrs Gordon said. 'My two dear granddaughters, aged six and eight. Perhaps Miss Alice would like to come to tea?' Her expression was such a mixture of smugness and alarm that Laura almost laughed. She could read the older woman's mind—an earl's daughter…but illegitimate. The chance of an entrée to the Big House…but the risk that her neighbours might disapprove.

Laura told herself that she had defended Alice and perhaps made some amends for her tactless remark about Lord Wykeham, which, whatever she thought about him, had been inexcusable.

'I am happy to accept on Alice's behalf,' he said.

Laura risked a sideways glance and encountered a pleasant, totally bland smile with just the faintest hint of mischief about it. Or was she imagining that? 'Well, this has been delightful, thank you, Mrs Trimmett. I am hoping to find Mrs Philpott at home,' she added as she got to her feet. Lord Wykeham stood, looming far too close for comfort in the feminine little parlour.

'I called on her about an hour ago,' Mrs Gordon said. 'So you will certainly find her at Laurel Lodge. Such a pleasure to meet you, Mrs Jordan.'

With a further exchange of civilities, and a slight bow to the earl who was holding the door for her, Laura left, hoping it did not appear such a flight as it felt.

A smart curricle with a groom in the seat stood outside the vicarage. The earl's, she assumed, sparing the pair of matched bays an envious glance as she passed. The groom touched his hat to her as she set off around the green that led past a group of cottages and towards the turning that Mab had told her led to Laurel Lodge.

Laura dawdled, hoping that fresh air and time would do something to restore her inner composure. She touched the inside of her wrist above the cuff of her glove to her cheek and was relieved to find it cool and

not, as she had feared, flaming with embarrassment.
What had possessed her? Probably, she concluded, a
desire to hear Wykeham abused by the other women,
to hear some scandalous gossip about him to confirm
her in her dislike of him. And now all she had done
was to ensure he would not dream of inviting her to
the Manor again. She had quite effectively cut herself
off from her daughter.

'Very rustic this, my lord,' Gregg observed, his arms
folded firmly across his chest; his face, Avery knew
without having to glance sideways, set in a slight sneer.

'That is one of the characteristics of the countryside,
yes,' he agreed.

'Hardly what we're used to, my lord.'

'No, indeed.' And singularly lacking in theatres, tav-
erns, pleasure gardens and other sources of entertainment for a good-looking, middle-aged groom with an
eye for a pretty girl and a liking for a lively time, he
supposed. 'We'll be off to London in a week or two,' he
offered his brooding henchman. Tom Gregg had been
with him for over ten years and enjoyed a freedom not
permitted to any of his other staff.

Gregg gave a grunt of satisfaction and Avery went
back to pondering the mystery that was Mrs Jordan. Just
what did she find so objectionable about him? Other
than his eyebrows, which could hardly be provocation
enough to make a well-bred lady express a dislike to
two near strangers. Her manner to him had been impeccable, if cool, and yet he was constantly aware of
a watchfulness about her and, ridiculous as it might

sound, a hostility. Perhaps she was like that with all men. It could be, he supposed, that her marriage had been an unhappy one, but his instincts told him it was more personal than that.

Which was a pity, as well as a mystery. Mrs Jordan was an attractive woman and Alice liked her. And, he supposed, with a wry smile at his own vanity, he was not used to ladies taking against him.

'You turn right here, my lord.' Gregg gestured towards a lane leading off the green.

So now he had a choice. He could allow himself to be routed by a sharp-tongued widow in drab weeds or he could endure her dislike for half an hour at Mrs Philpott's house. No, damn it, he thought, guiding the pair into the lane, Mrs Philpott had young relatives, so he had been told, and he was not going to deprive Alice of some possible playmates because of Mrs Jordan's prejudices.

And there she was, strolling along the lane in front of him as though she did not have a care in the world. No maid with her again, he noticed, and certainly no footman. But this was broad daylight in a placid little village, so perhaps there was no conclusion to be drawn from that about her resources, her respectability or her background.

His horses were walking, the ground was soft and it seemed she had not heard him. Avery allowed the pair to draw alongside her without speaking and noticed the start she gave when one of them snorted. She was so composed in voice and expression and yet her body seemed to betray her feelings as though she had no command over her nerves. He recalled the flush of pink at the nape of her neck when she realised he was in the room and must have heard her cutting words. He had wanted to touch that warm skin, he had wondered how far the blush had spread...

'Mrs Jordan. Good afternoon once more. May I take you up as far as Mrs Philpott's house?'

Her eyes flickered to Gregg's sturdy figure. 'Thank you, Lord Wykeham, but I am enjoying the exercise.' She turned and walked on.

So, she did not want to talk in front of his groom. Fair enough. 'Gregg, take the reins,' he said. 'Be outside Laurel Lodge in half an hour.' This needed settling.

She did not glance at it as the curricle passed her, but he made no attempt to keep his long stride silent, so her lack of surprise when he reached her side was only to be expected. This time she was completely in control of her reactions. 'My lord? I hardly feel I require an escort for a few hundred yards up a country lane.'

'But I require a conversation.'

'And an apology, no doubt. Please accept my regrets for my discourteous words at the vicarage, my lord.'

'I wish you would stop calling me *my lord*.' It was not what he had meant to say and her startled glance showed he had surprised her as much as himself.

'And what should I call you?'

'My name is Avery, Caroline.'

'And are we on such terms that we call each other by our Christian names? I believe I would recall it if we were childhood friends or cousins.'

'I would be friends. I am unclear what I have done

to make you dislike me. If I have offended you in some way, I would like to repair that.'

'How could you have offended me?' she asked without looking at him. 'We have only just met. And why should you wish me as a friend?'

'Alice likes you. More feminine influence in her life is desirable, I think.'

She caught her breath and something in the whisper of sound seemed to touch him at the base of the spine. *So that's what this is... I desire this prickly, difficult, wan-faced widow.* Avery stopped and, as though he had put out a hand to restrain her, she did, too. 'Look at me.'

Caroline half-turned to face him and studied his face, her own expression grave. As she had in the park, she seemed to look with an intensity that probed not just his appearance, but his thoughts and his character. Every muscle under the fine skin of her face seemed taut, there was wariness, almost fear in the dark eyes, and now something else. Something he would wager she did not want to feel at all.

'Whatever else there is between us,' Avery murmured, thinking out loud, 'there is physical attraction.'

'You flatter yourself!' She looked as outraged as he might have expected and also utterly taken aback.

'No, there is nothing to be vain about in an instinctive reaction. But I am right, am I not?' He had dragged off his right glove as they spoke and now he touched his fingers to her cheek. Warm, soft skin. The muscles flinched a little beneath his touch, but she did not step back, or brush his hand away or slap him. 'Has someone hurt you, Caroline?'

He read the answer in her eyes, an almost bottomless lack of trust, but her reply showed no weakness. 'Again, you flatter yourself to believe that my unwillingness to flirt with you is due to some flaw in my own experience.'

'I do not seek to flirt.' And he did not, he realised. Such superficiality would only make the itch to touch her far, far worse. 'I only want your company for my daughter and to understand what it is that sparks between us and yet seems to cause you so much pain.'

Her lids fell, covering the darkness of her eyes. When she opened them she seemed to have come to a decision. 'I have no reason to trust men, least of all strong, authoritative men who seek to order the lives of others. But it is a long time since… I cannot help it if there is some awareness in me of a virile man. I do not wish to discuss this.'

Or act upon it, that was very clear. *What manner of man had her husband been? A tyrant? A domineering bully? And yet a man who had awakened her sensually.* The two things were not mutually exclusive, he told himself.

'I do not seek to take advantage of you, merely, as I said, to understand.'

'And understanding people is your stock in trade, is it not?' Caroline Jordan began to walk slowly towards their destination. His uncharacteristically impulsive words had not, it seemed, deepened her distrust of him.

'It is. I study their motives, their strengths and weaknesses. The points on which they will yield and the points upon which they will stand fast until death.'

'I will visit Alice, if you wish,' she said, almost as though her words followed on from what he had just said. The charged intimacy still surrounded them like a mist and yet she seemed capable of ignoring it. 'Does she have a governess?'

'No, but I intend to employ one for her very soon. She is naturally very bright, I think. However, I do not want to stifle her enthusiasm and energy through rigorous teaching.'

'You must choose carefully.' She seemed calmer now, more at ease with him. Avery pulled on his glove and fell into step beside her. 'A young woman, one with a natural manner and energy herself would be best. Alice is just like I—'

'Yes?'

'Like I recall my best friend Imogen was at about that age. An older, more formal woman would stifle her character.'

It was not what she had meant to say, he suspected. 'Caroline,' Avery said and she did not react. 'Caroline?'

'Oh! I beg your pardon, I was woolgathering. You should not call me by my given name, you know.'

Woolgathering? In the middle of a conversation that started with a discussion of sexual attraction and moved on to a subject she professes an interest in? It was almost as though she did not recognise her own name...

'I was considering the question of governesses,' Caroline said. 'I know women are supposed to be able to think of seven different things at once, but I fear I cannot.'

It was the closest she had come to making a joke in

his presence. Avery reproved himself for his suspicions. That was what came of spending too much time in the company of professional dissemblers, outright spies and manipulative women.

He heard Caroline take a deep breath as though either shedding a burden or taking one up. 'That must be Laurel Lodge, Avery. Do you think it would be discreet to arrive separately?' Then she answered her own question even as he was masking his surprise at her use of his name. 'Foolish to pretend, for they will all get together and gossip about us anyway.' As he opened the gate for her she slanted a look at him. 'And foolish to allow them to think there is anything to hide.'

'You are quite correct.' Avery knocked, wondering at the composure Caroline layered over the vulnerability that lay like a brittle layer of ice beneath the poise. *Yes, there is nothing to hide except an awareness of each other at a very basic level that is, perhaps, nothing to be surprised about.*

Laura caught Avery's eye across the tea table and suppressed a smile. Their arrival together could not have provided Mrs Philpott, her daughters, two female callers and a youth making a cake of himself over Miss Maria Philpott, with more delicious grounds for speculation if they had planned it. The village was small, the pool of genteel company a mere puddle, a mysterious widow and an internationally well-known diplomat and earl would create a gossip broth that might last for months.

Avery. It had been a struggle to smile and to make

herself relax and allow the familiarity he asked for, but it was necessary if she was to spend time with Alice. Letting go had been like falling from the certainty of one position—dislike and distrust—to the uneasy foothold of distrust and...what exactly? Physical attraction, he had said. And he was right, she could not delude herself. He was a very attractive man to look at, he had intelligence, power, an unabashed masculinity. And he reminded her of Piers in some ways, but a Piers matured, and this man had never been the impetuous romantic his cousin had been.

One of the two female visitors asked her something and Laura made herself focus and smile. Yes, indeed, it was a delightful village and just what she wanted to recover her health. Yes, it was most kind of Lord Wykeham to escort her, although she was sure such a pleasant place was quite safe for a lady to walk alone.

His lordship was flattering Mrs Philpott on the subject of her nieces, who were playing in the garden under the eye of their governess. Perhaps she could advise him on the best way to find a governess for his daughter?

Mrs Philpott, Laura decided, was somewhat more sophisticated and worldly-wise than the vicar's wife. She did not bat an eyelash at mention of Miss Falconer and it was she who made the suggestion that Alice might like to come and play with the girls.

That was satisfactory, Laura decided. Alice would have the opportunity to make friends and she could leave now, the civilities achieved. After all, she would not be here more than another week, although she had no intention of saying so just yet, so she had no need to cultivate acquaintances now she had established her respectability.

Avery accepted another cup of tea and seemed to be handling the languishing looks of Miss Philpott, a fresh-faced brunette, with skill. Now would be a good time to make her escape, for he could hardly abandon both tea and young lady without giving offence.

Laura made her way home along the lane, repeating mentally, *Caroline Jordan, Caroline. Caroline.* She had almost been caught out by Avery when he addressed her by her assumed name. If she were to survive a week of close encounters, she must learn to respond to that quite naturally.

What was he hoping for with his remarks about physical attraction and his desire for first-name intimacy? Was this some unusual attempt at seduction? Laura shivered. It had not been easy to deal with that startling statement and the self-recognition that went with it. A man like him would treat a widow very differently than he would an unmarried lady. Perhaps he thought her sophisticated enough for a fleeting liaison.

And she had not lied when she had admitted that it had been a long time. There had been no need to spell it out, he knew they were talking about the last time she lay with a man. The awful thing was, the remembered image of Pier's face as he kissed her, as he lay over her, within her...that face was changing, shifting, becoming the face of Avery Falconer, Earl of Wykeham. Her adversary.

Chapter Five

'**A**stride! In *breeches?*' Avery sounded as scandalised as any prudish matron.

'Certainly astride,' Laura countered. 'Then she can learn balance and control and gain confidence before she has to deal with a side-saddle.'

Alice, clad in clothes borrowed from Cook's grandson, stood watching them, her head moving back and forth like a spectator at a shuttlecock game. The argument had been going on for ten minutes now and the groom holding the little grey pony's head was staring blankly across the paddock, obviously wishing himself elsewhere.

'Is that how you learned to ride?' Avery demanded.

'Certainly.' And she still did when she could get away with it. 'I am only concerned with Alice's safety.'

'Very well.' As she had guessed, that clinched the argument. Avery lifted the child and swung her into the saddle. 'Now you—'

Alice promptly slid her feet into the stirrups, heel

down, toes out, and gathered up the reins. 'Aunt Caroline showed me on the rocking horse in the nursery yesterday while you were out.'

'Aunt?'

Laura shrugged, her nonchalance hiding the warm glow of pride at Alice's quick learning, her trust. 'I appear to have been adopted.'

'So long as you do not mind the familiarity.' Avery took the leading rein from the groom. 'I will take her this first time, Ferris.'

'I am coming, too.' As if she would not watch her daughter's first riding lesson!

Avery cast a dubious look from the paddock's rough grass and muddy patches to her neat leather half-boots, but did not argue. *Sensible man,* she thought. *I wonder where he has learned to humour women.* But he would not be so casual about anything that actually mattered to him.

'Gather up the reins so you can feel the contact with his mouth, press in with your knees and just give him a touch with your heels to tell him to walk on,' Avery ordered.

Alice gave a little squeak of excitement as the pony moved, then sat silent, her face a frown of concentration.

'Let your hands and wrists relax.' Laura reached across to lay her hand over the child's clenched fingers just as Avery did the same thing. Their gloved fingers met, tangled, held. Alice giggled. 'Poor Snowdrop, now we're all riding him.'

'Relax,' Avery murmured and Laura shot him a stern

glance. It had not been the child he was speaking to. 'Shoulders back,' he added as he released her hand to correct Alice's posture.

'And seat in.' Laura patted the target area. 'That's perfect. When you ride side-saddle your back and posterior will be in exactly the same position as now.'

They walked around the paddock twice, speaking only to the child, hands bumping and touching as they reached to adjust her position or steady her. Laura was in heaven. Despite the looming masculine presence on the other side of the pony, and despite the crackle of awareness at every touch, she was with her daughter, able to help her, see her delight. She praised, she reassured, she smiled back as Alice beamed at her, and fought down the emotion that lurked so close to the surface. *Five days left.*

'I want to trot now.'

'No,' Avery said flatly.

'Why not?' Laura countered. 'It is hard work, Alice. You must push down with your heels, tighten your knees and rise up and down with the stride or you'll be jolted until your teeth rattle.'

'She'll not be able to post when she's riding sidesaddle,' Avery pointed out.

'Which is why you see ladies trotting so infrequently, but it will strengthen her legs. Pay attention to your balance and don't jab his mouth, Alice. Use your heels, that's it.'

Off they went, the tall man jogging beside the pony, the excited child bouncing in the saddle, *bump, bump* and then, 'Aunt Caroline, look! I'm going up and down!'

She stood by the gate and watched them until the circuit was completed and Avery came to a halt beside her, not in the least out of breath. For a diplomat he was remarkably fit. She had supposed he would spend all his day at a desk or a conference table, but it seemed she was mistaken.

'Enough, Alice. You'll be stiff in the morning as it is.' He lifted her down. 'Now run inside to Blackie and get changed into something respectable before luncheon.'

He took Laura's arm as the child gave her pony one last pat and then ran off towards the house. 'Thank you.'

'For what?' *For indulging myself with my daughter's presence for an hour? For reassuring myself that you really do care for her and will look after her?*

'For finding her those clothes and persuading me of the benefits of allowing her to learn to ride astride. She is very confident now and that's half the battle. In a week or two we can try her with a side-saddle.'

Laura was not aware of making a sound, but he glanced at her. 'We won't have to have one made. Ferris found a small one in the stable loft. You will stay for luncheon?'

'I—' *I would move in if I could, absorb every impression, every memory. In a week or two we could teach her to ride side-saddle...* Oh, the temptation to stay, to dig herself deeper and deeper into Alice's life, into her affections.

'You hesitate to come inside a bachelor household when I am at home? Alice and her nurse will be adequate chaperons, don't you think?'

'Of course they will. I would be happy to accept.' Not that she now had any worries about what the ladies of the parish might say if they found out. She would be gone in a few days and her purpose in meeting them, to help find Alice some little playmates, had been fulfilled. It was her own equilibrium she was concerned about. That and the man by her side.

Without Alice's presence to distract her Avery seemed to loom over her, tall, solid, an immovable object as much in her mind as in reality. Alice loved him; he, Laura was forced to accept, loved her. He was intelligent, good company, handsome and part of her wanted to like him, wanted...*him*. And yet he had stolen her child with every intention of keeping her from her mother. He had bribed another man's tenants into lying and he would ruthlessly do whatever it took to get what he wanted. She should hate him, but she could not. Instead she envied him, she was jealous of him and she feared him.

And none of those emotions were attractive ones. Hatred was condemned from the pulpit as a sin, of course, but somehow it seemed a more straightforward feeling. If one could express it, of course, Laura pondered as she walked beside Avery Falconer to the house. *Piers's house.* That was another pain, the way Avery had slipped so easily into the role of master here. And it was something else she should not resent, for the tenants were being treated well, the land was in good heart, the servants had employment. It was not this man's fault that his cousin had died, that Piers had broken his word to her, left her before they could marry, abandoned her for some romantic notion of duty and valour.

She was not wearing a bonnet and the breeze blew strands of her hair across her face. Laura pushed them back, wishing she could hold her head in her hands and think, clearly, rationally and not be filled with so many conflicting feelings.

She was conscious that Avery was looking at her, but she kept her eyes down, reluctant to meet his now she was the sole focus of his attention. Ever since he had made that remark about physical attraction he had said or done nothing the slightest bit improper or provocative. As a result Laura found she was constantly braced for words and actions that never came. And she was thinking about him as a man, an attractive man, a desirable man.

Was it a strategy? Was Avery playing with her, hoping she would be intrigued by that statement? Perhaps this was an opening gambit in a game of seduction.

'That was a heavy sigh. Are you tired?'

'Yes. Yes, I am,' she said before she could think better of it. 'I am tired of playing games. Two days ago you spoke of physical attraction between us and then nothing. You do not explain yourself, you do not flirt, you do not try to make love to me. I do not want any of those things, you understand. It is just very unsettling to have them…hovering.'

Under her arm his guiding hand tensed. 'I did explain. I said I felt that attraction and tried to understand it.'

'You had no need to mention it at all.' It had kept her

awake at night. 'It makes me uneasy. And I suspect you intended that.'

'Do you want me to flirt with you?' he asked. Then, when she did not answer, 'Do you want me to make love to you?'

'No!' Laura wrenched her arm away. Avery caught her hand in his, the impetus of her movement swinging her around so they were face-to-face. His face was serious, his eyes dark and intent and assessing. He desired her, she could read it in his face, could see it in his parted lips and the stillness of him. 'I do not flirt.' It was a lie. Her entire life away from this place was a game, a flirtation, an empty farce.

It was very quiet. The stable block was behind them and they had just entered the shrubbery that swept around the east side of the house, thick with laurels and box, the smell of the evergreens aromatic and astringent. A robin was singing high up in an ash tree and the gravel of the path crunched beneath Avery's booted feet. Her pulse was thudding.

'No, you have not done anything that might be construed as flirtation. I wonder then that I sensed what I did. Wishful thinking, perhaps,' Avery said and she saw from the faint smile that he had seen her colour rise. 'You said you did not trust men. Have you come to trust me a little, Caroline?'

'Yes,' she agreed, wary now, only half-believing what she said. Or what she felt. He was going to kiss her. And then what would she do?

'Why?' He was so close now that their toes bumped. She was aware of the smell of saddle soap and horse from his gloves and the warmth of his breath and the cock robin overhead flinging his challenge at every other bird in the vicinity. *Another arrogant male.*

'Because Alice loves you,' she replied with simple truth and watched his mouth, only his mouth, as the smile deepened, slightly askew so a faint dimple appeared on the right, but not on the left. And even then, even though she expected it, the kiss surprised her when it came.

Avery bent his head and brushed his lips across hers, an electric, tickling touch that made every hair on her nape stand up. He did not touch her or try to deepen the caress, but simply tucked her hand under his arm again and walked on.

'You are a wise woman to trust the innocent judgement of a child over your own fears.'

'I did not say I was afraid of you.' Her mouth trembled and she pressed her lips together. A proper kiss she could have dealt with. She would have returned it as an equal and then, as she always did, have made it very clear that nothing would follow. A crude attempt to do more she could have dealt with, too. She had no scruple about kneeing a man in the groin or biting an ear or whatever unladylike manoeuvre was necessary to leave him gasping on the ground in fear for his manhood. She had done that also, more than once.

But that brush of the lips—what was that? Was she being teased as she had so often teased? Best to ignore it, pretend it never happened, pretend that there was no heat in her belly and that she did not ache for his hands on her breasts and his mouth, open over hers. *Oh,*

Piers, how could I feel like this for another man? Was it because of the resemblance between the cousins? She pushed away the thought that she could be so foolish.

'I have drafted an advertisement for a governess,' Avery remarked as they came out of the shrubbery onto the lawn.

'Which newspapers will you put it in?' *So, he can ignore it, too, infuriating man. It should make me like him less, but somehow it does not. Yet I suspect he knows that. Games. We are both playing games.*

'All the London ones and the local press, as well. Will you check it over for me?' She nodded. 'In that case, if you would like to join Alice in the dining room, I will fetch it. Just through here.'

The long windows that faced the garden front were all raised to let in the balmy spring air and Avery helped her over the low sill into a blue-painted room with a table set for luncheon. As she stepped down onto the polished floor he continued outside, presumably to his study.

There was no sign of Alice yet. No doubt Miss Blackstock was scrubbing off every trace of pony and stables and dressing her in a suitable dress for a proper little girl. She should wash, too.

'Can you show me where I can wash my hands?' she asked the maid setting a bowl of fruit on the table.

'Yes, ma'am, this way if you please.'

It was an unexceptional way of exploring, although, disappointingly, all the inner doors off the hall were closed. The girl led her through to a small room with a water closet on one side and a washstand on the other and left her. Laura lingered over cleaning her hands, working up a froth of lavender-scented soap, trickling the cool water through her fingers.

A fantasy was forming in her mind. She would write to her solicitor, her steward, everyone, and explain she was going abroad for an indefinite period. Then she would tell Avery that she would become Alice's governess. He could not deny that the child liked her, responded well to her. He trusted her enough to ask her opinion, he knew from conversation that she was educated, cultured. A lady.

Laura blotted the wetness on a linen towel, watched the fabric grow darker, limp with the water from her hands. It seemed very important to focus on getting every inch of skin quite dry while her mind scrabbled at that fantasy like an overexcited child tearing the wrappings from a present.

And then, as though she had opened the gift and found not the expected doll or sweetmeats, but a book of sermons, acrid as dust, her hands were dry and her mind clear. She could not do it. How long could she live so close to Alice and not betray herself? She would be a servant in her own daughter's home, someone with no real power, no control. Sooner or later Avery would find her out and then she would have to leave and Alice would lose someone she might have grown very fond of. It was too painful to think the word *love*.

Avery was crossing the hall when she emerged, her hair smooth, her expression calm, even the trace of a blush from that kiss subdued by cool water and willpower.

'What do you think?' He handed her a sheet of paper. 'Will you look at it now in the study, before Alice comes down?'

He watched Laura as she stood, head bent over the draft. Her hair was rigorously tidy, each strand disciplined back into a severe chignon. It did not look like hair that relished control, it looked as though it wanted to be loose, waving, its colours catching the sun in shades from blonde to soft brown. Her cheeks were smooth, pale with less than the natural colour of health in them and none of the blush that had stained them when she had thrown that challenge at him in the shrubbery.

Her lips moved slightly, parted, and her tongue emerged just to touch the centre of her upper lip. He guessed it was a habitual sign of concentration, but it sent the blood straight to his groin. Those lips under his, smooth and warm. They had clung for a moment against his while he had wrestled with the urge to possess, feel her open under him, to taste her. He was confusing her and he wished he understood why.

'You state that the person appointed must be willing to travel.'

'Yes, that is essential. I expect to be sent abroad again before the year is out and I will take Alice with me.'

'You had best say it means to the Continent, then, and not simply on a tour of the Lakes.' Her lips quivered into a slight smile and were serious again.

Avery fought with temptation and yielded to it. 'I was

wondering... I know you said Alice would benefit from a younger governess, but I wondered about a widow.'

A shiver went through Caroline, so faint he saw it merely in the movement of her pearl earbobs. He held his breath. Was he being too obvious? And what, in blazes, was he thinking of in any case?

Chapter Six

What could he tell from Caroline's stillness? The downcast lids did not lift, nor the dark lashes move. Perhaps he had imagined that shiver, perhaps she had no notion he was talking about her. 'Not all widows are middle-aged,' she pointed out after a moment.

'No, indeed. Such as yourself.' Avery wondered just how old she was. The ageing effect of her black clothes, and the paleness of her skin, made it difficult to tell, but he doubted she could be much over twenty-five. 'I was just wondering if someone with more experience of children would be better.'

'And not all widows have had children,' Caroline said, her voice so lacking in expression it might as well have been a scream.

Hell and damnation. She told you she had lost a child. Get your great boot out of your mouth, Falconer, and stop daydreaming. It had been a nice little fantasy about Caroline Jordan as Alice's governess, but what did that make him, lusting after his daughter's teacher, a woman who would be under his protection in his house? *A lecher, that's what,* Avery told himself. He despised men who took advantage of their female dependants.

'You see how much I need you to stop me wandering off at tangents,' he said.

'It seems strange that a man who can steer the fate of nations at the conference table finds it hard to advertise for a governess.' Caroline sounded faintly amused, thank heavens.

'The devil's in the details,' he said, snatching at a cliché in desperation. He had told the Duke of Wellington to stop interfering before now. He had faced down the most powerful of the Emperor Alexander's ministers and he could negotiate in five languages, but this one woman, with her emotional buttons done up so tightly over whatever was going on in her bosom, had him in knots.

And that's because when you are dealing with Wellington you aren't thinking with the parts of your anatomy that are giving you hell now. Although it isn't simply desire.

'Papa! Aunt Caroline! Luncheon is ready and I am *starving.*'

'Coming, Alice.' Avery lowered his voice as he took the paper from Caroline. 'Do you suppose a governess will be able to stop her stampeding about like a herd of goats and shouting at the top of her voice?'

'Oh, I hope not.' Mrs Jordan's smile was curiously tender. 'Not all the time.'

Avery watched Caroline during the meal and Caroline watched Alice. Not him. Which meant he had either so comprehensively embarrassed her that she did not dare risk catching his eye or that she was completely indifferent to him. And yet his reckless remark about desire had discomforted her to the extent that she had challenged him about it this morning. She had neither screamed, nor slapped his face when he had kissed her, but she had given him no encouragement either.

So...not a merry window or even one sophisticated enough to contemplate an irregular liaison. He suspected she was not mourning her husband in anything but the outward show of black clothing and quiet living. There was a mystery there.

'Was your husband a landowner, Mrs Jordan?'

'In a small way. He was a military man.' She prepared an apple for Alice, scarcely glancing at him as she controlled the peel that curled from her knife.

'From this part of the world?'

'We lived in London when we were together.' Her hand was quite steady with the sharp blade. 'There, Alice. Now, I was careful to get it all off in one piece, which is very important for this magic to work. If you hold up the peel, very high, and drop it, it will make the initial of your husband-to-be.'

Alice giggled. 'That can't be right, Aunt Caroline. You peeled it, so you will have to drop it.'

'I have no intention of marrying again.'

'Please?'

Avery watched, amused that the wide-eyed green stare, combined with the faint tremble of the lower lip, worked just as well on Mrs Jordan as it did on him. He shuddered to think of the impact on young men when Alice was old enough to make her come-out. He would have to carry a shotgun at all times.

'Oh, very well. It will come out with a Z or an X or something improbable.' Caroline held up the peel and dropped it. She and Alice studied it with all the care of scientists with a lens. 'I cannot make anything of it,' she said at last. 'The magic obviously works and it knows I will not marry again.'

Avery leaned across the table. 'It is a lower-case *a,*' he said. 'It is facing me, that is why you cannot read it. See, the round shape and the little tail.'

'A is for Avery,' Alice exclaimed.

There was a deadly little silence, then Caroline said, 'Your papa will be marrying a titled lady, Alice. She is probably dropping her apple peel at just this moment and it is coming out as a capital A, the right way up.'

'You have the makings of a diplomat,' Avery remarked softly as Alice became engrossed in making letters with pieces of peel while she nibbled on her apple segments. 'I am sorry if we have embarrassed you between us this morning.'

'I am not embarrassed,' Caroline said and returned her attention to the piece of fruit on her own plate.

And she was not, he realised. But she was distressed. He was learning to read her emotions behind the calm facade and her eyes were sparkling as if with unshed tears and her hand shook, just a little, as she wielded the sharp little knife. What the devil had her husband done to her to make her so fragile on the subject of marriage?

* * *

He is going to marry some day and Alice will have a stepmother. She will call her Mama *and she will love her. They will be a family in some glamorous European capital while Avery is a diplomat and then they will host great house parties at Wykeham Hall when they return to England. Alice will grow up and another woman will help her choose her gowns and will share her secrets and those first tears over a flirtation. Another woman will... Stop it!*

It was self-indulgent and as foolish as prodding a bruise to see if it hurt. Of course it hurt, but her heartbreak was not important. Alice was what mattered. Only Alice. Laura glanced up and saw Avery was watching her. He knew she was upset and his face was grave. Strange how she was beginning to be able to read his face, the thoughts behind the skilful diplomatic mask. Would there have been as much subtlety and intelligence in Piers's face as he matured to the age this man was now?

He smiled at her, a little rueful, the expression of a friend who wants to help, but is not quite sure how. He would not look like that if he knew she was deceiving him or who she was, she thought with a kick of conscience.

'May I get down, Papa?'

'Ask Mrs Jordan's permission.'

'Certainly. Go and play, Alice.' Inevitably the door banged behind her. Then they were alone and she could say the thing her conscience was prodding her to say. 'I apologise.'

'Whatever for?' Avery was leaning back in his chair, but he sat up at that.

'I thought you arrogant and I made judgements about how well a single man could raise a child. It was wrong of me. Prejudiced.'

'And I apologise for making assumptions about how a widow might wish to flirt.'

'That is what it was? You must forgive me if I am a trifle innocent about these things.' She was not, of course, but she wanted to maintain the fiction that her world was not that of the *haut ton*. But while he was being so frank, she could seize the opportunity to remove a small worry about Alice's welfare. 'Do you not keep a mistress?'

The look he gave her was forbidding, but he answered without hesitation. 'I have done. Not very recently and not in this country. And I would never allow a future mistress anywhere near Alice, if that is what is worrying you.'

'So, when you were hinting just now that I might take the position of governess, that negated any chance you might offer me a very different position?'

'That is frankness if ever I heard it!' That question jolted him out of his composure, which was interesting. When he recovered his countenance, with a speed that spoke volumes for his self-control, she thought he might be faintly amused under the surprise. 'Allow me to be equally frank in return. I thought about that for a moment. And I am ashamed of myself, I own it, so you have no cause to look at me like that from those wide brown eyes.'

'Like what?' She had thought her emotions were well hidden.

'As though you are disappointed in me. Although perhaps I should welcome some heat in your regard after your usual Arctic chill.'

'You talk nonsense, my lord. I must leave now.' *Before this becomes any more complicated.*

'You will come tomorrow?' he asked as she retrieved her bonnet, reticule and shawl from the hall stand.

The servants had made themselves scarce. *Perhaps they know better than to intrude when their master is with a woman. No, that is unfair, I trust him when he says he would never expose Alice to one of his* chères amies.

'No,' Laura said crisply. 'It is not convenient tomorrow. Please say goodbye to Alice for me.'

Avery opened the door for her without speaking and she walked briskly down the drive, feeling his eyes on her back for every step. *That had been remarkably like a tantrum,* she told herself as she turned left into the lane in the direction of the village. *Or a lovers' quarrel. Only we are not lovers and he did no quarrelling.*

It was not difficult to work out what was upsetting her, only to know how to cope with it. The situation with Alice was clear enough, if painful. At least she had a clear conscience and the comfort of knowing she was doing what was best for her daughter, however much it hurt.

But Avery Falconer was tying her in knots. They had shockingly frank conversations about desire and yet she could be open with him about nothing else. She wanted him with a directness that was unmistakable, but she did not know why. Was it because he looked so much like Piers, but mature and reliable? Or was it that he was a devastatingly attractive man who was open about his attraction to her? Perhaps it was simply that she could not forgive him for stealing Alice, however well meant his actions, and therefore everything about him, good and bad, was exaggerated.

Whatever she thought of him, and however much he loved Alice now, she could not forget that love and concern for an unknown baby could not have motivated him to buy the child. Pride, arrogance and the certainty that he knew best for anyone who might be connected with the lofty Earl of Wykeham was what had driven him then and it was pure chance that good had come of it.

Oh, but she ached for him.

'Cutting off your nose to spite your face, are you?' Mab demanded over the breakfast table the next morning.

'Probably.' Laura bit into a slice of toast, chewed, thought, swallowed. 'Do sit down, Mab, you make my head ache stomping about. I have so few days left with Alice and I'm a fool to allow one mystifying man to stop me spending them with her.'

'Mystifying, is he?' Mab poured herself some tea and planted herself on the chair across the kitchen table. 'Not the word I'd use, myself. Downright—' She broke off and was lost in thought, searching for the word. 'Edible. I could think of other ways to describe him, but none of them decent.' She buttered a slice of toast and applied plum preserve with a lavish hand. 'Saw him riding past yesterday morning, first thing. Got a handsome pair of shoulders on him. And thighs,' she added. 'You'd know you'd got something in your bed with that one, right enough.'

'Mab!'

'Well, I'm female with eyes in my head and I've got a pulse, haven't I? Good-sized nose and feet...'

'Mab!' *Piers had big feet, too... Oh, stop it, you are as bad as she is.* 'All right, I am not dead either. Avery Falconer is very attractive. And intelligent. And he is good to Alice. And I like him. I just cannot forgive him.'

'Worse things to forgive a man for than giving a child a loving home.' Mab demolished the toast and picked up her tea. 'You and Mr Piers made a right hash of things between you, thinking with your...well, not thinking at all, if you ask me. You should have insisted he marry you before you got into bed with him and he ought to have cared enough about you not to have risked it. And don't look at me like that, you know it is true.'

It was like being slapped in the face. No, it was like having a bucket of cold water poured over a fragile sugar tower of illusion. Young love, passion, an undying, innocent romance—or two young people being thoughtless? She had built a castle in the air and inhabited it with her perfect knight, her gallant soldier, and hadn't the wit to think through the likely consequences of sleeping with a man off to a battlefield in the near future. And Piers had not fought hard enough to behave like a gentleman and not a randy young soldier.

More than time to let go of girlish fantasies. There

was no such thing as undying love or she wouldn't feel so much as a twinge of desire for Avery Falconer. And Avery was guilty of nothing more than a strong sense of family duty and an honourable obligation to the child of a cousin he was probably very fond of. He had taken Alice for Piers's sake.

Mab eyed her warily, braced, no doubt, for a blistering retort about the impudence of maidservants daring to speak their mind, or floods of tears. 'Thank you, Mab. You are quite right.' Not that it didn't hurt or was shaming to have the truth pointed out so bluntly, but it was probably like lancing a boil, she'd be glad later when the agony subsided.

'And you are quite right about today, too. I'll walk up to the Manor now. It is foolish to waste a minute with Alice.'

I will be pleasant and friendly and make it quite clear I want neither flirtation nor kisses, she resolved half an hour later as she negotiated the steps up the ha-ha and tackled the sloping lawn. Halfway she met Jackson, the footman, his hands full of a dew-wet hoop and ball.

'Miss Alice forgets her toys, ma'am,' he said with his friendly grin. 'Were you coming to see her? Only Miss Blackstock's taken her off to Hemel Hempstead in the gig to buy new shoes. You've just missed them.'

The disappointment was ridiculously sharp, not less for it being her own fault. If she hadn't been sulking over Avery she might have been in time to have joined the shopping expedition. 'I will just say good morning to Lord Wykeham, in that case,' she said, summoning a smile.

'He's in the Blue Sitting Room, ma'am. The window's open if you can manage the step.' He pointed. 'Or I can go in and announce you?'

'No, you continue your search for the contents of the toy box, Jackson. I can find my own way.'

Her footsteps were silent on the smooth flagstones. Laura stooped to look into the unfamiliar room and saw Avery. He was half-seated on the edge of a desk, his long legs out in front crossed at the ankles, his hands behind, bracing him. His head was down as though he was deep in thought. Laura hesitated, her hand on the window frame for balance, then caught her breath as he looked up, his face stark and naked as she had never seen it.

He must have heard her involuntary gasp, for he turned, his expression under control so fast she wondered if she had imagined the pain. 'Caroline. I was not expecting you today.'

'I know. I have missed Alice, haven't I?' She stepped down into the room. 'Avery, what is wrong?' The shadow of that inner agony was still on his face, now she knew to look for it. 'My dear man...' She went towards him, her hands held out and he stood, pushed away from the table and she was in his arms.

He said nothing before he kissed her, his mouth urgent and demanding, his tongue tangling with hers as she responded, opened to him as though they were old lovers who knew each other's bodies with utter familiarity. She knew how he would taste, how he would feel in her arms. She knew, as she kissed him back, how he would angle his head, how he would explore her mouth, how she would melt into him. He was everything her restless night-time imaginings had promised he would be and more. *And he is* this *man, not another, not Piers.*

He had turned as he kissed her and she felt the hard edge of the table press into her buttocks, the hard ridge of his arousal press into her belly. Desperate for air so that she could kiss him again, Laura dragged her mouth free. His eyes were dark and fierce and wild, the eyes of a man whose control was always perfect—until now.

'Caroline.' It was a growl, a statement, not a question.

Caroline? Who? Laura froze. Caroline was not her. Caroline was a lie and she could not be like this with a man she was lying to. 'Avery.' She slid her hands down so they rested on his chest. Under her palms his heartbeat thudded. He stared down at her and slowly the darkness of passion faded out of his eyes.

'Avery,' she said again. 'I cannot—'

'Hell. No, of course you cannot.' She blinked, confused. How could he know what she was going to say? 'I apologise. That was outrageous. I had no right to touch you. I'll leave.'

'No.' Of course, he thought she was saying she could not make love to him. He was not a mind reader. But thank goodness he had stopped before things had gone any further. 'You do not need to do that. It takes two to be as imprudent as we have just been. I take responsibility for my actions. And reactions,' she added with a smile in the hope of easing the tension that showed in his jaw and clenched hands. *Yes, this time, I will take responsibility and I will think of the consequences.*

'Thank you.' Avery turned and ran one hand through his hair. 'I was feeling a trifle blue devilled, not that it is any excuse for attempting to ravish you on the desk.'

She was never sure afterwards what she had intended to say to him. Laura looked up and saw the portrait on the wall behind him and the words simply dried in her mouth. *Piers*.

Chapter Seven

A very turned to follow her gaze. 'That is my cousin Piers Falconer,' he said. 'I inherited this estate from him. I do not wonder that you look surprised. It is uncanny, is it not? People often take it for a picture of me and remark that they hadn't realised I had ever been in the army.' He did not appear to find it amusing.

Laura looked into the clear green eyes in the youthful, unlined face in the painting and her feet took her, with no conscious volition, to stand on the hearth where she could reach up and touch the hilt of the sword. *Go away,* she willed Avery, but he did not move. 'He was killed in battle?' She knew the answer, but she had to say something.

'A stupid, unnecessary skirmish with the enemy where they were not supposed to be because of a failure in communications. Ironic that a man who dreamed of glory and great epic battles should die defending a ford over a stream that shouldn't even have needed defending.'

'Ironic indeed.' *That was what you left me for, Piers,* she thought. *I was so angry with you.* 'He was a romantic about war?' Her fingers slid off the leather of the hilt, still too new to have lost its grooves or to have softened and moulded to the hand of its owner.

'Piers was army-mad. But he was an only child, the heir. His father died when he was seventeen and I became his trustee, although I was not that much older— four years. I pointed out that he could not join, that he had responsibilities, that his mother would be desperately anxious, but he only laughed. She would be proud, he said, and of course he would not be killed. He thought himself immortal, I suppose. He was very young in some ways.' Avery sounded bone-weary, perhaps with the memory of endless arguments.

'But he joined anyway.'

'Oh, yes. As soon as he was twenty and came into some money from his godfather he went to London and bought himself a commission. There was nothing I could do and his mother, who had always indulged him, hid her fear. She died six months later. I suppose I cannot blame him for it, he never knew Aunt Alice's heart was weak.' Avery had wandered across to the window and stood leaning his shoulder against the frame, staring out over the parkland. 'He came back to England on sick leave. A combination of a minor wound and a fever. They gave him three months to recover and to settle affairs after his mother's death, although I'd handled that already.' He shrugged one shoulder as if to push away the memory. 'She was more like a mother to me than an aunt.'

'That is why Alice is named as she is.' Piers had never told her his mother's name or that she had died such a short time before they met. It seemed strange, she had thought they had shared everything. How little she had known him.

'Yes. Anyway, he recovered his health well and he was due to return on the next troop carrier, two days hence, when he told me he was going to make some excuse and delay.'

'Why?' Laura breathed, knowing full well why.

'He had become entangled with some air-headed chit and wanted to stay with her. I pointed out that by the terms of his father's will he could not marry without the consent of his trustees until he was twenty-one in six weeks' time and I was not giving my approval. He said in that case he would suffer a relapse and miss the ship.'

'She was so ineligible?' Laura asked. By some miracle she kept the shake out of her voice.

'No.' Again that shrug. 'Excellent family, no doubt a perfectly adequate dowry. But she was too young and he most certainly was, and they'd known each other a matter of weeks.'

Five weeks. Four weeks as lovers, long enough to create a child.

'Piers became very agitated, said he'd go sick for six years if it took that, let alone the six weeks until he could marry.'

'But he went back.' Laura held on to the back of the nearest chair. Piers had left, with only a brief note. *I have to go back to Spain. We cannot marry yet, but wait for me. I do not know how long it will be...* She had sat with it in her hand that morning, the morning when she had realised what the non-appearance of her monthly courses—usually as regular as clockwork—meant. She was pregnant and her lover had abandoned her.

'The boy was a romantic. A buffle-headed, muddle-brained romantic,' Avery said bitterly. 'He had broken his mother's heart by joining up, he had sworn an oath of allegiance, and the moment he fancied himself in love he would throw the whole thing over. He would lie to stay in England, pretend to be sick when his comrades went back to fight.

'I told him that to do what he was suggesting would be dishonourable, that his oath as an officer preceded any entanglement with some girl who could perfectly well wait for him—and if she could not, then she would be no wife for a soldier in any case. I asked him,' he said, his voice hard, 'if this was an excuse and he was too afraid to go back.'

Laura sat down, her legs boneless. 'You called him a coward?'

'By implication, yes.'

'And so he went back to Spain, abandoned the girl and was killed almost as soon as he returned?'

'Yes.' The stark word in the warm air of the room scented by the breeze from the garden was like the crack of a gunshot.

She had fallen from her horse once and the air had been knocked clean out of her. She had felt hollow then, but not as empty as she felt now. Laura stared at the dark head, still so firmly turned from her. What had that been? A confession? But he sounded angry, not remorseful, as though getting killed was Piers's fault.

Piers's sword rested almost within arm's reach. Laura saw herself pick it up and run it through that broad back as vividly as in a dream. She felt the jar as the steel hit bone and solid muscle, she felt the gush of hot blood on her hands. She blinked and it was still in its rack, she was still sitting down, her heart racing. When she spoke her voice came from a long way away and she wondered if she was going to faint. 'Do you regret it?'

'It was a matter of honour, it had to be said.'

'And you did not concern yourself with the girl he loved?'

'No.'

I had lain with a man I loved, because we loved. I was foolish and heedless, but does that make me worthless? It seemed that in Avery Falconer's eyes it did. *Hypocrite,* she thought. *I was... I thought I liked you.* Now she knew she had been right all along. He was arrogant, ruthless, judgemental and deeply unfair.

The clock struck, a thin, silvery note. 'My goodness, look at the time,' Laura said and stood up, half-expecting to find her legs would not support her. 'I must go and...and fetch something from the village. Something I promised Mab,' she added. She had the door-knob in her hand before he turned and she was out of the room before he spoke.

'Caroline—'

'Tomorrow,' she called back over her shoulder. 'I really must go now.'

* * *

He had shocked her. First by taking her instinctive concern as an excuse to kiss her and then by talking of battlefields and death. Avery watched the garden, but there was no sign of Caroline, so she must have taken the front path to the village lane. Tomorrow he would apologise. Now he had to shake off this mood before Alice came home.

Do you regret it? Caroline had asked. Regret was hardly the word, furious resentment was more like it. Damn it, he was not going to be plunged into this mental morass every time he came into this room to get a book. He could remove the portrait and the sword to the attic, but that would be cowardly. This had been Piers's home and his mother would have wanted them there. Alice must grow up knowing what her…her cousin looked like, hearing stories of his courage.

He had failed Piers when he could not stop him buying a commission and, somehow, he had failed him if the younger man had been capable of such muddle-headed thinking about where his duty lay. Avery found the book he had been looking for and deliberately sat down at the desk to check the reference he was looking for instead of taking it to his study. If he had caved in and let Piers stay and marry Lady Laura Campion, he might have been killed in the next skirmish after he landed in Spain. He could have drowned on the transport ship. He could have contracted a fever and died of that.

And he would have been leg-shackled to a chit of a girl who had been loose enough to throw her hat over the windmill for a handsome face in a scarlet coat and who then hadn't the backbone to cope with what being an officer's wife would mean. He had read the few bloodstained tatters that were all that remained of the letter that Piers had in his breast pocket when he was killed: nothing but anger and petulance. And yet his cousin had kept it against his heart and it was probably the last thing he read. No soldier deserved to have those words ringing in his ears as he fought and died. *Coward...betrayal...I hate...I'm pregnant...fault...Laura.*

There were not many young ladies by that name and fewer still who vanished from the social scene because of a family crisis at a distant estate. He had gone to find Lady Laura, telling himself that Piers would have wanted him to, driven by grief and anger at the fates and at himself. When he tracked her down, the word locally was that Lady Laura was not well and consumption was feared. That was enough to keep visitors away.

Avery had had to return to his duties abroad, so he had bided his time, watched the calendar, paid a skilful agent to spy, to intercept the mails before they reached the receiving office. The girl had sent the baby away, far away, he learned. After that it was simple. Wait a short while, then a few weeks' leave and he was back in Vienna with Alice.

The agent was rewarded well for his discretion and for the reports he continued to send about Lady Laura Campion. She had returned to London society, but not heartbroken, not crushed by the shame or by giving away her child. Of course she'd had to do it, no lady in her position could have survived it becoming public knowledge that she had given birth out of wedlock. Her reputation would have been shredded if she had kept the baby.

But surely she could have kept the child close and found a respectable family where she could visit without suspicion to watch over her growing daughter? To have sent her to the other end of the country, to a remote dale and the hard life of a small farmer's child, that argued a complete lack of concern for anything but a swift removal of an embarrassment.

Scandal's Virgin they call her, Lambton had written. *She's the fastest of all the débutantes, she spends money like water and they say she leaves broken hearts behind her like so much smashed crockery. The chaperons shake their heads, the matrons are scandalised, the gossip sheets love her and the men pursue. The betting books in the clubs are full of her name—but no one can claim on the wagers because, it seems, she always stops just this side of ruin. An arrant flirt...*

Avery could think of other words to describe Lady Laura Campion. Any guilt he might have felt at taking the baby vanished. If she had been heartbroken over Piers, if she had led a quiet, respectable life and married a decent man after an interval of mourning for Piers, then he would have experienced severe qualms about what he had done.

But Alice did not deserve a mother like that, a woman who showed no sign of mourning her dead lover or the loss of her child. He would move heaven and earth to make sure Alice never knew who she was. Sooner or later he was going to have to make up some fairy story for the child, create some perfect woman to be her mother and some satisfying, if romantically sad, reason why he could not marry her.

Not long now before he was in London and then he would see her, this witch who had so turned Piers's head that he forgot his honour and his duty, this lady with the heart of a harlot who had sent her own child far away so she could wallow in pleasure and break hearts as she had broken his cousin's heart.

'We are leaving. Now. Today.'

'What? Why?' Mab dropped the laundry basket onto the kitchen table with a thump.

'That man....' Her voice was shaking so much she had to stop, grip the edge of the table and breathe hard before she could steady it. 'That man forced Piers to go back to Spain before he could marry me. He called him a coward and he got him in such a muddle about his duty and his honour that he went—and he was killed.'

'Lovey, he might have been killed whenever he went back.'

'I know.' Laura sank onto the nearest chair. 'But he would have married me and Alice would be legitimate and Piers would not have died with that worry on his mind.'

'He knew?' Mab sat down, too.

'I wrote and it would have caught the next ship out. I think, from the timing, he could have received it. Perhaps I should not have done it, but I was so frightened and all I could think of was that I had to tell him.' *I feel such a coward. It seems like a betrayal of every-*

thing I told you I could be as a soldier's wife. I hate to worry you, but I am pregnant with our child. Please don't blame yourself, we were both at fault, but write, I beg you, tell me what to do... There had never been a response, only the news of his death.

'I dare not risk being near Lord Wykeham or I will say something I regret, I know I will. I cannot believe I kept my tongue between my teeth just now as it is.' She covered her face with her hands as if the blackness could somehow bring a measure of calm. 'The boy from the Golden Lion can take the gig into Hemel Hempstead and give a message to Michael to bring the carriage right away.' She got to her feet and ran to the front parlour to scribble a note for her coachman, who was waiting at one of the big coaching inns and enjoying a quiet country holiday while he did so. 'If you go to the Golden Lion now with this, I will start packing.'

Mab, her bonnet jammed on her head and her mouth set in a grim line, marched in and took the note. 'Don't you be putting your back out pulling that trunk out of the cupboard,' was all she said before she banged out of the front door.

Laura pulled another sheet of paper towards her and wrote as swiftly as her shaking hand allowed.

Dearest Alice,
I am sorry I had to leave without saying goodbye to you. I will always remember you and think of you. Please understand that not everyone who has to leave you wishes to do so.
With all my love, your 'adopted aunt'.

* * *

They had not brought much with them, for the cottage had been rented furnished and Laura's pose as a widow in mourning meant she could manage with a limited wardrobe. By the time Michael arrived in the coach—the one she had chosen specifically because it had no crest on the doors—she and Mab had the trunk filled and a neat row of portmanteaux lined up in the hall.

It was not a good time of day to leave, for they could not get back to London in daylight and would have to put up at an inn overnight, but Laura dared not risk staying another day. As it was, there seemed little chance that Avery could discover who she was, even if he wanted to. The cottage had been rented through her man of business in her false name, she had received no post and Michael had told no one who his employer was.

The note for Alice was dropped off at the inn for delivery the next morning. By then Laura would be on the road again, heading for London, the Curzon Street house, appointments with *modistes* and milliners, the re-entry into her world—the world of the Season and the *haut ton* and oblivion in a whirl of pleasure.

Avery Falconer could advertise for a governess and then pack his bags and go back to arranging the affairs of Europe wherever the government chose to use his undoubted talents for autocratically directing the lives and destinies of others.

He had cared for his cousin Piers and yet, when the young man had crossed Avery's line of what constituted honour and duty, he had bent him ruthlessly to his will.

He loved Alice: Laura told herself that she just had to believe he would never break her daughter's heart because he thought he was doing the right thing.

For two weeks Avery kept the tightest rein on his temper he ever had in his life. He interviewed governesses and found none to his liking, he arranged for the Berkeley Square house to be put in readiness and he dealt with a weeping child who could not understand why her new Aunt Caroline had vanished. And that was difficult to endure because he had the nagging conviction on his conscience that she had fled his kisses and Alice's distress was therefore all his fault.

After a few days of tears, followed by clinging, Alice seemed to settle down. After all, as she confided in Avery, poor Aunt Caroline had been sad, so perhaps it was best that she had gone home to her friends, the only excuse he had been able to come up with.

Now all he had to do was to find Alice a stepmama who would love her and she could forget a mother who had sent her away and a mysterious aunt who had vanished. He found he was quite looking forward to it. There would be no work, no worries, no sudden crises, simply a process of sociable, pleasurable wife-hunting and then marriage.

Must be getting old, he thought, studying himself in the pier glass and tightening the muscles of an already flat stomach. *No sign of grey hairs yet, but the prospect of a wife is surprisingly attractive.* There would be none of the expenses and tantrums associated with mistresses. *And none of the tension and guilt associated with respectable widows either,* his conscience added. But it was good that Caroline had gone, for an earl with diplomatic responsibilities could not offer marriage to the widow of some middling gentleman and the alternative would not have been honourable. Yes, it was fortunate that he would never see Mrs Caroline Jordan again. But he missed her.

Chapter Eight

'So who is chaperoning you? Hmm?' The Dowager Marchioness of Birtwell lifted her lorgnette to her eyes and fixed Laura with an unnervingly magnified gaze.

Laura paused in her wanderings through the crowds at Mrs Fairweather's May Day musical reception and dipped a curtsy. 'My cousin Florence, ma'am.' Laura reminded herself that one day she might be eighty with arthritis and managed a smile. She crossed her fingers behind her back—after all, Cousin Florence had promised to come and stay soon…she just wasn't here at this moment.

'Lady Carstairs? She always was an empty-headed peahen. If your poor dear mama couldn't keep you in line, what hope has Florence Carstairs?'

'I am resolved not to be a trial to her,' Laura said and was rewarded with a crack of laugher.

'Well, you are too pale to compete with this year's beauties—and you are getting to be too old for any nonsense into the bargain. Time to stop flitting about

and find a husband.' The dowager flapped her hands
at Laura as if she was a troublesome chicken. 'Go on,
there are enough of them out there. In fact, I saw just
the man a moment ago. Neither of you are in a position
to be too fussy. Now where has he gone?'

There were limits to polite toleration of one's elders,
Laura decided, murmuring an excuse and moving away
into the thronged reception room before the old dragon
spotted that Cousin Florence was nowhere to be seen
or located the rather less-than-ideal candidate she had
in mind for Laura's hand. She was too pale, too old
and had too much of a reputation to be entirely eligible
apparently, but what were the gentleman's faults, such
that he could not afford to be fussy either? she wondered. Buck teeth, a spreading waistline and a gam-
bling habit, perhaps?

'Lady Laura! You have returned to us and as lovely
as ever.' Lord Gordon Johnston placed one elegant hand
on his beautifully tailored chest, approximately where
his heart would be if he possessed one, and sketched
a bow.

'Nonsense, Lord Gordon. I have it on the best authority that I am too pale and too old and had best find
myself a husband before I am at my last prayers.' She
had known him for years and knew, too, that the only
way to avoid becoming the victim of his barbed tongue
was to show him no chink in one's armour.

Lady Birtwell was right: she *was* too pale, she had
lost her bloom and it was going to take sunshine, excitement and entertainment to bring it back and drive
away the memories of the past few months. Meanwhile

she must take care to seem as carefree and as secure as
ever if she wanted to hold her place amongst the *ton* and
not slip into being *that poor Lady Laura, on the shelf
and at her last prayers.*

'As white as the lily,' Lord Gordon agreed, running
the tip of one finger down her cheek. 'Such a duti-
ful daughter to shut yourself away in your blacks for
so long. And when will we be seeing the new Earl of
Hartland in town?'

'Very soon, I hope. The house is all ready for him.'
*Smile, don't let him see you care about another man in
Papa's place.*

'And you are ready for a whirl of pleasure, my dear?'

'Of course. Now who is new on the scene and lots
of fun?' *And why don't I care any more? Must pretend,
must keep up the mask.*

'Let me think.' Lord Gordon surveyed the guests
through narrowed eyes. 'How about Viscount Newlyn?
Fresh in town, still a trifle gauche, pots of money and
an itch to spend it. And such a pretty boy, if rather too
aware of it. He's over there, I'll introduce you.'

Laura allowed him to guide her through the crowd
to a group of old acquaintances clustered around a tall,
blond young exquisite who looked as though he was all
too conscious of every detail of his own appearance and
who had spent a good hour before the mirror preening
before he came out.

Irritating puppy, Laura decided, taking a mild dislike
to him on sight. Still, if he threw good parties and was
amusing she supposed she could tolerate him.

'Lady Laura!' He took her hand and pressed his lips

to it. Laura extricated it with some difficulty and smiled at the various acquaintances who were greeting her. A year ago she would have called them her friends, now, she realised, she had not missed one of them while she had been out of society. '…delighted.' The viscount was still talking. 'I had no idea I would be so fortunate as to be introduced to Scandal's Virgin herself within a week of arriving in London.'

The circle around him fell silent. The nickname was whispered but never spoken in the presence of Lady Laura herself. Miss Willmott, always nervous, gasped and gave a frightened little giggle, Lady Pamela Tutt started an abrupt, desperate monologue about the problems she was having with her maid and Lord Gordon's rather thin lips curved in anticipation of an explosion.

Laura waited a heartbeat, just long enough for Lord Newlyn to realise he had made a major error, then smiled. 'Why, my lord, I had no idea we were already on such terms as to be using pet names. What is yours? The Blond Blunderer, perhaps?'

There was laughter all round the group at that and the gentlemen, several of whom had stiffened, ready to intervene on Laura's behalf, relaxed. The viscount coloured, his expression rigid, but there was real anger in his eyes, she recognised. He was obviously not used to set-downs. 'My apologies, ma'am,' he said before he turned out of the small circle and stalked away towards the card room.

'A clumsy youth,' Lord Petersfield drawled. 'A mother's boy, no doubt, used to being the centre of attention amongst his little circle in Essex.'

'Oh well, *Essex*...' Lady Pamela tittered 'that explains it. Now, my dear Lady Laura, how are you going to amuse yourself now you are back amongst us? Mrs Bridgeport is promising the most delightful picnic next week if the weather holds...'

Laura finally found herself alone after an hour, talked out and rather weary. She was, she realised, thoroughly out of practice for late nights, hot rooms and constant conversation. Either that or the social scene was no longer enough to hold her attention, which was alarming. If she did not have that, her drug to stop her thinking, then how was she going to cope with the cold, empty centre of her life?

She didn't even want to flirt and tease now, to punish any more men for her abandonment by one of them. Because now she knew it was not Piers who had thoughtlessly abandoned her, but Lord Wykeham who had torn him from her and made her baby illegitimate. *He is probably to blame for Piers's death as well,* she thought, staring up at a lurid battle scene in oils that hung by the terrace doors. If Piers had not gone back just in time for that skirmish...

'Lady Laura, allow me to offer you this glass of champagne.' It was Lord Newlyn, a glass in each hand and expression of contrition on his handsome, boyishly smooth, face. 'Let me make amends for my blunder just now.'

She could have snubbed him, turned on her heel, or cut at him with some clever jibe, but, Laura thought with a sigh, it was not his fault she was in such a bad mood and perhaps she should give him the benefit of the doubt.

'Thank you.' She took the glass and sipped. 'Please, do not regard it. I know you are but recently in London.'

'Indeed. Please, could we not step out onto the terrace and talk? I am sure you could give me valuable pointers about how to go on.'

So that is to be my role in life, is it? Delivering wise words to young cubs. But it was too hot and too noisy and her head ached and her feet in the new satin slippers throbbed. 'Very well.'

It was a mistake. She realised it as soon as she set her glass down on the balustrade, as soon as Lord Newlyn moved in and trapped her in the angle of the stonework with far too adroit a manoeuvre for the green young man she had thought him. 'And who better to show me all the tricks but someone such as yourself?' he said as he put one hand on her waist and the other firmly on her left breast.

Laura was taken off guard for a vital second and by the time she realised what she was dealing with he had bent and was pressing hot kisses all over her face. She twisted her head away, jerked up her knee and freed one hand to give him a stinging slap around the ear. 'You lout!' she gasped as he crashed backwards, far too far and violently for the blow she had struck him.

'The very words,' a deep, hard voice agreed and she realised a man had taken the viscount by the collar and had sent him sprawling on the flagstones. 'Pick yourself up, apologise to the lady and remove yourself from this house before I find it necessary to deal with you further.'

They were all in shadow, but Laura pressed herself back against the unyielding stonework in one direction with as much desperation as Lord Newlyn was scuttling backwards on the ground in the other. With his back to her, obviously intent on shielding her, was a broad-shouldered figure she would have recognised anywhere.

'I…I'm sorry, ma'am,' the viscount managed. He got to his feet and hurried away, his tousled blond hair catching the light from the reception room as he stumbled past the doors.

'Are you all right?' The tall man turned, his face still shadowed. 'May I call your chaperon or a friend to you? It was perhaps not wise to have come out here alone with a young buck like that.'

'Thank you, no. I need no one.' It was impossible not to speak and impossible he would not recognise her voice, as she recognised his. 'Lord Wykeham.' What was he doing here, in London? In England, even?

'Caroline?' He went still.

'No.' Laura sidestepped and walked away towards the doors, stopped at the edge of the spill of light and turned to face him. 'No, my lord. That is not my name.' She could not make out his face beyond a pale oval against the blackness of the shrubs, let alone read his expression, but the shock and tension came off him like heat from a fire.

She lifted her chin and stood there, deliberately posed in the slender column of rose-pink silk overlaid with silver gauze. The neckline swooped low over her shoulders and bosom, the sleeves were mere puffs of ribbon and her hair was piled high in the latest style. She knew the rubies at her throat and in her ears would pulse in the light in time with her breathing because she had studied the effect in the mirror, and she knew she looked elegant, expensive and provocative, a hundred miles from the genteel respectability of the widow she had pretended to be. It was instinct to display herself and not to try to hide. Avery was here and there was no escape: she would stand and fight.

'Then who are you?' He took three long strides forward and confronted her. 'Step back into the shadow, we cannot be seen like this.'

Laura shrugged, a careless twitch of one shoulder that had his gaze dropping to the swell of her breasts as the silk shifted. 'No one will be surprised if I am seen on the terrace with a man.'

'Who are you?' Avery repeated. She could smell him, his familiar shaving soap, a discreet hint of cologne, the provocative warmth of a man who had been in a crowded room all evening. 'What are you hiding from?'

'I am not hiding from anything. Anyone.' She tipped up her chin. 'I am Lady Laura Campion.'

Avery went very still, the hiss of breath between his teeth the only sign of the shock she must have given him. 'How dared you insinuate yourself into my house under false pretences?' he said, the words low and even, at odds with the anger in the question.

'How dared you steal my child?' she flung back, unable to match his icy control. 'How could you accuse Piers of being a coward and send him to his death?'

'I sent him to do his duty. He made a choice when he took a commission and he knew the odds of being killed. If I failed him, it was by neglecting to teach him how to recognise a heartless wanton when he saw one. Just look at you now.'

'You hypocrite.' The stinging injustice of his words steadied her, gave her back some steadiness, even if it was only the rigidity of fury. 'You just like control, that is it, isn't it? You wanted to control Piers's life, you want to control his estate, you want to control his daughter's future.'

'I love that child.'

'I noticed. You love her so much that you let her think her mother left her.'

'Instead of telling her that you gave her away?'

'I—' Her parents had done it for the best of motives, she tried to believe that. 'It was the only thing to do.'

'Of course it was,' Avery said, his tone so reasonable that she gaped at him. He moved into the edge of the light and she saw his face, took a step back before she could control her reactions and stand her ground. 'The only thing if you wanted to forget about Piers, if you wanted to resume your gilded life, catch an eligible husband and had no care for your child.'

'What choice had I?' she flung at him and moved away, out of the light where he had her pinned like a moth against a lantern. 'You know perfectly well I would have ruined both my daughter and myself if I had kept her.'

'Of course I know that, but you could have gone to his family.'

'And what good would that have done?' Laura enquired. She groped her way to the balustrade and gripped the cool stonework, the dried lichen rough against the fine kid of her long gloves. 'His mother died shortly after he joined the army. There was no one to go to.'

'There was me. I came back.' Avery must have moved as she did, for he was very close now, the lepidopterist ready to skewer the captive moth with a long pin now she was fluttering, helpless.

'And what would you have done, pray?'

'Married you,' he said.

'*Married me?* Why? Why would you have helped me?'

'I would have not crossed the road for you,' Avery said dismissively. 'I would have done it for Piers and for his child.'

'Easy to say now,' Laura jibed. Inside she quaked. Where did the brave, defiant words come from? She was shaking so much she could hardly stand.

'You would not recognise a sense of honour if you fell over it.' The anger had finally surfaced and cracked his control. 'You sent the baby to the other end of the country to be brought up as a poor farmer's daughter. You had no intention of keeping watch over her, simply of getting rid of an embarrassing encumbrance. You might have found her a good home close at hand, but that is too late now. You will stay away from Alice, do you understand me?'

'Or what?'

'Or your reputation will suffer for it. It is bad enough

as it is, but I doubt even *Scandal's Virgin* could ride out that storm.' His lip curled. 'And that's the most inaccurate by-name I have ever heard.'

'If you betray my secret, then you ruin Alice,' Laura countered. 'No one would forget that story. All your scheming to make her eligible and respectable would go out of the window simply because of your spite against me. We are at check, my lord. If Alice is in London, then I will see her, even if you prevent me speaking to her.'

'I'll not let you near her. If you had loved her, you would have stayed in touch with the family you sent her to, not left her for six years and then arrived to play with her emotions on some whim.' All that hard-learned control had deserted him, she realised. Avery took a precipitate step closer, trapping her against the balustrade as Lord Newlyn had done.

'You cannot stop me—' Laura began. She had no idea what she was going to say, what she was going to do, for he took all her options away from her. His hands on her shoulders locked around the narrow bones as he pulled her towards him. Then his mouth took hers in a kiss that held nothing of sensuality or even simple arousal. This was punishment, anger, scorn and his own frustration at her defiance.

Laura stamped and kicked as Avery bent her back against the stonework. It took a few seconds to realise that there was cool air all around her, that his weight was gone, his hands had released her. 'There is no need to scream,' Avery said, his voice like a lash. 'I would not touch you again for any consideration I could imagine. Respectable widows are one thing, selfish pleasure-seeking chits are quite another. To think I was under the illusion I was rescuing you just now.' His laugh jarred, totally without humour. 'Just believe that I will do whatever it takes to protect what is mine—and Alice is mine in every sense that matters.'

It was on the tip of her tongue to tell him that she'd had no intention of trying to see Alice again, that she had resolved to leave her child in his care because she believed that was best for Alice. But now…now she would not admit that and let him think he had frightened her away, not if it killed her. Laura ran the back of her hand over her mouth and fixed him with a dagger glare that simply bounced off his disdain.

'We are all in London,' she said with a calm that belied her quaking knees. 'Unless you want to make a mystery of Alice and have people saying you are ashamed of her and want to hide her, then there is every chance I will see her again. I will not approach her because that would confuse her, but believe me, if I ever have the slightest suspicion that she is not happy, that you are not the loving father to her that you purport to be, then I will make such a scandal you would not believe and I will fight you in the courts for her.'

Laura gathered her long skirts in one hand and turned towards the house with all the poise of one of society's darlings. 'I will be watching you, Lord Wykeham. Never forget it.' She swept through the doors into the reception room again, into the heat and light and noise and almost stumbled with shock to find that this other world was continuing just feet from that encounter.

'There you are!' The dowager rapped on the floor with her cane as though she was rapping knuckles. 'Sent Newlyn to his rightabouts, I see. Good girl, he's a here-and-thereian, not worth dallying on the terrace with that one.' She looked around the room. 'Now where has he gone?'

'Newlyn, ma'am?' The astringent old bat was as effective as a splash of cold water in the face.

'No, you silly chit. Wykeham.'

'The Earl of Wykeham?' Had she gone white or scarlet? Was her face a picture of guilt? She felt as though the pressure of Avery's mouth must have branded her. Surely anyone looking at her would see her lips were swollen from his kisses?

'There's only the one. He'd do for you. Rank, money, good brain, although he's encumbered with that by-blow he insists on acknowledging. He won't do for some innocent girl straight out of the schoolroom, but you've enough town bronze to carry off that little embarrassment without any silliness. Eh? Men will be men.'

'Indeed they will, ma'am.' Laura agreed grimly. 'Will you excuse me? I feel quite exhausted—I am not yet used to town hours again.'

As she made her way to the exit she heard the old lady cackle behind her. 'No stamina, today's young misses. None at all.'

Chapter Nine

Damn it, I'm shaking. Avery summoned up every inch of control he possessed, thanked his hostess for a charming evening and strode out into the lobby. He looked down at his hands and willed them to stillness. He did not know what it was: fury at Laura Campion's deceit and defiance, the urge to shake the breath out of her or sheer frustrated lust. All three, he supposed.

Who the devil did he think he was punishing with that kiss? He was the one who was going to spend the night tossing and turning in frustration, not that deceitful, selfish woman.

'Your hat and cloak, my lord. Shall I call your carriage?' The footman waited impassively, too well trained to show that he found anything unusual about peers of the realm standing in the middle of the lobby eyeing their white-gloved hands and muttering.

I'll be a candidate for Bedlam if I carry on like this, Avery thought. 'Thank you. I'll walk. Find my driver and tell him to go home, would you?'

'My lord.' The coins hardly chinked as the footman palmed them. Of course, Avery could stand here threading the contents of the flower arrangement into his hair, provided he tipped well enough. The urge to do something totally mindless, utterly irresponsible, gripped him. Go to a hell off St James's Street and risk a few thou on the tables. Find a gin house down by the river and get stupid drunk and pick a fight. Or investigate a high-class brothel in Covent Garden and forget the taste of Laura Campion's mouth and the feel of her skin in a welter of costly, highly skilled flesh.

The gaming hells were closest, the thought of gin and a fight the most tempting and the brothel, he realised with a fastidious twist of his lips, the most distasteful. He began to walk, his stick casually in his hand, his senses, below the level that was furious and aroused, testing his surroundings for danger. Footpads abounded. Perhaps he could lose himself in violence that way.

It took him the ten minutes to Berkeley Square to cool down sufficiently to remember that he had a child to go home to. That would be behaviour to justify every one of Lady Laura's threats if he rolled in bloodied, drunk, stinking of gin and cheap perfume.

Avery turned around the square towards home and slowed his pace. Every night, whether she was awake or not, he went into Alice's bedroom and gave her a goodnight kiss. She was probably quite unaware of it—in fact, he suspected the only person gaining any reassurance from it was himself.

The fierce protective love he felt for the child still

shook him to the core. He had taken her out of duty and a nagging sense of responsibility—it was only in the small hours of the morning that he admitted to himself that it might be guilt—for having sent Piers back to Spain. Miss Blackstock had cradled the baby in her arms as they bumped down the rough track away from the remote farm and then, when they turned onto the smoother turnpike road, she had handed him the swaddled bundle without a word.

Avery had never held a baby in his life. He took her, looked down and was instantly riveted by the blue eyes staring into his. The baby looked at his face as though it was the only thing in the world, as though it was the entirety of her universe. Avery had looked back and discovered he had stopped breathing. *Is this love at first sight?* He could recall thinking that and then she freed one hand from the blanket, waved it, a tiny questing starfish, and found his finger. The grip was extraordinary. He looked at perfect miniature fingernails, at the smooth baby skin and knew, as his gaze blurred, that it was, indeed, love.

So much for setting Blackie up with a nursery and staff somewhere hidden away in England. Plans for bringing up the child at a distance in her own well-equipped, carefully staffed establishment went out of the carriage window. 'You will come with me to Vienna?' he asked Blackie and she had smiled and nodded, completely unsurprised by his instant infatuation. He supposed his smile must have been uncharacteristically sheepish, because hers had widened. 'You are sure?' he asked.

'Of course. A child should be with her father,' she had responded.

Her *father?* He had meant to be Cousin Avery, a remote guardian. He'd had vague thoughts of visits on her birthday and at Christmas, of gifts, selected by Blackie. Eventually a governess, a pony—all taken care of while he dealt with the important matters of international statecraft that filled his days.

But they did not fill his heart, he realised during that long journey. His new-found adoration survived even the unpleasant realities of travel with a baby and the transformation of a sweet-smelling, endearing little creature into a squalling, irritable tyrant who wanted the wet nurse *now,* who needed her napkin changing *now*— regardless of whether his lordship thought it might wait until they reached the next inn. He could get out and stand in the rain while the women dealt with it or he could grit his teeth and put up with it. Human babies, it seemed, were just like any other small mammal: they had their needs and they were quite ruthless about getting them filled.

Slowly the months had passed, the baby-blue eyes became greener and greener as Avery observed, fascinated, all the stages of growth. Weaning, the first tooth, the first words and steps. And still that wide, intent gaze would find his face and the smile would curve Alice's lips and he knew he was never going to be Cousin Avery. He was *Papa,* to Alice and in the eyes of the world.

Now, when he climbed the stairs to her bedroom, he found her awake and was glad he had resisted the mad urge to bad behaviour. 'Why are you not asleep?' he asked, shaking his head in mock reproof.

Alice blinked up at him, then rubbed her eyes and yawned hugely. 'I'm excited, Papa.'

'By London? But you are used to big cities.'

'I know.' She burrowed down, eyes already closing. 'But something exciting is going to happen, I know it is.'

'I hope not, pet,' Avery said and smoothed her hair before he bent to drop a kiss on the top of her head.

It was not until he was in his own chamber, shedding his clothes into the hands of Darke, his valet, that the question struck him. How the blazes had Laura Campion discovered that Alice was her daughter? Had the Brownes decided to make even more money and had contacted Lady Laura to tell her that they had handed over the child? But why had she left it so late? Then he recalled that her father had died the previous year. It must have been, as he had accused, a selfish whim. Now she was alone in the world, she would take a very belated interest in the fate of her daughter.

Or, he decided cynically, she had ignored Alice all these years, but had finally resolved to take a husband and wanted to make sure her secret was safely buried in that remote dale. It must have been a nasty shock to discover that someone else knew and that the child was not growing up milking cows, baking bread and learning her letters in the village dame school, but was under the protection of someone of influence and power.

'Am I a cynic, Darke?' Avery enquired, shrugging into the proffered banyan. 'Am I distrustful?'

'Of course, my lord. And very proper, too, in your

position, if I may say so. It doesn't do to think the best of people. You are a good judge of character, my lord. Very fair. But it is only right to assume the people you do not know well enough to trust will have only their own interests at heart.'

'Indeed. Just leave the hot water, will you? I'll sit up for a while.'

The valet effaced himself into the dressing room and eased the door shut. Avery lounged in the deep wing chair and followed his progress from tallboy to clothes press by the soft clicks and rustles until finally the outer door shut.

What exactly were Lady Laura's interests? He supposed that she had decided it would be wise to make certain that he would not betray her secret, but sneaking around disguised as someone else entirely would not achieve that—only a direct approach would have assured her of his silence.

Perhaps she had intended to find out more about him, see if he was the kind of man who would be a threat to her. He recalled her cool distance, the underlying *froideur* beneath her courtesy. And then she had met Alice and, he guessed, her plans had fallen apart. Unless she was a consummate actress she was deeply fond of the child...now. *Too late, madam,* he thought with a grim smile. *It is six years past the point where you should have discovered your maternal feelings.*

She knew now that he loved the child and would care for her and she had been correct to say that he would do nothing to cause a scandal. *Unless she strikes first and then she will be very, very sorry.* What he must do was to build the bulwarks up around Alice. He already knew he should marry and father an heir, but a woman who would treat Alice as a daughter, who would give her brothers and sisters and knit her into a normal family life, would benefit Alice as well as himself.

Avery got to his feet and tossed the banyan on the foot of the bed. Naked, he began to wash in the cooling water and pondered strategy as he worked the soap up into a lather. Picking out some chit from the flocks of them inhabiting every ballroom and park was too haphazard. He needed to study a prospective wife at closer range, assess her at nine in the morning as well as eleven at night, see how she interacted with servants and dealt with everyday setbacks and irritations. Watch her with Alice.

What he needed, in effect, was a house party. Avery scrubbed at his face with a towel and considered. He needed a hostess and he needed someone to suggest the guests. Which meant, he supposed with a sigh, he must ask his godmother. She was interfering and opinionated and she disapproved of Alice, but she was of impeccable *ton,* knew everyone and would not allow her disapproval to make her unkind to the child, only to lecture him on his supposed indiscretion. There was nothing for it, he was going to have to throw himself on the mercy of the Dowager Marchioness of Birtwell.

'And where are you going, my lady?' Mab demanded as Laura came down from her room after breakfast. 'You've got that look in your eye—you're up to mischief. And that outfit!'

'Really, Mab, any other employer would give you your notice. I am going out and I do not *get up to mischief.*'

'Then you'll want me along,' Mab said, refusing to be snubbed. 'You'll not be seen out without either maid or footman.'

Laura had no intention of being seen at all, hence the drab gown and pelisse that would not have been out of place on a governess, matched with a sensible veiled bonnet and sturdy half-boots. 'I am going for a stroll and dressed like this I am in no danger of being accosted by gentlemen on the strut.'

'You are going to find Miss Alice, that's what you're about.'

'I only want to see her,' Laura protested as she pulled on her gloves. 'I will not let her see me. You stay here, Mab.'

It was a sunny morning and no nurse worth her salt would keep a child indoors on a day like this. Alice would be going out to take the air, Laura would bet her new Norwich shawl on it. The directory had given his lordship's address and Berkeley Square, only a few minutes' walk away, had a large central garden that would be perfect to play in.

It was early, and quiet, without even a single carriage drawn up outside Gunter's tea shop in the south-east corner of the square. Servants were putting the finishing touches to the brasswork on doors and deliveries were in full swing. A florist's boy staggered under the weight of a vast bouquet, a dray dripped water outside Gunter's as men in leather capes unloaded ice, a milk-

man negotiated his hanging pails through the area gate
and down the service steps to the kitchen entrance of
politician George Canning's elegant house and a gig-
gling kitchen maid was flirting with the greengrocer's
delivery man.

Laura strolled into the garden and pretended an interest in the flower beds as she made her way towards the
north-east corner and a secluded bench opposite Lord
Wykeham's fine double-fronted house. She did not have
to wait long before the door opened and Alice bounded
down the steps. A bag bounced at her side and Miss
Blackstock followed her out. Her voice drifted across
to Laura. 'Walk, if you please, Miss Alice!'

They walked down past Gunter's, and then past the
high wall of the gardens of Lansdowne House into
Bolton Row. Laura hung back, matching her pace to
theirs, wondering where they were going. In a moment
they would be in Curzon Street, walking past her own
home. Then Alice scampered into Clarges Street and
Laura realised they must be going to Green Park.

It was not the easiest of the parks to hide in, she reflected as she watched Alice, hand in hand with Blackie
as they negotiated the traffic in Piccadilly. The nurse
gave her a coin to hand the crossing sweeper herself,
then they were through the gate leading to the narrow
rectangle of the reservoir. Alice ran to the end nearest
Queen's Walk where a group of ducks were clustered
hopefully and dropped her bag on the ground, spilling
what must be crusts of stale bread on the grass.

Laura walked in the opposite direction, to one of the
benches at the far end where the ride towards Consti-

tution Hill wound off around the gardens of the lodge-keeper's cottage. At this distance, veiled, she was safe from recognition, she was certain.

A few other nursemaids with their charges were walking towards the reservoir, all making for the end where Alice was surrounded by quacking and flapping ducks in the water and a flock of pigeons on land. Her laughter brought a smile to Laura's lips, even as her heart ached at the distance between them.

She glanced to the side as hoofbeats signalled the arrival of one of the park's rare riders, perhaps trotting back from an early morning gallop in Hyde Park. A raking black more suited to the hunting field than London hacking drew level with her and out of the corner of her eye she was aware of immaculate brown boots with tan tops, long legs in buckskin breeches and a gloved hand resting negligently on the left thigh as the rider guided the horse one-handed.

Her attention was still focused on Alice as she stood, intending to move her position to where a clump of bushed provided a little cover. The horse curvetted away, making her jump and she turned fully to face it as the rider swore. 'What in damnation are you doing here, Lady Laura?'

Avery Falconer brought the big animal under control without taking his gaze from her veiled face. *How can he recognise me?* Her immediate instinct was to bluff, to turn a haughty shoulder and pretend he was just some importunate rake bothering a lone woman in the park, but she realised at once that was futile. Something about her had jolted his memory, now all she could do was brazen it out.

Laura tossed back her veil and raised one eyebrow in haughty distain. 'This is a public park, I believe, Lord Wykeham. I do not require your permission to take the air in it.'

'Dressed like a governess and without your maid?' He brought the gelding sidling forward, so close it took a conscious stiffening of her spine not to back away. 'You are spying on Alice, you devious jade, and I told you I would not stand for it.'

'Indeed?' Laura lifted the other brow and sneered at him, as best she could, considering their respective positions. 'And just what do you intend to do about it, considering that I am nowhere near her and in a public place?'

'Do?' Avery jammed his riding crop into his boot and smiled. 'Why, remove you, of course.'

Before she could realise what he intended he leant out of the saddle, took her by the upper arms and hauled her bodily up in front of him. Laura kicked, twisted and found herself dumped unceremoniously to sit sideways across his thighs. 'Ouch!' The pommel jabbed into her. 'Put me down!'

'In my own good time.' He turned the horse's head away from the reservoir and shifted his arms so they caged her and he could take the reins in both hands. The gelding tossed its head as if in protest at the additional load, but walked on meekly enough.

'People will see,' she protested.

'Then resume your veil,' Avery said in a voice of sweet reason.

Laura contemplated wriggling free and dropping to the ground, but the animal was a good sixteen hands high and she risked a broken ankle if she tried that. Besides, the strength with which Avery had hoisted her up indicated that he would have little trouble subduing any attempt at escape. She was slender enough, but she was a well-built adult woman and no featherweight to be tossed about like a child. It was, she realised, fuming, rather exciting.

Crude, animal instinct, she told herself severely. *He is big, strong and muscular, any woman would be in a flutter under the circumstances. And he probably knows it, the wretch.*

His chest was broad and steady and it was impossible to lean away from it—in fact, she was squashed so close she could sense his heartbeat, infuriatingly steady. Beneath her buttocks his thighs were hard and, she realised with rising indignation as she worked out what was pommel, what was leg and what was…*something else,* that he was finding this arousing.

A middle-aged couple exercising a pair of Italian greyhounds on long leashes stared, mouths open in comic synchronisation. Laura dragged down her veil with something like a snarl.

'That is a truly ghastly gown,' Avery remarked.

'I did not wish to draw attention to myself.' *Oh, stop bandying words with him!*

'Which proves my point. You were spying.'

Laura firmed her lips over the retort she was about

to make and assumed as dignified a silence as a woman being abducted by a peer of the realm in broad daylight within a stone's throw of two royal residences could.

Avery guided the horse across the Mall and into St James's Park. Laura stiffened. This park was full of trees, avenues and groves of them, and at this hour it was even quieter than Green Park had been.

'Where...what are you doing?' It was shaming that her voice shook.

'I thought I'd take you into that secluded little grove over there and see what effect wrapping my hands around that very lovely white neck of yours would have in persuading you to leave me and mine alone,' Avery said with a grim edge to his voice that had her twisting round in alarm. His face was set, harsh and every bit as grim as his voice had been.

Laura opened her mouth to scream and he shifted the reins and clapped one hand over her mouth.

'I do not like defiance,' he murmured in her ear. 'As you are about to find out.'

Chapter Ten

Laura bit the big, gloved hand over her mouth and heard Avery mutter what sounded like a curse under his breath, then they were within the grove. He reined in and removed his hand, leaving her with the taste of leather on her lips and rage in her heart.

'I really would not bother wasting my breath if I were you,' he remarked as she dragged air down into her lungs to scream. She ignored him and found herself slid unceremoniously over the horse's shoulder to land on her feet, with the breath jolted clean out of her.

Avery swung down out of the saddle and the horse stood there, reins on its neck, like a statue. Laura was the only creature who ever dared gainsay Lord Wykeham, it seemed. Running did not seem to be an option, not faced with those long legs: she wouldn't get three feet before he caught her. *After all, what can he do?*

She lifted her chin and glared at him. 'Go ahead, strangle me, although I have no idea what you can do with my body, not having a spade handy.'

The sun shone through the leaves, the birds sang. Distantly, on Horse Guards Parade, a shouted order spoiled the illusion of being deep in the countryside. Avery's eyes flickered over her, his mouth set in a grim line. He might be finding abducting a woman in the middle of London's parks arousing, but it certainly did not seem to be giving him any pleasure.

He walked towards her, drawing off his gloves. 'I can think of several things to do with your *body,* Lady Laura, but it's your stubborn brain that requires dealing with.' He pushed the gloves into a pocket as he stopped, toe to toe with her.

Laura made herself stand firm. 'Really, this is positively Gothic! I am not afraid of you, Avery Falconer. Whatever else you may be, you are a gentleman and not a raving lunatic. You are not going to strangle me and we both know it.'

'Of course I am not,' Avery agreed. This close, without the slightest temptation to let her lids drop in erotic surrender, she could see how green his eyes were, a subtly different shade than Piers's had been. Gold flecks danced like fire. *Devil's fire.* 'I simply require your undivided attention for a moment.'

'Then you have it, my lord,' she drawled and gave him the look that worked very well with importunate gentlemen who became overamorous in conservatories. It always sent them off looking crushed. Avery merely appeared bored.

'I have said it once, but I do not think you have been paying attention. You will leave Alice alone. You will not watch her, you will not follow her, you will not contact her. Is that clear enough?'

'As crystal. And if I ignore your demands?'

'I will ruin you.' He smiled.

'Your threats are merely bluff. If you do expose me, then it will ruin Alice, too, you know that perfectly well.'

'Her name will not come into it, her parentage will not be an issue. You are not listening to my *threats,* as you describe them. Actually, they are promises. *I* will ruin *you*. Society will discover that *Scandal's Virgin* is actually *Scandal's Jade.*'

'That would be rape,' she flashed at him. 'I cannot believe it of you. Even of you.'

'It would, indeed, and *even I...*' his lip curled as he parroted her sneer '...even I would baulk at that. But fortunately for you, and for my scruples, all it needs is the appearance of the thing. Rumour, a whisper of scandal. A bet in the club books, a sighting of Lady Laura where she should not be, a few urgent and earnest denials on my part—and I will protest far too much, far too earnestly, just as a gentleman should—and the damage will be done.

'You have been very skilful, balancing on the edge, skating on thin ice. You dangle men on a string, leading them on. There's a nasty little phrase for women like you, Lady Laura Campion. Cock tease.'

On a gasp of outrage she stepped back and he lifted his hands from his sides, his palms open as though to demonstrate that he need not touch her, then he let them fall to his side, and smiled.

'Men have all the power,' she said as she found her voice at last. It trembled with anger, but she could not help that. 'You take what you want because the strength is on your side, the law, the double standards of behaviour. Men want my dowry, they want my bloodlines, they want my body and I do not choose to give those to *any* man because even the ones who protest undying love are unreliable. There is always something more important than a woman in their lives. I choose to entertain myself by playing the game with male rules and if that is uncomfortable for a *gentleman* I really do not care.'

She stopped because she was exposing herself and her pain all too plainly and his threats had the chilling ring of truth. He could ruin her with ease, just as he said, without laying a finger on her and without the slightest danger to Alice. 'You win, my lord.' She would not gratify him by squirming on his hook, she was too intelligent not to know defeat when she saw it. 'All I wanted was a few glimpses of my child. If you are threatened by that, so be it, I am not going to lose everything else in my life to your scheming.'

Laura turned on her heel and walked away before he saw the defeat in her eyes, while anger still gave her the strength to preserve the last shreds of her dignity.

'That could have gone better, Nero.' The gelding twitched an ear, but otherwise did not contribute anything to the one-sided conversation. 'She made me lose my temper. No...' Avery twitched his riding crop out of his boot and took a vicious swipe at some long grass '...she *did* nothing. I took one look, lost my temper and carried her off on my saddle bow like one of Scott's blasted heroes. And then what did I think I was going to do with her?' Nero cocked up one hind hoof and settled into the equine equivalent of a slouch. 'Kiss her senseless?'

Avery's body stirred, interested in this line of thought. The lack of control did nothing to improve his temper. 'How can I find her so damnably arousing when all I want to do is throttle the woman?' He gathered up the reins and remounted. As he moved, the scent of her rose from the front of his coat where Laura had been pressed against broadcloth and linen. Warm, angry woman blended with orange water.

Warm, frightened woman, he hoped. He had never threatened a woman in his life and it did not sit well with him now, but he'd carry out his threats without hesitation if he thought she was any danger to Alice's future. He would live with his conscience afterwards.

Laura Campion had courage, he'd say that for her. Avery dug his heels in and sent Nero back the way he'd come at the canter. Any other woman would have had hysterics, carried off like that. He recalled the look in her eyes as she'd faced him down. She had not flinched—yet how had she known he would not hurt her, one way or another?

But then she was a good actress with strong nerves— 'Caroline Jordan' had been proof of that. It was a miracle he had not become even more wrapped up in the young widow than he had, attracted by her air of mystery, her sensual allure, her cool distance and haunting air of sadness.

It was humiliating for a man who prided himself on being a good judge of character that he had found himself intrigued by a woman whose morals were loose, who had written that scathing letter to a man who was risking his life for his country and who had given away her child and had forgotten her for six long years.

Avery reined in as the reservoir came in sight. He needed a few moments to restore a calm, cheerful face for Alice. Just why was Laura interested in her daughter now? The question kept nagging at him. Perhaps she was coming to realise that she had lost the chance of a decent marriage with her fast behaviour and her smirched reputation. Perhaps, with maturity, she was coming to yearn for a child.

Well, it was too late to claim this one, he thought, catching sight of Alice playing ball with three other small girls, their bright dresses like so many large butterflies as they ran and laughed over the grass. Laura Campion was never going to get close to Alice again.

Pritchett, her butler, was too well trained to remark on his mistress's flushed face, crumpled skirts or scowl. He took Laura's bonnet and pelisse and remarked, 'You have a visitor, my lady. The Dowager Lady Birtwell arrived fifteen minutes ago. I informed her you were out, but she said she was fatigued and would wait.' He lowered his voice to a confidential murmur. 'I believe she is resting her eyes. Naturally, I sent in a tea tray.'

'Lady Birtwell? I wonder what...?' Laura looked down at her drab gown and shuddered. 'Please send my woman to me, Pritchett, and have fresh tea prepared. I will be ten minutes.'

She hastened upstairs, untying her bonnet as she went. What on earth did the old dragon want with her? 'Mab, I need to change quickly. The Pomona-green afternoon dress.'

Laura came down within the time she had allowed herself, neatly gowned, her hair brushed into a simple style, a Norwich shawl draped negligently over her elbows. She could only hope that the dowager did not notice that her hands were still trembling and she was fighting for composure with iron determination.

'Lady Birtwell, I am so sorry to have kept you waiting. I do hope Pritchett has been looking after you. Fresh tea is on its way.'

'No need to be sorry, child. You weren't expecting me. Glad of the chance for a rest, if truth be told. I've been running about like a scalded cat all day.' She accepted a fresh cup of tea and a macaroon.

'Nothing is wrong, I hope, ma'am?' Laura sipped her own tea and wished for a large glass of Madeira instead.

'I have the whim to hold a house party next week. Short notice, I know, but the weather is sultry and is doing my breathing no good, the Season is slacking off and I thought a few days in the country would put me back in prime fettle. Just a select company, a dozen or so. Get some of those girls out of the hothouse at Almack's for some fresh air and invite some of my old friends for a comfortable few days, you know the sort of thing. Hmm? What do you think?'

'I am sure you will find it restores you in no time, Lady Birtwell.' The dowager was famous for her relaxed, cheerful house parties with a range of guests, excellent food and informal entertainments from shooting at the archery butts to impromptu dancing.

'Excellent. You'll come, of course.' The rings encrusting her plump fingers sparkled in the sunlight as the older woman put down her teacup.

'Me? I, er…I would be delighted, of course, but I don't…'

'There's nothing on in town of any importance, or I would know about it.' She narrowed her eyes and studied Laura, head cocked to one side. 'You look flushed, my girl. You courting on the sly?'

'What? I mean, certainly not, Lady Birtwell!'

'I'm pleased to hear it. Do your reputation no good to be carrying on some clandestine flirtation—what you get up to in public is bad enough.'

'Yes, ma'am.' *And what would you say if you'd seen me an hour ago?*

Her instinct was to refuse, upset as she was, but Laura bit back the polite words as she made herself reconsider. *She is offering me a week in the country, a week away from any risk of seeing Avery.* Was it cowardly to run away? Laura found she did not care whether it was or not. She was tired of being brave and bold. 'Thank you, I would very much like to come to Old Birtwell House.'

'Excellent. Do you need me to arrange transport?' The dowager reached for her reticule.

'Thank you, no. I will use my own carriage and bring

my maid with me, if that is convenient.' Laura pulled the bell cord for Pritchett.

'Oh, yes, plenty of room in the staff wing and the stables. I will see you on Monday afternoon—bring the recipe for those macaroons with you.'

When the front door closed behind her guest Laura sank back on the sofa and closed her eyes. Lord Wykeham had defeated her, frightened her and humiliated her. He would keep her daughter from her and ensure she never got so much of a glimpse of Alice. Her only consolation was her conviction that he loved the child and would care for her.

Now all she had to do was to decide how she was going to spend the rest of her existence, because now her former life, the pursuit of pleasure, the *frisson* of being Scandal's Virgin, held no attraction whatsoever. Dry-eyed, Laura gazed at the row of stiff, engraved and gilded invitation cards that lined the mantel shelf. Her old life was dust, her heart felt as though Avery Falconer had kicked it and she had no idea what she was going to do next.

Except escape to the country and ride and gossip and eat too much and try, somehow, to imagine a future.

She had been to Lady Birtwell's house parties before and the sight of the house, its warm red brick glowing in the afternoon sunlight, was pleasantly familiar. The journey from London into the Surrey countryside had been smooth and uneventful, despite Laura's wish for something to take her mind off her emotional bruises. A minor riot, an escaped bull, even a highwayman, would have been satisfying. Instead, she and Mab had progressed in respectable comfort, on good roads, distracted by nothing more than unsatisfactory coffee at one inn and a slow turnpike keeper.

Other guests were there already. She saw a group of young ladies on the archery lawn attended by three gentlemen, one of them in scarlet regimentals. A carriage was being driven round to the stables as they drew up and Laura recognised Lady Frensham, one of the dowager's friends, being assisted up the steps to the front door by an attentive footman. It seemed that the party was an interesting mix of ages, if nothing else.

Her groom came to open the door and let down the step, the butler turned from delivering Lady Frensham into the housekeeper's hands to greet her and Laura took a deep breath, composed herself and entered the house, into a bustle of servants and luggage.

'Lady Laura, good afternoon, my lady. I am Rogers.'

'Of course, I remember you, Rogers. Good afternoon.'

The butler gestured to a footman. 'Lady Birtwell is receiving guests in the Chinese Room. Would you care to go to your chamber first—?'

The high-pitched screams of excited children drowned his words. The butler's carefully schooled expression slipped for a moment into something close to a wince. Laura realised she was wincing back. 'I beg your pardon, my lady. I trust the children will not disturb you. Lady Birtwell enjoys the sound of young voices.'

'It is lovely to hear them enjoying themselves, Rogers.' Laura forced a smile on her lips. She had not realised there would be children here, that echoes of Alice's laughter would haunt every room. 'I will just go up to my…'

Her voice trailed away as the noise grew louder. Half-a-dozen children ran from the garden door at the back of the hall to tumble to a halt as they realised where they were. A sheepish silence fell, broken only by the shuffling of feet and the sound of a hoop being dropped with a clatter on the marble floor.

'Now then, young ladies and gentlemen, this is not the place to be playing, is it?' Rogers chided. 'Lady Laura has only just this moment arrived and she must think this a menagerie.'

The biggest boy piped up, 'Sorry, Lady Laura, we didn't mean to disturb you. We'll go out.' He turned and ran back, his companions eddying around him, leaving one small girl standing staring at Laura, her mouth open.

The solid marble floor seemed to shift under Laura's feet. Behind her she heard the sound of crunching gravel and voices and realised the archery party was coming back.

'Aunt C…' Alice Falconer whispered, her eyes wide and hurt on Laura's face.

Chapter Eleven

Laura froze, then instinct took over. She raised one finger to her lips and shook her head at Alice. The words died unsaid on the child's lips as Laura crossed the floor to her side. She bent and whispered, 'I am not really Caroline Jordan—that was just a disguise.'

'You were hiding?' Alice whispered back, eyes wide. The sparkle of tears had become one of excitement.

'Yes, a bad man was after me.' As soon as she spoke Laura worried that she had frightened the child, but Alice's eyes were alight with excitement.

'Like an adventure story? Is that why you had to go away from Westerwood?'

'Yes, I am very sorry.' Laura crouched down so she could murmur without Rogers overhearing. 'We must pretend we do not know each other. Can you do that?' It was wrong to ask the child to practise deception, but it was for her protection, too. 'You may tell your papa, of course.' Even if her father *was* Avery Falconer, she could not allow Alice to lie to him or to encourage her in deceit.

Alice nodded vigorously, then whirled round and ran after the others, ringlets bobbing. As she reached the door she turned, put her finger theatrically to her lips and waved. She seemed thrilled with her new secret.

'My goodness, do you not know who that child is?'

Laura straightened up and turned to find Lady Amelia Woodstock surrounded by a group of young ladies Laura knew, more or less, from that Season's events.

'Good afternoon, Lady Amelia. I have no idea,' Laura lied with a smile. 'A pretty girl, is she not?'

'*That* is Lord Wykeham's bastard.' The other girls gave shocked giggles at the word. 'I think it is disgraceful that he brings her to a respectable house party like this.'

'She is an innocent child.' Laura kept her voice reasonable and pleasant as she held on to her temper with an effort. 'You cannot visit her parents' sins on her head.'

'Perhaps *you* aren't as worried about appearances as the rest of us,' Lady Amelia said with a toss of blonde curls. 'But those of us who are not still on the shelf have to maintain higher standards.'

The effort to remain pleasant was so difficult that Laura scarcely registered the insult. 'Provided her father is not intending to create any more babies while he is here I really do not think we are in moral danger, any of us.'

'Ooh!' squeaked one of the young ladies. They were loving the *frisson* of scandal and her bold words, Laura could tell. Now they would giggle and whisper together and pretend a delicious alarm every time Avery hove into view.

Avery. In her shock at seeing Alice every other thought had fled. Now she realised that the only reason the child could be here was because Avery was, too. Why on earth hadn't Lady Birtwell told her? And why hadn't she had the sense to ask who the other guests were in the first place? *Because I was so agitated about Avery and that encounter in the park, that's why. I just wanted to run away and I have run right into the enemy's lair.*

'Lady Laura?'

Laura blinked at the woman standing in front of her, hands neatly crossed over her lace-edged apron. It did not take the large bunch of keys hanging from a chatelaine to tell her this was the housekeeper, new since her last visit. *Run away now while you still can. Turn and say it is a mistake, you aren't staying...*

'May I show you to your room, my lady?'

Reality swept over her, stark enough to steady her reeling thoughts. She could not leave now—too many people had seen her and this flock of silly, gossip-mad girls would make a scandal broth of speculation if she fled moments after walking in through the door. Somehow she would have to find Avery and tell him what had happened, make him understand she had meant no harm.

'Yes, of course. Thank you. Come along, Mab.' *Smile, walk, behave normally. See? No one has noticed anything is wrong.*

* * *

The door had hardly shut behind the housekeeper before Mab burst out, 'That was her! Miss Alice—so his lordship's here, too. What are we going to do, my lady?'

'It is all under control.' Mab's unexpected panic calmed her, gave her focus as she reassured her. 'Alice will pretend she does not know me and I will seek a private interview with Lord Wykeham and explain.' She had said nothing to her maid about that last, disastrous encounter and Avery's threats. 'Now, help me tidy up because I must go down to see Lady Birtwell, it is only courteous not to delay.'

'What if he is down there?'

'Lord Wykeham will not make a scene in front of everyone, Mab.' At least, she hoped he would control his temper long enough for her to get him alone and explain.

Washed, tidied and outwardly composed, Laura made her way towards the head of the stairs. Someone moved in a cross corridor and she glanced along it to see a man close a door behind him and walk off towards the servants' back stairs, a coat draped over his arm. She recognised him from Westerwood Manor: it was Darke, Avery's valet.

Without giving herself time to lose her nerve, Laura turned into the passage. At the door she hesitated, hand on the knob, then the sound of voices from the direction of the stairs made up her mind for her. She could not be found standing alone on the corridor reserved for the bachelors outside a gentleman's bedchamber door.

With a twist of the wrist the door was open and Laura was inside, as breathless as if she had run. She closed the door and leaned against it while she caught her breath.

Avery, in his shirtsleeves, was standing with his back to her, head bent over the sheaf of papers in his hand. 'Yes, Darke?' he said without turning.

'It is not Darke,' Laura said.

He went very still. As the moment dragged on Laura saw the broad shoulders, the silk of his waistcoat drawn tight across his back, the point where the ties drew it in at his slim waist, the tight buttocks and the long line of his thighs, all exposed without the tails of his coat. He was a magnificent male animal and, much as she hated him, she knew she wanted him, too. And that made her even more vulnerable.

Avery laid the papers down on the dresser with care, knocked the edges together and then, only then, turned to face her. Laura realised with a flash of insight that he had needed the time to get control of himself, but whether he was controlling anger or lust, she was not sure. Both, perhaps.

'This *is* a surprise,' he drawled. 'Would you care to explain yourself or would you prefer to lock the door and undress first?'

'Is it necessary to be so crude?' she snapped. 'Or so arrogant? Your bed is the last place I want to be. I had no idea you would be at this house party, so I came to explain before you saw me and did something rash.'

'I do not do rash things, my dear.'

'Oh, yes, you do. You steal other people's children,

you kiss women you hardly know, you abduct people in parks…'

'I'll give you the kisses,' he said, a smile curving his mouth. It was not a reassuring sight. 'Those were rash, I concede.'

'Stop pretending to flirt, or threaten or whatever it is you are doing.' With an effort Laura stopped twisting her hands together. 'Lady Birtwell invited me here and I accepted because I wanted to get away from London. And from you. I should have asked her who else she had invited, but I did not.'

'So how did you know I was here?' Avery pulled the emerald pin out of his neckcloth, put it down on top of the papers and began to untie the elaborate knot.

'I met Alice in the hallway just now.' She seemed unable to stop herself watching the neckcloth slide through his fingers as he pulled it free.

'The devil you did!' He threw the crumpled muslin onto the bed. 'What happened?'

'I told her that Caroline Jordan was not my real name. I told her that I was hiding from a bad man.' His brows drew together in a frown and she added, 'She thought it was exciting, an adventure. She is going to pretend not to know me—you can make a game of it.'

'Can I, indeed? Or you can go right back to London. Now.' The waistcoat followed the neckcloth.

'Why should I? If I leave as soon as I arrive it will cause talk. I have already met several guests. In any case, I was only doing what you asked me to do, attempting to keep away from Alice. You go.'

'I am afraid I cannot do that, not without being extremely rude to Lady Birtwell.' He raised an eyebrow and began to unbutton his shirt cuffs. 'You did not know she was my godmother? She has put this house party together to help me find a bride.'

Laura sat down on the edge of the bed, the nearest flat surface. 'A bride? For you? Oh my goodness, she was hinting the other night at Mrs Fairweather's reception, but I thought she was just teasing me.'

'Suggesting you would make me a good wife, was she? She has a strange sense of humour, although she does not know the truth about you, of course.' Avery pulled his shirt free of his breeches and gathered the hem in his hands.

What he was doing finally penetrated Laura's jangling thoughts. 'Will you kindly stop undressing while I am in the room!'

'I have a bath cooling in the dressing room and I have no intention of getting into it clothed. Do I need to remind you that you are here uninvited?' The last word was muffled as he drew the shirt over his head.

Laura was confronted by a naked, muscled torso and drew a sharp breath. Tailoring could make a man look a lot fitter and slimmer than he was, she assumed, but Avery Falconer needed no help from either his tailor or his valet. The intake of breath had been a mistake. He had been riding, obviously, and his skin exuded the tantalising musk of fresh sweat over the faint traces of Castile soap and a tang of spicy cologne.

She found herself staring at the silky trail of hair that led down below the waistband of his breeches and, as if to indulge her curiosity, Avery's hands went to the fastenings of his falls.

'Stop it!' She closed her eyes, then slapped her hands over them for good measure. 'Go and check there is no one in the corridor so I can leave.'

He gave a faint snort of laughter and the bed beside her dipped as he sat down. 'In exchange for one kiss.'

'That is blackmail.' She opened her eyes and found he was removing his stockings. His breeches, thank heavens, were still fastened.

'Call it a forfeit.' He looked thoroughly amused now. No doubt this was highly gratifying, to see her embarrassed and at a complete disadvantage.

'If I let you take one kiss you will say nothing, you'll allow me to stay here?'

'I will speak to Alice. If she is not disturbed by having you here and I think she can treat your secret as a game, then, yes, you may stay. If she is upset or frightened by the thoughts of your *bad man,* that is another matter. I hardly feel you are going to enjoy this house party very much.'

'It will be amusing to watch you being pursued by a bevy of young ladies,' Laura said tartly. 'How will you decide—or will Godmama make that choice for you, as well?'

'I make my own choices.' The amusement had vanished, leaving his eyes hard, but not cold. There was heat there; he wanted her. 'And right now I choose to kiss you.'

Laura presented her right cheek, face tipped to the side. To her surprise he kissed it. Was she going to escape so easily? Then his lips moved, trailed to her ear and he caught the lobe lightly between his teeth. His breath was warm, fanning fires under her skin, teasing goosebumps along her arms. She gave a little gasp and he caught her in his arms, released her ear as he turned her and kissed her full on the mouth.

She wanted him to kiss her. She wanted *him,* despite everything that had passed between them, and she suspected he knew it perfectly well. Whatever else she could accuse Avery Falconer of, an assault on an unwilling woman was not one of them. But that did not mean she had to make it easy for him, or sacrifice her own self-esteem by simply melting into the kiss.

He growled as she put her hands on his bare shoulders and dug in her fingernails and paid her back by sliding his tongue between her lips so she was filled with his familiar taste. He shifted so that he fell back onto the bed, taking her with him to sprawl in wanton abandon over his half-naked body, her stomach pressed against his groin. She wriggled and he growled again and rolled over to pin her beneath him in a parody of mastery and surrender.

His weight and the slide of muscle under smooth skin beneath her palms was overwhelming. She wanted to yield and at the same time she knew she must not, did not dare. If she let him, he would burn her up, like tinder, leave her shattered. Leave her his.

Laura took hold of a double handful of hair and pulled. For a moment he resisted, his mouth still ravaging hers, then he let her pull his head up. 'Enough,' she gasped. *'Enough.'*

Avery braced his arms on the rumpled coverlet and then levered himself from her body. 'Enough,' he agreed. 'And now I have a cold bath waiting. How convenient.'

Laura got up, stalked past him to the mirror and began to push pins back into her hair. Her cheeks were flushed, her mouth looked as if…as if she had been ruthlessly kissed. Unable to meet her own eyes, she brushed at her skirts and retrieved her shawl from the floor.

'Kindly check the corridor.' If he so much as let his lips twitch, she would throw something at him, she swore, but Avery kept a perfectly straight face as he crossed the room and looked out.

'The coast is clear.'

'Thank you,' Laura said with awful sarcasm as she swept past him. And then, as she glanced back over her shoulder, he did smile.

A cool bath was certainly helpful. Avery dripped onto the bath mat afterwards and wondered whether he was bewitched or merely besotted. What was it about this infuriating, dangerous, flawed woman that attracted him so, against all prudence? It had attracted Piers, too, but his cousin had the excuse of being younger and a romantic. Now, on top of everything else, not only was she here, but she was expecting Alice to lie about her. He scrubbed his wet body dry, shrugged into his banyan and went to finish reading his correspondence while Darke set the dressing room to rights.

'Will you require me to shave you, my lord?'

'Hmm? Yes.' His concentration was all over the place, he'd probably end up cutting his own throat at this rate.

'Miss Blackstock said she would bring Miss Alice down to say goodnight early, my lord, at half past five. We understand that Lady Birtwell is holding a gathering before dinner to give the guests an opportunity to mingle.'

In other words, to enable her to parade her selection of young ladies before him, like fillies going down to the starting gate. 'You had better shave me now then and I'll get changed before Miss Alice arrives. She is capable of wrecking havoc with my attempts to tie a respectable neckcloth.'

'Quite, my lord,' Darke observed with some feeling. 'The hot water is ready.'

Avery sat back and closed his eyes as the razor scraped through the soap and the bristles of his evening beard. What the devil had his godmother been thinking of, to invite Lady Laura? She didn't know the truth, of course, but Laura's reputation was smudged enough as it was, even without the scandal of Alice's birth. Perhaps she had included her to throw the ladylike deportment of the other young women into relief by contrast.

It occurred to him that Blackie and Darke had both seen 'Mrs Jordan' at Westerwood. 'Darke, when Miss Blackwood brings Miss Alice, I would like you to remain for a few moments. There is something I must tell you both.'

* * *

Alice arrived as he was sliding his arms into the swallowtail evening coat with the assistance of Darke. She bounced into the room. 'Poor Darke is going red in the face, Papa,' she informed him.

'So would you, if you had to stuff me into this coat.' Avery tugged down his cuffs, added his watch, chain and fobs, stuck in a cameo tie pin and decided he was as fancy as he was prepared to make himself for the purposes of wife-hunting. 'Miss Blackstock, Darke, a moment please.'

Alice pouted. 'I wanted to tell you a secret, Papa.'

'Is it anything to do with Mrs Jordan?'

She stared at him, open-mouthed. 'How did you know?' She glanced from side to side at the servants. 'She said I was to tell you, Papa, but perhaps I shouldn't tell Blackie or Darke.'

'She told you to tell me?'

Alice nodded. That was a surprise. He had not expected Laura to do that. He had misjudged her. 'Miss Blackwell, Mrs Jordan, who visited while we were in Hertfordshire, is actually Lady Laura Campion. She has had a personal problem that required her to conceal her identity.'

'She said she was running away from a bad man,' Alice explained, her face serious with the responsibility of the big secret. 'It is very exciting and we must not betray her.'

Avery grimaced at his two expressionless staff. 'A man she wished to avoid,' he explained. 'It would be best if you give no indication that you have ever encountered her under any other name.'

'Of course, my lord.' Darke gathered up the discarded banyan and removed himself to the dressing room.

Blackie shot a look at Alice, who was busy straightening the fob that hung from Avery's watch chain. 'If Lady Laura should approach Miss Alice...'

'Treat her the same as any of the other guests,' Avery said and stooped to pick Alice up, making her squeal with laughter. 'You are not to be naughty and disturb the grown-ups, puss. But if you behave nicely I expect the ladies will want to talk with you.'

And if they avoided her, or made any derogatory remark, then they would be crossed off his list at once. Whoever he married must accept Alice without reservation.

'Off with you to your supper now.' He set her on her feet, noticing that she had grown since the last time she had worn that dress. Before he knew it, she would be a young lady. How would he cope when she was the age the girls downstairs were now and men were courting her? He would be forever sharpening a rapier or cleaning his shotgun. But before then he would have a wife to look after her, one who loved the child as much as he did. He just had to go and choose her.

Chapter Twelve

This was nothing like he had expected it to be. Avery, his features schooled into the expression that worked for sensitive, yet boring, diplomatic parties, circulated the room, displaying an outer confidence while he fought an inner sensation that was something akin to panic.

Young women swirled around him like so many birds in an aviary, charming in their pastels and frills, smiling and flirting and chattering. Previously he would have been civil to the plain ones and the dull ones—not that Godmama had invited anyone who fitted those descriptions—and then admired the pretty ones with an appreciative male eye for their physical features.

Which was just what he would be guarding Alice against when she was their age—men like him. Shaken, Avery kept his eyes firmly raised above collarbone level and set himself to assess character, not curves. There were ten eligible misses assembled for him, the mix leavened—or perhaps the better word was *disguised*—by three married couples in their early thirties, eight bachelors of his age and younger, a couple of older widowers and a handful of widows of Lady Birtwell's age. And Lady Laura Campion who was, he decided, neither fish, fowl nor good red herring.

'Lord Wykeham?' Lady Amelia Woodstock looked up at him through wide blue eyes, delightfully fringed by darker lashes. 'Is something amiss?'

'Am I scowling?' he enquired. 'I do apologise.'

'No, not scowling, merely looking a trifle thoughtful and severe. No doubt matters of state are weighing on your mind.' Her lips quirked into a confiding smile which managed to convey that she was hugely impressed by his importance, but also recognised that he was a man who might be charmed. By the right woman.

'To be frank, they are not.' Avery lowered his voice and leaned towards her. With a twinkle Lady Amelia inclined her head for him to divulge the secret. 'I was wondering what a red herring was and why, precisely, it is always referred to as *good* red herring.'

'Or why it is the term for a deceptive clue.' Lady Amelia pursed her lips in thought. Full, kissable lips, Avery noted. 'Perhaps Dr Johnson's *Dictionary* would tell us.'

Us, not *you*. A clever little trick to increase the intimacy of the conversation. Not only a lovely young lady, but a bright one, as well. Not that he was ready to go off to the library and snuggle up on the sofa with only a massive tome as chaperon. Not quite yet, not with the first promising candidate.

He glanced up and saw Laura watching him. No, watching Lady Amelia and with an expression he could not read on her face. It was not approval. Jealousy? After that kiss in his bedchamber any other woman would be expecting either a declaration or a *carte blanche,* but Laura knew full well why he would never offer either of those. The only kind of relationship they might ever have was a flaming and very short-lived *affaire* characterised by lust on both sides and liking on neither. And, as he was a gentleman and had no intention of carrying out his threats to ruin her, that must remain in the realms of fantasy. It was a very stimulating thought though and his body reacted to it with a shocking lack of discipline.

With an inward snarl at his inner primitive male Avery wrenched his thoughts back to reality and the sensible thing, which was to avoid the blasted woman, get his rebellious body under control and stop reacting like a green youth whenever the scent of her was in his nostrils. But in the confines of one house, and with an innocent child in the middle of the thing, he was not certain how avoidance was going to be possible. He wondered whether it was still possible to purchase hair shirts.

He was certainly no fit company just at the moment for an innocent young lady, not without a moment or two to collect his thoughts. 'Will you excuse me, Lady Amelia? It is almost time for dinner and Lady Birtwell asked me to take in Lady Catherine Dunglass, so I had better find her and make myself known.'

'She is over there by the window in the yellow gown. So brave to wear that shade of primrose with red hair.'

Little cat, Avery thought, amused by the flash of

claws. Lady Catherine had dark auburn hair and the primrose gown was a rather odd choice to complement it, but he doubted a mere man would have noticed without that little jibe. Was Lady Amelia aware of just why this house party had been assembled? Or perhaps she considered all single girls as rivals on principle and dealt with them with equal resolution. Perhaps they all did, he thought, startled by the notion that the ladies were hunting the single males with the same determination, although probably with rather different motives, as the gentlemen pursued them.

Parents were obviously searching for just the right husband for their daughters, but surely these girls, innocent, sheltered and privileged, were not ruthlessly seeking men? Weren't they supposed to wait passively to be chosen, exhibiting their accomplishments and beauty? He glanced across at Laura again. The fast young women like her were after excitement, obviously, but these other young women? He was obviously hopelessly naive in this matter of courtship and he did not like feeling at a disadvantage. It was not a sensation he experienced often.

Avery murmured a word to Lady Amelia and made his way across to the window and Lady Catherine, passing close by Laura as he did so. She turned and looked at him, her gaze clear, limpid and implacable. Was it only obvious to him that she had been kissed to within an inch of ravishment only a short while before? Her lips were full and a deep rose-pink and a trace of rice powder glinted on her cheek where he must have roughened the tender skin with his evening beard. Marked her.

Mine, something primitive and feral growled inside him. *Madness,* his common sense hissed back. This woman was a threat to everything that was important to him. He had tried to put aside the knowledge that she was Alice's mother, his daughter's blood kin, and that by following his instinct, to keep the two apart, he was both punishing Laura and preventing Alice from ever knowing and loving her own flesh and blood.

Of all the awkward times and places to have an attack of doubt! Avery moved behind an ornate screen to try to collect himself for a moment. Alice would never stop wondering why her mother had left her. As she got older she would speculate on why her parents had not married—and would doubtless place the blame on Avery's head.

I could tell her the truth—but then she will know Laura sent her away, completely out of her life. How could she face that rejection? She will know I am not her father. And if she blames me? I sent her father back to war and his death. I am stopping her mother from being with her. The shock would be terrible, her trust would be destroyed, not just in me, but in the whole basis of her life.

Fear was an alien emotion, except when he thought about Alice having an accident, being ill, being frightened. Now he knew he was afraid for himself. *If Alice discovers the truth, I will have hurt her. And if I lose Alice, I have lost the only person I love.*

Exerting all the control he had, Avery stepped out of cover and found Laura's eyes still on him. Hell, he wanted her. If he had not known all the things he knew about her he would have liked her as much as he had liked 'Mrs Jordan'. Her dubious reputation as Scandal's Virgin meant nothing to him now, he realised as he met her gaze, filled with pain and fear and pride.

It took a physical effort to break that exchange of looks, to move. Then he was past her and asking Mr Simonson, a club acquaintance from White's, to introduce him to Lady Catherine. Avery forced a smile and turned all his attention on the young woman.

She was shyer than Lady Amelia, but with a sweeter expression. By the time dinner was announced, with Lady Catherine seated to Avery's left, she was chatting quite naturally, with no little tricks of flirtation. They agreed that they both preferred the theatre to opera, that the state of the king's health was very worrying and disagreed over the paintings of the artist Turner, which Lady Catherine found inexplicable.

'I prefer the work of Sir Thomas Lawrence. Papa had Mama painted by him and it is very fine. And I like paintings that tell a story.' She smiled nicely at the footman serving her soup, which earned her points with Avery. 'But then I like novels and I expect you think that very shocking.'

'Minerva Press?' he enquired. 'Gothic tales of horror and romance?'

'Of course!' She laughed, then hastily put her hand to her lips as though anxious her mama would chide her for expressing herself too freely. 'Do you despise novels, Lord Wykeham?'

'Certainly not.' He did not read them himself and the plots of most Gothic tales seemed improbable in the extreme, but he knew perfectly intelligent diplomatic wives who adored them, so he was not going to cross this young lady off his list just because of her tastes in reading.

Avery passed her the rolls and butter and found himself meeting the quizzical gaze of Lady Laura, diagonally across the table from him. Her glance slid from him to Lady Catherine and her mouth curved into a faint smile before she went back to her soup. Had he imagined that burning look with all its agonising emotions a short while ago? It appeared Laura approved of Lady Catherine. Perversely, he began to find the redhead a trifle vapid.

Laura was partnered by Lord Mellham, one of the slightly older bachelors. She looked exquisite, beautifully coiffed, dressed in an amber-silk gown that skimmed lower over her bosom and shoulders than the styles worn by any of the other unmarried girls. And she was wearing coloured gemstones, yellow diamonds, he rather thought. A slightly daring choice for a single lady, just as her rubies had been that night on the terrace, yet her behaviour was perfectly modest and not in the slightest flirtatious.

Avery studied her partner. Mellham kept glancing at the creamy curves displayed so enticingly close to him and seemed a trifle disappointed that he was not receiving more encouragement for his sallies. Soup finished, he put down his spoon and one hand vanished under the table. Avery felt himself stiffen. If Melham was touching her... Laura bit her lower lip, shifted slightly in her chair and whispered something. Mellham grinned and both hands appeared above the table again.

Avery caught Laura's eye again. She lifted one dark brow and murmured something to Mellham, who went red. Obviously the lady had no need of protection tonight. Avery felt a curious sense of disappointment. Something in him wanted action, would have welcomed violence.

The soup plates were removed, the entrées brought out and Avery turned to his other side to make conversation with Mrs de Witt, the wife of a politician and a notable society hostess. With her he had to make no effort. The conversation flowed with the ease, and at the level, he was familiar with from countless diplomatic receptions. As his inner composure returned he reflected that it was tactful of Godmama not to surround him with unmarried ladies and settled down to enjoy Mrs de Witt's opinions of the vagaries of various ambassadors.

Laura turned from Lord Mellham to chat to Mr Bishopstoke, the younger son of an earl and an old acquaintance. This gave her an excellent view of Lord Wykeham's averted profile as he talked to Mrs de Witt.

'Lady Birtwell has assembled a very creditable number of guests, considering the Season is still under way,' Mr Bishopstoke observed.

'I expect we all need a little rest and, besides, she always gives excellent parties.'

'I suspect she has another motive than simple entertainment on this occasion.'

Laura, who had just popped a slice of lobster cutlet in her mouth, could only look the question.

'Lord Wykeham is her godson,' Bishopstoke murmured. 'I think she is wife-hunting on his behalf.'

Laura disposed of the lobster in two irritable bites. 'You mean at his request?'

Bishopstoke nodded. 'He's too downy a bird to find himself the victim of a managing old lady's matrimonial schemes. No doubt he has decided it is time to settle down.'

'I imagine he is perfectly capable of finding himself a spouse without help. He is not a green youth in need of guidance.' *Was he ever?* It was difficult to imagine Avery was once as unsophisticatedly open as Piers had been.

'He has been out of the country a great deal and can hardly be familiar with the field, shall we say.'

'The *field,* as you put it, must be familiar with Lord Wykeham's standing and reputation, though. They can mark out an eligible bachelor when they see one: titled, wealthy, intelligent, powerful and acceptably good looking. He only has to stand around and the pack will hunt him down, if that is not mixing our metaphors somewhat.'

Mr Bishopstoke gave a snort of laughter. 'If you find him only *acceptable,* then the rest of us must surely give up the contest. I have it on the authority of all my sisters that the man is a positive Adonis.'

'Hmm. Are you not a trifle tactless in discussing Lady Birtwell's motives with someone who might be one of the field, Bishopstoke?'

'Would you have him? You will never give any of the rest of us a second's serious consideration, cruel one.'

'Oh, poor Bishopstoke! And I never realised you were dying of love for me.' She spared him a teasing pout and flutter of her lashes before she recalled her determination to be done with such nonsense. 'I am sure I am too scandalous for Lord Wykeham. Besides, there is a slight problem with his impeccable credentials, is there not?'

'The child, you mean? Would that matter to you?'

'No.' She made a show of considering it. 'Not if I liked the man.'

'And you do not even like him?' Bishopstoke raised an eyebrow. 'You amaze me, Lady Laura. Wykeham is being held up as a paragon of desirability.'

'I find him arrogant, manipulative—'

'Both useful characteristics in his profession, wouldn't you say? The hauteur to maintain his country's position and the ability to turn people and events to his will.'

'Admirable in a diplomat, but not comfortable characteristics in a husband, though.'

'Aha! Wicked girl, you want a man you can dominate.'

'Of course. And if I found one that I could, then I would despise him for it. Do you wonder I have not married?'

'It will have to be a marriage of equals for you then, Lady Laura my dear.' He raised a glass. 'Here is to that impossible creature, a man who is your equal.'

Laura forced a smile and touched her glass to his. 'To a mythical beast, I fear.'

* * *

Lady Birtwell withdrew with the ladies after dessert, leaving the gentlemen in no doubt that they were not to linger over their port and nuts. Laura drifted over to the married ladies, unwilling to join the unmarried ones who, she was certain, would be chattering about the gentlemen and comparing their virtues. *Or lack of them.*

'Lady Laura, how pleasant to see you again. Such a sad business, the loss of your parents.' Lady Herrick patted the sofa next to her. 'Come and tell me how you get on these days. Who is chaperoning you?'

'My mother's cousin, Lady Carstairs.' She really must write and confirm the arrangements with Cousin Florence or word would get around that she was living scandalously alone with only the servants to maintain the proprieties and that would just about finish her reputation. Lady Herrick looked around and Laura added hastily, 'Lady Birtwell is chaperoning me here. I hardly liked to impose another guest on the party when I know I can rely on her.'

'She is a notable matchmaker, our hostess. I have hopes that she will steer someone suitable in the direction of my Emma.' Lady Herrick nodded in the direction of her daughter, a very shy brunette who was hovering on the fringes of the group of girls.

'There are a number of eligible gentlemen here, certainly.'

'And one for you perhaps, my dear.' Lady Herrick lowered her voice. 'Lord Hillinger, perhaps?'

Lord Hillinger was forty, a widower with two daughters and a passion for racing. His looks were distinguished, his stomach flat, his hair all his own and his fortune large. 'He is certainly a most eligible gentleman, from what I hear,' Laura agreed with caution.

'You have not met him? He is a connection of my husband's family, I will introduce you. See, the gentlemen have returned to us.' She waved to the third man through the door and he bowed slightly and came over. 'Max, my dear, may I present you to Lady Laura Campion? Lady Laura, Lord Hillinger.'

They exchanged greetings and the earl took the chair opposite them and launched into perfectly unexceptionable small talk. Laura reciprocated with half her attention. She could discuss the Prince Regent's latest building projects in her sleep.

'I'm not certain Nash is the man for the job, though,' Lord Hillinger remarked. 'What do you think, Wykeham? Is Nash the man to create what Prinny wants down in Brighton?'

Laura was sure the hairs on the back of her neck were standing up as Avery's deep voice came from right behind her. 'Depends whether Nash can pander to the Regent's shockingly bad taste. If he can, then he'll do as dire a job as any architect. If he tries for restraint or elegance, he'll be out on his ear. He's got an eye to the main chance though, so no doubt he will prostitute his talents to order.'

'Lord Wykeham!' Lady Herrick turned with a shake of her head for his choice of words. 'How nice to see you again. It seems an age since we met at the Congress, does it not? Come and sit down, do.'

He could hardly refuse, Laura realised, not without

being unacceptably rude to the older woman. Avery came round the end of the sofa and took the other armchair in the little conversation-grouping.

'Do you know Lady Laura, Wykeham?' Lady Herrick was obviously more than happy to introduce Laura to men she would not consider suitable for her own, very young, daughter.

'We are acquainted, yes, ma'am.' There was nothing but polite acknowledgment in his slight bow to Laura and she flattered herself that no one could read a thing in her careful social smile in return. 'Do you have an opinion on the planned works to the Pavilion, Lady Laura?'

'They will certainly add to its entertainment value for those who spend the summer in Brighton. Whether it is an aesthetic experience or a circus show remains to be seen. Are you familiar with Brighton, Lord Wykeham?'

'Only on the most fleeting visits when it has been necessary to report to his royal highness. I may consider it for a summer break this year. I imagine my daughter would enjoy the seaside.'

Beside her Laura felt Lady Herrick stiffen so she kept her voice light. 'The beach is pebbles, unfortunately. But it is safe for swimming and her governess could take her out in a donkey cart. And there are delightful walks.'

The older woman relaxed, reassured, presumably, that Laura was not going to faint at the mention of the scandalous love child. 'Will you excuse me? I see my daughter wishes to speak to me.' The men rose and then sat again as she swept off.

'And boat trips,' Laura added, rather desperately. She

really did not want to be talking to Avery at all, not in public and certainly not in front of anyone else. 'And the air is very healthy. Do you not agree, Lord Hillinger?'

He did not have a chance to respond as a pleasant baritone voice remarked, 'The air is always healthy and fragrant wherever you are, Lady Laura.' Mr Bishopstoke dropped into the newly vacated seat beside her. 'Never tell me you have identified *two* mythical beasts?'

'Sir!' Lord Hillinger was looking decidedly put out.

'I beg your pardon, my lord. A little joke Lady Laura and I were sharing, as old friends do. She seeks a husband who is her equal, one who she is neither dominated by, nor can dominate. I tell her that she seeks a mythical beast.'

'I do not find your humour amusing, sir.' Lord Hillinger got to his feet, favoured Laura with a stiff bow and stalked off.

'Philip, you wretch,' Laura hissed, unable to look at Avery.

'He is a stuffed shirt, as well to get rid of him for he won't do for you, my girl. Now you have only got one mythical beast to deal with.' He flashed his charming, mocking smile at Avery.

Laura braced herself for Avery's crushing retort. There was silence. She risked a glance.

'What sort of mythical beast are you imagining?' Avery asked. He seemed faintly amused. Or perhaps that was simply the smile of a man about to knock another man's head off. 'I have wyverns on my coat of arms. Would that suit you, Lady Laura? Wings, scaly legs and a dragon's head? No doubt it would be a fair contest.'

'My goodness! That sounds like a proposal, Lady Laura.' Bishopstoke appeared to find his own dubious wit hysterical. 'Or a deadly insult. Shall I call Wykeham out for you?'

'Do go away, Philip,' Laura said with acid sweetness. 'Or you may find that both Lord Wykeham and I will upend our teacups over you.' He went, chuckling, leaving only Avery for her to be angry with. 'A fair contest? What kind of creature do you consider me to be, to equal a wyvern?'

'Perhaps they are like unicorns and will lie down at the command of a virgin.' He watched her from beneath heavy lids, like a big cat contemplating a dead antelope and wondering if it could be bothered to get up and eat it. 'Or no,' he added in a low voice that would not reach beyond their little space, 'that will not work, will it? A mermaid, do you think?'

Laura knew the symbolism as well as he did. 'The female embodiment of lust? The creature that lures men to their doom?' Why did he dislike her so? What was it about her relationship with Piers that seemed to anger him beyond reason? She found her hands were shaking and clenched them in her lap to still them. 'Sending you to your doom seems very tempting, Lord Wykeham.'

'I would like to see you try.' He looked completely relaxed, that faint, infuriating smile still curving his lips. *Those lips...* No one glancing in their direction would guess he was mortally insulting her.

'Then I would be delighted to oblige you, my lord.'

Laura got to her feet, inclined her head and swept over to join the single ladies where she could retrieve the rags of her temper unobserved amongst their self-absorbed gossip.

Avery Falconer was going to pay for his insults. Just as soon as she worked out how to punish him.

Chapter Thirteen

The next day was sunny and Lady Birtwell swept her guests outdoors. 'The children need to run off their high spirits, the girls can renew the roses in their cheeks and the gentlemen may impress the ladies with their prowess at the archery butts and on the lake.'

There were canvas awnings set up in sheltered corners, with rugs, comfortable seats and footstools for the older guests and they were soon joined by the mothers who were glad to hand over their offspring to the small army of nursemaids on duty.

However, it seemed that the unmarried ladies had decided that a demonstration of their maternal suitability might be a good tactic, given that the bachelors were all assembled outside, as well. The babies were soon removed from the nurses to be cooed over and the little girls' dolls were admired. The small boys, far less appealing with their grubby knees and tendency to fight, received no female attention and were marshalled into an impromptu game of cricket by some of the fathers.

Laura felt a strong inclination to go and fire arrows into one of the straw targets, imagining the bull's eye painted on Avery's chest, but the opportunity to play with Alice was too tempting and, besides, she wanted to keep an eye on how the young ladies interacted with her.

Lady Amelia had apparently overcome her scruples at being seen with a love child. Laura put that down to her success with Avery the evening before when she had held his attention for at least ten minutes before dinner and had coaxed several smiles from him. Now Amelia was posed prettily on a rug, her pale pink skirts spread about her, a Villager straw hat perched on her curls to keep the sun from her face as she helped Alice dress her doll. She kept sending sideways glances towards the lower part of the lawn where Avery, coat and hat discarded, was fielding cricket balls.

Laura strolled across and sat down next to Amelia and Alice, her own forget-me-not-blue skirts overlapping the pink muslin. Amelia gave her own gown an irritable twitch to display it better.

'Good morning, Miss Alice.'

'Good morning, Au…Lady Laura. Lady Amelia thinks Clara needs a new sash.'

'I think so, too. That one is sadly frayed. You must ask your papa for a new ribbon.' Laura turned to watch the cricketers. 'He is working very hard.' Avery sprinted for a high ball, jumped, caught it in one outstretched hand and sent it back, fast and true, to hit the stumps.

'Oh, well caught, my lord!' Amelia applauded and Avery turned and sketched an ironic bow before walking back closer to the players.

'I wish I could play cricket.' Alice put down her doll and watched, her lower lip sticking out in a pout.

'Girls do not play cricket,' Amelia reproved. 'It is not ladylike.'

'We could play rounders if we can find enough players,' Laura suggested, knowing that Alice's natural energy would not last for many more minutes of sitting on the rug being good. 'I saw a bat and a soft ball with the cricket things.' She counted heads. 'Who would like to play rounders?' she called and found herself with five girls and four other ladies. Lady Amelia remained alone on the rug, looking decidedly put out.

They moved to the other end of the lawn from the cricketers, improvised four bases with branches from the shrubbery and began to play.

After ten minutes Laura had discarded her hat, rolled up her sleeves and was poised with the bat raised as Miss Gladman threw the ball to her. She had watched her bowling and was sure this ball would be as feebly delivered as all the previous ones. It was. Laura hit it perfectly, sending it flying away over Alice's head and towards the cricketers.

Alice ran for it, one stocking falling down, hair streaming behind her. Laura ran, too, straight for first base. Alice reached the ball and came running back, directly towards second base, which was closest to her.

'Don't run!' Lady Catherine at second base squeaked.

'Run!' Laura ordered, picked up her skirts to her knees and sprinted. It was a dead heat. Laura hurtled into the branch just as Alice did. They both went flying.

Alice landed on her bottom, ball still clutched to her chest, hiccupping with giggles. 'You're out, you're out!'

Laura, twisted, threw herself to one side to avoid the child and landed in an awkward, jarring, heap. 'Alice, are you all right?'

She nodded enthusiastically and bounced to her feet. 'That was such fun!'

Bless her, she doesn't know enough other children to play games like this, Laura thought as she tugged her tumbled skirts down and began to get up. 'Ouch!' Her right ankle gave way under her and she sat back down with a thump.

'Lady Laura!' Alice dropped the ball and crouched down beside her. 'Have you hurt your poorly ankle?'

'Shh!' Laura warned. 'Yes, I must have twisted it.'

'I will get Papa and he can carry you again.' Before she could stop her, Alice ran off towards the cricketers. 'Papa! Papa!'

And this time it really is twisted, Laura thought grimly as the other players, realising at last that something was wrong, gathered round her. 'No, no, I will be all right, just a sprain, I think. Oh, thank you, Miss Gladman, I would be glad of a hand to rise.'

'Stay exactly where you are, Lady Laura.' Avery stood over her, coat and neckcloth discarded, sleeves rolled to his elbows. His shadow blocked out the sunlight as she looked up at him. 'I will carry you inside.'

Time seemed to slip back as he bent and slid one arm beneath her bent knees, the other behind her back, and lifted. The awareness of her body, of her femininity, was heightened by the thin barrier of his shirt, by the sensations of fine fabrics over the bare skin of his forearms. They were both hot from exercise and the scents of two warm bodies mingled in his nostrils. *It would be like this if we were making love.*

Lady Amelia hurried up. 'Your skirts, Lady Laura! Here, allow me.' She smoothed them about Laura's ankles with a show of concern that effectively drew the attention of anyone who hadn't noticed to the display of Laura's legs to the knee. Somehow the little tricks did not seem so amusing when they were directed at Laura. Perhaps Lady Amelia really did want him and was jealous. He could understand jealousy...

'Now, don't fret, Miss Alice,' Lady Amelia, said. 'You take my hand and we will go in with Lady Laura and Papa. You are so active, Lady Laura, I do so admire your energy, but you have quite spoiled that pretty dress. How fortunate it seems to be an old one.'

She really was a little cat, Avery thought, unable to suppress a rumble of laughter, deep in his chest. Laura must have heard it, or perhaps felt it, for she moved in his arms and he caught her to him more securely with a murmur of reassurance before raising his voice. 'So kind of you to assist, Lady Amelia. Perhaps you and Alice would walk on ahead a little to alert the staff?'

'Of course, Lord Wykeham. Come along, Miss Alice.'

Laura held her head as upright as possible, stiff and unyielding. She was not going to allow herself to relax against his chest. Perversely Avery tightened his grip and slowed his pace. 'Let go, Laura. I have you.'

It was a mistake. She gave a little gasp that wrenched at something inside him, provoked a wave of helpless tenderness, just as he felt when Alice fell and hurt herself. And yet it was nothing like that feeling. He did not want to offer hugs and a sweetmeat and a bandage with bunny ears. He wanted to lay Laura down on a bed and pour out his doubts and fears and confusion until he understood them himself. He wanted to make it all right for all three of them. He wanted Alice safe and happy. He wanted to keep her and her innocent, unconditional love. He wanted this woman who could destroy all that with one word.

Laura was watching Lady Amelia as she moved ahead of them, her pretty skirts swishing on the grass, her parasol tilted elegantly and one of Alice's hands was linked with hers. *The perfect picture of modish motherhood,* Avery thought.

'Cat,' Laura muttered, echoing his thoughts of a minute before.

'Jealous?' Avery murmured in her ear, the merest brush of her skin on his lips sending goosebumps down his spine.

'Of her gown? Certainly not. I do not begrudge her all the help her dressmaker can give her. I have plenty of new gowns, I just do not choose to flaunt them all the time,' she said tartly as he shifted his grip to negotiate the steps to the lower terrace from the lawn.

'Of my attentions to her, then?' What the blazes was he doing, putting his thoughts into words?

'Certainly not. You are implying that you and I have a relationship that might be threatened by her.'

But we do have a relationship, of sorts. We have a child in common. We have those memories of Piers. We have our own different guilt and our own needs. We have desire. Surely I am not the only one that feels that even after what has happened between us? Don't be a fool, Avery told himself harshly. He was keeping what she wanted from her—the thing most precious to him was threatened by her very existence.

'I am sure Lady Amelia will make some lucky man an excellent wife,' Laura said. Her voice was tight with an emotion he could not read. He could not tell whether she was flustered by being in his arms, furious with Amelia or simply in pain. 'However, you should be aware that she disapproves strongly of Alice.'

'Nonsense. Look at them now,' Avery said. *Jealousy, that is all it is.*

'You did not hear her in the hallway when I arrived, telling the other ladies that it was shocking to bring a bastard to a respectable house party.'

'That is low, even for you, Laura, to make up such a thing.' Yes, he had been correct. She was jealous at the thought that Lady Amelia might be Alice's stepmother, that the child might grow to love her.

'How dare you! I am not a liar—'

'Of course not,' he said. *'Mrs Jordan.'*

Laura ignored the jibe. 'She is making up to Alice because she has set her sights on you.'

'On the contrary, I imagine she cannot be unaware of my interest and is very sensibly finding out how she gets on with my daughter.' It was time to stop this agonising and self-doubt. He was right to keep Laura from Alice. His plan to marry, to give the child a new mother, was the right one.

Avery strode across the upper terrace. At any moment they would be at the side door into the house and he could put Laura down, get her out of his arms.

'You have heard how she makes snide remarks—'

'I have heard no more than the sniping that seems commonplace between young ladies in the Marriage Mart. And amongst married ladies, come to that.'

'You have made up your mind that she is perfection, in other words!'

'By no means, if by that you mean I intend to fix my interest upon her. Frankly, my dear, your antagonism towards her makes me incline towards Lady Amelia. I doubt I would wish to marry someone who had your approval.'

'And why, exactly, is that?' she demanded, twisting in his arms in an attempt to face him.

'Because you are inconstant, flighty, deceitful—' They were at the door. Avery bit off the words, smiled. 'Ah, thank you, Lady Amelia. Lady Laura's maid is just the person we want. And two footmen with a chair. Excellent.'

'You sanctimonious libertine,' Laura hissed and pushed against his chest as he turned to place her in the chair. It was so unexpected, he was so off balance that his grip slipped and she slid free. Avery reached for her, his wrist cracking down on the carved wooden arm with a sickening thud.

Laura landed on her feet, clutching at him. She gave a gasp of pain as her injured foot took her weight and then she was slipping down. This time he caught her, held her tight despite the pain in his wrist.

'I never faint...' she whispered, and passed out.

'That's a new pair of half-boots ruined. And a good pair of stockings without a single darn in them covered in grass stains and as for this gown, I don't know I'll ever get it clean.'

That was Mab. Laura turned her head on the pillow and squinted against the light. She was lying on the bed with her foot propped up and something cold and wet draped over her ankle. She wriggled her toes experimentally. 'Ow!'

'You're awake then.' Mab came over and peered down at her. 'What a pickle. His lordship's none too pleased, believe me.'

'And what has it got to do with him, pray?' Laura reached behind her for more pillows so she could sit up.

'Miss Alice was frightened and was in floods, saying it was all her fault that you hurt yourself, so he had to cope with that until Miss Blackstock arrived. Then he banged his hand on the arm of the chair, trying to catch you, and it must have hurt like the devil, but being a man, he can't or won't admit it. And on top of that he's surrounded by silly chits all of a-fluster because he was striding about carrying you, like some fool in a poem, and they were ogling his arms and his chest and cooing about how strong and noble he is... Well, you can imagine, I'm sure.'

'Only too well.'

'Like I always said, he's a fine figure of a man. But

with his coat off I can see what they were carrying on about. Buttocks you could bend a sewing needle on, I'll be bound.'

'Mab!' But a snort of laughter escaped her.

'That's better. No use you looking like a dying duck in a thunderstorm, that ankle's bad enough without you getting yourself in a pother about a man.' She scooped up the discarded clothing. 'We had to cut that half-boot off. I'll take these downstairs and have a word with the laundry maids, see what we can do with the grass stains. I'll have some tea sent up, shall I, my lady?'

Alone, Laura lay back with a sigh. Now she was doomed to be an immobile audience as Lady Amelia wormed her way into Avery's favour. She did not trust her one inch over Alice, for surely no one went from spluttering with disgust over the presence of a love child to finding themselves charmed out of their prejudice in a matter of hours.

A tap on the door heralded a maid with a tea tray and, hard on her heels before Laura could think of the words to deny her, Lady Amelia.

'I thought I would come and keep you company as your woman is struggling to salvage your wardrobe,' she said with a sweet smile. 'Put the tray there.' She nodded to a side table and sat beside it, regarding Laura across the chinaware with perfect composure.

'How kind.'

'Not at all? Milk and sugar?'

'Lemon, thank you.' At least it would give an excuse for a sour face.

Amelia stood to place the cup on the bedside table,

inconveniently, and no doubt deliberately, at the exact angle that ensured Laura must twist inelegantly to pick it up. 'Miss Alice is quite unharmed by the incident,' she remarked as she resumed her seat, sweeping her pretty skirts around her with some emphasis.

'I had no reason to suspect otherwise. She seems a sensible child who would say something if she was hurt.' Laura managed to pick up her tea without slopping any in the saucer and took a sip. 'You seem very concerned about a child who you referred to as a bastard and whose presence you deplored only yesterday.'

'Naturally, a lady is concerned for the well-being of any creature.'

'Especially if she is intent on ensnaring the creature's father?' *There, at least we both know where we stand now.* 'Might I trouble you to pass me a biscuit?'

Amelia stood again, placed the entire plate on the bedspread next to Laura and returned to her place. 'Do have them all. Ensnare? I have no need to aggressively hunt after a gentleman. They come to me and seek my approval.' She gave her skirts another twitch. 'After all, in addition to breeding, connections and style, I have an impeccable reputation.'

'Which I do not. That is understood. But this is not about me, Lady Amelia.'

'I could not agree more. You may throw yourself at Lord Wykeham, but a gentleman of his nature would have only one use for a woman demonstrating that kind of behaviour.'

'Are you suggesting that Lord Wykeham would set up a mistress?' Laura ate a biscuit without tasting it.

'They all do,' Amelia said with a shrug. 'A lady ignores that kind of behaviour. And the women involved,' she added with a faint smile. 'The child is evidence of his proclivities.'

'And yet you would accept his offer if he makes one?'

'Certainly he will make one. And I may well accept it. After all, I doubt the other gentlemen are any different.'

'And Alice?' The teacup rattled in the saucer. Laura set it down awkwardly on the bedside table. 'It is rather difficult to ignore a child.'

'Once I am in control of the household the child's place will be clearly established. As soon as I give Wykeham a legitimate heir then he will lose interest in her, I will make certain of that. A separate establishment would be necessary. Naturally, one would not want her mixing with one's own children.'

'Naturally.' A biscuit snapped between Laura's fingers. 'And yet you have sought out her company here.'

'But of course. Wykeham might hesitate to press his suit if he thought she would be an obstacle, which is why he has brought her here. I realised that after the first shock, as soon as I was able to give it some thought. And I would not be unkind to the poor little thing. She will soon learn her place—it is not her fault she is a bastard.'

'Love child,' Laura snapped.

'So sentimental. Everyone has to learn their station in life.' Amelia dabbed carefully at the corner of her mouth with one of the tiny linen napkins. 'I thought we ought to have this little chat because I would like to avoid unpleasantness as much as possible, as it seems I cannot rely upon you exercising restraint when it comes to the gentleman for whom I am easily the most suited partner.'

'Lord Wykeham is quite well aware that some call me *Scandal's Virgin*,' Laura said. 'I doubt he has any illusions about me, nor any intentions towards me.' *Not respectable ones, that is for certain. Should I warn her that I will tell him what she says about Alice? That would be the honourable thing for me to do. On the other hand it would allow her to prepare some lies.*

'And do not think to tittle-tattle to Wykeham about me.' Amelia took a final sip and set her teacup down with a firm click. She was apparently a mind-reader. 'I have already confided in him how jealous you are of me and I confessed I was a little taken aback and surprised when I first realised Miss Alice was here. He is assured of my complete understanding and support and I believe he is impressed by my frankness.' She got up and regarded Laura with a complacent smile. 'Do rest, Lady Laura. I'm sure it would be a great disappointment to you if you were unfit for any boisterous activities that might take place.'

'You witch,' Laura said to the unresponsive door panels as they closed behind her visitor. 'You scheming, clever witch.' Was Avery taken in by her? Very probably he was. A frank confession of prejudice, followed by a touching demonstration of motherly care for Alice, was just what might convince a man who was desperate to see his child accepted. It might have convinced Laura, if she hadn't heard the spite in Amelia's voice in the hallway and if she hadn't known her motive for befriending Alice.

'Over my dead body are you going to become my daughter's stepmother,' Laura swore. But how on earth was she going to prevent it?

Chapter Fourteen

Laura insisted on going down for dinner. She sent Mab in search of a cane and, by dint of leaning on her maidservant's arm, hobbled downstairs, muttering unladylike curses under her breath every time she had to put weight on her injured foot.

'Why you insisted on this gown, I'll never know,' Mab grumbled as they paused for breath on the first landing. 'Thought we were saving it for the big dinner before the musical performance in two days' time.'

'I am trying to counteract the impression that I am a hoyden without an outfit in the latest mode to my name.'

'Hmm. One doesn't follow from the other. That Lady Amelia been poking at you, has she?'

'Yes,' Laura admitted.

'Pads her bodice, she does,' Mab confided. 'Saw her woman adjusting one of her gowns in the sewing room.'

It shouldn't have made any difference to her mood, but, reprehensibly, it did. 'Thank you, Mab.' Now, every time the witch batted her eyelashes at Avery, Laura could imagine a handful of wadding escaping to peep above her neckline.

Everyone was very kind when she limped into the drawing room and several gentlemen offered her their arm to go in to dinner. Laura made light of the accident and forced a smile when Lady Amelia studied her gown and then smirked. She had risen to the bait and her opponent knew it. It would have been better not to have shown she cared and to have worn a less fashionable outfit.

Avery came over after dinner and enquired politely about her ankle, Laura replied with equal courtesy and he strolled away to discuss carriage horses with some of the other gentlemen.

'Oh, this will not do! We are all so quiet this evening after our energetic day in the fresh air.' Lady Amelia clapped her hands and laughed. 'We should play a game, do you not think, Lady Birtwell? Charades, perhaps or, no, I have it—Truth or Forfeit!'

Immediately her bosom friends joined in, urging that they play the game. Lady Birtwell beamed approval. 'An excellent idea. Now, all you young people bring your chairs into a circle, and, yes, I do mean you bachelors skulking in that corner.'

She organised them with jovial ruthlessness. The elderly and the married remained seated on the sofas, the unmarried were chivvied into the middle of the room. 'You begin, Miss Gladman. Chose your victim.'

Miss Gladman went pink, but turned readily enough

to Mr Steading on her right. 'What is your worst night-mare, sir?'

'Playing round games where pretty young ladies put me to the blush,' he said without hesitation.

'That is a fib, sir,' Miss Gladman said severely. 'What forfeit shall I impose?'

The unfortunate Mr Steading was forced to stand in the middle of the circle and sing all the verses of *God Save the King* in his wavering tenor, but he was greeted with loud applause when he sat down.

'My turn again,' Miss Gladman announced, looking to her other side. 'Lord Hastings, what was your child-hood nickname?'

'Podger,' the reed-thin viscount replied. 'Believe it or not, I was a fat child.' That was accepted as being so unflattering it had to be the truth and Lord Hastings chose the next person to question. 'Lady Amelia, what characteristic do you admire most in a man?'

She swept the room with her wide blue gaze, lin-gering for a moment on Avery's face. 'Why, integrity, of course.'

Laura would have liked to challenge that. Wealth and status would have been nearer to the mark, but there was no way of disputing the answer.

'Now, who shall I…? Lady Laura, what do you de-sire most in the world?'

Taken off guard, Laura realised she did not have a believable, safe answer. *What do I want, most of all? Why, Alice, of course.* And she would do anything to have her, she realised. Anything. A murmuring in the room jerked her attention back and she found that she was staring at Avery and that everyone was staring at her.

'Something that was stolen from me years ago,' she answered directly to Amelia.

'Whatever was it?' Amelia demanded. Laura realised she must have hoped the answer was a gentleman, and, probably, Avery, which would have produced blushing confusion and no answer.

'I will not say.'

'Forfeit, forfeit!' one of Amelia's friends called. 'What shall it be?'

'A poem,' Avery said. 'We cannot expect Lady Laura to exert herself, not with an injury to her ankle.'

Amelia pouted. *I expect she hoped for something embarrassing,* Laura thought. 'I will recite a verse a young friend of mine wrote,' she said. *'I wish I was a little star, Right up in the sky very far. I would twinkle with all my might, And make everybody's dreams come right.'* She finished off the piece of doggerel with a flourish, amidst general laughter and applause. From across the room Avery's mouth curved into a smile. Alice had written that out in her very best handwriting and drawn stars at the top and a sleeping figure of her papa at the bottom and Laura had helped her paint it.

'How charming,' Lady Amelia murmured.

I shall have to be careful, Laura thought. *She is so suspicious of Avery and me. The slightest indiscretion and she will make a scandal.*

Make a scandal... What do I desire most in all the world? Alice. And how can I have her without any scan-

dal that would risk hurting her? By marrying Avery, of course.

The thought was so shocking she almost gasped aloud. The game continued, but she heard none of it, laughing and clapping when the others did, joining in the choruses of disbelief like an automaton. Avery desired her physically, but that was all. For some reason she could not fathom, he held her in implacable dislike. Yet he had liked her when she had been Mrs Jordan. If she was living with him, surely she could convince him that his prejudice against Laura Campion was misguided and that he could find again what he had enjoyed in the company of Caroline Jordan?

Could she simply ask him to marry her? No, he had made it clear that the only union he could imagine with her was an irregular connection, so she would have to entrap him. Laura shifted uncomfortably on her seat at the thought. It was an unpleasant word, *entrap*. It was an unscrupulous thing to do.

But she was not contemplating it for material gain, to secure a title or wealth. There were three people in this: herself, Alice and Avery. She would be happy if she had Alice. Alice would be happy with a stepmama she liked and Avery, surely, would be content when he saw Alice was well looked after and flourishing. And Laura would make him a good wife. She had social poise, languages, experience in running both a large household and a country estate. She had given birth once, so there was a good chance she would give him an heir.

He was not in love with anyone else, for his feelings for Lady Amelia were surely only the result of a practical assessment of her suitability. *But can I make him happy?* She wanted to, she realised. She wanted Avery to be happy. She wanted him to love her and to feel loved in return. *And I can do that. I can love him. I am more than halfway there already if I could only get beyond the fear for Alice and my anger at his mistrust of me.*

Yes, Laura concluded, trying to put aside that tantalising fantasy of love, marriage to her would be at least as satisfactory for Avery as marriage to any of the other women assembled here for his choosing. He would be angry with her, any red-blooded man would be, but he would simply have to get over it for Alice's sake, she told her conscience firmly. It was still making uneasy sounds, but she tried to ignore them. The discomforting thought intruded that the last time she had ignored her conscience she had ended up in bed with Piers and, ultimately, become pregnant.

She glanced across at Avery, her resolution shaken. She had liked him, admired him. He was, for all his faults, a good man and she was thinking about seducing him into matrimony. Then she saw Lady Amelia watching him and thought about her plans for Alice. *I want and need him,* she admitted to herself. *Alice needs a mother who will love her without condition, without reservation.*

'Are you cold, Lady Laura? Or in pain?' Lord Mellham was at her elbow. 'You shivered.'

'I am a trifle tired, that is all. Would you be very kind and ask a footman to fetch my maidservant so she can help me to my room?'

'I could carry you,' he offered with a grin.

'I think I have been carried enough for one day, thank you, Lord Mellham.'

Even so, when Mab came in he helped Laura to her feet and supported her across the room to the door, watched with sympathetic interest by the company and by Avery, whose thoughts might have been a complete blank, judging by the absence of expression on his face.

Avery watched Laura limping from the room on Mellham's arm, smiling up at him, leaning so that when he looked down it was at her white shoulders and the lace that scarcely veiled the swell of her breasts. She had made the man blush over dinner last night, although he was showing no discomfort in her company now. After that she had been whispering with that fribble Bishop-stoke, as thick as inkle-weavers, the pair of them. And later she'd been giving Hillinger the benefit of that other low-cut gown at close quarters, the hussy.

It seemed that Scandal's Virgin had decided to retire from the field on the arm of an eligible husband. The bachelors that Godmama had invited to give some cover for his search for a bride were providing Laura with an excellent choice of gentlemen, although she was going to have to find one who was so blinded by love or lust that he either did not notice, or did not care, that she had borne a child.

She'd tell some tale, he supposed, as the game broke up with the arrival of the tea tray. A youthful betrayal that ended with the child dying. Or perhaps she would not trouble with arousing sympathy, perhaps her wealth and her name would be enough for someone like Bishopstoke.

Or I could marry her. The thought hit like a thunderbolt.

Avery drank a cup of tea that he did not taste, excused himself and went upstairs to the nursery wing. Alice had a small room off the main nursery where a nursemaid slept, one ear alert for the charges in her care in the rooms on either side and in the cots around her.

As he expected, Alice was fast asleep, one hand tucked under her cheek, her hair in its bedtime braids, her favourite doll on the pillow. He watched her in the dim light of the glass-covered nightlight, marvelling at the perfection of her skin, the curl of her lashes, the pout of her lips. Perfection, until one saw the scratch on her hand where she had been teasing the stable cat, the tiny smudge of mud under one ear that bath time had not dealt with, the stubborn tilt of her chin, even in sleep. She was a real person, not a doll, and he found her endlessly fascinating.

She was his world. He had taken her out of duty and out of guilt and she had rewarded him with unconditional love and trust and all she had asked in return was the love he felt for her. And all that was missing from her life was her mother and an end to the fear that he knew she had buried deep inside her, that somehow it was her fault that her mother had left.

Unable to resist, Avery stroked her hair, so soft under his hand. He could give her that mother, although how they could ever explain the circumstances of her birth and Laura's rejection of her, he did not know.

He tried to think it through logically, assess the facts as though they were terms in a treaty. Laura had behaved shockingly, thoughtlessly, with Piers and she had turned on him when he had returned to war and his duty. She had sent her daughter away, as she was bound to do or face ruin. But instead of finding her a home close by, one of ease and elegance, one where she could watch over her, she had sent her to a remote dale and a life far removed from her rightful place.

And she had simply forgotten her for six long years while she lived a life of pleasure and reckless enjoyment. *But,* he struggled to be fair, *she had been very young. She loves Alice now. Can I take the risk that she will be a faithful wife and a good mother? Can I take the risk that she will not steal Alice's love from me and then hurt the child?*

Selfish, he castigated himself. *This is not about you, this is about Alice. She will not stop loving you. Will she...?*

He stood there, wrestling with his demons, watching the child. The prickling sensation at the nape of his neck came on gradually, then the unease crystallised into the sound of another person breathing in the room. Someone was behind him.

Avery turned, swift and silent on the balls of his feet, and saw Laura sitting quite still on a low chair in the shadowed corner. 'What are you doing here?' he hissed.

'Watching her, as you watch her. Loving her while I can.' The breathy whisper was quite clear in the still room.

'You cannot stay here.'

'No,' she agreed softly, a ghost in pale ivory and dark shadows. 'Will you help me to my chamber?'

Avery bent to drop a kiss on Alice's cheek, then turned and lifted Laura out of the chair and into his arms. She gasped and clung and he murmured, 'Quieter this way, there is less chance of you stumbling.' That was true. So, too, was his need to have her in his arms again, soft and fragrant and dangerous. Desirable and vulnerable. Yes, he would ask her to marry him. And pray he was right to trust her.

She did not struggle, only curled her arms around his neck and was silent as he nudged the door closed with elbow and hip and strode to the top of the stairs. Her room, and his, were on the floor below. He had taken the precaution of discovering which was hers—why he was not certain, unless it was to help him sleep more easily at night, knowing she was not close.

The stairs were dimly lit and the froth of her skirts and petticoats were enough to stop him seeing where he was putting his feet. 'Keep still.'

'I am,' she murmured, and he realised that she had not moved. Only his body was reacting as if she writhed against him, his skin sensitive as though every nerve was exposed, the fret of linen against flesh almost intolerable. There was a tightness, a weight in his groin, and he set his teeth to ignore it and to ignore the whisper of her breath, warm against his shirt front, the tickle of her hair against his chin, the subtle assault of some expensive, elusive perfume in his nostrils.

It seemed to take an age to negotiate the stairs. He

was two from the bottom when she murmured, 'I am sorry, Avery. I wish…'

He stopped. 'Sorry for what?'

'For this antagonism between us.' Her voice was husky with something that his body recognised at a visceral level. *Desire. For me, or simply for physical pleasure?* 'I wish…' She twisted in his arms and lifted her face. Her lips grazed his chin and then his throat, and fire shot through him. 'Please, Avery.' He felt the words more than heard them. Then she tipped back her head. 'You are right, I tease. But I am not teasing now.'

Avery did not speak. This was no time for words. Nor place, not here. He had decided to offer her marriage, now it was as though the Fates had been listening to his mind. He took the final steps to the floor, then turned left to his bedchamber, not right, to her door. In his arms Laura gave a little sigh and curled herself closer.

He held her one-handed as he turned the knob, then froze at a faint sound. It was as though something had fallen. But there was nothing to be seen and he shouldered open the door.

Darke had gone, as usual, leaving a lamp turned down low on the dresser. Avery disliked being attended at the end of the day. He preferred to undress himself and wash slowly in cool water, taking his time, thinking over what had passed and what the morrow would bring, shrugging on a banyan and taking a book to the fireside chair until his eyes were heavy with sleep.

Now he carried Laura to the bed and set her carefully on her feet beside it before returning to the door.

His hand hovered over the key. 'I will lock the world out, not you in.'

'Leave it, I trust you.' She smiled faintly at his raised eyebrow. 'In this, at least.'

'Why, Laura? Why have you come to me?' *Propose to her now, or afterwards? Afterwards,* instinct told him. *Do not complicate this moment.* In passion, in the aftermath of passion, surely he would see the truth in her.

She half-turned from him and ran her fingers pensively over the old chintz bedcover, tracing the twining flowers and stems that some long-dead lady of the house had embroidered. The curve of her neck, the elegant line from bare shoulder to ear, was exposed to him, pearl-pale in the lamplight. Between her breasts was a shadowy, mysterious valley where a gold chain glinted.

'It has been a long time,' she said finally, without looking up. 'You think me loose, but there has not been anyone since…since before Alice was born. And there is this thing between us. This desire. I feel cold inside almost all the time. Flirting and laughing is no longer enough. And with you there is heat, even if there is nothing else but dislike and suspicion.'

Avery had not expected this frankness, this simple confession of need. His body stirred, eager, but he did not move. She spoke of nothing but desire, dislike, mistrust. Could he ever replace that with even the basic tolerance marriage would require? He probed a little, testing how open she would be. 'You know you are fertile. Why take such a risk again?'

Laura did look up then. The brown eyes that could

look so cold seemed pansy-soft in the lamplight. 'We were young and foolish. We were to marry, so what did it matter? And Piers was inexperienced. You, I think, are both experienced and not inclined to be careless.'

Avery could argue that all the care in the world was sometimes not enough, but somehow his prized self-control was slipping away, sand through his fingers. Tomorrow he would take that huge risk with his life and his heart and with Alice's love. Tomorrow he would disregard all the lessons of his own parents' disastrous marriage.

Tonight he would lie with this woman who was ruining his sleep, haunting those dreams he could snatch from a few hours of slumber. He would not get her with child and he would purge himself of this obsession, replace it with clear-eyed logic. A small, cold voice of common sense told him that neither could be guaranteed by force of will, but he was sick of common sense.

'You will be missed from your room.' The handful of sand had almost trickled away.

'I told my woman to leave me. As you have sent your valet away. It seems we value being alone—that is one thing we have in common, you and I.'

'Beside Alice there is little else,' he said as he crossed to her side. 'Except this.'

She quivered as he trailed one finger down her neck, over her breast to lift out the golden chain, warm from her flesh, but she did not speak, only turned so her back was to him.

Avery lifted the weight of hair and kissed the nape of her neck as he began to unfasten the gown. He was slow because his fingers were not steady and slow because he wanted to prolong this moment, this silent surrender, this unexpected trustfulness. Under his lips the delicate skin over her spine was cool satin vanishing into fragile lawn and lace.

He unfastened the gown and pushed it from her shoulders to pool at her feet, brushing down his legs, covering his evening shoes. The wisp of a camisole was next and he followed it down with his hands, over the hardness of the corset, down to the feminine curve of her hips, then back up to free the laces.

Laura sighed as he loosened the garment, tossed it aside and bent to kiss the red marks it had left on her tender skin. Only then did he allow his hands to circle her waist and then drift up to cup the weight of her breasts, his thumbs sliding over the hardening tips. She murmured something too softly for him to hear and tilted her head back to rest against his shoulder and he closed his eyes while he struggled to find control and finesse and care.

She lifted her hands and pushed down the remaining petticoat, then turned slowly, within his embrace, to stand naked in front of him. There was colour on her cheeks and her eyes were lowered and it came to him that, for all her directness and bravado, Laura was shy. *It has been a long time,* she said. Six years for a sensual, beautiful woman who had known physical passion was indeed a long time. Time to ache—and time to grow reticent.

'Would you like me to put out the light?' he asked.

She looked up at that, eyes wide. 'Oh, no! I want... I

want to see you.' A smile trembled on her lips. 'I want to be very bold and I fear to shock you.'

'Shock me?' Avery tugged his neckcloth free and stripped off coat and waistcoat. 'I would love you to shock me, Laura.' He finished undressing, arousal stoked by her unwavering gaze. When she ran her tongue along her lower lip he almost lost control like a callow youth. He dragged a deep, steadying breath down into his lungs. 'Show me. Let me show you.'

Chapter Fifteen

It had worked. She was naked with Avery in his bed-chamber, all that remained was for them to be discovered and she had done what she could to ensure that. Now she had to deliver what she had promised and her courage was failing her for so many reasons.

He looked so like Piers and yet so different, so unsettlingly different. This was no idealistic, lovestruck youth, still growing into his body and his confidence. This was a man, self-assured, experienced and physically in his prime. And the overwhelming masculinity and sexuality he exuded shook her own poise. She desired him, he, very obviously, desired her, but it was six years since she had lain with a man. Could she entrance him sufficiently that he allowed her to stay the night, that he became careless of discovery?

She was acting out of calculation, acting against every instinct except the one that propelled her towards Alice. And yet she could not hate this man. She still could not find it in her to forgive him taking Alice, sending Piers back to war, but in everything else she desired and liked him. *I love him,* she realised, her breath taken by the realisation. *I love him and I am going to betray him.*

The only way she could go on was by drugging herself with lovemaking. Laura reached out and laid her palms on his chest, curled her fingers and raked down, lightly scoring. Avery closed his eyes and growled, deep in his throat, but he did not move as her hands moved downwards, winnowed through the coarse curls on his chest, circled his navel. She felt the skin tighten under her fingertips and she stayed still, deliberately tormenting him. Who would break first?

To her amazement he did. 'Touch me,' he ground out and opened his eyes, green and intense.

So she did, not tentative and not gentle, taking him in a bold grasp, stroking hard from tip to root and back. 'Like that?'

'Like that,' he agreed and lifted her, both hands under her buttocks, and pushed her back onto the bed so her legs dangled over the side as her shoulders hit the mattress. It was outrageously arousing after the memory of Piers's tentative, gentle caresses. Heat flashed through her and when he stroked between her thighs with arrogant possession she knew she was already wet for him.

'Now,' she gasped and reached for his shoulders as he bent over her, his feet planted on the floor, the high bed presenting her wantonly to him. Her conscience stirred and she blanked her mind to it the only way she knew how. 'Now. *Avery.*'

He did not hesitate. One thrust and he entered her,

filled her, shocked her into startled awareness of him, only him. Avery froze, poised over her, deep within her. 'Did I hurt you?'

'No.' He had not, only overpowered her with his size and his certainty. 'I am not sure I can move, though.'

'Curl your legs around my hips,' he prompted and, as she obeyed, ignoring the stab of pain from her ankle, the pressure eased. *'Ah.'*

Avery began to move slowly, his arms braced either side of her, his eyes never leaving her face as though he was reading her thoughts, her soul. It did not occur to Laura to close her eyes and escape that gaze as he remorselessly drove her higher and higher, tighter and tighter until she began to writhe and sob beneath him, begging for release. He shifted the angle and growled, 'Come for me', and she did, shockingly, suddenly.

When she surfaced out of the darkness and back to herself Avery was still moving within her, but he had shifted again, brought her up with him to lie on the bed. 'Again,' he ordered.

'I...I can't.'

In answer he bent his head to her breast, kissing, licking, nipping while she reached helplessly to caress the autumn-leaf hair, threading her fingers through the springing strength of it, holding him to her. The careful, sliding penetration had changed into a demanding rhythm that built the need back up in her, hot and swirling and tight almost to the point of pain.

'Avery.' And she was lost again. This time she heard him gasp, felt him go rigid and then withdraw before

the swirling light and dark left her with nothing but the awareness of her own body, her own disintegration.

She came to herself to find him cleaning her with a cloth and cool water from the washstand. It was a curiously tender gesture from him. Laura realised she would not have been surprised if, having done with her, he had put her from the bed and left her to her own devices. *As I deserve. Finally I have earned my reputation.*

He had better manners than that, Laura concluded. She should be shy, ashamed even, to lie there naked amidst the tumbled sheets while a man showed her these intimate attentions, but she was too sated with satisfied desire to move. *I love him and he has made love to me as I never could have imagined. Oh, Avery, I love you so much.* Could she tell him, risk everything, admit what she had done and why? Would it convince him of her desperate need for Alice or would it simply disgust him? *He will never believe me if I admit how I feel.* She had done this all wrong, she realised. She should have told him she loved him, told him she trusted him with Alice. She should have loved both of them enough to risk letting them go.

And now she had to stay here, stay in this bed or this, this beautiful, stupid, wicked mistake, would have been in vain. She had chosen the wrong path, but now she had to follow it to its end.

'Thank you,' she murmured as Avery tossed aside cloth and towel. She reached out and touched his arm. 'Come back to bed.'

'You can hardly keep your eyes open,' he said, his own heavy-lidded gaze resting on her face.

'We can sleep a little and then later…' Laura let her voice trail off as she held out her hands to him. She did not have to act. Avery smiled and slid down beside her, pulled the covers over them both and settled her against his side, her head on his shoulder. It felt so good to be held by a man again, to be held by this man. His skin was salty and musky with their lovemaking, warm and soft over hard-strapped muscle. She wriggled closer and tried to turn a deaf ear to her conscience. *It is too late. Too late to go back, too late to say* I love you. *Too late for trust.*

Laura closed her eyes and finally slept.

They had woken twice during the night and reached for each other without words. Laura woke for the third time to the delicious drift of kisses across her stomach, then lower. Light was streaming through the open curtains, early morning light that showed her Avery's broad shoulders and the top of his head as he eased himself between her wantonly spread thighs.

'Avery?' She had heard of this, but Piers had never touched her in that way. Avery silenced her with a kiss so deep, so intimate that her whole body arched off the bed. His hands held her ruthlessly while his lips and tongue and teeth destroyed every last inhibition she had. Her hands were fisted in the sheets, her breath was sobbing from her lungs and her voice was hoarse with pleading, but he was implacable. Laura convulsed, shaking and ecstatic, her blood thundering in her ears.

Then Avery cursed savagely and she realised the noise was not her blood pounding, but knocking on the door and an agitated female voice. Avery threw a sheet over her and twisted one around his waist as the door she had persuaded him to leave unlocked flew open to reveal Lady Birtwell, Mab and the indistinct shapes of other figures in the corridor behind.

Lady Birtwell slammed the door behind her, leaving everyone else outside. 'Avery Falconer, how could you?' she demanded, brandishing something at the bed, the evening slipper Laura had managed to drop from her foot the night before as Avery opened the bedchamber door. Her plan had worked and now she felt sick with nerves and self-reproach. *Alice, think of Alice.*

'And Laura Campion, I am shocked and disappointed. Thank heavens your poor mother is not alive to hear of this. Well?' She turned her furious gaze on her godson. 'What have you to say for yourself?'

'Who knows of this?' he asked coolly. Laura, close to him, could see the tension in his jaw, the clenched fist on his thigh, but his voice betrayed nothing but bored enquiry.

'*Who knows?* The entire dratted household, I should imagine!' Lady Birtwell snapped. 'Lady Amelia found the slipper when she was on her way to Miss Gladman's room to borrow something and she brought it to me immediately, which was very proper of her, for, as she said, something must have happened to you if you were wandering about with only one shoe.' She glared at them both. 'Well, Falconer? What are you going to do about it?'

'I can do little about the fact that Lady Amelia is a

prurient little busybody,' Avery drawled. 'My immediate plans are to get dressed and have breakfast.'

The infuriated dowager raised both hands heavenwards as if in supplication for more strength. 'What are you going to do about Lady Laura?'

Avery swivelled round to look at Laura, as unconcerned by his near-naked state as some pasha disturbed in his harem, she thought with unreasonable resentment. The irritation helped her meet his green eyes with some semblance of calm while she waited for the outburst. 'Why, marry her, of course,' Avery said calmly.

'Thank merciful Providence for that.' Lady Birtwell did not sound very thankful. She opened the door a crack, hissed an order and Mab sidled into the room. 'Take your mistress in there.' Lady Birtwell gestured towards the dressing room. 'Get her clothed while I make sure no one else is still wandering about.' She went out, closing the door behind her with a decided snap.

Laura swathed the sheet around herself, slid off the bed without looking at Avery and hobbled painfully after Mab, who had been gathering up scattered garments. The maid closed the dressing-room door and leaned against it. 'What were you thinking of?' she demanded.

'Getting Alice. It worked,' Laura said, pulling on her petticoat. If she sounded confident and pleased, then perhaps she could convince everyone else that was how she felt. It was a pity she could not convince herself. For one night she had known how it felt to be loved by the man she was in love with. Now, although she would lie with him for the duration of their marriage she had forfeited the right ever to tell him how she felt, ever to expect his love in return. 'Stop lecturing and fasten my corset.'

'But the scandal!' Mab jerked the strings tight and shook out the chemise.

'Lady Birtwell will squash it and he will marry me. I will be Alice's mama-in-law.' She turned on her maid who was unrolling stockings. 'What are you muttering about?' she demanded and sat down to take the weight off her ankle. She must have twisted it again during the night for it was throbbing like the devil.

'You are getting Alice, but you are also getting a husband who is going to hate you—and he didn't care for you too much to start with!' Mab knelt to roll on the stocking, tutting over Laura's swollen ankle.

'Avery will not show his feelings for Alice's sake,' Laura said, praying she was correct. 'And I will make him a good wife.' *Somehow I must make amends.*

'He'll not forgive you,' Mab warned. 'He's a proud man used to having his own way, used to being in control. You've trapped him in a net of his own honour.' She stood and began to stick pins into Laura's tangled hair with emphatic force. 'You've got a tiger by the tail, my girl. Let go and he'll eat you alive.'

Avery waited until Laura had been bundled out of the room by her maid, waited until Darke put his head round the door and retreated, wary and silent, to fetch hot water, and then swore viciously and inventively until he ran out of words. When he looked down, the sheet between his hands was ripped across.

Thank heavens he had not asked her to marry him before she had revealed her true nature, not let her glimpse the feelings he had not been able to acknowledge to himself until those moments when he had held her in his arms and thought he had read truth and pain and some stirring of emotion for him as a man.

Now his questions had been answered. He could not trust her, she was as manipulative and deceitful as he had feared. She had told him yesterday evening as clearly as it was possible that the thing she wanted most in the word was the thing that had been stolen from her. Alice. Avery smiled, with a bitter kind of satisfaction. Laura thought she had trapped him, cock-led him into matrimony. All that had happened was that she had betrayed herself, armed him thoroughly against her future wiles. There was nothing she could negotiate with now and he had what he wanted, a mother for Alice whose devotion to the child was assured.

Darke eased himself in from the dressing room and cleared his throat. 'Your shaving water is ready, my lord. Will you require me to shave you this morning or...?'

'I will shave myself.' Avery looked down at his clenched hands. 'No, you do it, Darke.'

Twenty minutes later he sat back in the chair, chin raised while Darke negotiated the tricky sweep around his Adam's apple, and resumed the outward calm that had seen him through one duel and numerous diplomatic crises. Laura Campion was just one more crisis to be dealt with.

'My lord!' Darke stepped back, the razor dangling

from his hand. 'My lord, I almost… I am so sorry, I do not know what came over me.'

'My fault, I moved abruptly.' Avery dabbed gingerly at his throat and regarded the bloodstained towel with a rueful smile. 'I hope you can dress the cut or the guests are going to assume I would rather cut my own throat than wed.'

'Hah, hah,' Darke rejoined, clearly uncertain whether that was a jest or not. 'I am sure no one could think such a thing. A very delightful young lady, if I may be so bold as to offer my congratulations, my lord.'

'Yes, thank you, Darke.' Avery sat back in the chair and allowed the nervous valet to complete the shave. *Laura.* He had thought himself armoured against her—it seemed his nerves were not as steady as he had thought.

Avery went down for breakfast with a dressing on his throat under his neckcloth and an expression of complete blandness on his face. The breakfast parlour was almost full of house guests all eating very, very slowly in the hope of catching the scandalous lovers when they came down.

He smiled amiably, returned mumbled *Good mornings* with studied calm and sat down. 'Something of everything,' he said to the footman. 'And coffee.'

'You have a good appetite this morning, Falconer,' Simonson said and then blushed when two ladies giggled and several gentlemen cleared their throats noisily.

Avery regarded him steadily for a moment. 'Indeed I have. This excellent country air, I imagine.'

Lady Birtwell entered and the men got to their feet as she cast a repressive glance around the table and announced, 'The carriages will be at the front door at ten for morning service. For those who wish to walk, it takes twenty minutes and one of the footmen will direct you.'

From the expressions around the table it was obvious that the fact this was Sunday had escaped almost everyone, swept up in the delicious scandal bubbling in their midst. Avery accepted a plate of eggs, bacon, sausage and kidneys and made himself eat. He could not recall ever being so purely angry.

There had been fury mixed with grief and guilt over Piers's death, he had been more than annoyed when he discovered Laura Campion in London and realised what she was doing, but now he was conscious of little else but a desire to shake her until her sharp white teeth rattled in her head. It did not help that some of the anger was directed against himself.

He made himself converse with his neighbours on topics that were suitable for a Sunday which, eliminating horse racing, royal scandal, the latest crim. con. cases in the courts and most plays, none of which would have been approved by their hostess, rather restricted discussion.

There was a desultory exchange underway about the death of an ancient royal cousin and whether court mourning would be decreed when the door opened and Laura came in, leaning heavily on the arm of one of the footmen. The gentlemen rose to their feet and then sat again when she took her place, reminding Avery of a flock of lapwings, alarmed at a passing hawk, rising off a ploughed field and then settling back.

'Good morning,' she said generally, then, 'Tea and toast, please,' to the footman.

'You are very pale this morning, Lady Laura,' Lady Amelia said with sweet smile. Avery regarded her with dislike. How the blazes had he thought this sharp-tongued cat might have made a suitable wife? Laura's judgement had been quite correct.

'My ankle is very painful,' Laura said. 'How kind of you to be so concerned.'

Avery almost smiled before he recalled how furious he was with her. The wretched woman looked, pallor aside, completely calm. *Actress,* he thought. *No shame, not an iota.*

The room had gone very quiet except for the scrape of knives on plates and the rattle of cups in saucers. The other guests did not appear to know where to look—at him, at Laura or at their plates. What did they expect—that he was going to fall to his knees at her side and ask for her hand? Well, he might as well give them something to twitter about.

'With your injury I imagine you would wish to drive to church, Lady Laura.'

All eyes moved to her. 'Certainly I will not be able to walk,' she agreed and took a sip of tea. Over the rim of the cup her eyes met his, brown, unreadable. Last night he could have sworn he could see into her soul. Last night he had believed he could love what he would find there.

'Then perhaps I may take you in my phaeton? It is

not a high-perch one, so I imagine you will find it easy enough.'

'How very kind, Lord Wykeham. That would be delightful.'

Not a blush, not a moment's hesitation, the hussy. 'Excellent. It will be at the door for ten.' He would drive her to church and make only the most banal conversation. He would sit next to her in the pew and find the hymns for her. He would behave impeccably until her nerves were as tight as a catgut violin string and then he would drive her into the depths of the park and... settle this matter.

Chapter Sixteen

They think I am brazen and immoral, Laura thought, watching the avid faces around the breakfast table. Only a few of the guests had the decency to make conversation. Lady Birtwell seemed frozen and Avery, damn him, looked like a cobra waiting to strike.

When was he going to say something? It was obvious he wanted to torture her with suspense, because he could hardly propose to her in the phaeton with Alice there. It was beginning to dawn on her that Avery Falconer had reserves of self-control that made her own seem like those of an hysteric.

Laura came down for church in a sombre deep-brown pelisse over an amber gown with a new French bonnet.

'Put your veil down,' Mab whispered as she helped Laura descend the stairs.

'I am not going to hide from them,' she murmured, then raised her voice. 'What a charming bonnet, Lady Amelia. So harmonious with your complexion.'

The bonnet was green silk. Miss Gladman tittered, Lady Amelia showed her teeth in what might have been taken for a smile. 'And yours is delightful, too. I always think fawn is so flattering with an older skin.'

'Very true,' Laura agreed warmly. She moved closer and added, low-voiced, 'And one of the benefits of passing years, as you will inevitably discover, Lady Amelia, is the awareness of the danger of making gestures which, however satisfying they may be for a moment, actually work against one in the end. All that effort to attach a certain gentleman, thrown away in one moment of spite. Oh dear.' She smiled. 'Look, Mab, Lord Wykeham has just arrived in his carriage. Help me to the door, if you please.'

And not a moment too soon, she thought as she heard the sharp hiss of indrawn breath and saw Lady Amelia's gloved fingers turn to claws on her prayer book.

The tiger was at the horses' heads and Avery stood waiting for her with Alice perched up on the seat. There would be no room for Mab.

'Allow me, Lady Laura.' He put a hand either side of her waist and lifted her up to sit beside Alice, then walked to the other side, climbed up and took the reins. The tiger ran round and scrambled up behind.

'Good morning, Lady Laura.' Alice, bandbox-neat and clutching her prayer book, peeped up at Laura from under her bonnet brim. 'Are you safe now?' she whispered. 'From the bad man?'

'I hope so,' Laura whispered back.

Alice slipped her hand into Laura's and gave it a

squeeze. 'Papa will protect you,' she said confidently. 'Are you having a lovely time? I am.'

'Do you get on well with the other children?' Laura asked, conscious of Avery's silent figure looming on the other side.

'Oh, yes. Tommy Atterbury was horrid because I do not have a mama, but I said I would rather not, if mine dressed me up in such a silly way. His mother makes him wear a velvet suit with a floppy bow at the neck and he has ringlets, you know. Anyway, the others all laughed at him and Priscilla Herrick said I was a good sport and they've all been very nice.'

Laura could feel her lips twitching into a smile and bit her lips until she could answer with a straight face. 'That was very quick-witted of you, Alice. Well done.' Given Lady Atterbury's own appalling dress sense poor Tommy's outfit was no surprise at all.

She glanced sideways and found Avery looking at her. 'I can't be with her all the time,' he remarked mildly.

'Of course not. Self-defence is important. No doubt Alice has learned her quick wit from you.'

'And the sharp edge of her tongue is doubtless inherited.' His eyes were on the road again, fixed between the heads of the pair of handsome greys he was driving.

'Attack is often the best form of defence,' Laura remarked. 'Especially for a woman. We have fewer natural weapons.'

'I would beg leave to disagree,' Avery remarked, looping his reins as he guided the pair down the lane to the church. 'Men are constrained by honour from retaliating.'

'Given their natural superiority of strength and the unfair advantages law and society give them over women there has to be a balance somewhere.' With Alice listening Laura struggled to keep her tone light and free from the anger she felt. *Honour! What a hypocrite he was.*

'Papa, may I have the money for the collection plate?' Alice asked, cheerfully unaware of the battle raging over her head.

'When we get down, sweetheart.' Avery reined in and waited for the tiger to jump down before he descended and swung Alice to the ground. 'Allow me, Lady Laura. I trust the ride did not jolt your ankle.'

'Not at all.' Laura took his arm and limped into the church. Eyes followed their path down the aisle towards a box pew whose door was held open by one of Lady Birtwell's footmen. 'Not that one. I will sit there, with Lady Atterbury,' Laura said, recognising the towering confection that her ladyship considered suitable as a church bonnet.

'I imagine Lady Birtwell has given instructions on who is to sit where.' Avery continued down the aisle, her hand trapped against his side.

'But we look like a family group,' Laura hissed.

'And?' Avery let Alice go in first, then ushered Laura through. 'That is your aim, is it not?'

'But not yet,' she hissed. Without creating a scene there was little she could do except sit down on the embroidered pew cushion. Laura leaned forward to place her prayer book on the shelf and said, 'I would prefer to be asked first.'

'You have already done the asking,' Avery remarked. He picked up a hymn book, consulted the numbers on the board and rifled through until he found the first before placing it before Laura. 'I am merely trying to exhibit some dignity by not screaming and thrashing about in the trap you believe you have sprung.'

To her horror her eyes began to sting. Laura dropped to her knees on the hassock and buried her face in her hands until she got the urge to cry under control.

The congregation came to their feet and Avery put a hand under her elbow to hoist her up. 'Or do you propose to remain there, praying for forgiveness?'

Laura ignored him, sat down and remained seated through the entire service. She helped Alice with her hymn book, moved her lips as though she was singing and fought her temper and her fear.

Finally the vicar and choir processed out and the congregation gathered their possessions and began to file down the aisle towards the south door. Laura had no idea what she said to the vicar as they left, although she must have said something reasonably coherent because he smiled and shook hands and no one seemed shocked.

Avery waited for his phaeton. 'Gregg, take Miss Alice to Miss Blackstone, please. If she has already left, then walk Miss Alice back to the house.'

With a sinking sense of helplessness Laura allowed herself to be helped into the seat and waved to Alice with the best imitation of cheerfulness she could manage. Avery got in, took the reins and sent the greys off at a brisk trot in the opposite direction to the house.

'Where are we going?'

'To hell in a hand basket, I imagine.' Avery turned into a lane and drove on until it widened into a little meadow beside a stream. The sun was shining, the birds were singing and the brook plashed cheerfully amongst its stones. An exquisite spot for a proposal, Laura thought, wondering if Avery's sense of irony had led him to select it for that reason.

He pulled off onto the grass, stuck the whip in its holder and tied the reins around the handle. 'I have to give you full marks for tactics, my sweet.' The endearment was like a slap in the face. 'The slipper on the floor outside my door was masterly.' She did not trouble to deny it had been deliberate, but concentrated on aligning the markers in her prayer book as though the fate of nations depended on their straightness. 'And as for your performance in bed, why, that was positively professional. Anyone would have thought you were actually enjoying yourself.'

The book fell to the floor of the carriage, the markers blew away in the breeze that did nothing to cool her burning cheeks. 'I was not pretending and neither were you. You know there is something between us. You said as much back in the village after we first met. Desire.'

'I am impressed by your ability to separate your emotions from your passions, then.' Avery looked down at his hand, opened his clenched fist and began to strip off his gloves. Laura saw one had split along the seam. 'The general wisdom is that it takes a kick in the groin or a bucket of cold water over the head to stop a man performing, but that ladies are far more sensitive. I doubt I could have lost myself in the moment quite as thoroughly if I was engaged in such a masterpiece of deceit at the same time.'

'You drove me to it.' She turned her shoulder to him. If she could just spring down from the carriage, confront him face-to-face instead of being forced to sit passively next to him. If only she had the courage to tell him she loved him. 'If you had not forbidden me any access to Alice, I would have been content, but you had to take her from me utterly. Utterly. How could you be so cruel?'

'Well, you have got what you wanted, for I doubt any respectable woman is going to accept an offer from me now, with this on top of the prejudice about Alice's birth.'

She had to be certain. Laura swivelled on the seat to look at him. Avery had leaned forward, rested his forearms on his long thighs and was staring at his clasped hands. 'You…you will marry me?'

He looked up at that and his lips curved into a smile that chilled her to the marrow. So must a master swordsman look when he was about to run through some hapless opponent. 'But of course.'

'And we will live together, with Alice? Be a family?'

'Of course,' he repeated. 'Your powers of acting are established and you will find mine are almost as good. Alice will not be affected by any household rift. As for when we are alone, my dear, we will keep separate suites. I will come to you when I wish to get you with

child, for as long as it takes, and, how shall I put this…
doing only what it takes. I think I will settle for the
conventional heir and a spare. You need not fear my
demands will be onerous.'

The ice congealed around her heart so she could almost hear it cracking. 'I imagine your mistress will be
glad to have so much of your company, then,' Laura
said. She could almost feel pleasure that she sounded
so indifferent.

'I keep my vows,' Avery said, and now she could hear
the anger beneath the even, slightly mocking tone. 'I
have no mistress now, nor will I take one. You may be
sure I will be faithful, my dear.'

'So you expect us both to suffer?'

'Suffer?' He shrugged. 'Sexual release is a mechani-
cal matter, I do not expect to experience any pain of
deprivation.'

'But we could have had so much more,' Laura flung
at him and took hold of his lapels, shook him, desperate to crack the mocking facade.

'We could have had,' Avery agreed. 'You have ensured we never will.'

When her hands dropped away from his coat he dug
in his pocket and produced a small box. 'You see, I came
prepared. Think of the pleasure of displaying this to
Lady Amelia and her friends.' The square-cut diamond
glittered in the sunlight. Beautiful, cold, expensive.

'Thank you,' Laura said steadily as she drew off her
left glove and held out her hand. 'I must obviously take
my pleasures where I may. You can be sure I will gloat
in the most ladylike manner.'

He said nothing, but took her hand in his and slid the ring onto her finger. It was a perfect fit. Laura looked at the arrogant, masculine, beautiful face and did not flinch when he raised his eyes and met her gaze. *I love you,* she thought. *I would have shown you that love, heart and soul.*

Avery's eyes narrowed as if he saw something in her face, then he turned away with a slight shake of his head. He pulled on his ruined gloves, unwound the reins and clicked his tongue at the horses.

Laura kept her eyes on his profile and felt the ice crack even further until the pain told her everything she needed to know. *It is too late. What have I done?*

She had her composure intact when they returned to the house. She smiled and thanked Avery prettily for the lovely drive, she laughed gaily at her own clumsiness as she hobbled up the front steps on his arm, she lowered her lashes demurely when she saw her hostess approaching and let her see the great diamond on her finger.

The reaction was most gratifying. Or it would have been if all she cared about was securing a husband and suppressing gossip. The sideways looks, the sharply indrawn breaths, the tutting disapproval, all vanished as if they had never been. Lady Laura Campion had secured the hand of a most eligible nobleman and all was as it should be.

Even the young ladies who had hoped to receive a proposal from Avery and who had sniggered with horrified delight over her disgrace that morning had the sense to hide their chagrin now. Lady Wykeham was going to be a power in society and they had no intention of earning her enmity now.

Laura could only feel relief at the change, although she gave no sign of her feelings about their hypocrisy. After all, she was the greatest hypocrite there. She showed off her ring, feigned modest delight, fluttered her eyelashes at Avery when he was not looking at her and did everything expected of her other than summon up a blush.

'Yes,' she agreed, dabbing at her dry eyes with a lace-edged handkerchief. 'It is so sad my parents are not here to share my happiness. No, I have no idea where we will be married. I will leave that decision to Lord Wykeham.'

'St George's, Hanover Square,' Avery said, strolling up to the tea table in time to hear her. 'I intend to stay at the town house for the remainder of the Season and I can see no reason to delay the ceremony, can you, my dear?' His look of polite enquiry dared anyone to so much as think an early date might be a necessity, not a matter of choice. 'Have you finished your tea, Laura? I think it time we shared our news with my daughter.'

'Of course.' She stood and took his arm and allowed herself to be guided from the room, but instead of walking through to the garden entrance and the terrace where the children were playing Avery opened the door to a small sitting room.

'In here. I need to make something very clear.'

'Well?' Laura shook off his hand and swung round to face him. 'What is your latest demand?'

'You will give me your word that you will never, under any circumstances, tell Alice the identity of her mother.'

Laura stared at him. The thought that she was now in a position to tell Alice the truth had never occurred to her, she was just so happy that she would be with her, despite Avery's loathing. Now she realised that it would be the most natural thing in the world to tell her daughter the truth.

'But I must tell her! Not yet, of course, but when she is of an age to understand. She has the right to know her mother loved her, always.'

'She has the right not to be hurt any more than she has been,' Avery said.

'Why, you are afraid I will tell her you are not her true father! That is it.' His expression became even stonier. 'You coward, you think she will cease to love you.'

Avery moved like a snake striking. His hand fastened around her wrist like a manacle and her pulse jolted so he must have felt it like a hammer-strike. 'Tell her who either of her parents is and you will regret it. Alice has a hard enough path to follow in order to shake off the legacy you bequeathed her and establish herself as an accepted member of society with the hope of a decent marriage. Will you shake her understanding of who she is, destroy everything she accepts as the truth in order to satisfy your own need for forgiveness?'

'No! I need her to understand she is loved—'

'She knows that already.'

His fingers encircled her wrist, not tightly, just keeping her there. Laura tugged. 'Let me go, you are hurting me.'

'It hurts when you resist me, not when you do as I say.' He waited until she stopped pulling and established his point for him. 'In our marriage you will find the same thing. Obey and you will be happy enough. Run counter to me and suffer the consequences. Now swear.'

He did not spell out what those consequences were. To banish her from Alice, she supposed. He was intelligent enough to know an unspecified threat would work more uncertainty on her mind.

'I am surprised you would accept my word, but, yes, I swear not to tell Alice the truth about her parentage. Let me add another promise. I will never let her realise that the man she loves as her father is a blackmailing, unscrupulous tyrant.

'Now, let us go and tell her our joyous news.' She smiled at him, the glittering smile that had always masked her deepest hurt. *And I swear you will never discover my greatest weakness: my love for you.*

Chapter Seventeen

They sat together on a broad garden bench under a lilac bush, well away from the laughter and shrieks of the playing children. Alice stood in front of them and listened, wide-eyed, her hand clasped in his as Avery told her that he had found her a stepmama and that Lady Laura would be his wife. He had hoped she might be pleased, but he was unprepared for the emotional kick in the gut when she wriggled her hand free of his and threw herself into Laura's arms with a shriek of delight.

Alice's joy should not have been a shock, he knew she liked Laura, had seen their rapport when the child had grown to know her *Aunt Caroline*. Surely he could not be jealous, or worse, resentful that the child had found another adult to love? Avery shifted that uncomfortable, unworthy thought away and watched Laura. He was not prepared for the tears on her cheeks, nor the fierceness of her embrace in return for Alice's. She had protested all along that she loved her daughter and now he knew he had to accept that was the truth. No actress, however skilled, could feign the depth of her emotion and, in his heart, he had always known it.

And, despite her fierce independence, her dislike of him and her desperate need to be with Alice, she had yielded on every occasion when he had put pressure on her for the sake of the child.

Now, against his every prejudice, he had to accept she would do anything for Alice. Even, it seemed, marry a man she detested. But why leave it so late to try to claim her child? It could not even be that she had refrained from making contact while her parents were alive for their sake, because it was not until over a year from their deaths that she had sought Alice out. And the conventions of mourning would not have kept her from the child, he could see that. There had to be some good explanation, he wanted to believe that.

But could he trust her with anything else? She had turned on Piers, furious and full of spite, when he had simply been doing his duty. She had flaunted herself amongst the fastest set in society for years, earning a reputation that had been an inch from ruin. And she had lied to him, disguised herself, wormed her way into Alice's affections with a charade she could never have sustained. Even when she had come to him, acknowledging the dangerous sensual attraction between them, it had been a lie, a stratagem, a cold-blooded manoeuvre to trap him. It had not been her fault that she had delivered exactly what he had decided he wanted.

No, he could trust neither her word nor her virtue. She was a danger and he knew he did not understand her. Last night as she lay in his arms and had yielded with passion and fire to his lovemaking he had almost believed he was falling…

Avery gave himself a sharp mental shake. He could not afford weakness. He had gone to her room this morning when it was empty and he had taken that pair of evening slippers. Now one was locked in a dresser drawer, a physical reminder of a deliberate betrayal.

'May I call you *Mama?*' Alice asked.

Laura looked at him over the top of the child's head, her face tranquil, her eyes stark. 'Of course, darling. As soon as I am married to your papa, then I will be your mama.'

'Do you love Papa?' The innocent question startled him, and Laura, too, from her expression. Her gaze switched instantly to Alice's face and she smiled. It was not the smile she kept for him, edged with icicles, and not the genuine warm one that transformed her face whenever she looked at Alice. This, Avery realised, was a smile that hid something very deep.

'He will never know how much,' she said.

There was nothing he could return for that, not with Alice listening. For a moment he had thought it sarcasm, directed at him, and then he saw the glimmer of a tear as the dark lashes lowered to veil Laura's eyes. Her teeth caught her lower lip for a second and then she was calm again. She had not responded about her feelings for him, but for Piers, Alice's real father. But then she had written that letter to Piers. He shook his head in an attempt to clear it. Had he somehow misunderstood her? The woman tied him in knots.

'Is it a secret or may I tell everyone?' Alice was

already off the seat, hopping from foot to foot in her eagerness.

'Yes, you may tell,' Laura said and sat, her hands lax in her lap, watching Alice as she raced across the lawn to the other children.

'You loved him, then?'

She turned to stare at him, a frown of puzzlement between her arched brows. 'Him?'

'Alice's father.'

'Piers?' Her confusion puzzled him. 'Why, yes, of course I did. I would never have lain with a man I did not love.'

'Really? And last night?'

'What do you think?'

'That you overcame your revulsion very well.' He got to his feet and took a few angry paces away from her, furious that he was letting his guard down, that she might suspect he cared.

'I am not an innocent girl barely eighteen years old any longer.' She kept her eyes on the children, over by the house. 'And you are an attractive man and, as I expected, skilled in bed.'

Avery felt himself flush at the dispassionate description. 'I am glad I gave satisfaction.'

She looked at him then and this time there was more than a hint of tears in the brown eyes. 'You know you did. Stop trying to sound like a...a...as if I was paying you.'

'You do not have much good fortune with your lovers, do you?' He had not meant to mention Piers, ever again, but that last accusation splintered his resolve.

'How did you feel about Piers when he left you? Went back to do his duty?'

'Bereft,' she said and stumbled as she got to her feet. Avery put out a hand to steady her and she hit it away with a swiftness that betrayed the depths of her turmoil. 'In the moment when I read his note I felt betrayed, alone and frightened. You would have been proud of what you had achieved, sending him back to his honourable death and making me hate him, if only for a second.'

Laura turned and walked away from him, away from the house, into one of the winding walks through the shrubbery.

His hand hurt like the devil. She had slashed out with the edge of hers and caught him on the side of the palm. He stood rubbing it while he watched the laurel branches sway and then settle in her wake. *Innocent girl, barely eighteen. Bereft, alone, frightened.* Pregnant. The wave of guilt swept through him, leaving the taste of bile in his mouth as it had so often in the months after Piers's death. *What had I done? Was I wrong? Should I have listened, helped?*

Too late now and, however hurt and frightened she had been, surely no woman who was truly in love could have written those cruel words to a lover facing battle?

Avery turned from the shrubbery and went towards the house. He needed a glass of brandy and straightforward male company with its certainties and its emotional directness.

'You may kiss the bride.'

The church swam into focus as Avery lifted the veil

and folded it back over the wreath of myrtle and orange blossom that crowned her hair. Laura closed her eyes as he bent and touched his mouth to hers and a sigh went round the sophisticated, fashionable congregation. An excellent marriage of equal status and a great deal of land and money. How very satisfactory.

She clung to the cynical thought as Avery's lips moved over hers, warm and possessive. Her hands were on his lapels and she had no recollection of placing them there, but it was a good gesture, one that confirmed her affection and her submission to him in front of witnesses.

They went arm in arm to the vestry and she signed her new name carefully, as she had rehearsed. Laura Caroline Emilia Jordan Falconer, Countess of Wykeham. Beside her, Avery made a sound, quickly bitten back, presumably as he realised she had not lied about her name at least, those days in Hertfordshire.

Then they were in the chancel again, surrounded by faces in the pews and peering down from the wide, dark-panelled gallery. Her hand felt heavy with the broad gold band as she lifted her skirts to negotiate the steps to the nave and the great organ over the west door thundered into life, making her jump. All her senses seemed to be alert, raw. But not her feelings—those were numb.

On the steps she smiled and threw her flowers and waved as she sat in the open carriage and was driven away into New Bond Street and no one seemed to notice it was all an act.

'You look beautiful, Lady Wykeham.' Avery resumed his tall hat and sat back beside her.

'Thank you.' He looked exceedingly handsome, barbered and groomed to perfection, dressed with elegant formality, his patrician features suited to the grave solemnity he had projected all through the service. 'Alice behaved very well.'

'She was feeling so grown up in her miniature version of your gown that I think she was afraid to move.' Avery's face relaxed as he smiled. 'Do you mind not having a proper honeymoon?'

For a moment she could not follow his train of thought. 'Oh, you mean taking her with us tomorrow when we go to Westerwood? No, of course not.' Conscious of the groom clinging on behind she lowered her voice. 'After all, it is hardly as if we would wish to be alone together, is it?'

Avery was silent, occupied for several minutes with pulling off his gloves and smoothing them flat over his knee. 'We did not get off to a very good beginning with our relationship,' he said eventually, equally low-voiced.

Was this a flag of truce? Or a trick? 'No,' Laura agreed. 'We did not. However, I keep my word. You may be certain that I will do my utmost to be a good wife and you know I will do everything in my power for Alice.' He sighed, just on the edge of her hearing. 'What more do you want?' she demanded sharply, then caught herself before the groom could hear. Avery did not answer.

The wedding breakfast went exceptionally well. Laura knew everyone and, with the confidence of maturity, knew how to make a social event a success, even when her brain seemed numb and the house, her new London home, was unfamiliar. The guests retired to the vast drawing room after the meal, champagne continued to flow, the noise level soared. It was, people were saying on all sides, the wedding of the Season. And, of course, it was spiced by the speculation about how Avery Falconer would tame Scandal's Virgin.

At six o'clock Laura went searching for Alice and found her curled up asleep on a sofa.

'I'll carry her up,' Avery said behind her.

'But—'

'Blackie will put her to bed, you can look in later. We cannot both disappear together.' His expression became sardonic. 'Not this early, anyway.'

Laura watched him lift the child in his arms and remembered the three occasions when he had carried her in his arms, the feel of his body and the strength of his hold. She bent to kiss Alice's cheek and felt an answering pressure on the top of her head as if he had laid his cheek there for a moment, or pressed his lips to her hair in a kiss. Her heart fluttered, then she realised he must be acting for their guests.

The smile was perfect on her lips when she straightened and she did not look back as she swept back into the centre of the room. She could act, too, be the loving stepmama who was still less to the child than Alice's papa was. Someone made an observation and Laura nodded in agreement. 'Indeed, Mrs Nicholson. Such a delightful child, so pretty and affectionate. So easy to love.'

* * *

Three hours later Laura sat bolt upright in the big bed with its froth of lace and net hangings and tried to decide what to do. Avery would be coming in soon, she had no doubt. He would insist on his marital rights until she was with child, of that she was certain.

But she was equally certain he would not force her. She could say *no,* but that would be to break her word to be a good wife, and besides, she wanted him to make love to her.

A somewhat humiliating realisation, that. But she loved him and she desired him and she knew he made love with toe-curling skill: she would have to be perverse indeed to recoil from him because he did not love her.

She could do what ladies were supposed to do, or, at least, what some young ladies were told was proper: lie still and allow one's husband to do what he wanted. Laura suspected that Avery, if he did not laugh himself sick at the sight of her apeing a virtuous lady, would treat that response as the equivalent of a refusal.

A draught of air amidst the draperies was the only clue that the door leading from hers into Avery's bedchamber had opened. Laura stiffened, unprepared and with no plan at all for what would happen next.

Her husband appeared beside the bed clad in a vivid red-and-green banyan, a tight smile and, apparently, not a lot else. Laura swallowed.

'Shall I put out the candles?' He must have noticed the convulsive movement of her throat.

It was a tiny kindness, but it made up her mind. 'No, thank you. I want to see you.'

Avery lifted one eyebrow, untied the sash, dropped it to the floor, shrugged out of the heavy silk and stood regarding her quizzically. Laura stared back, then let her gaze slide slowly down over the sculpted muscles of his chest, the flat belly, the dark hair, to the inescapable evidence that whatever else her new husband was feeling it was not rampant sexual desire for his wife.

Laura closed her mouth and studied her interlaced fingers on top of the satin coverlet.

'I have discovered,' Avery said drily, 'that it is one thing making statements in the heat of anger and another altogether to carry them out.' He tugged on the banyan again and sat on the end of the bed, his back against one of the carved posts. 'It occurred to me that you would be lying there expecting me to march in and... Hell, I can't find a word that isn't downright crude or—'

'You certainly do not want to say, *make love*,' Laura agreed.

His mouth tightened at the sarcasm. '—*have you*, whether you want it or not. You wouldn't be aroused, I would hurt you.'

'Many, perhaps most, men would, without a second thought.'

'I am not most men.'

No, my love, you are not and that is why I love you, despite everything. 'I cannot think of an unexceptional euphemism either. Would it help if I said I would like to have sex with you?'

'You would?' The unfastened banyan fell open as he shifted to look directly at her. He was not so very far from arousal after all, or perhaps her frankness was stimulating.

'I think you would have noticed if you repelled me. Despite everything, I enjoyed lying with you before. You must have noticed *that*.' Laura pulled the ribbon tie of her negligée open. Catlike Avery watched the moving silk. 'Women do enjoy sex, you know. They don't have to fool themselves by imagining they are in love, or have to be wanton and abandoned.'

It was half the truth. She wanted him, badly, yet just as badly did not want the suspicion and hostility that lay between them like a hedge of thorns. She needed tenderness and affection and the slow slide of those long brown fingers across her flesh, the gentle torture of his mouth on her body.

'Then let us, as you say, *lie together* and whatever follows from that.' Avery flipped back the covers and shifted up the bed to prop himself on one elbow next to her. She could not imagine speaking so frankly with any other man under such circumstances. Somehow that very ease made her sadder. They could have so much, share so much if only they did not have this history between them.

Bold, because she knew what she wanted and needed him to want it, too, Laura pushed the heavy silk from his shoulders and ran her fingers into his hair, pulling him down to kiss her. Avery obliged, his fingers deft in the ties of her negligée, the urgency in contrast to the slow, almost lazy sweep of his tongue between her lips.

Avery disposed of her nightgown with an efficiency that made her smile against his mouth. One warm hand moved down her body, slid between her thighs. She was ready for him, embarrassingly so if she had a particle of shame left in her. Laura pressed against the questing fingers, arched into his palm to find it gone. He shifted his weight over her, nudged her thighs apart with his knee and entered her in one hard stroke.

Surprised, yet excited, Laura curled her legs around his hips and looked up into his face. Avery's eyes were closed, his face stark, the tendons of his throat taut. He thrust steadily without kissing her, his hands still on the pillow beside her head. Laura struggled to meet his rhythm, to pace her own pleasure. Then he stilled, groaned deep in his throat and thrust hard, hanging over her, his face contorted into a mask of effort. She felt the heat of his release deep inside her, braced herself for his body as he relaxed onto her and held him to her when he subsided, crushing her breasts against his chest.

Her body was throbbing and tingling with unsatisfied desire, but part of her was flattered and titillated by his urgency. She rubbed her cheek against his hair as he lay, his face buried in her shoulder.

Then, taking her by surprise, he rolled off her body, rose from the bed and pulled on his robe. 'Thank you,' Avery said politely, as though she had poured a cup of tea or hemmed a handkerchief for him. 'Goodnight, Laura.'

Chapter Eighteen

The pattern continued for four days and four nights. Avery was unfailingly polite, mildly affectionate to her in front of Alice and the servants and consulted amicably about what changes she might wish to make to the house. In the evening he listened intently to Alice's news, courteously to Laura's description of how she had spent her day and made unexceptional small talk over the dinner table.

At night he came to her bed, ensured she was adequately prepared for him, which, to her humiliation, was easy enough, and removed himself to his own chamber as soon as he had obtained his own release. Laura was furious and frustrated and had no idea what, short of chaining him to the bed, she could do about it. Easy though she had found it to speak frankly to Avery about desire, she found her tongue stuck to the roof of her mouth when she tried to ask him to stay and actually make love to her.

'You're as cross as crabs,' Mab observed on the

fifth morning when Laura managed to upset her trinket bowl on the dressing table, sending ear bobs and silver chains flying. She knelt on the floor, muttering curses under her breath, and tried to gather them up while her maidservant nagged. 'What's the matter with you? You've got little Alice, you've got a lovely home and a fine husband who isn't lacking in his attentions to you…'

Laura sat up abruptly and banged her head on the underside of the table. 'Ow!' She crawled out and glared at Mab. 'I will thank you not to refer to private matters of that sort. Nothing is wrong.'

'Then sit down and let me do your hair.' Mab was, as usual, unsquashable. She swept the brush through Laura's hair, provoking a gasp of pain as the bristles found a tangle. 'There, of course! I know what's wrong, its that time of the month. I lost count, what with the excitement over the wedding and all. That's why you're so down in the mouth, just like normal.'

'So it is.' Laura rubbed her back, which now she thought about it, was aching. She did some rapid calculations. 'Tomorrow.' Now she had the knowledge that she was not pregnant to add to her usual monthly misery. She would be fine by the day after, once she had got through a day of being clumsy, achy and prone to tears and another day of cramps. Tonight, she thought, with the feeling of someone glimpsing a small patch of silver lining in a very dark cloud, she could tell Avery to keep to his own bedchamber for a few nights. He'd be hoping he had got her with child, she was sure, gloomily pleased to be spreading the misery.

* * *

By the time she went downstairs she had talked herself into a more positive frame of mind, although she was grateful that Alice was going to be spending the day with her friends, the granddaughters of Mrs Gordon. Avery had ridden out early to inspect some distant woodland with a view to selling some of the timber, Pritchett informed her.

She had been reluctant to turn off any of her old staff so Avery had agreed to Pritchett taking over at Westerwood while his own butler remained in control of the town house and the Westerwood butler, who had been feeling his rheumatics, moved to the easier duties at the Leicestershire hunting lodge.

Pritchett refilled her coffee cup. 'Which room do you wish to look at today, my lady?'

The rooms at Westerwood Manor were all in excellent condition, but some seemed dated, others were not very comfortable. Laura had been working round them, making notes and listing necessary work. It made a neutral topic of conversation with Avery and it was helping her learn his tastes before they moved to his main country house, Wykeham Hall. It was best for Alice, they had agreed, for her to become used to the changes to her family in a house she was familiar with.

'This room, I think… No, the Blue Sitting Room.' Avery was away, that was the safest time to investigate the room where Piers's portrait hung.

'Very well, my lady. I will send Jackson and one of the maids along to assist you.'

'No need for that, thank you, Pritchett. I do not expect to have to change anything around. I just want to familiarise myself with that room.'

It took an hour of procrastination before Laura finally shut the door behind her and went to sit at the writing table that faced the fireplace and Piers's portrait. This was the table where Avery had kissed her with such passion, the place where she had learned the truth about Piers's return to Spain and his death.

Laura folded her hands on the blotter and made herself look steadily at the picture until she felt her calm return. He looked so young, so unformed in that flamboyant red jacket. Had he really loved her or was it simply a boy's first calf love? If she had refused to make love with him, would they have drifted apart naturally?

Yes, she thought, sadly. *Yes, what we had was sweet and strangely innocent. Or perhaps naive is the better word. If he had lived, we would have married because of the baby and by now we would have outgrown each other and yet be tied together for life.*

She got up and went to lift down the heavy cavalry sabre from its stand on the mantelshelf. It was not even scratched, Piers had owned it for such a short time. A bullet in the chest had killed him before he was able to raise his sword in anger at the enemy. Laura touched the tassel that hung from the finger guard, then set the weapon back in place.

It felt as though she had said goodbye, finally. Laura went back to her seat at the table and straightened the blotter, the paper knife and the inkwell automatically, unable somehow to leave the room yet. Presumably there should be writing paper and sealing wax in the drawers, she had better check that was all in order.

She opened the shallow right-hand drawer and found expensive paper, a knife for trimming pens, a taper and a coil of wax. All as it should be. She pulled at the left-hand drawer and it stuck. When she bent down to check she realised it was locked, although the wood of the drawer had shrunk so that the tongue of the lock was visible. Impulsively she picked up the paper knife and pushed it into the gap. The flimsy lock popped open and the drawer slid out.

It was empty except for a tattered, much folded, piece of paper. Curious, Laura picked it up and flattened it out on the blotter. It was not even a full sheet of writing paper, just a torn quarter of a page, ragged at the edges, covered in a brown stain with only a few words visible.

Then she realised she was looking at her own handwriting and that this must be part of that desperate letter she had written to Piers when he had left for Spain and she had realised she was carrying Alice.

These brown stains must be blood, Piers's blood. She snatched her hand back, then, ashamed at her squeamishness, traced the few faintly legible words with her fingertip, seeing again the full message she had tried to send. Her fear, but her trust in him despite his apparent desertion. Her anxiety and her desperate need for reassurance.

She had no idea how long she sat there or when the realisation came to her that he must have kept her letter beneath his uniform against his heart, and that was why it was rent and bloody, just as his body had been. He had died knowing she loved him, knowing he was to be a father. She hoped he had been happy at the news, even if, like her, he would have been apprehensive.

Something dripped onto her hand and she realised she was weeping, the tears sliding silently down her cheeks. Laura found her handkerchief and mopped her eyes.

'How very touching.'

She started and the paper fluttered to the desk, as brown and tattered as a dead leaf. Avery ducked under the raised window and stepped down into the room, just as she had all those weeks ago when she had found him here.

'This is the last letter I wrote to Piers.' Why was Avery's face so set and hard? Because she had opened the locked drawer? She answered the unspoken accusation. 'I know the drawer was locked. I did not intend to pry, it must have been instinct.'

Avery shrugged. 'I wonder you care to touch it.'

'Because of the bloodstains? If he was wounded and in my arms I would not care about the blood.' She looked down at the scrap again, away from her husband's hard, inexplicably accusing, eyes. 'Piers must have carried it against his heart.'

'A strange thing to do, considering what you wrote.'

'I do not understand.'

Why did she sound so confused—surely she recalled what she had written in that last letter? Avery reached across and picked up the fragment and stared at it again. 'It was how I found you, and Alice,' he said absently as his mind grappled with the puzzle. 'Your name is not common.' It was like trying to read the occasional coded message that had come his way when abroad, the sort where individual words and the spaces between them had to be shuffled and...

The spaces between. God, had he been so blinded by his own guilt and grief, the need to blame someone? 'Read me what you wrote.' He thrust the paper at Laura.

She stared at him as if he was drunk, but she was prepared to humour him, so took it and laid it in front of her. One rounded nail traced the first line as she read, hesitating out of forgetfulness or emotion, he was not sure which.

'*I feel such a coward. It seems...like a betrayal of everything I told you I could be as a soldier's wife. I hate to...worry you, but I am pregnant with our child. Please don't blame yourself, we were both at fault, but write, I beg you, tell me what to do... Please look after yourself, with all my love, Laura.* There was only the one page. The beginning of the letter was me thanking him for his note and hoping he was safe.' Her voice trailed away.

'You really did love him, didn't you?' He was trying so hard to stop his voice shaking that it came out harder and more abrupt than he meant. What had he done? Instinct should have told him to look deeper. To have trusted this woman. Prejudice, guilt and fear. What a toxic mix.

'Yes, of course. I told you how I felt about him, I would never have made love with him if I had not.' Laura's hands clenched into fists. 'I am sorry, but the fact that I loved Piers does not mean I cannot be a faithful wife to you.'

'That is not why I asked.' *Hell, this was difficult.* 'I have a confession to make.' He made himself meet her startled gaze. 'When I found that letter all I could read were isolated words, negative, angry words. Together they sounded like a diatribe from a woman who felt bitter and betrayed, who was writing to accuse Piers of abandoning her. I thought those were the last words he received from England, that he had gone to his death not with a message of love over his heart, but one of furious rejection.'

Laura gasped and stared down at the letter. '*Coward, hate, blame.* But…you condemned me on those isolated words alone? How could you!'

He almost said it aloud, spoke of the grief and the guilt, the awful guilt, but how could he excuse himself when he had done Laura such an injustice? It would sound as though he was trying to justify the unjustifiable. 'I am sorry. I was wrong and I was prejudiced.' *I love you. How am I ever going to be able to say those words to you now? How will you ever accept them from me?*

'I should have been open with you from the start. Told you what I thought, asked you to explain.' He was unused to being in the wrong so completely. *The great diplomat, the man who can read faces, delve into minds. Look at you now.* 'I should have been totally open and honest.'

'Open and honest,' Laura echoed, almost to herself. When she stood she seemed paler than normal, frailer somehow, as though she was in pain. 'I cannot speak of this any more now. It is too... Excuse me.'

Avery was still standing on the same spot when little Annie, the downstairs maid, came in, her hands full of feather dusters and polishing cloths.

'Oh! I'm sorry, my lord. I thought the room was empty when I saw her ladyship come out. I'll come back later.' She bobbed a curtsy.

'No, I am just leaving.' Avery folded the bloodstained letter into a piece of fresh paper and took it with him. He would lock it in the desk in his bedchamber where there was no risk of Laura finding it and being upset all over again.

Who am I trying to deceive? I was the one who upset her, not the letter. She was weeping, yes, but that was simply normal grief. The pain came later when she realised what I had thought, how little I valued her. I thought all I was risking with this marriage was my place in Alice's heart. He had glimpsed something more than he had ever hoped for. A wife he loved and who might love him, a family built on truth and trust and not lies and secrets. And he had thrown it away.

Laura did not appear at luncheon, although it was not unusual for them to miss each other for that informal meal. Perhaps she had gone to collect Alice early so she could enjoy the company of someone who trusted her, he thought, spearing a slice of ham with unnecessary force. But how could he tell what she thought or what she wanted? He was coming to realise he did not understand her at all and that she might never trust him enough to let him try.

Laura had been still pale and quiet during dinner. She had left him to his port and was sitting with a book open on her lap when Avery joined her in the drawing room. After ten minutes of stilted conversation she announced she was going to her room, said goodnight and left him standing on the hearthrug with no idea of how to reach her.

After half an hour spent brooding Avery came to the conclusion that they had only two things in common. Alice could not be involved in this, but perhaps they could talk honestly in bed. He felt a glimmering of optimism as he shed his clothes and donned his banyan.

Laura was sitting up in bed, pale against the white pillows. When she heard him she opened her eyes and said, quite simply, 'No.' Then she closed them again and lay back.

Avery found himself out on the landing with no very clear memory of how he had got there, only the knowledge that he had never been with an unwilling woman in his life and he was not going to start now with his wife. Even persuasion was unacceptable.

He thought about the library and its decanters, only to be jolted out of his inertia by a snort right behind him. When he turned Laura's woman Mab stood there regarding him with disapproval over an armful of clean linens.

'Yes?' he enquired in the tone that normally had staff scuttling for cover.

'Have you been bothering my lady?' Before he could tear her off a strip for impertinence she added, 'You men! And now of all times.'

'What do you mean?' Was Laura sick? 'Come in here.' He steered her into his bedchamber where Laura would not be able to hear them.

'I mean, she'll be feeling poorly for a couple of days, bless her. Always has taken her badly. And it's no good you glowering at me. You might be upset she's not going to give you your dratted heir this time, but I expect she's not too pleased either.'

'Poorly? Heir?' Light dawned. 'You mean it is that time of the month?' No wonder the poor woman had looked so drained. He could not have found a worse time to distress her if he had tried for a year.

'Yes,' Mab said baldly. Her face softened a trifle. 'I'm sorry if I spoke out of order, my lord, but I worry about her. She might seem as if she's hard sometimes, but she's not. Not as sophisticated as her reputation makes out and not as strong either.'

'I cannot fault you for caring for your mistress.' He should not be gossiping with servants, let alone taking one into his confidence, but he had to ask. 'You've known her for years. She loved my cousin, didn't she?'

'Aye,' Mab agreed. She shifted the laundry onto her hip and scratched her ear as if deep in thought. 'Doubt it would have lasted though. Calf love.' She eyed him up and down, a purely feminine appraisal that brought the colour to his cheeks. 'He wasn't the man you are, if that's what's worrying you.'

'It is not. Thank you, Mab.' He opened the door for her. 'Is there anything I can do for her?'

'Stay in your own bed for a few nights.' He heard the wretched woman laugh softly as she padded off down the corridor.

Avery abandoned thoughts of the brandy, went to bed and lay awake, brooding on the enigma that was his wife. He had misjudged her badly over Piers, but why had she rejected the baby? Perhaps her grief for Piers was the cause. Or she simply could not face the scandal and then, if she feared she was never going to marry and have children, a belated maternal instinct had driven her to seek out her daughter. But if scandal worried her, why had she returned to society and behaved in a manner that was certain to brand her as fast, to put it mildly?

But he could hardly demand an explanation now, not when he had so obviously destroyed whatever shreds of trust she had in him. He shifted uncomfortably, going back in his head over her shock and hurt that he had so misread her letter. It seemed that she was right not to trust him and yet he dare not risk trusting her utterly either, not when he loved her like this. It felt like baring his throat to a sword.

Alice had been his only vulnerability, his only weak spot. In everything else his life was his to command and he could rely on his determination, his intellect, his ambition, to achieve what he wanted. He was not used to failure. Somehow he had to turn this around for all their futures.

Chapter Nineteen

Laura took breakfast in bed the next morning. It was easier to yield to Mab's bullying than face Avery over bacon and eggs that would simply make her queasy. She was uncomfortably aware that he was probably very angry with her. No man would take a monosyllabic refusal with equanimity, she was certain. She should have explained, however embarrassing it was and however hurt she was by his interpretation of her letter to Piers.

And that did hurt, deeply. No wonder Avery had thought so little of her if he could believe she was fickle enough to send a letter full of accusations and recrimination to a man facing danger and death. He was a hypocrite, too, she told herself, stoking her anger. He had virtually forced Piers to go back to Spain when, who knows, if he had sold out to marry her and be a father to their child, he would be alive now.

What if, what if... No, it was a futile game to play. Piers might have walked out of his house and been run over by a cart, or have been struck down by typhoid.

Every second of every day everyone made choices that could result in life or death. If Avery felt guilty, then that was his burden to carry and she had to learn to forgive him.

It was curiously difficult to do, even when she loved him. Perhaps that was the penalty of becoming older, one saw the shades of grey in everything, in everyone.

'Mama?' Alice peeped around the door. 'Blackie and Mab say you are poorly and I mustn't come and bounce on the bed.'

'But you may come in and sit beside me.' Laura patted the bed. 'I will be better soon, it is just a tummy ache.'

'Papa has written you a letter. He said I could bring it.' Beaming with importance, she handed over the note, folded but unsealed.

Laura opened it and read: *I have accepted an offer on the timber in the far woods and I must go to St Albans to my lawyers to finalise the sale and for other business. I may also need to go to Buckingham, but I will be back in four, or at the most seven, days.* There was no salutation, no signature beyond his initials.

'Papa has gone away for a few days on business,' Laura said and managed a big smile. 'So the ladies of the house are in charge. What mischief shall we get up to while Papa is away?'

That did make Alice bounce, until Mab wagged a finger at her. They would have a picnic with nothing but cake, go riding all day, buy a puppy...

Laura let her rattle on and told herself that it was only her present condition that made her feel so miserable. But she knew she wanted Avery back, needed to talk to him, needed to find a way through this suspicion between them.

Alice followed Mab into the dressing room to 'help' her sort out Laura's shoes and Laura smiled at Miss Blackstock, standing quietly in the corner, waiting with her usual patience. 'Do you think we should find Miss Alice a governess, Miss Blackstock? My husband was speaking of it a while ago.'

'That was when he did not know who he would be marrying so soon, if I might be so bold as to put it that way. He hasn't said any more about it to me, my lady.'

'She is still a little young. I could undertake her lessons for a year.'

'That would please Miss Alice, my lady. But might it not be a problem when his lordship wishes to travel with you and not always take Miss Alice? You haven't had your bride trip yet, for one thing.'

That was true. Somehow Laura could not imagine Avery wanting to whisk her away alone on a romantic journey, but he might want her to act as hostess if he was sent on a diplomatic mission and Alice was becoming rather old to take around the capitals of Europe with parents who were distracted by matter of state.

'A governess would give her continuity,' Laura agreed. She stretched and rubbed her back. The cramps were easing, by tomorrow she would feel her usual energetic self. 'Which carriage has Lord Wykeham taken?'

'The small one, my lady.'

'Well, in that case, I think I will take the travelling carriage and we can go up to London tomorrow and set about finding someone. Mab, Alice!' They looked around the door, one head above the other, and made her smile. 'I think we will have a ladies' trip to London, just the four of us, and we will see if we cannot find Alice a nice governess. What do you think of that, Alice?'

The child came in, her face scrunched up in thought as she considered this hard question. 'Will she be fun?'

'Of course. She will be young and cheerful and she will teach you all kinds of exciting things.'

'And you won't go away, just because I've got her?'

'I will have to go away if Papa is travelling and needs me, but I will always come back, Alice. If we choose a governess now, then you will have plenty of time to get to know her before I go anywhere with Papa. And Blackie will be here, as well.' Alice nodded approval. 'In that case, ladies, this afternoon we will pack for London!'

Avery had intended to stay away a week, time for Laura to recover from her temporary indisposition and from her distress over the letter. Time for him to decide how to deal with a wife he desired, whom he had, undoubtedly, wronged and yet, somehow could not quite bring himself to trust. *She has wronged me,* a mutinous voice reminded him. She had never explained how she could shut Alice out of her life for six years. She had acted a part as Mrs Jordan. She had tried to entrap him into marriage. *And yet I love her.*

Avery gritted his teeth and looked out of the window at the sight of the park rolling past the carriage windows. The sun was just setting and the stands of beech trees cast long, lovely shadows across the grass.

He was in no mood to appreciate natural beauty. Four days he had managed to stay away, not long enough to get his own guilt and resentment under control and not long enough, he was sure, for Laura to be feeling very kindly towards him.

His mood was not helped by Pritchett's expression of surprise as he walked through his own front door. 'My lord!'

'Yes?' Avery raised an eyebrow. 'Why the surprise? I believe I live here.'

'Yes, of course, my lord. It is just that her ladyship—'

Something cold ran a finger down Avery's spine. 'What is wrong with her?' *Was she sick after all? He would forgive her anything. Anything at all—*

Pritchett took a step back. 'Nothing, my lord, I assure you. It is only that her ladyship and Miss Alice left for London the day before yesterday. I assumed you knew, my lord, and would be joining them.'

'Of course.' *Whatever else was happening, preserve appearances in front of the staff.* One of his mother's favourite rules. Appearances are all, never mind the hell beneath. 'I will be joining them in London. To-morrow.' *If they are there. Stop it. Trust her. Of course they will be there.*

'I feel confident we can find someone suitable from these five, don't you?' Laura conned the list of young women she had asked for interview the next day.

'I think so, my lady. I particularly liked that one and

that one.' Miss Blackstock touched two of the names on the list that Laura held out to her. 'They all have the qualifications you are looking for, and are under thirty and seem to be of a kind and cheerful disposition, but those two gave me the impression of a natural firmness.'

'Which is what they will need to handle Alice,' Laura agreed with a chuckle. 'Miss Blackstock, I hope you do not feel that I am attempting to detach you from Alice. You have been such a major influence on her and she loves you very much. But I am hoping that perhaps there may soon be someone else for you to look after…'

'That is wonderful, my lady. His lordship—'

'No, not yet, Miss Blackstock, but I hope it will not be too long. And I do not want Alice feeling that not only has her little nose been put out of joint by a new baby, but her Blackie has also been taken away from her.'

'Of course, my lady. That seems very sensible and farsighted.'

'Thank you.' The carriage lurched as they rounded the corner into the square. 'Almost home. I wish now I had not told Alice we were seeking a governess for her. When they call tomorrow and meet her I have no idea how she will react to them.'

'Ah, well,' Blackie said with a smile, 'if the worse comes to the worst and she is difficult it will scare away the faint-hearted ones.'

Laura met Blackie's gaze over the top of Alice's head and raised an eyebrow. The nurse nodded the merest fraction. On the other side of the room Miss Pemberton, candidate number five, was deep in discussion with Alice over whether, as Miss Mirabelle was a French doll, Alice ought to learn some French words so she could talk to her. The young woman's references were excellent and all from ladies Laura knew. She was quiet yet cheerful, bright-eyed, intelligent and decisive, and Alice took to her from the start.

'Miss Pemberton.'

The woman looked up. 'Excuse me, Alice.' She came and took the chair next to Laura. 'Lady Wykeham?'

'I would like to offer you the position. Do you need time to consider the offer?'

'No, I would be delighted to accept. Thank you very much, I greatly appreciate your confidence, Lady Wykeham.'

'Excellent. So when would you be able to start?'

The door opened. 'Lady Wykeham, what the blazes are you—?' Avery stopped on the threshold apparently silenced by the sight of his usually elegant drawing room. The table was littered with dolls and their clothes, the Chinese carpet was obscured by a drift of drawing paper, the side table bore evidence to a hearty tea and Alice was bouncing with excitement.

'Papa!' She threw herself into his arms as Blackie and Miss Pemberton got to their feet.

'Good afternoon, my lord,' Laura said with a calm she was far from feeling. 'Alice, please stop squealing, I wish to introduce Miss Pemberton to Papa. My dear, this is Miss Pemberton, who is to be Alice's new governess. Miss Pemberton, my husband, the Earl of Wykeham.'

'Delighted, Miss Pemberton.' He offered his hand, she took it with a calm, well-bred manner that made Laura want to cheer. Apparently cursing earls disturbed Miss Pemberton's composure no more than noisy six-year-olds did.

Avery was wearing his best diplomatic blank face, but she could not worry about that now, nor the butter-flies fluttering in her stomach, nor the sharp pang of desire at the sight of him, windblown despite his im-maculate riding gear, eyes sparking with tightly con-trolled temper.

'Do allow me to show you out, Miss Pemberton.' Laura stood and ushered the governess towards the door. 'If you would like to come with your trunks in two days' time?'

'Thank you, Lady Wykeham. My lord.' She dropped the slightest of curtsies. 'Goodbye for now, Alice. Miss Blackstock.'

Laura said goodbye in the hall and left Miss Pember-ton to the butler to show out. When she went back into the drawing room Avery was hunkered down, talking to Alice. 'No, I have not brought you a puppy. Are you not glad just to have Papa home?'

'Of course.' She looked up winsomely from under her lashes. 'But I'd have been even gladderer if you'd brought a puppy with you.'

'You are a minx, young Alice. Don't try those tricks on me, I've had older ladies than you flutter their eye-lashes at me and none of them has received a puppy as a result, let me tell you. Now off you go with Blackie, I must talk to Mama.'

He waited, smiling and apparently relaxed until the door had closed and the sound of Alice's excited chatter had faded. When he turned the smile had vanished. 'What the devil is going on, Laura? What are you doing gadding off to London without so much as a by your leave?'

'I have come to our house with my maid, our daughter and her nurse, using our carriage and leaving our staff fully informed of our whereabouts. I have engaged a suitable governess for our daughter as we have discussed in the past. I am not certain which part of that programme counts as *gadding,* but I am certain you will enlighten me.' Her knees were knocking and the ginger snaps she had eaten with her tea were lying heavy in her stomach, but at least she managed to sound both composed and polite.

'You did not consult me.'

'Neither did you, when you took off for a week with only the courtesy of a scribbled note.'

'Damn it, Laura, I was taking myself off while you were…indisposed. Mab told me.'

She raised her eyebrows at his language, but did not protest at it. 'I see. So having discovered that you were unlikely to get any sex for a few days you could think of nothing else to keep you at home.'

'There is no need to be so crude about it,' Avery snapped.

'Forgive me.' Laura got to her feet in a swirl of sea-green muslin. 'I was pleased to note that Miss Pemberton is able to withstand your violent language without flinching. She will obviously need to.'

'And to the devil with Miss Pemberton!'

'Miss Pemberton is not going to the devil, she is coming here. Alice, Miss Blackstock and I all agree she will be an excellent governess.' She pulled the bell cord. 'I would like some more tea. Will you join me and tell me about your business and I will tell you about Miss Pemberton and how Miss Blackstock and I decided upon her?'

'And Alice?' He sat, crossed one booted leg over the other and regarded her steadily. All the anger was under control. She wondered if she would ever penetrate that composure more than a fraction.

'Alice was very helpful in sorting out the final five candidates, you may be sure.' The door opened to reveal the footman. 'More tea, please, and another cup for Lord Wykeham.' *How very wifely I sound. How very hollow I feel.*

Miss Pemberton and her trunks arrived two days later. With Blackie's help she turned part of the nursery into a schoolroom and then Blackie went on a long-overdue holiday to her family in Somerset. She and Laura had discussed it at some length and concluded that not only did the nurse need the rest, but it would be best for Alice who would not be able to play Miss Pemberton off against Blackie, who warned Laura that she was quite bright enough to do so.

Laura saw no reason to inform Avery of Blackie's holiday. It was, she concluded, well within her remit as mistress of the household and he did not seem to notice her absence which was far less noticeable in town than in the country house.

The household settled down to a few more weeks in London as Alice adjusted to a new routine. It was best to remain there, Laura was certain. Alice was less familiar with the town house, the opportunities for distraction were fewer and it gave Miss Pemberton time to exert her gentle but firm authority.

Whatever else she was doing Laura made certain she was at home for nursery tea and games and Avery, even if he could not be at home then, made a point of being there for a bedtime story.

He was perfectly amiable, drove Laura about, took her to the theatre, walked in the parks, hosted a small informal dinner party. He took an intelligent interest in Alice's lesson plan and approved the light touch with much play amidst the learning.

What her husband was not, Laura thought resentfully on the fifth evening after he came to London, was in her bed. She dragged the brush through her hair, counting under her breath, but it was not enough to distract her from the fact that he had not come to her room once. It was, she supposed, retaliation for her blunt accusation about why he had left Westerwood so abruptly.

She dropped the brush onto the dressing table, tossed her hair back over her shoulders and snuffed all but the bedside candles. A new novel sat on the pillow where her husband's head should be lying. She frowned at it and then felt a sudden resolve that however sensational it might prove to be, it was not how she was going to spend another night.

The connecting door was firmly closed, but not locked. She had tried it an hour ago, eased the handle down while she laid her ear to the panel and listened. Avery had been speaking to Darke, a desultory conversation. Then she heard the valet say *Goodnight*. It was not even as though Avery had an evening engagement.

Laura looked from the pristine white bed to the door and back again. No, she was not going to climb between the covers and lie there patiently waiting on his lordship's pleasure. She smiled ruefully. That was what she had been waiting for all the nights of their marriage. His pleasure, not hers.

As she walked to the door and pressed down the handle she asked herself what was the worst he could do. Order her back to her bed? Without knocking, she opened the door and went in.

Chapter Twenty

Avery was not in bed. He lounged in the chair reading, his bare feet propped up on the fender, a leather-bound book in his hands.

'Laura?' He dropped the book to the floor and stood up. 'Is something wrong?'

'It occurred to me that I had spent rather too much of my marriage lying in my bed waiting on my husband's pleasure. Literally, *his* pleasure. Certainly not mine.'

'Laura!' He sounded so shocked she almost smiled.

'I do not think I need to mince my words with a man who uses his wife for his carnal needs without any consideration for hers,' she retorted.

'The devil you say!' Avery strode across the room and confronted her. Laura took a step back and found her shoulders were against the door. 'Are you saying that I take you without your consent?'

'No, you pig-headed man,' Laura snapped. 'I am saying you leave me unsatisfied in order to punish me for trapping you into marriage. When you condescend to come to my bed at all, that is. There, is that plain enough for you?'

'You are saying that you want me even after I said those things about coming to you only to get an heir? Even after the way I leapt to assumptions over that letter to Piers?'

Suddenly she saw a vulnerability that she had never glimpsed before. Perhaps because she had never looked, perhaps because all she had been filled with had been her own needs—her need for Alice, her need to somehow survive loving this man who thought so little of her.

'Yes, I am saying that. We have always known it, you and I, haven't we? That there was an attraction, despite everything.' She reached up and touched his face, trying to convey a tenderness that she dared not put into words. 'I am a grown woman, Avery. A married one.' Laura looked deep into the troubled green eyes. There it was again. Avery needed something and perhaps, just perhaps, she might be it. 'You want me, too.' She did not dare risk saying *need*.

He did not answer and for a despairing moment she thought he would turn from her. Then his mouth came down over hers in a kiss that was hard and unapologetic and demanding. She fisted her hands into his hair and kissed back with equal force. There was the metallic taste of blood in her mouth, his, hers, she did not know, or care. She would probably have felt no pain if a bullet had hit her.

Avery put his hands on her waist and lifted her up, heedless of her hold on his hair, his mouth still fastened on hers. Pushed back against the door, all she could do was wrap her legs around his waist as her nightgown rode up and she felt silk, skin, coarse hair and blessedly hot, hard, fierce heat against the soft skin of her inner thighs.

He lifted her higher, freed her mouth, then with relentless control, let her slide down, down until their foreheads rested together and he filled her. They clung to each other, joined tighter and deeper than they had ever been before, the only sound their shuddering breaths.

Then he began to move. They were so locked, the position so strained, that he could make only the shortest withdrawals and thrusts, but the very constriction and restraint inflamed her beyond bearing. Laura found Avery's mouth and pressed her own to it open, her tongue searching and twisting against his, her breasts crushed against his chest, each movement fretting the hard, aching tips of her nipples against the lawn of her nightgown.

He growled deep in his chest and lifted her, holding her higher so he could thrust harder, making the door rattle at her back, merciless until everything knotted, broke, shattered and she screamed against his mouth, convulsing around him, until she felt him shudder and collapse against her, the spasms of his release sending her over into a second crashing climax.

He must still be supporting her, she realised hazily, otherwise she would have poured down the wall, boneless and limp. Avery was so still she might have thought him unconscious, the thud of his heart against her breast and the heat of his breath on her bared shoulder the only indications that he lived.

After a long moment he lifted her, shifted her in his arms and carried her to the bed. He laid her down and then simply collapsed on the covers beside her, limbs sprawled, eyes closed. Laura found strength from somewhere to roll over and push back the sides of his robe. The belt had been lost somewhere. She folded her arms on his chest and studied his face. His hair was dishevelled and there was a smear of blood on his lip. She wondered if he was asleep or simply as shattered by the experience as she felt.

Cautiously she sat up and dragged her nightgown over her head. It was torn and crumpled and she tossed it to the floor and went back to contemplating her husband. The dark lashes lifted and he regarded her steadily. 'Did I hurt you?'

'I don't think so. I did not notice if you did. Did I hurt you?'

'I have no idea.' His lips twitched into a fleeting smile. 'I had other sensations to deal with.'

'Mmm.' She curled up against his chest, a satisfyingly broad and strong pillow.

Avery tugged until he could flip covers over both of them. 'I regret that I may need to lie here awhile before I can repeat any part of that performance.'

'I will contain my impatience,' Laura murmured and heard his chuckle. 'Part of me wants to know where you learned to make love so skilfully, part of me does not want to hear the answer.'

'What happened just now was not skilful.'

'It was thrilling beyond words.' She wriggled so she could trace kisses across the flat pectoral muscles and feel his skin quiver at the touch. 'And the first time...'

'You mean that the way you responded to me that first night together, that was genuine? At the time I believed it was, hoped it was, but then when I knew why you were there, I did not know.'

Laura sat up abruptly. 'How good an actress do you think me, Avery?' *And how cynical? But he said* hoped. *Does he care?*

'I do not know.' He sat up against the pillows, turned so he could look her in the face. 'Your—'

'My reputation?' Her heart sank. So that was it, not the uncertainty of a man who cared, but the doubts of a man who thought he was dealing with an experienced lover. 'I was a virgin when I first lay with Piers. Thinking back, I expect he was, too. We made love six times. I told you I have been with no one else, Avery, whatever the gossip says. They called me *Scandal's Virgin,* did they not? That was the truth. I flirted, I kissed, I permitted liberties that I should not have, but that was all.' Part of her rebelled against justifying herself, part of her desperately needed him to understand.

'Why?' he asked. 'Why risk your reputation like that?'

'Frankly?' She shrugged, embarrassed by telling someone she cared about what had motivated her. 'I was angry. Angry with men, angry with society. Angry with myself. Piers had taught me to love, but then he left me. I know it was not his fault, that my anger was not rational, I understand that.

'I wanted a lover, but there was no one I could bear to be with and besides, I dared not risk falling pregnant again. Society expected me to return to the Marriage Mart after my *illness,* but how could I counterfeit an innocent little virgin? Besides, if I married, the man would have to be very naive indeed not to notice I had carried a child.'

'If he wished to marry you, you could have told him first.' Avery's thumb stroked the sensitive skin of her inner wrist. She doubted he realised he was doing it, he seemed so absorbed in her story.

'And have him break it off? Risk the truth getting out? No man would marry me knowing that.'

'I did.'

'I trapped you,' she flung back.

'Perhaps,' he said, puzzling her with the small, almost secret smile that touched his lips. 'You certainly secured the two things you wanted: your daughter and a man in your bed.'

'A man in my bed is a matter of no importance beside my daughter. I would have become a nun if I thought that would make Alice happy and secure,' she protested.

'That would be a waste,' Avery said. Had she wounded him, asserting that a man—he—was of no importance? 'It took you a long time to seek her out.'

There was a question in the statement, one she could not bring herself to answer. How could she tell him her parents, whom she had loved and trusted, had plotted and lied, had planned to take her child and break her heart, all in the name of respectability? She loved them still, but she could not forgive them, or bring herself to speak of that betrayal, the way they must have put respectability and appearances beyond care for their own grandchild and before her own wishes.

'The time was right,' she said abruptly. 'Avery, make love to me again.'

It seemed he was rested enough. There was no opportunity then, nor until they fell asleep finally and deeply at dawn, for questions, truths or lies.

Avery could not remember ever feeling so physically satisfied before. His muscles felt as though they had been massaged, his whole body was relaxed and yet sensitive, tingling with remembered orgasmic pleasure, the anticipation of more to come a constant awareness.

And yet, as another week passed in apparent harmony and the nights in mutual pleasure, he could not settle, could not be easy in his mind. He knew what was wrong, or, at least he could see the shape of the problem, looming like a nightmare beast in the corner of his vision. Lack of trust. Laura had lied to him and, he was certain, lied to him still. There was something she was hiding, something she was not telling him. He no longer believed that she feigned delight at his lovemaking, but he had been deceived by her too often to yield to the emotions that he feared would make him blind to more lies, more deceptions.

He loved Laura and if she ever discovered that weakness she had the intelligence and the ruthlessness to exploit it unmercifully. His own mother had been quite conscienceless in manipulating his father, who could never bring himself to believe the woman he loved was the wanton his friends tried to warn him about. She had smiled and charmed and, occasionally, confessed to a fault with tears and ingenious excuses. The poor devil had believed her until he was confronted by undeniable proof.

Avery had never believed the story of how the shotgun had gone off accidentally when his father was climbing a stile. He had gone to his Aunt Alice and she had simply accepted him into the family, treated him as an elder brother to Piers. His mother had shrugged, no doubt, and gone her own self-obsessed way. The accident that left her with a broken neck at the foot of her latest lover's grand staircase had been hushed up. Avery, aged just seventeen, had wept for the last time in his life and faced the fact that his mother had killed any scrap of love he had ever had for her.

Now, over breakfast, he watched his own wife and tried to force the lid closed on the feelings that left him vulnerable to hurt and disillusion, just as his father had been.

Why had she left it so long to come for Alice and why, when she did, had she disguised herself and lied about her identity? Why had she not simply come to him, told him who she was, confessed her wish to become part of her daughter's life? Why, when she knew he was seeking a wife, had she not suggested to him that they wed in order to provide Alice with a loving home?

Her first deception had risked confusing and hurting the child. It had certainly confused him. He could accept that now and knew why he had been so angry when he had discovered who she really was. Her second piece of scheming could have wrecked his reputation.

Was that it? Startled by the sudden thought, Avery lifted his newspaper to hide his face. The sheets rattled against his cup and he threw it down. Did she hate him so much that she would risk upsetting Alice, hazard her own, fragile reputation in order to punish him?

He had taken her daughter, then she discovered he was instrumental in sending her lover to his death. Once he knew her identity he had forbidden her any contact with the child until the house party had thrown them all together. Had she manipulated her invitation to the house party, relying on his godmother's cheerful love of entertaining to ensure her welcome?

The enormity of it made him dizzy. Avery made himself breathe deeply until the charming, happy face of his wife came back into focus. She was coaxing Alice into eating some egg before the child attacked the jam and toast. The picture of perfect motherhood. The ideal wife who had every reason to hate him.

He had never found the words to convince her of his deep regret for the misunderstanding over the letter to Piers. And Laura had never mentioned it again. Was that because she did not *want* to forgive him? Yet there was no way she could wound him, not now they were wed.

'Papa?' Alice's clear voice cut through his churning thoughts.

'Yes, sweetheart?'

'Do you like my new hair ribbon?'

'Yes, sweetheart.' She could hurt him through Alice. If she took the child away…

'I don't seem to have seen Blackie for an age,' he said.

'No.' Laura smiled at him. Clear-eyed, innocent. 'I gave her a long holiday with her family. Now Miss Pemberton is with us I thought it was time she had a rest.'

Miss Pemberton, his wife's choice made without reference to him. His wife's employee, loyal to her. Avery schooled his expression into bland approval. 'Of course, my dear. She deserves her holiday.'

He waited until the next morning. It was Miss Pemberton's half-day and Laura went out shopping, taking Alice with her. Avery waited for the front door to close behind them, then he climbed to the nursery floor and tapped on the door of the governess's sitting room.

She was sitting at the table, darning stockings, but she got to her feet when she saw who it was. 'My lord. Please come in.'

Avery left the door ajar in case she felt uneasy about being alone with a male employer. 'Miss Pemberton, I hope you will excuse me interrupting you in your free time, I will not take much of it, I hope. Shall we sit?'

She took the chair opposite his and folded her hands neatly on the table. A self-contained, intelligent young woman.

'I do not interfere with my wife's running of the household, you understand. And, naturally, your appointment is within her sphere of influence.' She looked a trifle puzzled, but she nodded. 'However, Alice is my daughter. She is my wife's *step*daughter.' The governess nodded again and sat a little straighter in the chair.

'Naturally she is very fond of Alice, but she is not her guardian, not her mother.' His tongue almost tripped him on the lie.

'Yes, Lord Wykeham. I am aware of that.' Miss Pemberton was cool.

'I am sure you are. I wanted to make it clear that my daughter does not leave the house without my knowledge and consent. She most certainly does not go on carriage journeys without it. Do you understand?'

'Your instructions are very clear, my lord, although I confess I do not understand.'

'Lady Wykeham is prone to occasional flights of fancy that usually manifest themselves as erratic journeys. It would be unsettling for Alice.'

'I see.' She looked very perturbed. 'I can assure you, my lord, that if there is any suggestion of such a thing I will inform you at once.'

'Thank you.' Avery stood up. 'I can rely on you not to mention this to my wife? She becomes very distressed when we argue about these...whims.'

'Of course, my lord. I greatly respect Lady Wykeham, I would not wish to upset her in any way.'

Laura barely made it downstairs in time before the sound of footsteps on the upper landing sent her headlong through the first bedchamber door she came to. She closed it gently and leaned back, one hand pressed to her lips to stifle the sound of her panting breath.

She had come back into the house because Alice had forgotten her gloves and, leaving the child in the carriage, had run lightly upstairs in her thin kid shoes to fetch them herself. It was much easier than trying to explain to a footman where they might be.

The sound of Avery's deep voice coming from Miss Pemberton's room had caught her attention. What on earth was he doing there? Not interfering in the carefully constructed lesson plan, she hoped! She tiptoed along the landing and found the door ajar, so she stood and listened, indignation at interference swept away by horror at the tale Avery was telling about her.

She was within an inch of sweeping in and demanding to know what he meant by it when she realised what was happening, what he feared. Despite the lovemaking, the appearance of friendliness, the pleasant partnership that she was so hoping would blossom into something else, he trusted her not one inch.

He believed she would betray him. He thought she wanted to steal Alice from him.

Chapter Twenty-One

Laura listened to the sound of Avery's footsteps dying away, then she heard the door to their bedchamber open and close and she ran down the stairs, jerking to a walk when she reached the hallway.

'I couldn't find them,' she said to the footman. 'Never mind.' She had to get out of there before Avery realised she had been in the house. 'I couldn't find them,' she repeated to Alice and sank back against the squabs as the carriage moved off.

Was Avery insane? He knew she had no hope of setting up a separate household with Alice. He could simply walk in and claim them both, order them back home. She had no legal power and, now she was married, virtually no money either.

Then she realised. He was perfectly sane, perfectly logical. He genuinely thought she would snatch Alice away from him to hurt him. To punish him for Piers, for the things he had said about that letter and for taking her daughter in the first place. He thought she would do something so rash simply to wound him, make him suffer. After all, she had jewels, pin money, so she could, she supposed, vanish and manage for weeks, if not months, before he found her. If she told the child the truth about her parentage she might be able to do it in such a way that Alice would come to regard Avery as some kind of monster, so that when he eventually caught up with them Alice would hate him…

'Mama, are you all right?' Alice bounced across to sit beside her. 'You look frightened.'

'Do I?' Laura conjured a smile from somewhere. 'Not at all. I was just…thinking.'

Pretending to be Caroline Jordan had been a dreadful mistake. But there was no going back from it, even if it proved fatal to her marriage. Avery condemned her for entrapping him, lying to him and she could not find it in her to blame him. Somehow she had to convince him that he could trust her and hope he might come to understand why she had done what she had. Would he ever forgive her? She had no idea, but she had to try, she loved him too much not to.

Laura swallowed panic as Alice prattled happily about the shops as they passed and she contemplated the desert in front of her, the arid marriage of her own making. She had fallen in love with Piers with all the impetuosity of a girl, heedless of consequences, unknowing of what love truly meant. Now she loved Avery with a woman's understanding and a woman's heart. The heart that would be broken when he cast her off, for surely that would be what would happen unless somehow she found a way to reach him.

* * *

The realisation of what to do came to her as she helped Alice choose ribbons. 'The blue to match your new dress and the green for the new bonnet,' she agreed, her mind half a mile away where one tall, brown-haired gentleman dealt with his correspondence and perhaps contemplated ways of ridding himself of his untrustworthy wife.

The answer came with a jolt as she gave Alice the coins to pay for her purchases. *Tell him the truth. Tell him everything, however painful it is, however it reflects on Mama and Papa. Be utterly and completely open without trying to work out whether it will make things better or worse. If he forgives me, I will tell him I love him, tell him the new secret that is still just a hope. If I tell him first he will think I am trying to wheedle him into forgiveness.*

And I will forgive him, however hard it is. I will learn to understand and forgive, for Alice and because I love Avery.

'Avery?'

Avery turned from the bookshelves he had been staring at for the past ten minutes. 'Laura.' She was the last person he wanted to see, not while he was wrestling with his conscience over what he had said to Miss Pemberton. It was probably a sensible precaution, a rational part of him said. *You love her,* his heart urged. *Trust her.*

'You want to talk to me?' He pulled a chair round so she could sit, but she stood in the middle of the floor, her hands clasped in front of her like a defendant in the dock.

'Yes, I want to talk.' She was very pale, but her voice was steady. 'I overheard you speaking to Miss Pemberton.'

'Hell.' He did not try to justify himself or to touch her. There was a core of inner steel there, he realised as he met her steady gaze. It was not hostile or tearful, just…strong.

'I had thought that we were…that things would be all right. It wouldn't ever be perfect, but we could be a family even if you did not love me, even with everything that had happened in the past. But I did not realise until I overheard you how little you trusted me, how little you understood why I had lied to you, why I had trapped you into marriage.'

'There are things you have not told me. There are still secrets,' he said and Laura nodded, slowly, accepting the accusation. 'But I should not have spoken to Miss Pemberton.' Her eyes widened at the admission, but he pressed on. 'I should have talked to you instead.'

'I did not trust you with everything I need to tell you. And you do not trust me and I cannot blame you for that.'

Avery turned away sharply, one hand fisted in the silk window curtain, his back turned, unable to meet the honest pain in her face. If he touched her now he would kiss her, lose this chance of honesty in the flare of passion that overcame him whenever he felt the softness of her under his hands, caught the scent of her in his nostrils.

'I would happily die if that would make Alice happier or safer,' Laura said. 'I do not know how to make you understand what I did and allow me to be a proper mother to her. I want us to be a family, a happy one,' she added, her voice a whisper he had to strain to hear.

Avery unclenched his hand from the curtain, leaving it criss-crossed with creases like scars. 'Tell me what happened when you knew Piers was dead.'

Behind him there was the rustle of silk as Laura crossed to the chair and sat down. 'I told my parents I was with child. They were…aghast. Will you forgive me not repeating what they said? It is very painful.'

'Of course.' His voice sounded rusty.

'We agreed that I would pretend to be ill and go to one of our country estates to recover. Luckily there were all sorts of fevers going around that year. I coughed and moped for two weeks, then apparently succumbed to the infection.

'It was a healthy pregnancy.' Her voice trailed away, then she said, almost angrily, 'You want to know why I waited six years to find her, don't you? That is what you cannot understand or forgive.'

'I can forgive if I understand,' he offered and turned. This was the sticking point, the thing that Laura found most difficult to tell, he realised. He took the chair opposite her and sat down, leaning forward, his forearms on his knees, just out of touching distance.

'My parents told me she was dead,' Laura said abruptly. 'When my baby was born my mother took her, wrapped her. I heard her cry, once. I thought Mama would give her back to me to hold, but she gave her to the nurse and they went out of the room. Then Mama came back and said she was dead.' She stopped and drew a deep, shuddering breath.

'I watched her from the park the day before you found me there. That was the first time I had heard her voice from that day. They told Mab her name in the village. A shopkeeper knew my daughter's name and I did not.'

Avery found he was on one knee in front of her chair, both her cold hands clasped in his. 'How did you find her?'

'I was going through papers, months after they died, because I was moving into the Dower House and I needed to make sure I was taking the personal documents and leaving all the estate papers for Cousin James. There were letters from the Brownes in a locked box. I thought she was alive and I could find her. And then they wrote to say she was dead.'

'Oh, God. I told them to do that.'

'I went there anyway. I wanted to see the grave. They told me everything, gave me your card.'

'How could your parents do that?' Avery demanded.

'I suppose they thought it was best for me. I tell myself that. Why, after all this time, the hurt should be so sharp, I do not know. They did it for the best,' Laura repeated on a sob, then caught herself, her hands over her mouth.

'Oh, my darling.' Avery reached for her. 'My poor darling.' By all that was merciful she stayed in his arms and her own went around him, her forehead resting on his shoulder.

'When I found you had taken Alice it was bad,' she said, her voice muffled. 'Then when you told me about Piers I thought I hated you. I will never know how I managed to say nothing to you that day under his portrait. I saw myself in my mind's eye with Piers's sword in my hand, running you through.'

The vision was so vivid he almost felt the blade of the sword, the sickening pain. 'I understand.'

'You do?' Laura released him and sat back, her eyes enormous and dark as she stared at him. 'You might understand now why I let Alice go in the first place, but still, I deceived you and then entrapped you.' Laura forced a smile that caught at his heart. 'You are only human, after all.'

'I am only human,' Avery agreed. 'I understand why you had to pretend to be Mrs Jordan, why you mistrusted the man who had taken your daughter. I understand why you could not bring yourself to suggest marriage directly.' But now she had told him the truth and he could be honest with her in his turn, he realised. Tell her things he had never told another soul.

'My father adored my mother,' Avery said, his tone conversational, as he sat back on his heels. 'We were such a happy family, I thought.'

'You thought?' Laura was still shaken from her own confidences. He could see her struggle to comprehend what he was telling her.

'She'd had lovers for years. She'd lied and deceived, she had wound my father around her little finger. I thought she was perfect, too. And then he found a letter and it all came out. I saw her change—it was like something from a medieval myth. One moment there was Mama, beautiful, loving, sweet. The next there was a bitter, mocking creature hurling contempt with her back against the wall, confronted with evidence she couldn't twist or hide. She had been acting for years.

'She left without saying a word to me—I was eight. She went to her lover and my father died in an accident with his gun a few weeks later.'

'An accident?' she ventured, her voice appalled.

'Everyone agreed it was best if it was. I found him,' Avery said. *He looked so small huddled there in the bracken and the blood.*

'Avery!'

'She died a few years later. It seems it has left me finding it difficult to trust,' he said with a wry twist of the lips. 'I suppose somehow I see myself in Alice, fear for her if her love is betrayed, just as I fear for my own heart.'

'Oh, my love. Oh, Avery.' Laura found herself on her knees, reaching for him without conscious volition, before her words or his came together in her mind. 'You fear for your own heart?'

'You called me your love?' Avery's voice clashed with hers. 'You love me?'

She could lie, but then she had lied to him so often. She could pretend, but she had done that, too, and it was hollow. Summoning all her courage, Laura held his gaze and said, 'I love you, Avery. Whatever happens, whatever you feel for me, I will always love you.'

'Thank God. I lost my heart to you, my love,' Avery

said. The tautness had gone from his face and there was nothing in his smile but genuine, wondering, happiness. He gathered her in to him, his cheek against her hair. 'I had a glimmering of it. That night we first made love I was going to ask you to marry me. I was going to wait until the morning and do it properly with the ring. And then, what happened, happened, and I closed off all those new feelings for you, sank back into suspicion. How could I let old history teach me so wrongly about trust and truth?'

He felt so good, so strong and solid and male. Her man. *My husband.* 'When I met you again unexpectedly in London, I thought I hated you,' Laura murmured into his shirt front. 'But there was always something there between us though, right from the start. I thought it was simply desire.'

'I do not think there is anything simple about desire, my love.'

Laura twisted so she could drop a kiss on his wrist, feel the pulse beat against her lips. He loved her. Miracles happened. 'Perhaps that connection between us made the mistrust more extreme.'

'It would take a better philosopher than I am to understand the mysteries of the heart,' Avery said. 'Who would have thought that I could fall in love with Alice's real mother?'

'Who would think I could learn to love the man who stole her from me, the man who told the world he was her father?' Laura laughed at the sheer wonderful inevitability of it.

'Papa?'

The small voice from the doorway had them twisting round, clasped in each other's arms like guilty lovers in a melodrama. Alice stood there gazing at them, her face pale, her eyes wide, hair ribbons trailing from her fingers like some misplaced carnival decorations. 'You are not my father? I don't understand.'

Chapter Twenty-Two

'Alice!' Avery got to his feet and held out one hand to the child as he helped steady Laura with the other. 'Come in. We need to talk.'

Laura's heart bled for him as she saw the look in the child's eyes: doubt, anxiety, trust wavering on the edge of betrayal, but this was no time for displays of uncontrolled emotion. They had to reassure their daughter, nothing else mattered. She moved briskly across the room, closed the door and took Alice by the hand. 'Come and sit down, Alice,' she said with as much calm firmness as she could muster. 'This is going to be a very big surprise and it is a good thing you are such a big girl now and can listen carefully and try to understand.'

'We'll sit on the floor,' Avery said, folding down to sit cross-legged on the carpet. 'Then we can all hold hands and look at each other.'

'I am your mother,' Laura said without preamble when they were settled, Alice's cold little hand in her right hand, Avery's big warm hand in the left. 'Your real mother.'

'You left me.' Alice bit her trembling lower lip.

'I lost you,' Laura corrected gently. 'You know that people have been unkind to you sometimes because Papa was not married?' A nod. 'People get very cross if a man and a woman make a baby before they are married and I'm afraid that is what your father and I did. We loved each other and he had to go to war. And then, darling, I'm so sorry, he was killed. He was very brave and he was doing his duty.' Avery's hand squeezed tight around hers.

'Like Cousin Piers?' Alice was looking steadier now.

'Cousin Piers was your father, sweetheart,' Avery said. 'So I thought I must look after you. Only when I found you I knew at once that I loved you and that I wanted to be your papa. So I let you believe that I was.'

'But…' Alice turned to Laura, her forehead crinkled with the effort of working it all out. 'If *you* are my really mama, why didn't you marry Papa?'

'Because I didn't know where you were,' Laura told her. 'You see, my mother and father thought it was best if they sent you away so no one knew I had been in love with your father and that we had had a baby.'

'Because silly people get cross because of you not being married.' Alice nodded, obviously having sorted that out to her satisfaction.

'It took me six years to find you,' Laura explained. 'And I pretended to be Mrs Jordan because I didn't know what your papa would think of me.'

'So why didn't you tell me? And who was the bad man you were running away from?'

'Er…'

'Mama did not tell you because I was cross with her, too, which was exceptionally silly of me,' said Avery firmly. 'And the bad man frightened Mama in the park, but he has gone now and will never come back.'

'So it is all right now?' Alice asked, the anxious quaver back in her voice. 'Even though Papa isn't my really father and Mama is…Mama?'

'It is perfectly all right,' Avery said. 'Grown-ups make a lot of muddles about things sometimes and we can't tell everyone about who really is who because otherwise some people will be horrid to Mama. But now we are a family and nothing is going to spoil that.'

'Would Cousin…Cousin Piers be pleased? Can you tell me more about him?' Alice jumped up and put her arms around Avery's neck and kissed him. 'I don't love him like you, Papa, but I'd like to know about him.'

Laura found she was looking at her husband and daughter through a mist of tears. Avery appeared to have lost the ability to speak. 'We will talk about him lots,' she promised. 'And he would have been very, very proud of you, Alice.'

And then Avery opened his arms and pulled them both close and they clung together, murmuring disjointed reassurances to each other. There were tears, but when Laura finally stood up and took her daughter's hand and went upstairs so they could wash their faces and brush their hair it seemed as though none of them could help the smiles and the laughter of sheer happy relief.

'Are you tired?' Avery asked when finally Alice, who had been allowed to stay up for dinner, had fallen asleep with her head on the tablecloth and had been carried up to bed.

'Exhausted,' Laura admitted as she walked unsteadily into Avery's bedchamber and collapsed on the bed. 'I can't face going downstairs for tea. But I do not think I will ever sleep either.'

'Happy?' Avery asked. He kicked off his shoes, then leaned against the bedpost and began to untie his neckcloth. The dressing-room door opened and he called, 'That will be all for tonight, thank you, Darke.' It closed again and he joined her on the bed.

'Happy? I do not think I know the name for it. It is as though someone has swept away all the doubts and worries and pain and loss and I'm like a newly whitewashed house. Empty. And yet full. Confused,' she added when he laughed. 'Happy, content, terrified I will wake up and this is all a dream.'

Laura turned on her side and propped herself up on her elbow. Avery was lying on his back, eyes closed, mouth curved into a smile of pure content. 'How do you feel?'

He opened his eyes and studied her for so long that Laura felt herself grow rosy with the intensity of the look. Then Avery sat up. 'There are not the words. Let me show you how I feel.'

Time stood still as he kissed her, caressed the clothes from her body, then lay and allowed her to strip him and caress in her turn. All the urgency, the heat, that had driven their lovemaking before had gone, replaced with a tenderness that went far beyond the erotic. Avery made love to every inch of her body with lips and teeth and tongue and gentle, relentless fingers.

Laura was swept from one peak to another, her body saturated with sensation. When he finally took pity on her and fell back beside her she summoned what remained of her energy and moved on top of him, straddling the narrow hips. He closed his eyes as she rose up and took him into her body, sinking down until they were joined, perfectly, and she felt a tide of feminine power sweep through her, meet and meld with his maleness.

He let her set the pace, lay and watched her through heavy-lidded eyes, his lips parted, his breathing ragged as she slowly, slowly built the tension, twisting the rope of passion between them until he reached out, gripped her wrists and thrust up, taking them both over the edge, into the storm.

They lay there, blissfully relaxed, drifting in and out of sleep, for hours. Eventually a clock, somewhere deep in the house, struck three.

'I am awake,' Avery said. 'And hungry.'

'So am I. Shall we raid the pantry? There is plum cake and cheese.'

'A recipe for indigestion,' Avery teased, but he belted his banyan and followed her downstairs, through the sleeping house. They filled plates and made tea and then tiptoed out again.

'Goodness knows what we are going to have to tell Miss Pemberton,' Laura said as they curled up against the pillows and tried not to get cake crumbs in the bed.

'I will tell her that I was a foolishly suspicious husband. Miss Pemberton will consider me a brute and will probably order *A Vindication of the Rights of Women* from the library for you.'

'Poor Avery,' she teased and then, suddenly anxious, added, 'Are you truly comfortable with Alice realising you are not her blood father?'

'I am very happy. It has done my conscience no end of good, confessing. She'll have lots of questions, but we will deal with them honestly as they come up.' He put an arm around her shoulders and pulled her close.

'Thank you for agreeing to let Alice have a puppy,' Laura said.

'I had forgotten I had a bone to pick with you, my lady,' Avery said sternly. 'Whatever possessed you to promise Alice a puppy at dinner time? I foresee months of puddles on carpets, shredded upholstery and missing slippers.'

'Um…' Laura wriggled free and caught Avery's left hand in hers, fiddling with his wedding ring, keeping her eyes fixed on it. 'I thought it might be a good idea, because her nose is going to be very out of joint in a little while, I suspect, bless her.'

There was a moment when she thought he did not understand, then Avery pulled her round to face him, his fingers tipping up her chin so he could look into her face, his own intent and flushed. 'You are with child?'

'I think so. So does Mab. But it is very early, just weeks, and I have not seen a physician yet.'

'Oh, my love.' His arms around her were strong, possessive yet strangely tentative. 'You should be resting... You shouldn't have had all the strain and anxiety. You—'

'Avery.' She gave him a little shake. 'I am pregnant, not sick! Are you pleased?'

'Pleased?' He sat back and regarded her as if she had asked whether he had a head. '*Pleased?* I am delighted. Why did you not tell me before?'

'Because I thought I would never find out your true feelings for me once you knew,' Laura admitted.

'I see.' Avery rolled off the bed and got to his feet in one fluid motion and turned away. Her heart sank. 'Trust. It keeps getting in the way, doesn't it?'

'Lack of it does,' Laura admitted.

'You thought I would lie to you, pretend an affection I did not feel, if you gave me a child?'

She swallowed the lump in her throat. 'I wondered.' Surely, after all that had passed between them, she had not had lost him again? Trust was so important to him and so fragile and she had shown she doubted him. Her hand went instinctively to her belly. She shouldn't have said anything yet. It was to soon, she could be wrong and then he would think—

Avery paced back to stand in front of her. He looking down, his face shadowed. 'I wonder if perhaps we are being too hard on ourselves,' he said. 'We are going to make mistakes, hurt each other, I am certain. But that is part of it, part of growing together. Love cannot be a magic potion, can it? One moment we are just two fallible human beings full of faults and fears, the next we are in perfect harmony? No, this isn't a fairy tale, this is real life and real love.'

He reached out and pulled her gently to her feet. 'I love you. You love me. We will work it out, Laura. We will learn how to trust and how to tell each other of our fears. We will learn to argue and make up and not see that as a sign of failure.'

Her hand was still pressed over where she hoped his child lay. 'I may not be...'

Avery caressed her cheek. When he spoke his voice was husky. 'I think you are.' He laid his hand over hers. 'But if not, then we have time and love and what will be, will be.' He bent closer to look into her face. It was shadowy under the bed canopy, but the candlelight threw his face into relief, showed her both the strong man she loved and the tender lover she was coming to know. 'Are you crying? Oh, Laura, my love.'

She found her voice from somewhere. 'Only because I am happy. Ever since Alice was born there has been an empty, hollow place inside me. When I found her again it was filled and yet, somehow, something was still missing. I was not complete. Avery, I am complete now, with you.'

When he pulled her into his arms and kissed her there was no need for words. Impossibly, when she had given up all hope of happiness she had it all. A husband she loved, who loved her. Her daughter and the hope of all the years ahead would bring.

'Tomorrow, shall we pack and go to Wykeham Hall?'

'Start afresh?' Avery asked. 'Yes, my love. That house has been long neglected. It is waiting so we can make it ours. Let's go and build a home together. Raise a family.'

As he embraced her she saw their shadows, strong against the subtle silk of the wall hangings. *Two figures entwined, two hearts as one,* Laura thought as Avery began to kiss her and her eyelids fluttered closed. *Finally at peace.*

* * * * *

Join Britain's BIGGEST Romance Book Club

50% OFF your first parcel

- **EXCLUSIVE** offers every month
- **FREE** delivery direct to your door
- **NEVER MISS** a title
- **EARN** Bonus Book points

Call Customer Services

0844 844 1358 *

or visit

nillsandboon.co.uk/subscriptions